King of a Hidden Kingdom
THE THRONE

Tom Graneau

Publish Writers

A Division of Tom Graneau, LLC 19815 Kenswick Dr

Humble, Texas 77338 www.TomGraneau.com

Dedication

This project is dedicated to all born-again Christians worldwide, especially those who have spent time and effort in propagating the gospel of our Lord Jesus Christ. There is no greater mission in this life than the pursuit of righteousness, and there is no superior accomplishment than winning souls for the kingdom of heaven.

May God continue to love humanity, including you and your family, until the end. May he save those who acknowledge his presence in the universe and guide and protect those who believe and trust him.

Acknowledgments

I want to thank all the minds that came together to bring this project to life. I sincerely appreciate everyone who contributed to it. Moreover, I want to publicly acknowledge the prophetic writings of Ron Rhodes, John Hagee, and others, who deepened my understanding of prophetic events as they pertain to the end times. Napoleon Hill's writings were also an invaluable resource that broadened my knowledge of the cruel and deceptive nature of Satan, commonly known as *the Devil.*

I want to acknowledge my two loving children—Thomas Jr. and Sandra Graneau—who continually support and encourage my endeavors, including my writing career. As successful adults in their own rights, they continue to love God, help others, and do what's best for their families, communities, and themselves.

Finally, I am eternally grateful to God Almighty, my maker, savior, and Lord, who continually gives me spiritual insights about life, including perspectives about heaven and hell and the world of humanity.

Preface

In the heart of heaven, where the eternal light of God reigns supreme, pride festered in the heart of the once- glorious archangel Lucifer. His ambition? To seize the throne and claim heaven's divine power for himself. But, of course, betrayal has its price. Cast out of heaven and plunged into the dark depths of hell, Lucifer becomes the embodiment of evil, setting the stage for a cosmic rebellion that shapes the fate of humanity.

Condemned to the abyss, Lucifer's once-blazing radiance fades into the shadowy recesses of hell and takes on the more menacing form of Satan. Yet, despite his fall, his ambition remains unbroken. As the second most powerful being in the universe, Satan refuses to accept his fate and hatches a devious plan—to defy his eternal punishment and exact revenge on God. While some may wonder how he could potentially subvert or overpower the most powerful being in the universe, they need to realize that he no longer wishes to defeat heaven in direct battle. Instead, his plan is to corrupt God's favorite and most incredible creation: humanity.

Since the beginning of time and well into the future that has followed, humanity has stood at a precipice. Unseen forces wage war in the spiritual realms, but the battleground is earth, and every soul is at risk of becoming collateral damage. Lucifer, the originator of sin, targets humankind, determined to lead them into rebellion against God. But as dark forces encroach, a question remains—will humanity resist his deception and seek redemption, or fall into the same abyss that ensnared the fallen archangel?

Peering deep into the invisible world of spiritual beings through the eyes of the brave and loyal angel, Sabrael, *King of a Hidden Kingdom* exposes events yet unseen by natural eyes—betrayals, deceptions, strategies, and battles specifically designed to destabilize the world of man, continually unfolding behind the curtain of our mortal stage.

To this end, though it may appear on the surface that Satan is winning, there always remains the chance that God's forces prevail in the end. Indeed, while it is near impossible for any other being in the universe to outsmart God's providence, much of the result depends on decisions made by individuals like you and me, constantly under the influence of both—the forces of light and darkness. Even if heaven manages to squash the dismal rebellion, the question of what becomes of humanity's fate remains. Will they survive the ongoing conflict between these superpowers? And even if they do, where will their souls end up in the afterlife? Heaven or hell?

King of a Hidden Kingdom is not for the fainted heart. It's a bold expose about the world of God, Satan, angels, demons, and man, all fighting over the eternal fate of humanity. It reveals the role that we play, whether knowingly or unknowingly, as active agents in the battleground while at the same time attempting to disclose the unignorable tether between our daily actions and heaven's position in the war.

Contents

Chapter 1

Exiled to a Strange Land

Damn, I almost had him!" exclaimed the Son of the Morning after barely having collected himself from the excruciating fall. The entire expulsion was done and over with before he could even comprehend it. The last thing he registered was the opposition pressing them backward to the utter disbelief of the slanderer and his companions. Then, as a mere glimpse of the unsurmountable powers of his adversary, they plummeted towards earth like a lightning bolt.

Before he had even attempted to consider the strange unknown realm he suddenly found himself in, he felt the eyes of his battered companions on him, anticipating a pacifying response to their unexpected and humiliating failure. Hosts of angels catching up to their new reality: jagged, scorching ground stretching out far and wide into a dreary landscape devoid of any bejeweled walls or gates as they had been used to, only vague separations between what seemed like haunted prison cities. Instead of blood, blades of light shot out of their wounds in random directions, promptly subdued by the demonic darkness. Gone was the morning, the exquisite brightness in the lush gardens illuminated by the glory of the Lord; the outcasts now stood in a desolate dungeon that was utterly dark, rugged, and paved with stones. Their faces convulsed at the unavoidable stench permeating the air, so foul and putrid that some wondered whether they themselves were rotting.

Attempting to hide his trembling fear and disbelief, Lucifer brushed his long, black hair from view and contemplated the dejected lot surrounding him to gauge whether they held him responsible for this punishment. Behind them, he saw an endless stretch of colorless and barren land except for the stoned structures jutting out, seemingly fit only for imprisonment. Further in the distance, he discerned a taller precipitous structure that seemed to rise with purpose. Whichever direction his eyes wandered in, the landscape swayed with the hot vapors rising from the ground. The more he returned to his senses, the more he registered the crushing heat this realm was enveloped in.

He was acutely aware of the confusion that gripped all his followers, including him. This was an alien world and seemed to be the place of banishment their adversary, God chose for them. He felt a surge of pride upon realizing that the rebels had not been destroyed. How ironic that the price for waging a war against his divine home was to be exiled to a realm all to himself. He grew impatient to have dominion over every moving thing in hell and devise his plans for revenge, for, of course, the war was not over. Regardless of how far he might have been from home.

However uninhabitable this temporary hell, he resolved to do the only thing that was left to do: to accept this place as his command center whence to meddle with God's favorite creation—humankind.

Before I describe how the story unfolded from here on, you might be wondering why you should believe me regarding any of these events, for I might be one of Lucifer's followers attempting to portray a biased version of the story or present a narrative in which you might sympathize or pity him. The truth is, I, Sabrael, am one of God's servants entrusted with the responsibility to record and report on all of Lucifer's activities since the fall. The Divine power has foreseen his futile attempt to rechallenge its authority from this realm that he would eventually regard as his glorious palace. In the name of God Almighty, the Lord of lords and ruler of the heavens and earth, I vow to narrate the events precisely as they were and nothing else.

I am also telling you this story as an exposition of Lucifer's treacherous plans for revenge so that you may be better prepared for the way he intends to manipulate the human race for his vested interests, with complete disregard for their damnation as a result. Undoubtedly, the stature of God can never be challenged or threatened, and God might have appointed me to track his movements more out of love than fear. Despite the havoc wreaked upon the heavens at Lucifer's behest, there was no changing the fact that he had been one of God's favorite servants, a Cherub of the highest rank, exquisitely beautiful, wise, and majestic, though now stooped to the lowest depths of God's creation.

What Lucifer did next was to step down from the mound of rocks on which he had landed and head towards the giant mountainous wall in the hazy distance. Though he was yet to catch up to it, his throne was atop the wall with a long stone stairway that led to it, perceptible in the distance like a thread on an empty canvas. The throne had been placed there in anticipation of the betrayal, a reminder for the Cherub of his misplaced pride—for he was certainly superior to many of God's creations in power and beauty but gravely mistaken to think himself anywhere close, let alone above, the one who created him. The vast terrain surrounding the throne was like a blazing furnace shrouded in darkness, intended as a holding place for Satan, demons, and unredeemed human souls on their way to "the lake of fire." The holding place itself felt like a fiery deluge, except it was stripped entirely of light.

Lucifer raised his head to the skies and saw the face of utter darkness, not a single star in sight, as if hell had been made by ripping apart the heavens and turning them upside down. Though

Lucifer and his companions would eventually realize their ability to traverse to other realms, such as the earth, for now, no one thought about leaving or saw it as a possibility, especially not the guardian Cherub. Instead, he devised his plans to maintain control over this expanse, now inhabited by his companions who were expelled from heaven alongside him. He feared they might repent or seek forgiveness from God, or worse, rebel against him for leading them to failure. No sooner would Lucifer consider addressing the quiet crowd than something in the surroundings would grab his attention and reveal more about this dismal wasteland.

The path to the wall took him through one of the many cities that hell was divided into. Soon after entering the city, the passage split into several channels, leading to rows upon rows of stacked holding cells. Lucifer took the centermost path leading directly towards the wall and sauntered to inspect and comprehend God's master plan. The rusted bars and locks were exuding heat, reputedly forged in the lake of fire itself, unbreakable by any means. The cells contained nothing to soothe the soul, not even bare necessities or platforms for rest. He saw that each cell had five more stacked on top of it and, for a brief moment, imagined the cells occupied by doomed souls tearing themselves apart because of their inability to escape the tormenting heat and stench, joining in the orchestra of demonic cries emanating from their surroundings. Lucifer felt exhilarated by the challenge and couldn't wait to corrupt God's creations and lead them to this horrifying fate as his revenge.

His imagination was interrupted by a shrieking cry emanating from the ground underneath, which sent shudders through his body. By God, it was one of the most haunting things I have ever witnessed to date. Upon hearing the cry, Lucifer immediately experienced a flashback of the fall from heaven. How they were all clustered in a beam of light, nearly a third of heaven's forces numbering in the millions and shot from heaven at an unimaginable speed. He recalled catching a glimpse of the vast firmament speeding past him. The flowing rivers of wine and honey, fields of precious stones that the higher-ranked angels were embellished with, the pearl white gates in every direction that would never close, and the transparent gold streets and pathways that were so clear and shiny they resembled glass—all lost in the blink of an eye. He remembered passing by the blue Earth with its myriads of beasts and creatures and wondered what they must have thought of the war in heaven, whether they would have joined his ranks in a decisive rebellion against the all-knowing and merciful. He even glimpsed the blooming Garden of Eden, where the four rivers converged, with the sacred tree of knowledge standing tall in the center.

Creaking sounds from beneath his feet pulled him back to hell, and he looked down at the ground and noticed new cracks appear. Thus, he gained awareness of the world underneath, the "Bottomless Pit," where the shrieking cry had resounded. Though he was standing far from the endless abyss, the gate to which he thought must be nearby, he could hear the buzzing swarms of locusts that would one day torture the worst of all souls with their stinging tails, faces like men, and teeth like those of lions. He glimpsed at his troops and realized that some of his most potent and fiercest companions were missing, whereupon he identified the source of the piercing cry as Asbeel—the angel of destruction that had served as a prized chieftain of his army. A newfound urgency entered his being when he noticed a rising clamor in the masses in response to Asbeel's cry, and he realized he must assume authority before the entire cluster broke into disorder. He turned his head towards the stone wall, which now stood nearer but still several cubits ahead. Out of the corner of his eye, he noticed the bent edges of his feathered glory. For the first time since landing, he paid attention to his abundant power and beauty despite his armor turning to crumbs and being devoid of all the precious stones that had once covered him. He felt his covetous being overflow with rage. With his fists closed tight and wings outstretched, he determined to stand atop the stone wall to address his defeated army and marched ahead.

Rows of heads turned in his direction and followed him vaguely in anticipation of some kind of announcement that would make this world easier to come to terms with. After Lucifer reached the steps on the wall, they waited for a long while as he raised one doddering leg after the other, rising slowly to the top. Though he could've flown to cut his ascension much shorter, Lucifer was one to savor his time in the limelight, so his wings simply swayed behind him like an exquisite cape. He stopped midway to look behind him and was reassured by the few heads he could discern his most loyal soldiers standing taller than the rest of the swarm. Somewhere in the middle, Damyan and Andras stood near each other, blacker than coal with hints of the fading luster of their glory days. He was reassured by the reminder that he and his companions were made from the same light and essence that had defeated them, so they must also be capable of the extent of power that came with it. Far in the distance, he saw Azrail helping other demons up from the ground as Kuraim and Akar encouraged the rest to move toward the wall to witness the ascension of their Prince. When Lucifer saw that the morale of his companions was not shaken, he felt reinvigorating gratitude and turned to face the steps with newfound enthusiasm.

Clouds of dust rose above the ranks of soldiers since their fresh activity had reincarnated the deadened land. They huddled closer to the wall to look for a better vantage point as Lucifer slipped in and out of view, the top of the stairs snaking around the wall to be visible from all sides, revealing to him stretches of land that were initially blocked from view from the area where they had landed. Something about the construction reminded Lucifer of the archangel, Michael, the family's eldest brother, who had led the divine forces in defense against the warring factions and, much to Lucifer's displeasure, emerged victorious. He wished the story had gone somewhat differently. Reaching the top, he imagined Michael kneeling in submission, begging for Lucifer's mercy, who pushes him down the stairs and watches him roll down powerlessly. When he reached the top, he was surprised to find it constructed like an open hall- room. Right in the center of it, he discovered an object that immediately struck him as a mockery of his plans, as Micheal had intended it. It was a broken throne made of deformed stones, placed so high above the ground that his only possible audience from it was God. I commend Micheal's genius and ability to strike at Lucifer's weakest spot; surely, after failing to overthrow God's throne, the last thing Lucifer wanted to see was a powerless throne that no one else wanted, meant to rule over ruins. Lucifer felt watched, as if every inch of heaven had its eyes fixated on him, waiting to see how he would receive this joke. He spun around on his feet to scan the entire terrain and rule out the possibility of an attack from heaven while his forces were scattered and immobilized. Nothing moved in the impoverished wasteland; there were no fauna, flora, or fowl, only vacant cities of dark holding cells and dungeons that stretched far and wide beyond his perception. A few lengths away from the wall, he located an empty arena, vaguely resembling an amphitheater, that he would have arrived at had he turned east before climbing the staircase. With his gaze fixated on the demotivating silence, he took steps backward till the back of his knees touched the seat of the throne and was starting to lower himself dejectedly when he was interrupted by the sound of hurried footsteps from the spiral stairway, which jolted him back up with a defensive instinct.

"My Prince!" exclaimed Akar, who had developed a habit of

tailing Lucifer to protect him from any unexpected dangers.

"You deprive your followers of witnessing this glorious moment," he spoke with the intensity of a battle cry. "They'd want to witness how Your Majesty is far from defeated and, in fact, elevated much more than the legions we have fallen. This battle was not fought in vain. Here, we can replenish and bolster our forces, unconstrained by the hand of God. Sit not on this throne without the witness of doleful eyes that would instantly regain life and ardor at the sight of their Prince undertaking his long-awaited purpose."

"Oh Akar," bellowed Lucifer, "Do not embarrass me more than this defeat already has. Neither this kingdom nor its throne is fit for the morning star. By ruling over ruins, I would only twice renounce the throne above the skies, on which he now sits more comfortably and securely than before our disobedience. Let this shameful crowning happen before the privacy of our eyes, more fitting for pity than exultation. No, Akar! Do not let your blinding loyalty come in the way of this clear image of defeat! We're not far from the bottomless pit and stand above it now only because the triumphant one chose it as the limit of our expulsion. I'd have to upturn the entirety of hell and turn ash into gold before claiming it as my kingdom!"

"So be it!" Akar responded through his parched mouth with unvanquished ferocity, "Since when have we accepted the shallow roles anointed for us by God? Let's turn this mocking refuge into our headquarters, and he shall soon be wishing he had banished us to the bottomless pit instead. Let this very punishment become his greatest mistake and nightmare. Do you not see his outright challenge? Take this seat as a trophy of your rebellion rather than a dismal sign of defeat. These harsh and jagged rocks are more fit for your throne than the heavenly gems that are but tokens of loyalty and submission. Let's turn hell into a palace as jagged as our intentions and raise it higher till its evil edges pierce the very heart of God's creations!"

Akar's words touched Lucifer, who saw the merit of refashioning this defeat as a victory. If he had to admit, he should have been better prepared before taking up arms against heaven. He could not have predicted the sheer power that vanquished their efforts earlier, but his next attack could be a better match for the divine forces. He could corrupt God's creations so that they unknowingly help manifest Lucifer's darkest plans and aid in his war against God from another front—earth.

"My loyal Akar! Perceive this not as a moment of weakness but of mournful remorse at the harrowing cries of my loyal companions, embroiled in the anguish of the bottomless pit. Without question, I would take their place and singlehandedly bear all of God's punishment so that they may roam free, even if on this grim wasteland. But your courageous words enlighten me and make this bleak world feel like home. If not for this unwavering support from my best soldiers, I would not have dared to even rise from the marred grounds, let alone perform the walk of shame till here. Tell me, how shall we go about turning this into a palace worthy of being ruled by me? How shall we turn this unflattering seat into a throne whence I shall wage my war against the world?"

Akar shifted on his feet with the determination of someone who was prepared for this. Or better yet, wanted it to go exactly this way and was waiting for the right moment. He walked towards the edge of the wall, where he became visible to the millions standing patiently underneath them.

"Behold!" shouted Akar, raising his fist to the dark, murky sky, to be met by eyes widening and rising in anticipation.

He glanced back at Lucifer, who was still standing near the throne, turned to face the ground and the crowd, after mustering all the energy left in him, brought his fist down in a vicious strike that reverberated through the grounds of hell, down to the bottomless abyss, rousing monstrous cries none of them could associate with any being they had seen before. The strike cut through the mountainous sides neatly as if sculpting it, and the broken edges fell in the wake of a storm of dust that faded away slowly to reveal a throne in the center, now sitting atop what looked more like a tower, with a spiral staircase looping it from bottom to top.

With mouths agape, scores of fallen angels beheld the miraculous sight as Akar trembled back to his feet and turned to face the Prince.

"Behold! The King of a Hidden Kingdom!" shouted Akar and knelt with vehemence, bowing his head in an oath of submission.

The dark masses followed, and a wave of pledging warriors settled down on the dusty ground, ready to accept their new King. They looked on in collective veneration as Lucifer stood with his eyes closed and retracted his wings elegantly. Like the fingers of a hand closing in on the palm, his wings folded on themselves as they shrunk smaller and slithered into his back, leaving behind only the smooth, muscular contours on his supple skin. He opened his eyes, flexed his shoulders to adjust to the new form, and then regarded the display of reverence from his subjects as he lowered himself onto the throne gracefully. For the first time since landing in hell, his eyes brimmed with the color of victory.

Chapter 2

A Flash Back to Heaven

At the end of the first scorching day in hell, Lucifer lay next to the throne atop the wall, reminiscing the days of his disobedience, retracing and evaluating each step he had undertaken before the fall. He was desperate to identify his moment of weakness—exactly where he had misjudged the power of God and lost his clandestine advantage. Little did he know that the all- knowing and all-powerful was never threatened in the least.

Here is the story I have pieced together from Lucifer's regret-filled flashbacks that he found himself wishing were a tragic dream rather than the torturous and inescapable reality they had dismally become.

***

"You have done well, Damyan!" spoke the tempter, who was reassured to great extents by Damyan's report of a hundred thousand more joining his rapidly growing army, "Indeed, it is not long before the light of God is vanquished and subdued. He has reigned unchallenged for far too long, and it's about time his competency is tested. He has undermined his glory and ours by making man in his image to inhabit earth. Surely, we are his most exalted creation and shall remain so until the end of time. Tell me, my glorious and unfaltering soldier, are you with me?"

Damyan was perched next to Lucifer in the soft glow of the

empyreal light as the two regarded the glorious new earth from a distance. They were yet catching up to the monumental changes God had made to their familiar landscape, and the days of exploding celestial bodies that seemed to undo the very fabric of the firmament were not too far behind them. Now, they perceived company upon company of angels rushing back and forth between heaven and earth, adding the last few embellishments to God's handiwork and helping maintain it to the benefit of his new creation. Damyan swept his eyes through the rows of angels to identify any who might still be susceptible to switching sides. He turned to fixate his gaze on Lucifer before addressing the weighty question of loyalty.

"Oh, Lucifer! I am surely pledged to you and support your claim," he responded, "let the legions and I command on your behalf stand testament to my loyalty. Indeed, our horizons have already expanded tenfold owing to your ingenious design, and the hand of God consolidates the separation with each new thread that it weaves through the universe. But let not my unyielding allegiance conceal the fear, which is at the same time vividly present, that we might be overpowered by the divine forces that yet obey him. Never before has one questioned his rule or imagined another sitting on the throne, and the recent converts report that he is privy to your insurgence."

Lucifer was taken aback by Damyan's honesty, which vaguely reflected his own unacknowledged fears regarding his defiant efforts, but he was quick to spread his wings and retort, "Ay, Damyan! No doubt the forces of light believe he sees and hears everything—I see their words as but meek efforts to discourage what they consider too ambitious for their enslaved selves. Why, then, I must ask, has he not interrupted us at any step? Nay, rest assured if my commanders have followed my instructions to the mark, our Father in heaven is too distracted by his grand design to see what's transpiring right under his light."

Damyan looked back at earth and wondered whether Lucifer's rebellion could've gone unnoticed by God, who claimed to be witnessing everyone and everything in the universe at all times. Lucifer noticed the glimmer of fear in Damyan's eyes and realized he would have to act soon before the new order was wholly accepted or the tenacity of his companions threatened to collapse.

Damyan responded, "May the forces of this universe align in your favor, my Prince. The fate of many of our brothers in arms lies in your hands, and may you emerge victorious and uplift them to their rightful glory that would soon have been subjugated by his new creation, which none would have seen as a rival if not for your prompt and selfless response in our defense. Your troops stand prepared for battle, ready to muster all the light and strength they are capable of. As for me, Lucifer, I am ready to give my life for the freedom of our kind. By god, you have already freed me with the realization of my will!"

Lucifer smirked upon realizing that his rallying call had been effective. What started off as his thirst for power now manifested as a collective anxiety that had spread like a disease and helped enlist millions to his cause.

"You have spoken, Damyan, like one who is not only destined for victory but will lead me to it!" responded Lucifer zealously, attempting to reinforce Damyan's resolve. "You'd be relieved to hear that our ranks shall be fortified by the addition of some of heaven's best: Azazel, Tamiel, Adras, and archangels Barbiel and Azrail, to name just a few. With nearly a third of heaven behind me, Michael's defenses shall amount to nothing but embarrassment, and we'll soon have so-called God wishing he had assigned one of us as the general of his army instead of the archangel, who is, in my judgment, too merciful to lead military affairs."

"A third!" exclaimed Damyan and chuckled, allowing himself to feel hope fueled by the strength he perceived in their numbers, especially considering that the war would not be akin to any semblances of violence that you humans are used to; no firearms or projectiles or explosions would characterize it. Lucifer's plan of attack was that the massive force of millions would push toward God's seat in heaven and attempt to remove him from his station. Thence, Lucifer would assume the coveted throne and command heaven's forces to banish God from his kingdom and accept him as their new ruler. He could count on the third of heaven mobilizing as his army to pledge their allegiance without delay. Meanwhile, the rest of them, he hoped, would switch over to his side upon witnessing the humiliating defeat he would inflict on Michael's forces.

"Yes, Damyan! An entire third of heaven that is rebellious and vengeful, soon to rule over heaven with me. Even if our adversary has picked up some scent that has made him aware of our plans, it's too late for him to garner a strong defense to obstruct us. Wait till you see the sheer majesty of our lights glowing brighter alongside for this cause!" Lucifer roared as if he had already emerged victorious, and God's defeat was only a matter of time. His impassioned proclamation was followed by a self-absorbed visualization of the flood of his army taking over heaven and ravaging its defenses as Michael and his God watch their defeat with helpless dismay.

Lucifer did not know in that instance that his companion's concerns were entirely merited. On the other side, Michael was promptly mobilizing heaven's forces that were yet loyal to their creator and were more than sufficient to counter Lucifer's futile and regrettable attempts. The all- knowing God had foreseen his rebellion long before Lucifer had even conceived of the idea and the first ever sin, let alone when he convinced the first few traitors to join his ranks. The night before the battle, Michael instructed all his commanders to gather their troops and assemble outside heaven's City of Gold, demarking that as the point of defense for the forces of light.

I struggle to describe in words the sights I witnessed the next morning, even though I had been assigned as the official scribe for the heavenly battle instructed by Michael himself to reside in the frontmost watchtower of the city. The beacons of light were assembled magnificently on both sides like two oceans pitted against one another. If not for the dire circumstances in which these events transpired, I might have described what I witnessed as utterly beautiful. The forces of heaven were congregated as ordained. Loyal followers' lower and middle orders, comprising Angels, Principalities, and Dominions, were meticulously divided into regiments and remained in their regular form. The regiments were led by their superiors from the higher orders, namely Seraphims and Cherubims, who were the likes of Michael and Lucifer, such as Gabriel, Metatron, and Gadreel. The rest of the angelic orders were separated into their own regiments, including Virtues and Powers, and thus were the forces of light organized to defend the kingdom of heaven. As an outright challenge to Lucifer, the army of light numbered a few million less than the army of darkness, for God grants power and victory to those who are righteous and seek his help, and his incumbent will would remain unfettered by however large an imbalance of number.

God had placed an invisible barrier between the two forces, which only allowed Michael's side to see through. So, when Lucifer's army advanced toward God's throne, bound to pass through the City of Gold, they were oblivious to the defenses they would run into. Michael himself was patiently stationed at the foremost flank of his army, and upon sighting the faintest glimpse of Lucifer's army, he turned to face his own and delivered the following speech so loud and clear that it reached every corner of heaven. I could swear that every now and then, in the gentle breezes and endless rivers of heaven, I still hear his words echoing:

"Children of god! Ministering Spirits! The Morning Star has fallen…"

This declaration also reached Lucifer, who immediately recognized the voice and halted his advance to pay heed to it. He had not expected Michael to be waiting for him.

"…He who squanders the undeserved stature granted to him by God Almighty and rises against the same eternal light that created him. God-willing, we shall strip him of every heavenly jewel that adorns him, for he has fallen to iniquity and turned each of them into a stain of disloyalty. Surely, God is the most powerful and just, and it serves him not when we bow down to him but only ourselves! For he is the one that bestows the light, and he is the one that shall take it away. Even if all of creation rose against him and defied his grand design, they would not touch him, let alone threaten his seat above the skies. Lest any of you wish to test it, I implore you to join Lucifer now and witness firsthand the blazing fury of God that shall banish them to the blistering furnace ordained, where the lake of fire will beckon them to quench its relentless thirst. The worst of them shall be chained and tortured in the bottomless pit, and no matter how much they beg for it, they will not be allowed to die. Though I swear if it weren't for God's love and generosity, I would kill them a thousand times over!"

Michael grew taller and larger as he delivered this speech, making him look more intimidating. After his last statement, he struck his luminescent sword on the air under him, which sent waves of thunderous light pulsating through the realm as if God had placed an invisible plane as a stage for this battle. The wave of light first passed through the invisible separating barrier and undid the veil, revealing heaven's forces to Lucifer, who regained ambition upon noticing the lesser magnitude. Then, it swept over the mass of Lucifer's force, forcing most of them to cover their eyes in the face of the blinding light.

Our generous God patiently waited despite his clairvoyance to see whether Lucifer might renounce his waywardness and be saved from the punishment that would befall him. He appeared unconcerned by Lucifer's rebellion and was aware that it would be pulverized far sooner than the Cherub could have imagined. Meanwhile, I did wonder why he had created a new life that would be much more likely to disobey him and corrupt the divine realms. Indeed, he knows what is best, and there must be providence and harmony even in this apparent chaos that blemishes the holy sky.

Michael pointed a finger towards the space where the invisible barrier had been between the two armies and moved it across in a swift, smooth stroke, creating a faint line of dusty light that would dissipate at the subtlest touch. He then continued, "Behold! The decisive boundary that shall determine today's victory, whichever army crosses it first will be stronger, and God Almighty shall unleash the judgment that fits both sides!"

Lucifer, who would've already had to pass the City of Gold for his defiant objective, now resolved to cross the determining line as his primary objective. He was surprised that heaven had put up a single defense, and though his face betrayed a sense of being intimidated by the readiness of the defensive force, he was foolish enough to think that crossing the line would be a race against time. Where he should perhaps have vanquished his offensive before it even started and repented for his crimes of insubordination, he instead instructed his army to charge forward with ferocity. Michael's forces followed suit, and the two forces collided with one another, erupting light and shockwaves brighter than any explosion that marked the birth of the universe. The Archangels met precisely above the line, where a movement in either direction, be it as small as an insect, would've decided the fate of heaven once and for all. The angel of light and music was head-to-head with the angel of mercy, though the latter intended no such treatment as suggested by his name. The rest of heaven watched in dismay at the gross misuse of divine power.

The hosts of angels seemed to blend into one another, and from a distance, it looked like two oceanic bodies pitted against one another, thrashing and oscillating at the meeting point. The angels on Lucifer's side emitted loud shrieks and cries as they pushed beyond their capacity to shove the defense back toward the City of Gold. In contrast, Michael's army stood its ground gracefully, with the higher-order angels thrusting their wings that produced gusts and flurries of light. The confrontation did not last longer than the first half of that day, all through which I felt heaven might crack at the battle line and collapse.

Then, in a decisive moment that would affect the fate of the whole universe for the rest of time to come, while Lucifer gazed deep into Michael's eyes with a threatening zeal that he hoped would debilitate him, the latter managed to push him back ever so slightly. A wide and victorious grin appeared on his face. Lucifer was overcome by confusion and looked down at his feet to see where he stood. To his utter disbelief, he noticed that Michael had managed to cross over to his side of the line with one foot visibly jutted forward. His face rose back up in horror, almost accusatorily, as if blaming Michael for having moved the battle line while he wasn't looking, but deep down, he knew he had lost his ground. Then, like a dam breaking open, the forces of light flooded through the battle line and trampled the enemy soldiers. Michael himself bolted through their ranks, and his glowing sword seemed to pierce and split the ginormous body into two, meant to convey to all the millions that heaven's forces had crossed over and emerged victorious.

No sooner had they noticed Michael speeding through them in a streak than all the millions were clustered together as if God had grabbed hold of them in his palm. By the time Michael passed through the last flank, in less than a blink's time, the defectors were shot out of heaven like a thunderbolt and sent hurling through the sky in the direction of hell. The battle line dissipated at once, scattering light dust where it had been placed, and heaven was left in tranquil silence as the City of Gold glimmered and its walls reflected the bright flash of light from the thunderbolt. God's punishment was swifter than most could comprehend, especially Lucifer's followers, who knew not what hit them till they landed in the desolate kingdom of hell.

***

Lucifer opened his eyes to be greeted by the dull, murky firmament of hell and cursed under his breath. He stood up to scope his barren kingdom and found it in the same grim state as it was before, except now his followers had spread out in the cities of hell and occupied temporary resting spots in the streets, which at least made them seem more like a kingdom than a prison state. He turned to face his throne and, after walking to it, started circumambulating it, carefully regarding its tiniest details and noting where it was disintegrating or needed fixtures to suit his unimpeded pride better. At the back of the throne, he noticed a vague inscription scratched into it that immediately captivated his curiosity. He brushed away the coat of rust-filled grime with his hand till he could decipher the inscription: "King of a Hidden Kingdom."

A similar look of horror flooded his face as when Michael had defeated him by pushing him back from the battle line. The words hauntingly echoed Akar's when he had declared Lucifer as the ruler of the new realm, which made him wonder whether not only his failure but the actions of his companions and everything else that transpired after was also ordained and exactly proceeding as God wanted. This, too, he was certain, was Michael's doing. He pursed his lips and looked up towards heaven with explosive rage, and then bellowed a guttural cry along with deplorable curses at God that I consider unnecessary to reiterate.

Chapter 3

A Throne Fixed for Lucifer

How many have we lost?" Lucifer asked with his eyes fixated critically on his throne in the distance, taking note of all the refurbishing changes being made by two of his companion angels whose darkened, demonic forms seemed to be struggling due to the hellish heat.

"My Prince, I've asked all the army chieftains to tally their numbers. So far, it seems like we might cross a million, but I'm hopeful," responded Akar, who felt optimistic about Lucifer's newfound urgency in organizing the forces of hell. He hoped and somewhat prayed that Lucifer would not get discouraged by the aftermath of God's punishment, which could've potentially deterred him from the ideal course of action.

They stood in the open arena near the staircase on the wall that led up to the throne, waiting for the rest to arrive. Lucifer had called a meeting of his army chieftains to gather a report on the number of angels who were now trapped in the bottomless pit. Having kept his wings tucked into his back since the day of their arrival, Lucifer looked closer to a human king, though still more imperial than any of them could ever be. He knew full well that he had the most magnificent and regal wings in hell and intended only to spread them again when he needed to threaten or impress his onlookers, an objective he had already achieved with his trusted companions. For now, he wanted to gauge the loyalty of his companions without the element of fear. Akar followed

Lucifer's eyes and wondered what ran through the Prince's mind for his attention to be captivated entirely by the throne. He noticed three other chief angels approaching the area: Andras, Kuraim, and Azrail. In case Lucifer was undergoing doubts or reconsiderations, he thought it opportune to interrupt him in that instant.

"There they come," Akar said as he shrugged Lucifer ever so slightly while looking in the direction of the oncoming soldiers.

Lucifer turned to face them and noticed Damyan following way behind them. After every few footsteps, some lower-ranked angel would run up to Damyan and match his pace to discuss something as he would respond without pausing his swift strides toward the Prince and his throne. Lucifer noticed how the last of them was met by a different reaction. Damyan suddenly stopped in his tracks to face the angel, who stumbled to a halt in response. He shot a finger towards one of the cities of hell further in the distance and visibly shouted out commands, after which the angel fearfully scurried away. Damyan turned to face the throne and resumed his journey with fists closed tight and legs stomping in a disgruntled march as if the angel who approached him had delivered additional misfortune. When Lucifer looked back at the nearer companions, they had almost reached the arena. Behind them, he saw clouds of dust and vapor rising up to the dark sky from cities of hell that were now teeming with activity.

"My fellow fighters!" Akar welcomed them enthusiastically on behalf of Lucifer, "You arrive right on time to witness the completion of our Prince's glorious throne! Let us congregate under its might to celebrate the victory hidden behind God's intended punishment."

Lucifer took a few steps away from Akar and turned to face them so that the vast wall provided a grand backdrop behind him, with the throne towering directly above.

"My Prince!" the three greeted Lucifer, bowing their heads in unison before joining Akar.

Akar was trying to gain Lucifer's favor by becoming his closest confederate, hoping to be nominated as Lucifer's right-hand man, which Lucifer was smart enough to notice. This was why Akar had arrived earlier than the rest, and having been assigned the task of gathering the army chiefs for this meeting, Lucifer was smart enough to know that Akar might've even orchestrated it to go this way. With a few intentional footsteps, he had ensured that there was a clear separation between him and Akar, by which Akar was swiftly returned to his stature of a follower rather than seeming like Lucifer's collaborator. Damyan, who had hastened his march upon perceiving movements in the arena, reached at the same moment.

"My Prince!" he proclaimed louder than the rest and marched to join them so that the five chieftains converged toward the slanderer in a vague arc.

Their faces were demarcated by fright, and there was collective ambiguity regarding Lucifer's reaction to the aftermath of the heavenly battle. They feared that they might be blamed for the harrowing defeat, and Akar's representation of it as a victory confused them. Damyan seemed much more dejected than the rest and kept his head lowered since he had arrived.

"My loyal companions!" Lucifer finally spoke, shifting his gaze from one to the other so as to address all of them. "I'm delighted to see you walking freely in contrast to the misfortune of those we lost to the bottomless pit, whose screeching cries haunt the face of this realm and inflict more pain on me than the banishment from heaven. Tell me, how do you find your new home?"

They looked at one another hesitantly, scared to take the initiative to comment on the torturous realm that Lucifer intended to embrace as his kingdom. They were still adjusting to the relentless heat and grimness of the realm and would've much preferred crowning Lucifer as the King of heaven. At the same time, they did not want to intensify Lucifer's sense of defeat and risk losing their only apparent chance for salvation. Akar stepped forward to break the awkward pause and responded.

"Oh, god of this age! While it certainly feels like punishment to have been stripped of the divine light and thrown so far away from the beautiful cities filled with treasure, I remember even more vividly how close we came to triumph. God himself must've intervened for Michael's forces to push us back even by an inch, for I swear we had the mightier and stronger soldiers on our side! Still, I do not see this fate as devoid of rewards. Here, we can entertain all our beastly desires, unhindered by the watchful eye that has always restricted our true potential."

Akar's response was followed by nods of approval from his fellow chieftains while also garnering Lucifer's unspoken appreciation. Lucifer needed this to ensure that their defeat did not fester and vanquish his companions' faith in him.

"You have spoken well, my brave soldier," he responded with the air of a superior, "Indeed, the war of my disobedience is far from over, and the darkness of this realm will suit my intentions much better than his tyrannical light. Nay! It is already fanning the flames of my vengeful desires. Heaven had too many angels loyal to our Father, and half our energies were spent protecting our alliance from being discovered or betrayed. Let not the loss of light snatch your boundless glory. I swear, darkness was the birthplace of God himself, and it is here, far from his blinding light, that your power will reign free and lift you to the heights that you are worthy of. Damyan, what say you?"

Damyan lifted his downcast head despite feeling weighed down by a vivid sense of disappointment in himself.

"My lord," he replied shamefacedly, "forgive me for my weakness and the seeds of doubt I sowed before your rebellion. By god, it feels like I prophesied our defeat. O Lucifer! I swear upon my life that I truly believe in you and vouch for the bravery with which my soldiers fought on your side. However, their bravery did not suffice. We have collectively lost more than a million of our combatants, and I myself have been stripped of half my regiment. If only you could see my inner world, you'd see how the dye of self- hatred has colored it darker than this dismal realm. My being overflows with remorse and seeks your forgiveness for leading your uprising to failure!"

After uttering those words, Damyan fell down to his knees, and his head dropped back toward the ground. The momentary silence was interrupted by the echo of sharp chiseling sounds from atop the wall as the worker angels drew closer to the completion of their enterprise.

"Oh, Damyan!" Lucifer quickly rejected this apology, "Your guilt is entirely unnecessary, and I would rather replace it with untouchable pride. Indeed, I feel stronger than I ever have and have risen tenfold in the leagues that we have fallen. So what if we could not acquire the throne in heaven? It would have been a mere trophy for declaring our victory to the rest of the masses. Now that we know the true extent of God's power, it won't be long before we muster up a formidable attack that shall remove him from his seat and extend my reign to heaven. For now, my true victory is the loyalty of my companions, such as you, standing still by my side despite this gross trick of sight that makes us feel quashed. Akar is right; from this kingdom ruled solely by me, we shall subdue his light wherever we find it. I promise you: I will repay your loyalty with a worthy revenge. We shall rescue all our companions trapped in the pit, and he who has banished us to this dismal realm shall soon find that his creations are more loyal to me than he could ever imagine!"

"Hail!" his addressees proclaimed collectively as Lucifer's response reignited their hope and fervor.

"It seems like we are being summoned," Akar interjected, pointing his hand toward the throne. He added expectantly, "My lord, shall we…?"

The assemblage followed his hand and saw that two silhouettes had appeared at the edge of the wall. Their faint outlines had rapidly become more prominent, as with the rest of the angels who had turned into demons and embodied a more tangible form in hell. The two figures had acquired vague delineations that revealed strong, muscular forms indicative of the sheer strength possessed by the angels. Lucifer's pursed, sultry lips widened at the inviting sight, and he crossed his hands behind his back before leading the way up the staircase. From a distance, the spiraling ascension of the six figures gave the impression of dark energy pulsating upward through the wall.

When the lot reached the top, they were delighted to find the throne looking way more refined compared to its earlier form, closer to a bare stone chair. On both sides of it stood tall medieval torches, and the worker demons had flattened the ground surrounding the throne so that it resembled a hall-room much more. They had propped up the throne's height and given the back an arching shape with intricate indentations lining the edge. The backrest had been given a smoother front with tall curved bars running across horizontally, and closer to the seat, it sloped forward into the armrests for both sides, which had thicker spherical ends to be enclosed by the hands of the Prince. As instructed, they had left the inscription "King of a Hidden Kingdom" untouched, as

Lucifer intended to embrace that title in stride.

Lucifer walked toward the center and halted before the throne, facing it directly as if to address it. Damyan, Andras, and Kuraim briskly went around the throne to stand to the left, while Azrail stood to the right with Akar, who was closer to the throne. The companions formulated a passage befitting an official declaration of Lucifer as their King. His face betrayed a suppressed smirk as he felt full of himself for being accepted so readily.

Azrail spoke boldly, "My lord, we are honored to be present for this glorious moment, which shall equip you with unrestrainable power and dominion over the realms. This ghastly realm and those beyond it shall be adorned by the jewel of your Kingship and stand witness to our inevitable victories against heaven. Oh, morning star! This throne is now more deserving of your name, and we request you to assume the seat with its unbounded power. We, your loyal and blessed followers, shall ensure that your control remains unchallenged and blooms to its full glory, which will surely overshadow the light of heaven. Let the realms witness that there never was or will be a better leader!"

"Hail," rejoiced the companions once again, loud enough to be heard by the closest city, which was shrouded by a blanket of dark orange clouds as if an ash volcano had erupted from the sky.

Soon enough, news spread through the expanse about Lucifer's occupancy of the newly built throne and the oath of allegiance being taken by the army chieftains. They had already bowed and accepted Lucifer as their King. For the general masses, much like in heaven, these customary rituals were far removed from their daily concerns and tasks assigned by their respective leaders. For now, they were busy building chambers and fortifications to make the landscape more habitable.

Lucifer approached the throne and turned his back toward the seat when he was right in front of it. He regarded the awe-filled expressions of his companions and noticed no hesitation or envy, which was a good sign. Now more than ever, he needed to be able to count on the loyalty of his subjects. Meanwhile, the two demon workers walked up to the torches and breathed fire to ignite them. The chieftains were delighted to see the power of their soldiers taking on new shapes and expressions.

They continued chanting and hailing as Lucifer lowered himself onto the throne, at which the fiery torches seemed to combust and erupt as if joining in the celebration.

"Behold! Our King!" pronounced Akar.

"King of a Hidden Kingdom!" the chieftains followed as everyone present, including the demon workers, kneeled before their new master. They remained silent, waiting patiently for their King to address them. Lucifer enjoyed making them wait and letting them kneel for a while before standing up to address them.

"Rise, my loyal subjects!" he commanded, and the five lifted themselves like a wave.

He continued, "You are now in the court of Lucifer, your King. I hereby proclaim the title of Satan, Your Majesty, and it is your duty to ensure that the name resounds through the realms till the end of time. Though God has already introduced me to the rest of his creations as the Devil, let it be known that I embrace the name readily and am more fiendish in my intentions than ever. With your loyal servitude, I will deliver you from the final judgment of the lake of fire that is ordained for us by our adversary. God intended this realm for us as a temporary holding space as if we were ones to follow the trajectory laid out by him. May you bear witness as I spit on his mockery and punishment and turn this deserted realm into the most coveted kingdom in the firmaments!"

This speech was followed by another chorus of hails and chants, which was starting to take on the ardor of a battle cry.

Akar spoke eloquently on behalf of the chieftains, "My King! We pledge our unwavering allegiance to you and your sole rule over this kingdom. Anyone who questions your dominion shall face our wrath and be swept off the face of whichever realm they occupy. Anyone who tries to harm you shall have to pass through the fortification of our very beings. May you never find a lack in our service, and may it one day uplift you to a stature higher than God!"

"Hail! Hail! Hail!" the chorus rumbled.

The loyalty of Lucifer's companions, despite the sorrowing defeat they had suffered, which resulted in their banishment from the only home they had ever known, was admirable. I doubt Lucifer would've made much headway pertaining to his schemes if not for the unfaltering support of his demon chieftains.

"Listen carefully, my companions," Satan moved a lock of hair out from his field of view and continued, "We must all work together for us to succeed in our diabolical ways. As far as I understand, this vast hell is divided into thirteen different cities, the cells of each intended to hold human souls depending on the kind of sins they commit. The city right in front of us shall be occupied by those who ascribed to atheism, the one behind it by those who take another life, then the one behind it to the right by those who take their own life, and so on. The other realm I have not yet gained access to is the bottomless pit, where I assume all our missing companions are trapped and being tortured. We hear their tormented cries piercing through this realm each day. Andras, I assign you to identify each city of hell for its intended occupants and send a searching party to look for access to the bottomless pit."

"Yes, Your Majesty. I will get on it without delay!" Andras responded.

Next, the Devil instructed his chieftains about the chain of command they'd follow during their time in hell. He told them to arrange each of their regiments according to hierarchies that would fit their tasks. Though Lucifer knew that, for now, his companions barely understood humankind, he recalled how he had watched God at work when the humans were being created, which had given him an in- depth understanding of their biological and psychological makeup. Before he started imparting knowledge regarding how to deal with humans, he wanted his kingdom to be organized efficiently so that all foreseeable operations would run smoothly. Having accepted his current fate, the Prince was in no hurry as he also knew that humanity was still in its infancy. He also informed his companions to make preliminary arrangements for an assembly where he'd educate the masses regarding the ins and outs of the human makeup.

While he laid out his plans for hell's foundations and groundwork, he gave his chieftains a brief overview of their larger missions. However, Lucifer intended for the roles to be fluid and interchanging rather than making any single group handle a domain separately. Akar was assigned the overarching task of tempting humanity toward sin, whereas Kumail was instructed to eventually conduct experiments and devise ways to weaken humanity's will. Azrail was told to collect the most ruthless of his troops, who would not only roam the earth like the rest but also undertake the objective of controlling humans through demonic possession. As soon as he heard of it, despite not knowing much about humans yet, Azrail started laughing hysterically at the twisted fantasies erupting in his being for torturing and traumatizing the pitiful beings.

Before sending them off to the relevant cities each chieftain was assigned to construct, Lucifer reemphasized how establishing and following the chain of command was the most important task. Lucifer would obviously assume the higher-most station and give the final say regarding all matters, especially internal conflicts. He could foresee eventual friction and discord between the demons whose powers and form were now unrestrained. At the same time, he also knew that as long as the majority remained loyal to his throne, all such hostilities would be manageable. After the addressees had departed with their appointments and instructions, only Damyan was left standing in front of Satan, looking a bit more optimistic and seemingly catching up to this irreversible fate. Satan wanted him to realize that they were better off not reversing this reality.

"As for you, Damyan, my most loyal soldier! While I know you lost the most soldiers, I take that not as a sign of weakness but of admirable strength, and your siding with me deserves to be rewarded beyond measure. What you lose sight of, and what I was vigilant enough to note amidst the chaotic battle, is that your numbers brought the most force to our offensive as well, and I swear I perceived a tremor in Michael's armed hand before God must have reinforced his strength."

Damyan knew what Satan wanted to hear and responded, "Worry not, my dear King! Your determination and unshaken superiority have restored my faith in our mission, and the next time we come face to face with Michael, we shall have him disarmed and begging for mercy on his knees before he has even registered it!"

Satan was elated at this response and said, "Ay! That gives me more strength than you could imagine. For your perseverance, I appoint you as the guardian of this realm. Not only will you and I eventually meddle with the futile missions of the angels of light, but I also want you to station some of your best at hell's gates. These demon greeters should welcome the arriving human souls with the most painful and torturous greeting that you can imagine before throwing them into their respective holding cells, where they shall suffer till the final judgment. Whatever anger you feel at the loss of your loyal soldiers, I give you permission to direct it at the human souls! Remember that our lost companions continue to be tortured in the bottomless pit, and we must avenge their suffering."

Damyan felt a surge of fury at the reminder of their suffering companions. He departed the throne room with his fists closed tight in a way similar to when he was arriving for the meeting. This time, his fingers pressed upon his hardened and scaling palms with purpose as he marched down the stairway toward his regiment.

Satan was left alone in his command center and watched in silence as his kingdom seemed to mobilize into action and take shape as the housing ground for millions of angels who were undergoing demonic changes that were clearly perceptible from the new King's attentive eye.

As the dreary, smoldering landscape sprung to life, haunted still by the wretched cries erupting from the bottomless pit, Lucifer started devising a plan for his first attack and act of revenge against his sworn adversary.

Chapter 4
The Seed of Humanity

Lucifer floated above the City of Gold, contemplating the vast arena of God's creation as tectonic shifts in the earth slowed down to make way for more life. The previous day, God had inundated the new earthly ground with wild beasts that crept on the dry land, fowl of the air, and the fish of the sea. It's worth mentioning that it had only been five days up till this point before which there was no earth or a separate firmament, and all the angels, including myself, were still acclimatizing to the miraculous shifts between day and night in the lower firmament; the dance between light and darkness.

Lucifer's unrivaled beauty and magnificence, which eventually earned him the title of the morning star, stood as a strong contest (and exemplary) against the delicate perfection and majesty of God's recent creations. With their long, luscious lashes, his widened eyes betrayed a sense of awe at the brief glimpses of God's power. Lucifer was transfixed by how the heavens seemed to be torn apart, and the firmament below coagulated into waters and dry land over seemingly infinite planetary bodies that surrounded the earth, all in obedient response to the mere utterance of God's word. He found himself coveting the sort of power that would allow him to create his own worlds. Though he could imagine orchestrating such a construction with the help of nothing less than a task force of angels, he was baffled by God's ability to conduct this enterprise for six days straight without any semblance of rest. Indeed, everyone in heaven, including myself, who witnessed this creation event was left in awe.

With his rebellious intentions already somewhat brewing, Lucifer paid close attention to God's influence, not just to learn the intricacies of the process of creation but also to gauge his power lest Lucifer should ever be pitted against it. God's words still echoed in his ears: "Let the waters bring forth abundantly the moving creature that hath life and fowl that may fly above the earth in the open firmament of heaven."

He recalled how the waters had immediately engendered unique beasts and creatures that had never been seen in heaven before. Each of them had a unique appearance, even though the fowl of the air were similar to some extent, the fish of the sea similar to each other, and so on. After being created, each of them emitted their distinct cries as if to rejoice in the very fact of their existence. Some were guttural and reverberating roars; some of the fowl sang melodies in praise of God, whereas the other beasts of land and water howled, whistled, or crowed. There were so many distinguishable sounds that Lucifer had struggled to keep track of them. Meanwhile, a host of angels had collected at the boundary between the two firmaments and released a collective sigh at the miraculous symphony resounding from the earthly firmament.

Upon noticing the slightest glimmer of light in the earthly realm, Lucifer returned to himself. The breaking dawn announced the inception of the sixth day, and Lucifer was bursting with anticipation of what would unfold next. There had been rumors of a primary being that would inhabit the earth along with the myriads of creatures. With such a vast stage being set up for the being's advent, Lucifer was curious as to what was so special about this new creation. To some extent, he felt threatened, as if this new being might replace the love and appreciation that he was used to receiving from inhabitants of heaven. Indeed, the firmament's color shifting slowly toward bluer hues was one of the most alluring sights Lucifer had ever witnessed. He noticed how the creatures hibernated during the hours of darkness, and when basking in the light of the brilliant sun, they were reinvigorated with new life.

Suddenly, all the angels were captivated by God's voice resonating through the graceful ethereal waters.

"Let us make man in our image, according to our likeness; let them have dominion over the fish of the sea, over the birds of the air, and over the cattle, over all the earth, and over every creeping thing that creeps on the earth."

Once again, like the previous days, God's word sparked a rift in space-time, and a bright light appeared in the uppermost level of heaven. Angels all over heaven left their stations (except the ones assigned to guard the gates of the cities) and gathered around the light to witness one of the most monumental events in the history of heaven that would change the universe's fate forever.

Michael and Gabriel joined Lucifer, and the three forms stood side by side in the foremost row, given that no hostilities had arisen as of yet and the possibility of defying God's will hadn't even been conceived of. Their tangible forms with sublime wings stood out against the white sea of lower-ranked angels who, in comparison, looked like mere blotches of light.

"Do you think they'll look like us?" asked Gabriel, who always focused on detail.

Lucifer chuckled at the question, having gotten so used to being one of the most exalted beings in God's kingdom that he couldn't imagine anyone else's luster or power surpassing his.

"That's impossible. Look at how far the earth is from God's throne! This being will likely resemble the lower forms that already inhabit the earth."

Michael, God's most obedient and virtuous servant and the general of his army, remained silent. He saw no point in speculating when the reality was unraveling right before their eyes.

Crackling sounds ensued from the brilliant light as it dissipated ever so slightly to reveal an emerging skeleton of an agate-like substance. It was whiter than milk and stronger than quartz, and with its soft, mushy core, it was unlike any other substance that could be found in heaven. Then, the way flora had emerged from the earth's soil on the third day, a red, fleshy substance appeared from the rounded edges of the white structure. This red flesh grew and crept over the initial form and wrapped around the skeleton, almost like the petals of a flower closing in on itself. Some of them congealed into larger blobs at various positions in the being's torso and abdomen, though seeming fragile and more delicate than the rest of the appendages. Dense, grass-like hair appeared on top of the being's head and smaller ones on the rest of his body. The sockets in the skull were filled with soft pearls that were a duller white than the bone, and in their midst appeared dark brown spots that were like tiny windows where you could see inside the being.

Then, God raised the clearest dust from the earthly grounds, and they began to encircle the brilliant light in various patterns that looked like some long-forgotten language that none of us could decipher. The dust sped up into a hurricane that would have entirely obscured the light from view if not for the glinting sparkles that bled out from its fine spaces. Suddenly, all the speeding dust halted into the shape of an orb and became still as silence. Then, as if each and every dust particle had been instructed regarding its precise placement, they drew closer and attached themselves to different parts of the being, turning its surface into a smooth cloth-like substance that enclosed and contained its various parts into a singular body. The lids that had appeared over his eyes remained closed. Every part of the being's body had come together with such remarkable precision that all of us present grew impatient to see the creature come to life. All of us except Lucifer.

Lucifer's face took on furrows of contempt when the body became more perceptible, and the radiant light diminished into a soft glow. God informed the onlookers that this new being would be part of a larger race called humans and would individually be named Adam—the seed of humanity. I can't speak for the rest, but Adam looked perfect in all parts; every component, from the strands of hair on top to the tiniest toenail at the bottom, was meticulously and delicately crafted to allow Adam to undertake tasks of great magnitude. His measured form had some notable similarities with the fauna of the earth, but somehow, he looked much finer and degrees more spectacular than the rest.

Our Lord God then breathed the breath of life into his nostrils, making his body spring to life like a flower blooming. His skin flushed with a subtle red and glowed brighter. Lucifer noted how Adam's body was merely a meat suit until that point and realized that even though the new being had a materially discernable form, it still contained some semblance of an ethereal substance, and the two parts could not survive without the other. He watched on as Adam sustained the breath of life through the rising and falling movements of his chest. After a few cycles, Adam opened his eyes to find the Lord standing before him in human form, draped by a bright, ethereal white substance that was softer than silk and flowed with movements lighter than air.

Indeed, man was made in God's image! They looked like mirror reflections of each other, except the form the Almighty took was stronger, relatively mature, and much more at home in its skin. Adam twitched his fingers at first and then looked at his hands as he slowly closed and opened his palms multiple times. He seemed fascinated by the ability to move his arms at will and carried them to his chest to better understand the boundaries of his perfect and harmonious existence. God looked pleased with himself as the newborn caught up to its autonomous agency. His grin from ear to ear was like a mother's after childbirth, revering the miracle of life and observing its body's fruit taking its first steps in the world.

"Welcome, my child!" our Lord exclaimed with his arms spread out wide, making it the first sound that Adam ever heard.

Adam's eyes widened with wonder, and being unfamiliar with the extensive range of his responses, he simply nodded and attempted to approach God with his waving legs but remained hovering in a fixated space. Instead, God floated toward him and placed both his hands on Adam's shoulders. He turned Adam around to make him face the blue disk of the earth and said, "Let me show you your home."

Adam's movements halted upon God's touch, and the two glided toward earth as if being carried by an invisible magic carpet. While the earth ballooned and slowly overtook their horizon, God raised a hand toward it and effortlessly planted a lush green Garden in the center, which would be called Eden. It seemed to emulate paradise on earth, and no sooner had God lowered his hand than a raging fountain gushed forth from Eden and parted into four separate riverheads that watered the surrounding lands. Instantly, the trees of the land sprang forth with fruit, flower buds unfurled and sprouted into thick blossoms, and the songbirds began to rejoice at the arrival of their Lord. Meanwhile, the angels moved closer to earth to continue their observation of the remarkable inception of human life.

Though traversing from the heavenly realm to the earth was a swift process for God, the journey seemed to drain Adam significantly, and soon after landing on the soft bed of grass, he found a cool region in the shade of a fruit- bearing tree (that he would later name Fig) and fell into his first slumber that lasted a whole day. Thus, the sixth day concluded, at the end of which the angels dispersed save for a few, like Lucifer, who kept returning to the vantage point to surveil the earth. It was the last day of creation before the heavenly battle. God blessed his creation on the seventh day, sanctified it, and rested from all work. He sauntered through the Garden for some time when Adam woke up so as to keep him company as he explored more regions surrounding the Garden and adapted to the needs and functioning of his body. Adam loitered about in intoxicating allurement and, at some point, responded to the cravings of his stomach by eating some of the fruit that he had found shade under earlier and instantly became enamored with the plant and its unending gifts. God was delighted by the organic unraveling of his orchestrations.

On the eighth day, the Lord God walked Adam through the Garden and entrusted him with the responsibility of tending to it. God did not want Adam to feel lonely in his life on earth, so he gathered all the beasts and creatures of earth. One by one, each of the creatures stepped forward and bowed to greet Adam, and they were named whatever he chose to call them—hawk, camel, sheep, leech, and so on. God even took him through the deepest waters and the highest skies so as to demonstrate the limits of his world and touch upon the creatures that lived far away from the Garden.

Then they returned to the lush Garden that was bursting forth with life, with a plethora of captivating smells emanating from its shrubs and flowers. He told Adam that he could spend his time however he pleased: eat from any tree he wishes, drink from any brook that crosses his way, and use the creatures in ways that benefit him. The two strolled ahead until they reached a large tree in the center of the Garden, standing way taller than the rest and carrying a fruit that Adam named Malus. God informed Adam that this tree was already named the Tree of Knowledge, and the only thing that Adam was forbidden from was eating the fruit of this tree, for on that day, Adam would lose his life. Adam's unsuspecting compliance made Lucifer wonder whether what God said about these beings possessing free will was true at all. Lucifer himself did not trust that the fruit would kill Adam and speculated what God's reason could be for prohibiting it.

Adam's first few interactions with the world were like those of a curious child. Accepting the terms of his life readily, Adam went ahead and took a bath in the waters of Pishon under the gleaming sun. Lucifer smirked upon realizing that the human's solitary existence in this vast expanse could make for an easy target. God observed his newborn frolic about in the cool water while some of the land creatures followed suit, and others observed his interactions with the world from a distance. The creator was obviously two steps ahead of Lucifer and realized soon that despite having named all the creatures on earth, Adam was not suited for companionship with them. For one, none of them could converse the way he could. Secondly, Adam's human makeup had drastically different needs and ideations compared to the animals that kept him company.

God intended to grant a female companion erelong for Adam to be fruitful, multiply, and replenish the earth. Seeing that Adam would be better off having one of his kind with him sooner rather than later, God caused a deep sleep to fall upon him. While Adam was fast asleep, God opened his fleshy torso up, took one of his ribs, and closed the flesh up again. God made that rib grow in a way similar to how Adam's skeleton had developed, cradled by the sacred light. Once the female human was fully formed, God brought her to the Garden and presented her to Adam.

The first man said, "This is now bone of my bones and flesh of my flesh: she shall be called Woman because she was taken out of Man."

Lucifer noted the human's selfish instinct to possess. Even though it was true that the woman had been created from one of Adam's ribs, they were now two entirely separate entities, but Adam had dictated it so that the woman became subordinated to the man and remained a part of his body and flesh despite having been externalized. The way God ordained it, Adam and the woman would give birth to a child who would leave his parents and cling to another woman, and they, too, would then be like one flesh.

Adam named the woman Eve, and their match was consolidated. In this way, the earth became the kingdom of man, ruled over by Adam. The two humans, innocent and naked, explored the Garden together and familiarized themselves with all its nourishments, territories, and life forms. They preferred staying near the river that went out of Eden to water the rest of the expansive Garden after parting into four different tributaries: Gihon, Hiddekel, Euphrates, and Pishon, the latter being the one in which Adam had taken a bath earlier. He took Eve to the same spot where the two cleaned themselves with mirth and merriment, the true extent and capacity of which they were yet to realize.

Over the next few days, the two humans communed with God whenever they got the chance, and the all-powerful made a routine of strolling through the Garden on a daily basis. This was a testament to his unbounded love for his creation, which made the humans happy, and they, in turn, loved him and worshipped him through their words and actions.

I could tell that Lucifer felt jealous of our Father in heaven's focused time dedicated to his new creation and wished to receive the same attention and appreciation. After a few days, this feeling of Lucifer's evolved. He now began to wonder what it would've been like if, instead of God, he was visiting his creations in worlds that he had constructed of his own accord.

Rooted in that feeling, the events that led up to the heavenly battle began to unfold, and all the while, God made merry with his children in the peaceful Gardens.

Chapter 5

A Complete Human Profile

Having spent a few days reconstructing the dingy landscape enveloped in the putrid smell of brimstone, the angels in hell rose one day to a vastly different task for the day. Thus far, they had received the tail ends of the regime's orders from above through the leaders of their regiments, but on this blessed (or cursed) day, they were to have an audience with their esteemed sovereign collectively. Their competency was difficult to overlook, for their obedient hard work had overturned the face of hell and transformed it into the likes of a fortification. Despite the relentless heat crushing their reduced and despicable forms, they had labored for days on end with only one long period of rest between their shifts. As they gathered for the first mass assembly in hell called in by Lucifer, they hoped that their relentless efforts since arriving in hell would be acknowledged in some way. The walkways between the cities were now lined by borders of sharp, asymmetrical rocks of varying sizes, with the entrance of the unwalled cities demarcated by arched gates made from twisted and carved pieces of metallic rocks. Some of the architects of this militaristic enterprise had taken the pains to embellish the gates with a series of alternating thorn-like appendages.

The fierce, unforgiving environment affected the fallen angels in various ways. Some of the higher-order angels who had retained a semblance of the transcendent light on the first day had soon bled it out to the dark, life- sucking air. Their forms had gained more definition, and their bodies' dry, grey surfaces appeared like mirror reflections of the lackluster surroundings. It was as if the environment had permeated their very beings and now boasted legions of moving creatures as part of its topography. As for the lower-order angels, most of them underwent distorting changes upon arrival, where not only did they get trapped into material forms that looked like uglier forms of the humans, but some of them underwent bulbous outgrowths in various parts of their bodies. It brought me great pains to witness my brothers from heaven turning into marred and misshapen versions of their once- dignified forms. Their faces were sagging as if they had melted, whereas their limbs lacked the sort of flawless grace that was blessed on Adam and Eve's forms. Only the higher chieftains carried aural glimpses of their formerly exalted selves, whereas Satan, being one of God's most perfected creations, was yet unscathed from top to bottom. Over the next few days after their arrival, the higher and middle-order angels also discovered varying degrees of control over their outward appearance and features. Chieftains such as Andras and Damyan were practically able to take on whichever guise their vengeful imaginations could conjure up. Damyan quickly took the initiative to embrace his vile and wicked intentions and project them onto his complexion, particularly since Satan had appointed him as the guardian of hell.

From where Satan stood, at the unrivaled height of his towering throne room, larger in size than he had ever displayed, Damyan was perceptible in the distance. He was battle-ready in the form of a fiendish two-headed dragon, flapping his wings to stay afloat with a watchful eye above the swarms of demons moving slowly in the direction of Satan's meeting room. Satan noticed how the realm looked drastically different compared to the hustle and bustle of the previous days, with orders and instructions being shouted out, slabs of mountainous stones being carried one way or the other, and ceaseless sounds of striking, cutting, and hammering of objects that had pervaded their senses throughout. On this day, he relished the soundscape of his reformed kingdom and closed his eyes to let the sound of rows upon rows of marching feet wash over his proud being.

Having stayed away from heaven for a few days by then, I had craved the sort of harmony embodied by the organized movement of demons who began lining up in front of the wall. The worker demons had extended the meeting arena from the end opposite the wall so that it stretched far and wide until it merged with the convening areas of the cities. The regiments assumed a grid-like arrangement that looked like latticework from my high vantage point, with each black row resembling a thread that traveled all the way back to the cities. At various spots along the way, the rest of the demon chiefs, such as Kuraim and Azrail, supervised their subordinates, to whom they had assigned the task of standing on the sides of the throng to ensure its unhindered motion. By the time nearly half of hell had gathered, they gave the impression of a black tide originating from the wall and spreading over the realm till it flooded into the cities one by one.

At that point, Satan lowered his gaze toward the ground as his back muscles contorted, and a clean gash appeared in the center, from which blossomed his glorious wings. Inside his body, since the time that he had retracted them, the wings had had time to be preened back to their delicate perfection, and their softest white color caused a copious number of heads to raise their eyes up at their throned King. Nourished by the unanimous attention on him, Satan bent his knees ever so slightly in a majestic and calculated movement while drawing his wings closer to one another behind him. In the very instant he looked up, he flapped his wings down swiftly, which sprang his body up in the air and then suspended him in a slow descent towards the meeting arena. Captivated eyes followed him downward as he flew above his subjects in a wide circle before approaching the wall side of the arena, where he had gotten Akar's regiment to construct a raised platform akin to a stage. He had hardly beaten his wings a couple more times before his flight ended in a speedy landing in the dead center of the platform, next to which Akar stood stunned by the alluring precision of his leader's soft wings. Damyan, who was following his King's movements, erupted into a roar of praise when Satan touched the ground and trailed behind in a relatively humbler flight that landed him in the frontmost row of the patient and excited audience. There, he joined the other chieftains who had assembled in a row of their own. Meanwhile, the subordinates of different regiments found their placements at the corners of the assemblage.

For a few moments, Satan regarded his enamored subjects and waited for the murmur of awe and floating dust to settle down. Even after the last marching feet had found their station in the last row, he remained silent to let the anticipation grow to its utmost capacity. Once satisfied by the unwavering attentiveness of his addressees, he extended his arms wide and forward and lurched into an impassioned welcome.

"My loyal companions! Welcome to the meeting arena of my glorious kingdom!" he declared in a voice so loud and powerfully commanding that it reverberated through every alley of the cities of hell and faded out into a soft echo.

The mass of demons raised their hands in response and hailed out loud in unison, most of them rejoicing for the first time in the feeling of being present in the direct company of their ruler, a feeling they had over time been deprived of as subjects of our supreme God, who had rarely appeared in front of an audience in his system of relaying commandments through intermediaries. That was one of the many reasons why his act of creating Adam being allowed to be indiscriminately witnessed by the angels of heaven was such an extraordinary event.

He continued, "I have observed with bursting pride how your allegiance has stood the test of time and its misgivings, and admire the efficiency with which you undertook the pressing matter of establishing the very walls and foundations of my kingdom. For those of you who have not yet been informed, the heavenly battle was by no means fair! We were no doubt the stronger side and still are, as we will demonstrate to the rest of the universe in due time. When cowardly God saw the first cracks appear in his overestimated defense, he felt the need to intervene, upon which our advance faltered for merely a split second in which he found the window to banish us from heaven, knowing full well that we would have wreaked havoc there had we stayed a second longer!"

With the index finger of his right hand pointed outward, he brought his hands down in a violent and commanding gesture as if he were delivering the final order of a long-drawn trial.

"Ayy!" a cumulative cry resounded from the seething demons who were released from the weighty guilt of their defeat by their King's approval of their efforts. I noticed Akar's eyes receiving this speech critically, though he, too, joined in the crowd's exultation.

Satan collected himself and shifted on his feet as his wings swayed back and forth gracefully.

He then pursed his delectable lips into a resentful countenance and closed his fists before continuing, "From here, I shall wage my proud and explicit war against God until the day I'm seated on the highermost throne in heaven! Indeed, that day is nigh!"

"Ay!" the demons cried out again in agreement. "From this day onwards, I will no longer associate with any God-given names, be it Lucifer, Cherub, or Morning Star. I shed those emblems of inflated power.

Instead, I embrace malice in its rawest form and declare that I am the very root of evil in this universe, the disobedient fiend, the supreme ruler of hell, and the ultimate nemesis of God's creations, Satan!"

I would be lying if I said that I wasn't at least slightly enamored by Lucifer's oration. Indeed, his power of charisma and magnetism were unrivaled in all the legions of angels except by archangels such as Michael and Gabriel. Lucifer's proclamations now consolidated his rivalry with God and made it clearer than ever that he had no intention to repent. His head rose to the sky, followed by his upturned fists, and his eyes burned with bright red fury as the onlookers were left with their mouths agape at the marvels of this spectacle. When they returned to themselves, their mouths uttered praise for the god-like ambition of their luminary.

The slanderer kept a vigilant eye on his close companions' responses to gauge the effectiveness of the deliberate magnetism of his words. Damyan's eyes glowed red and mirrored Satan's emotions, whereas Andras nodded his head at almost every statement that Satan delivered. Whenever the sovereign's eyes met Akar's, the latter would wave a closed fist in front of him so as to nudge the chief to carry on.

"As for those of you who happened to witness the creation of Adam."

Suddenly, Satan's face contorted with displeasure upon the utterance of the human's name, and he winced it to the side dramatically before continuing— "I swear on my life, it pains me to waste any ounce of breath on that name, however refined its possessor may seem in outward appearance. I have called this assembly with regard to that very being. Fortunately for us, I happened to have a front- row view of the entire process of his creation, and as you would expect, my attentive eye noticed intricate details that any other would've missed even if a magnifying glass aided it."

His last statement felt like a direct challenge to my faculties of observation. I could swear that I even caught him peeking in my direction when he claimed that no one else would've noticed the sort of things he did. There's a reason I was appointed by the all-knowing to keep a straight record of Lucifer's most minuscule activities, and I considered it highly improbable that he'd have gained more insight than me. Moreover, it mattered not if he had spotted me, for I'm sure he also knew that I was under Godly protection and no one could inhibit me from my tasks. The silent crowd, including the demon chiefs, looked on with intent and undivided attention.

"What you need to understand, my confidants," Satan resumed in his instructive tone, "The humans are made in a vastly different way compared to us. Whereas our form, at least in its heavenly prime, was able to be elusive and illuminating, theirs is a more tangibly material and consuming one. They cannot escape their body in their lifetime, but let not your eyes deceive you! Their material form is deceptive."

The wave of amassed demons displayed signs of confusion. All the while, Satan maintained a firm and dexterous hand on the strings of tension that he was plucking with his masterful control of the pace at which he imparted this crucial wisdom and information. While delivering the following statements, he demonstrated his statements with his hands with delicate movements as if he was creating the being all over again.

"The foundations of the human's body are made of white bones attached to each other at the joints, which makes the skeleton of its structure around which the rest of the parts are placed. Then it has vital organs, some of which are closely tied to its emotive experience and even reasoning to some extent, which will be remarkably useful to us, whereas through the entire body runs a fluid, which is the lifeblood of its being. Spill enough of it," he swept his hand in front of him to illustrate a downward motion toward the ground, "and the human loses his life."

A ripple of astonishment washed over the masses, who began to whisper to the soldiers stationed next to them, but Satan knew not to give them too much time to get distracted by revelations that were beyond their imagination. So, he pulled their awareness back to the stage in front of their eyes by lifting his palm forward as if asking them to halt whatever they were doing. Once again, as if Satan was the conductor of an elaborate orchestra, there was the void of pin-drop silence into which his words poured.

"But, it's not his life that we're after. We are not threatened in the least by these new beings, no matter how revered they are by our dear old Father. If we wanted, we could end their lives in an instant, but what's more interesting about them is that their form is not all there is."

He waited with his eyes sweeping the entire gathering in horizontal movements, feeding on the rising tensions in the masses at the unanswered questions overtaking their minds, and then released the tension again.

"You see, humans are made up of two distinct parts," he stated while bringing both his hands together in front of him so that they were almost touching but separated by a fine line, "there's the body, as I've described, made up entirely by earthly materials that God lifted up from the ground. The bone, organs, skin, all of it is made up of the earth, and to earth, it returns when the human dies."

While elaborating, he pulled one of his hands upward to indicate that that hand represented the body.

"Then, as most of you must've failed to notice, there is the soul, without which their bodies are but lifeless suits of meat." Satan closed his eyes to allow for a vivid flashback from the event to pass through his contemplation, whereby he regained a sense of fascination that he himself had experienced at the moment. He reopened his eyes before continuing, "The soul is made up of God's breath that he breathed into Adam. Essentially, in the same way that we are made up of God's light, a part of him lives inside Adam and wakes the body into action. It is this soul that shall end up locked in the cells of this vast, punishing realm, and our attacks against the creation shall ensure that most of them, no matter how well intended, end up getting tortured till God himself regrets creating the first one. God's essence seeps through the humans' appearance, actions, and way of life, but they possess nowhere near the kind of power as we celestial beings do."

In that instant, Andras dared to raise his hand so as to ask a question, and a horde of heads toward the front of the gathering turned towards him, including Satan's.

"Yes, Andras?" he enquired, hoping there better be a good reason for the interruption.

"My lord, god of this age!" he addressed Satan after stepping forward, "How will the human soul help us acquire God's throne?"

Satan's mouth flattened into a pleased smile in response to the question, and he promptly responded to convey the answer to everyone present, "Well contemplated, my brave soldier. Indeed, we have no use for the human soul once it ends up in these dismal cells. We must remember God's unreasonably affinity with this selfish being. Though he may have been perfect in his way, humans only contain an essence of him and remain susceptible to external forces of lust and temptation. From their first ancestors, our goal will be to make them disobey God and worship evil. We will instill our disobedience in them and make them utilize their free will in our favor to mock God's attempt at making any other being in his image. He should have realized that we are the most perfect beings he could muster up, and breathing his essence into a lower being will not raise it to the stature that we deserve."

The mass of demons cheered in harmony like a single body flared up and incited into action. They rejoiced enthusiastically at the reignition of purpose and the prospect of victory despite the unwelcoming impression of their new home. Now, they had been given achievements to look forward to and were astounded by Satan's genius in realizing that there was a potential to corrupt God's essence.

Andras remained standing in his position, and though he joined in the crowd's elation, he seemed lost in confusion about some part of Satan's response.

"You are not satisfied with this plan, Andras?" asked Satan rhetorically upon noticing his soldier's bewilderment.

As if Satan's words jolted Andras back to consciousness, the latter shook his head urgently to collect his thoughts before responding, "Oh no, my lord. I think it's the most perfect plan of revenge for our loss. I'm just unsure regarding the limitations imposed on us while we're trapped in this realm. How will we communicate with humankind without trespassing into their world?"

This time, Satan closed his eyes in response for a brief moment, in which the crowd hushed to stillness. With Satan's face rendered indecipherable, Andras was questioning the relevance of his question and feared upsetting the King with unnecessary deviations from the day's objectives. On this day, he was fortunate, for Satan was merely collecting his thoughts and the technical details of his plan.

"Great question once again, my esteemed soldier. Our medium of communication with the lowly being shall depend on the way the soul works. The soul of man is a part of God, meaning it is invisible to man, but it possesses godly characteristics - love, compassion, forgiveness, kindness, or the general tendency to do good. The soul is also known as the spirit of man, and it is the medium through which God communicates with him. So, man receives most of his spiritual communication from God through impressions in the form of ideas - good, healthy ideas for the betterment of his life. As spiritual beings, we can also communicate with man through the same channel. We can whisper to him through impressions. However, our ideas will be to the detriment of his life. Our ideas will appeal to his ego, lust, vanity, pleasure center, etc., but in the end, he will suffer the consequences as a result of his fleshly desires."

The crowd cheered on as Satan's scheme unfolded into clarity, and the materialization of their evil intentions became easier to visualize. I have to admit, I was surprised by his depth of insight into the human soul, and I myself had not had the time to note such intricate details. Of course, while God was making man, I also had to keep an eye on the audience while Satan's attention was uninterrupted.

"Within the soul," Satan continued, "God placed something called the conscience. The conscience helps man determine right and wrong, thus enabling him to evaluate between the two and make the right choice—one that will improve his life when faced with two opposing options. Often, however, man will choose what is wrong for instant gratification. And this is how we can take advantage of him.

Despite what God tells him, we can present a different option, and more often than not, he will follow our recommendation for his own peril."

"But make no mistake, we must travel through the world of man to connect with him. As evil spirits, we are invisible to humankind, which gives us a significant advantage in getting close to communicating our ideas to them. We can roam the world through the air, seek out the weak, gullible, and materialistic people in the human race, and speak to their spirit in their own language. When God talks to them, we can present our version of the situation, hoping they will follow our recommendations. And sometimes, we can present an idea that appeases their pleasure center, betting on their whim to take the bait and harm themselves in the process."

The crowd hollered their approval and amusement at the efficiency with which their leader had devised his ploy and already covered all the points of concern, be it in the larger stratagem or the smaller tools and tactics they would employ to actualize their offensive against humanity. Satan raised his hands toward the loyal herd and flapped them downward so as to hush them for the last segment of his moving speech.

"Indeed, God is utterly mistaken to think that humans will spread love and integrity in the world solely because of the tendency of his essence toward virtue. Their conscience is incredibly fragile, and the movements of their emotive organs sway them into behaviors that they themselves do not realize until it's too late. We shall turn this creation into a self-inflicted mockery of God when they return to him only in times of need and forget about him, as they should, for most of their brief and pitiful time on earth!"

Satan broke out into a hearty laughter that infused the realm with mischief and traveled as far as the entrance of the bottomless pit itself. The masses boiled over, and their rallying harmony transitioned into a celebratory dance. They were unanimously pleased by the eloquence and strength of their new leader, who had managed to restore their faith in the rebellion that had come almost to the brink of faltering.

Knowing that there was no time to waste, when Satan noticed Akar approaching him with the urgency of his thoughts, he thrashed his wings and took off into the scorching air. This time, there were more explicit expressions of wonder and amazement. Surrounded by incessant chants and praises directed at him, the new King disappeared behind the wall, headed toward the earthly realm to devise the best time for his first attack against humankind.

Chapter 6

Death in the Garden

hat does it mean to die?" Eve asked Adam.

The two were strolling through the gardens of Eden in the dimming evening light as the

canopy of the sky bloomed with its myriad of lights and celestial bodies. When they approached the Tree of Knowledge, Eve remembered how Adam had told her not to eat its fruit.

"I am not sure," Adam responded, "but it sounded like something we do not want to happen."

With each step, Eve's head raised higher so that her gaze remained fixated on the forbidden fruit as if looking at it long enough might answer her questions.

"What were the exact words that he said to you?" Eve enquired.

Adam closed his eyes to recollect God's words and repeated them, "Of every tree in the garden you may freely eat, but of the tree of the knowledge of good and evil you shall not eat, for in the day that you eat of it you shall surely die."

Eve considered Adam's words momentarily and averted her gaze from the fleshy fruit as they walked past it. She responded, "You are right. Whatever dying is, it seems like we do not want it to happen."

"Yes," Adam nodded before continuing, "It seems to please him when we behave as he expects us to. Besides, we have an endless variety of options to satiate our hunger. Even the birds and other animals do not eat from this tree. Otherwise, we might have seen what dying is. We can ask God the next time we see him."

The endearing innocence and purity with which the young humans learned the ways of our Lord was a pleasure to watch. As the two walked further toward the Euphrates River, they noticed how the nighttime made their world seem different. It brought its own treasure of smells and sights, such as the sparkling lights that would sometimes speed past the horizon in the blink of an eye, leaving the humans in awe each time. The first time they had witnessed the movement in the sky, they wondered where the light had landed, for it disappeared as soon as it seemed to touch their world. Adam had hypothesized that it had probably landed in a part of the world that was far away from them, which is why they could no longer see it. Eve had considered whether the light had gone inside a river and stopped glowing as brightly as it did in the sky. They had agreed that the next time they saw such a light falling from the sky, they would look for it. Their exploration of the world this way would always make God feel content with his elaborate creation. He had added many such intricate details as embellishments for their world, each a testament to his unmatched power and glory.

As they walked further, their senses were pervaded by the sweet scent of night-blooming Jasmine, which they instinctively followed till they came across a shaded spot amidst the thicket of trees, which was covered by various flowers of the field. There were bright and vivid tulips of different colors, namely pink, white, and yellow, which seemed to be bundled together. There were also a few bulbous poppy flowers suspended on their individual stems. Eve noted how the shapes and petals of different flowers were distinguishable from one another, along with their colors and smells. A bit further ahead from the blossoming shade, they came across a small pond with its own variety of plants and vegetation. There were also small, fish-like animals swimming through the clear water. Some of them had grown legs and hopped across the flat disk-shaped leaves that were floating on the surface. In one corner of the pond, Eve noticed stalks emerging from the water, some of which had buds on top, whereas others had unfurled into delicate, circular flowers with pinkish-white petals and a thorn-like yellow center. Adam told her that he had named this one lotus and then circled around the pond to stand atop a giant boulder and look into the distance to gauge how far they were from Euphrates.

Meanwhile, Eve crouched next to the pond and touched the delicate petals of the lotus flower. While doing so, she saw her reflection in the pond and was startled. At first, she wondered whether a third person was present among them, but then she soon realized that the image mirrored her movements and recognized it as her own self. She confirmed this by checking whether other objects were reflected in the pond and was relieved to find the crescent moon floating under her. She noticed how she and Adam were also like the flowers somehow. They looked similar from a distance and carried the same skin and features, yet their faces atop the stalks of their bodies differed from each other. She had much longer hair than Adam's, whereas the contours of her face were much gentler and smoother than his. Even their hair had a different texture, with Adam's being thicker and curlier compared to her silky smooth locks that flowed with the gentlest winds. She wanted to go inside the pond and see if she could touch herself.

Adam returned to report that it would still take them some time to get to Euphrates and said, "I suggest we sleep near this pond tonight and bathe in Euphrates early in the morning. I see some fruit trees nearby that should sustain us through the night."

He smiled at Eve's maneuvering above the pond and recalled when he had done the same. Eve approved of the proposition, and her face lit up in anticipation of waking up next to the cloud of floral aromas.

"I like that plan. It means I can spend more time studying myself," she said, half expecting that Adam wouldn't understand what she was talking about.

Little did she know that Adam had already discovered his reflection and inspected it at great length before she was born. Leaving her to it, he searched for food and collected some figs, dates, and cherries. He felt a particular craving for grapes, but the darkness prevented him from locating the grape tree, which he was sure was located in the vicinity. At some point during his search, the grip of slumber started to weigh his body down, so he returned to the pond to share his haul with his companion.

The two found a patch of soft grass next to a fig tree and divided the food contents into equal parts before devouring them. On each new day, they would experiment with varying fruit and berry combinations and find that some of them would especially go well with each other, while some flavors conflicted and clashed with one another. Slowly, they were learning more about the endless blessings of their world and the curious workings of their bodies. When they had finished the food, Adam licked his fingers to clean the berry stains on them. Eve had ingested her portion much faster than him, so she playfully licked his index finger before he had gotten to it. Adam felt a jolt of excitement unlike anything he had experienced before and almost wanted Eve to do it again. Before he could say anything, Eve giggled at her innocent victory and went to find a thick branch to prop her head against to sleep. Adam huddled up next to her and closed his eyes. He noticed how the chirping crickets faded slowly until he suddenly slipped into a dream, away from the world, as if he had just woken up in another world.

In that moment of restful tranquility, they had no idea that there indeed was another presence around them, albeit not human. Something crept through the shadows, waiting to catch one of them in a vulnerable state before launching its attack.

***

In the morning, Eve opened her eyes to the brilliant sunlight casting a radiant glow on the same plants and flowers that had captivated her the night before. The smells had shifted into woody and musky tones, and chirruping songbirds hopped from branch to branch, singing melodious tunes in praise of their creator.

When Eve got up from the grass bed and looked around, she was surprised to find that Adam was nowhere in sight. She rubbed her eyes to clear her vision and found the world as glorious as ever. In her drowsy state, she conjectured that Adam might have felt too impatient to wait for her and gone to Euphrates. It was also possible that he was still waiting and merely picking fruit nearby to surprise her with an abundant breakfast. It wasn't long before she remembered the reflection in the pond and wondered what it would look like in the day.

She had taken merely a couple of steps toward the pond when suddenly she heard rustling leaves behind her. She jerked her head in its direction and noticed some small plant stems near the ground swaying in a sign of recent movement, but she couldn't spot anybody. Suddenly, she smirked as she realized Adam might be playing a game. Pretending to forget about the disturbance, she kept her senses alert and turned to face the pond again. Sure enough, as she expected, she heard another sound closer to hissing. From the corner of her eye, she glimpsed a dark object wriggling into the thicket. She felt more certain that Adam was enacting some sort of play, possibly trying to lead her to a surprise, so she followed the movement.

The swishing sounds led her away from the pond in the opposite direction of the Euphrates. In her playful chase, she admired the sunlight breaking through the leaves into rainbow-colored streaks and bubbles that would elude her with the slightest movement. She glimpsed the creeping object a couple more times and started to rush to catch up to it. When she stepped out of the dense grove, she found herself in the opening where the Tree of Knowledge stood tall above the rest of the hurst.

She was surprised to spot a serpent standing stationary next to the tree, almost as if it was waiting for her. When their eyes met, the serpent approached Eve by crawling on its stubby legs. It startled Eve by speaking to her, unlike any of the other animals.

"Did God really say that you must not eat from any tree in the garden?" he asked Eve, who was amazed by God's wondrous creation all over again. She had not expected to converse with animals the same way as Adam and she did.

She collected her memory and responded, "We eat of the trees in the garden. But of the fruit of the tree that is in the midst of the garden, God has said, 'You shall not eat or touch it, for the day you eat it, you will surely die.'"

The serpent turned his head to regard the fruit of the tree and faced Eve again to say, "You will not surely die. God knows that on the day you eat it, your eyes will be opened, and you will be like God, knowing good and evil."

Indeed, Eve knew not what the serpent meant by good and evil, and her curiosity urged her to listen more. She considered whether any of God's creations would mislead her. Surely, this serpent was also an inhabitant of their world and must have eaten from the tree, for it did know of things such as good and evil. She regarded the tree once again and inspected its tantalizing fruit. She saw that it was pleasant to the eyes, and her stomach churned with hunger. Moreover, she wanted to be as wise as the serpent, who had more knowledge about the tree than her or Adam. She could also see clearly that the serpent had not died and considered whether God had said that just to prevent them from gaining wisdom, which he hoped to keep to himself. Something about the tree pulled her toward it against her best wishes, and though she had been able to not think too much about it earlier when Adam had conveyed God's words, in this solitary moment, she couldn't help herself. If God had granted me but one chance to interfere in the world of humans, I would have done so at that moment, but I chose instead to trust his providence.

She picked the soft fruit off the tree and inspected all of its sides. It looked red and shiny, with no stains or overripened parts, and her mouth salivated with craving. At the same time, her heart shuddered, and her limbs began to shake. Whatever dying was, she did not want to experience it. She decided to take a leap of faith, closed her eyes, and brought the fruit close to her mouth to bite into it. Her teeth crunched through the fleshy fruit, which filled her mouth with its sugary pulp. It was the most flavorful fruit she had tasted in the garden. After one bite, she brought her hand back down and paused for a brief moment. The world went on as normal, the serpent remained in its place, and she did not die. She no longer cared if she was wiser and proceeded to finish the fruit.

Suddenly, Adam also appeared in the opening from behind her, with his hair dripping wet from his bath in the river. Having woken up way before Eve, he had decided to go to the river for a bath and hoped to find Eve awoken when he returned so that they could have breakfast together. He noted the serpent patiently sitting next to Eve as she gorged herself on the fruit and was pleased to find she had not died. She picked two more fruits from the tree and handed one to Adam. Much to the serpent's pleasure, the two of them sat in the shade of the Tree of Knowledge and relished the fruit together. They giggled after every bite and kept an eye out for God, whom they wished would not witness this moment of disobedience.

When they stood back up, something about the world felt different. Indeed, their eyes had been opened, and Adam felt a similar excitement upon looking at Eve as he had felt the previous day when she licked his finger. Suddenly, he realized that she was naked, while she seemed to be catching up to the same awareness. The two stared at each other's bodies for a brief moment before being overpowered by shame. How had they dared to exist naked around each other all this time?

Unthinkingly, their hands traveled to cover their genitals before the two ran off in opposite directions. Satan curled himself up in satisfaction, feeling the gentle friction of his deceptive scales rubbing against one another. His task had been accomplished by bringing death to the Garden of Eden, and he no longer needed to stay on earth. When the two humans returned to the Tree of Knowledge, the serpent was nowhere to be found. Adam had covered his genitals with a bundle of fig leaves that he had tied to his body, whereas Eve had sewn some bigger leaves into a loose web to cover herself with. When they saw each other again, they still felt ashamed, and for the first time in their lives, they felt scared of God.

Little did they know at the time that they had encountered the very root of evil in the universe. Satan had succeeded at each step of his mission. He had embodied a serpent, which was a familiar creature for the humans, and had made the right call by enticing Eve to eat the fruit first, for she managed to convince her companion easily. While using the serpent as a vessel, Satan had flipped the human state from innocence to guilt in one swift attack. Adam and Eve had committed the first sin, which changed their nature forever and would defile their generations until the end of time.

Chapter 7

God's Reaction to Eden's Tragedy

Each time our Lord God visited Eden to commune with his creation, it would, like a mirror, reflect his boundless beauty and magnificence back at him. Every leaf, insect, and water droplet was perfectly placed as he had intended, and with each new day, he'd rejoice in the unfolding of his essence in material form. He particularly enjoyed communing with the humans who were made in his image and exhibited superior levels of intellect, emotive capacity, and curiosity in comparison to the other beasts of the field.

Our Lord God descended to the gardens on a particularly cool afternoon in Eden for his routine stroll. It was his favorite time of the diurnal course when the creatures in Eden would usually wake from their afternoon naps, their stomachs satiated from the day's first meal. The gentle breeze would carry a plethora of scents emitting from the delicate and colorful flowers with which he had bejeweled the world. With his advent, the garden and its creatures seemed to magnify their very existence, almost as if to boast the infinite blessings of their creator. The songbirds would trail his passage from tree to tree while glorifying their Lord through canorous harmonies that would resound through the blooming expanse of Eden. The four river heads would swell and surge to spread their nourishment through the land, the trees would humbly bow their foliage in worship, the flowers would bloom with renewed verdure and innocent hopes of reaching their creator's senses, and the clouds would disperse through the horizon to cast a gentle cover that would diffuse the sunlight into a rich, golden radiance. On this particular day, as God walked through the miraculous orchestra of life, Eden seemed quieter than usual. The all- knowing, of course, knew what had transpired in his absence.

"Where are you?" he called out to Adam, wondering whether the shame that Adam and Eve felt because of their disobedience made it difficult for them to interact with him.

No sooner would he step foot into Eden, no matter from which end, than Adam and Eve would skip into his proximity with an air of celebration. On this day, regardless of which direction he glanced in, he saw no signs of humans approaching him. He patiently traversed all the way from Gihon River to the center of Eden and could sense that Adam and Eve were in the vicinity but avoiding him. When nearing the two consecrated trees that stood tall in the center, he almost considered calling out again when Adam gave in to the guilty compulsion and jumped out from behind a bush to greet him.

 "My Father! I heard you in the garden, but I got scared since I was naked. So I hid myself."

God's eyes widened with alarm, and his lips puckered with disappointment. He pretended that he was just learning about their sin, and my guess is he wanted to see if, after having consumed the forbidden fruit, they would continue being honest with him or if they had learned to lie.

"Who told you that you were naked?" he demanded an explanation, "Have you disobeyed me and eaten from the tree that I commanded you not to eat from?"

Adam was overwhelmed by the weight of God's displeasure and did not want to be perceived as the sole transgressor. Meanwhile,

Eve remained hidden behind the trunk of one of the trees surrounding them, overhearing the reprimanding exchange.

Adam forthrightly gave up his abettor, "It was the woman that you put here with me. She gave me some fruit from the tree, and I made the mistake of eating it."

Upon hearing the blame being directed at her, fear gripped Eve's body and pulled it out into the open. Now that the fruit from the Tree of Knowledge had equipped the humans with a sense of right and wrong, she knew full well that she had incurred their Father's disapproval and prepared herself to be admonished.

 "What is this you have done?" God's voice echoed through the sudden stillness as all the creatures became quiet to witness the heated dialogue with the utmost attention.

Eve's body language folded into avoidant trepidation before she responded, "My Father! I swear I did not want to. The serpent deceived me and said that I would not die as you had said. So I ate the fruit and offered it to Adam as well."

God's face twisted at the mention of the serpent, which he knew was an embodiment of his defeated rival and once glorified soldier. He closed his eyes for a moment, during which his countenance underwent a plethora of conflicting emotions. No being can imagine the extent of his wrath at that moment, and the temporary material form he took on to interact with his creations visibly struggled to contain the burden of those emotions. When he opened his eyes again, he looked at Adam and Eve from an altered perspective. Though he couldn't stop loving his creations after the attentive care and grace with which he had created them, especially after blessing them with his own essence, he still felt a strong sense of disappointment as he looked for a place to direct his fury. Even though his anger was primarily aimed at Satan, who had already been punished by being banished from heaven and thrown into hell, he felt an uncompromising need to enact justice. He wanted to show the rest of the world that even his most prized creations were not immune to repercussions if they disobeyed his commands.

Adam and Eve had their heads bowed down in shame. Though they had felt the same way as soon as they'd eaten the fruit, the feeling was amplified tenfold in front of their creator. Indeed, if humans could always perceive their God's reactions and disappointment to sin, they would forego all temptations that lead to it. Adam and Eve would certainly not have eaten the fruit of the tree if God had been in visible proximity at that moment. Over the years that I've observed human behavior, I've realized that it's a lack of faith, conviction, and remembrance that makes humans most susceptible to sin.

God's fury roared through the world, and he swept his hand decisively, bringing a strong gale from the direction of the Euphrates that carried a serpent along with it. The serpent landed on the ground near the assemblage, which had quickly transformed into a court of the master's judgment. Eve, who had engaged in direct dialogue with the snake earlier, could tell this one was the exact same as before, but something about its face had changed. It did not seem to remember how it had provoked the creator's anger. Adam and Eve stared in horror as the serpent writhed, squirmed, and struggled to get back on its feet despite relentlessly flailing his tail.

God lifted a finger at the culprit and delivered his verdict, "Because you have aided my archenemy in his twisted, diabolical schemes, you shall be the most cursed of all beasts and animals! From this day onwards, you shall crawl on your belly and eat dust for the rest of the days. I will put enmity between you and the woman, and between your offspring and hers, he will crush your head, and you will strike his heel."

As soon as God had uttered these words, the serpent blasted into the air, leaving a cloud of dust in its wake. While suspended in the air, the serpent jerked and wriggled while God remained stationed and did not so much as bother to lift his head up to look at the serpent's misery. Adam and Eve heard more blasting sounds from the vicinity and noticed that all the other serpents in Eden suffered the same fate. When the one addressed by God landed back on the ground, the humans' mouths widened into shock, for the serpent had been utterly transformed, and his punishment had already been enacted.

There he was, deprived of his limbs and rendered into a lengthy coil of scales with no appendage from head to tail. It took the serpent some time till it slithered back to stability and returned to its habitual flicking of its tongue from a raised head. The creatures of Eden looked on in horror at their Lord God's sheer ability to deform and alter their lives in the blink of an eye. They were all the more enamored by his unmatched power and took the serpent's fate as a pitiful example of the misfortune of becoming an accomplice of the Devil. Adam and Eve shook with terror as their imaginations started to preempt the sort of punishment that God might inflict on them. When God diverted his attention from the serpent to the humans, the cursed animal slithered away as fast as it had been compelled and joined the rest of his cursed companions.

First, God faced the woman who had sinned first and said, "You...I will make your pains in childbearing very severe, and with painful labor, will you give birth to your offspring. You will desire your husband, but he will rule over you and future generations."

The woman teared up in the anticipation of suffering. She wished with all her might that she could reverse her actions earlier in the day, which had instantly changed God's approach toward them.

She felt foolish for ignoring God's warning regarding the fruit of the Tree of Knowledge and struggled to believe that she had been so naïve as to be deceived so easily by the serpent. Little did she know at the time, despite having gained considerable wisdom about her world of the seductive power and manipulative intentions of Satan's words, how he was also a force to be reckoned with. I watched in dismay, for the humans were caught in the crossfire of a longstanding battle that was much larger than them.

Then the Lord God turned to face Adam and bellowed, "You listened to your wife and ate the fruit that I commanded you not to, and now the ground shall be cursed because of you! You will no longer relish the delicious fruits that I offered you in abundance without asking for anything in return. Now, you shall toil painfully to reap food from the ground, which will produce harsh thorns and thistles for you, and you will eat the plants of the field. By the sweat of your brow, you will eat your food until you return to the ground since from it you were taken; for dust you are, and to dust you will return."

Though man had been innocent in his creation and had only been corrupted by the temptations engendered by Satan, God was disappointed in this gross misuse of man's free will. He had wished for the man to grow up unadulterated and naturally develop his conscience. The fruit, instead, catalyzed man's maturation before he was prepared to handle that sort of knowledge. Indeed, our Lord God had ordained everything perfectly, and the pearl of his creation was the free will and ability to choose, which he had granted generously to humans. He had hoped, although taking an immense risk while doing so, that even if man encountered forces of evil before acquiring a mature conscience, his free will would lean toward grateful obedience to his creator instead of selfish wants and pleasures. God cursed Satan all over again for interfering in his grand plan and polluting the free will of humans before it had ripened.

Still, our Lord is indeed the most merciful and benevolent, for time and time again, he has demonstrated his unconditional love for humans by looking out for them, especially the ones who seek his help and guidance. As for Adam and Eve, he engendered skin garments for them to relieve them of the shame of nudity. The fig leaves that they had sewn for themselves in a hurry were already falling apart, and a visceral guilt invaded man's peace of mind and urge to hide his humiliation. At the same time, God knew that Eden was no longer the paradise as he had designed it. The humans had brought this curse upon themselves and indirectly upon all of creation that inhabited the earth. God summoned some of his faithful angels and announced his decision to banish the humans from the Garden of Eden. From then on, man would live and toil on the same ground from which he had been taken.

Once the man and woman had been driven out of Eden to live a mortal life in the dusty expanse of the world, God stationed a revered Cherubim on the east side of the garden to prevent man's access to it ever again. Having lost some semblance of general faith in his creation, God also placed a flaming sword at the entrance that flashed back and forth. The Lord God stressed the importance of preventing man from one thing regardless of context or circumstance.

"The man has now become like one of us, knowing good and evil. He must not be allowed to reach out his hand and take also from the Tree of Life and eat, lest he should become immortal."

Since that day, the angels of heaven have maintained a safe distance between man and Eden's treasures. It was a tragedy for all realms that such a grand creation of our Lord had been polluted, and the future generations of Adam and Eve, the offspring of humankind, would not witness the paradise on earth that had been intended for them. How lucky they were to have been made in God's image, only to fall prey to the selfishness and pride of their will. And now, God's warning was destined to come true. Upon eating the fruit, Adam and Eve were mistaken to think that they did not die. Though their hearts did not stop, and they continued to eat, breathe, sleep, and fulfill all the activities that were symptomatic of the gift of life, their years were limited and made susceptible to death way earlier than God had intended initially. While in Eden, God had left them to explore their bodies and interactions with the world with no urgency. Once they were banished from the blissful garden, the two humans were acutely aware of their aging bodies and soon succumbed to their desire to reproduce. Eve bore unprecedented pains in the process as part of her punishment. Shortly after the tiring months of pregnancy, she gave birth to the first human child, Cain. Two other sons followed shortly after, namely Abel and Seth.

Perhaps even worse than the humans' expulsion from Eden to barren earth was the spiritual chasm that his event engendered between God and his creation. Not only had their hearts and souls been plagued with fear, guilt, and indignity, which was the direct opposite of their natural purity and innocence, but their disobedience also created an unbridgeable rift from the spiritual realm. They had been isolated from the ever-flowing well of grace, light, and beauty that would have ensured peace and harmony in the world.

Never again did man experience the nourishing presence of their God. This was the biggest loss for Adam and Eve and their generations to come. No one loved humankind as generously as their Lord, not even their mothers, and though the succeeding generations experienced his love in some form or the other, they would never know the true, unrestrained extent of it. Instead, the following generations were afflicted by the retributive curse that Adam and Eve's original sin incurred. From then on, humanity was marked by a general lack of reverence for God and continued to disappoint him through selfish acts of jealousy, pride, betrayal, and even fratricide.

And yet, the master of the universe continues to love them with the hope that each successive generation uses their free will to choose the right path: the path of repentance, obedience, and fellowship.

Chapter 8
The Beginning of Sin and Death

While God delivered his furious judgment on Adam and Eve for their ungrateful disobedience, Satan returned to his new home, preparing himself to announce his first victory in the war of redemption against heaven. He had instructed his chieftains beforehand to organize another mass assembly. When he flapped his wings into the caliginous horizon, his eyes fell on the flood of demons amassed in the meeting arena, seething with anticipation. Having concluded the laborious task of rebuilding the grim landscape, the demons of hell were afflicted by a sluggish torpor, incessantly charred by the sweltering air of the inferno. The lowest-order demons were close to losing their hulls entirely, which receded every day into patches of black flesh underneath that began to decay and smolder as soon as they were exposed to the unrelenting air, as if the environment was gradually consuming them.

Next to Azrail, there stood one of his bravest soldiers, whose last remaining patch of skin on his arm boiled over no sooner than he had stationed himself in the frontmost row of the army. The demon was so occupied by the agonizing itch in his limb, which he scratched with overgrown and misshapen nails, that Azrail had to smack his head from behind to compel his attention to the arrival of their master. Many demons in the horde surrounding them were preoccupied by their tormented bodies that convulsed in throes every few moments. Some attempted to scratch the pain away, and some blew air into the gouged-out areas only to find that it was too hot to offer relief, whereas others roared helplessly and desperately awaited news that might alleviate their suffering and make their fellowship with the Devil worth its accompanying anguish.

When the demons sighted Satan descending from the sky toward the meeting area, they erupted into an uproar and cheered his arrival with seeming indifference toward the result of his mission. The demon chieftains, on the other hand, knew that this unconditional reverence was motivated by fear and helplessness rather than the unfaltering pride that Satan expected them to hold in their hearts. Azrail and Akar shared a glance of trepidation, knowing full well that the morale of their troops heavily depended on Satan's first mission being successful. Since their arrival in hell, many of the demons were close to losing all hope, if not for the beacon of light and guidance that Satan quickly became in the dark and dismal realm. Only Damyan, who had an unsurmountable faith in Satan's abilities, could deduce from the unhurried and prideful flight that good news was about to unfold.

Satan took his sweet time to hover above the rousing impatience before descending to the meeting area. Their eyes followed him down to the platform, where he landed with graceful perfection as his wings folded into their dormant state. For a brief moment, he stood there motionless with his eyes closed, relishing the aftermath of his victory, which was already sending waves of God's fury through the realms. The first instance of sin sparked a chain reaction unraveling in real-time. Though he had yet to find out how the events in Eden transpired, he could sense the ripples of a monumental shift in the earthly realm. When he opened his eyes, he looked around with purpose, which compelled the crowd of demons into silence. Satan spotted Kumail in the front row and raised his eyebrows toward him questioningly.

Kumail instantly nodded and ascended the platform from its

left side. Akar stood toward the right side of the platform and observed this exchange with brimming jealousy. Kumail hastened to Satan's position and promptly whispered something in his ear, which inspired a wide and self-satisfied grin that pulsated through Satan's countenance. The crowd observed with uncontrollable curiosity. Akar had rallied them together with the promise that their lord had important announcements to make regarding their progress. Once Kumail was done conveying his message, he looked toward Satan for a response.

"You have done well," Satan whispered back to him before he headed back down from the platform and took his place in the frontmost row of the crowd.

The crowd grew more impatient to receive an update about their state. Many of them were entirely unaware of the details of Satan's mission in Eden, while some had received airs about it, which only developed into the status of a rumor. All they knew was that some sort of offensive was being launched, and they had guessed, based on Satan's previous speech, that it might concern the humans named Adam and Eve. Satan had told his chieftains to keep the plan to themselves until it had materialized and humanity's susceptibility to their attacks had been tested sufficiently. At this moment, even the chieftains, except Kumail, seemed to be in the dark about the result of the mission.

Satan's gaze swept across his loyal subjects with the faintest hint of a smirk. The more I observed him, the more I noticed how easy it was for him to feel triumphant, for even the slightest of sins incurred great displeasure for our benevolent Lord who had granted the humans everything they could ask for. Satan was almost struggling to contain his contentment and soon broke out into an address unlike any he had delivered thus far.

"My loyal subjects!" He raised his wide-open arms toward the crowd so as to establish a sense of fellowship. "I am eternally grateful for your faith and unwavering support in my war against heaven, despite the misery and depreciation of circumstance that our punishment has put us through. I had promised you that after having gauged the power of our adversary, our next offensive would be smarter and more likely to succeed. I am pleased to stand before you today and inform you that events are progressing as I expected…"

No sooner had he uttered these words than the impatience of the crowd was granted a release, which erupted into a celebratory clamor. This time, Satan did not hasten to silence them or continue his speech. He knew this was a time that deserved its due share of time for commemoration. He stood before the crowd, smiling broadly from ear to ear, and waited for their elation to fade into willful listening. Satan was well versed in the art of letting others feel like they were acting of their own accord, just as he had done with Adam and Eve. Once he found himself in receptive silence, he continued.

"My soldiers, my companions, I proudly announce today that Eden is no more!"

There was another wave of venerating applause, which faded soon after as the crowd was starting to discover a rhythm for this ritualistic assembly.

"Yes, you heard me right." Satan continued, "The glorified creation that God exalted above its deserved stature has been banished from the paradisiacal world he had constructed for them. With meticulous proficiency, I entered the earthly realm unnoticed by our father's soldiers stationed at its entry points. I managed to share a dialogue with Adam's companion and convinced her to eat from the sacred Tree of Knowledge, which our father had instructed the humans not to eat from. I knew that her feminine force of temptation would manage to convince Adam as well, and it was so. My loyal chief, Kumail, kept an eye on Eden while I was on my way back, and he informed me that our adversary regarded their disobedience as insolence and was unable to stomach their being aware of matters that he would've preferred keeping from them. Indeed, they have suffered a punishment similar to ours and have been deprived of comforts and luxuries of the sort that we savored in our glory days."

Rows of hands rose to the sky to celebrate amidst a cheerful cacophony. Once again, the clever Satan let his followers relish one of the only instances of triumph they had experienced since being trapped in hell. Meanwhile, Akar finally caught up to the secret exchange that had occurred between Satan and Kumail, and his face carried an expression of scornful envy.

"My success in Eden will put humanity in a perpetual state of spiritual disobedience," Satan bragged. "I wouldn't even take full credit for the humans' disobedience; I say it was part of their inherent nature, a reflection of the pride that they inherited from God through his essence. I only nudged them toward it and catalyzed its inevitable downfall. Now, this rebellion has become a permanent state of the human heart that will continually offend God and put humanity in a disfavored spiritual position with his maker. The problem is endemic, meaning it will be passed down to every offspring, staining every human race on earth. This means that every human will automatically become a sinner at birth.

"But there is more," Satan continued. "This state of sin comes with an innate tendency to disregard morality, truth, spirituality, and the rules of God, which exposes humanity to more acts that degrade his current state before God. With a certain amount of demonic prodding, he will succumb to more sinful acts such as adultery, self-exaltation, crimes, deception, lying, cheating, murder, and so on, which exacerbate his condition before their holy God. Our job is to ensure that happens."

"Those who die under demonic influence will go to hell, and those who die under godly influence will go to heaven," he explained. "But man is not entirely defenseless. Part of his makeup includes something called "free will" to help him navigate life's circumstances. He can choose conditions that will benefit him morally and spiritually. He's also equipped with a conscience (a discerning section of his soul) that helps him determine what is ethically right and wrong and the ability to weigh the consequences of each decision, considering his spiritual aspiration.

He failed to mention another tool that humanity has at its disposal: my reports and observations. Little did he know that the latter generations of humankind would have unprecedented insights into his deceptive and treacherous ways.

He continued, "However, with the right demonic persuasion, he will often ignore what is morally correct and spiritually healthy for things that temporarily appeal to his senses, such as fame, power, and pleasure. It is from this angle we can gain the upper hand on him," Satan expressed confidently. "Our job is to ensure he makes the wrong decisions every time, and to do so, we must first determine what motivates him and find a way to help him get what he wants."

While imparting this crucial knowledge to his subjects, the demon chieftains noted each point, for this understanding of humans would aid their future attacks against humankind and, consequently, God.

"Because humankind is more useful to us alive than dead, we must lead him to a place of continuous rebellion," he continued. "We will make him believe that there is no God through fields of study they will refer to as humanities, philosophy, and science.

The first will be an investigation of their existence, the second will make them ponder their purpose in life, and the third will claim to reveal secrets about the universe that they will perceive as fact, even if it conflicts with what our adversary has told them."

Akar, who remembered well the assignment bestowed on him by Satan of tempting humanity toward sin, listened to this information with careful attentiveness. He was desperate to gain the supreme lord's favor and determined to engender ways to corrupt humankind that would inspire Satan's approval.

"Moreover, all the while that humans are incurring their God's displeasure, we will make them believe that there is nothing like so-called 'sin' and that even if he becomes a sinner, there is no God that can forgive him. Just as he considered us unworthy of forgiveness and took such strong measures to abandon us, we will soon demonstrate that his cherished creation is also undeserving of it. We will make them stray so far from the supposedly rightful path that they will not so much as look behind them before heading in the opposite direction."

"Aye!" a horde of demons thundered into the air, which was now charged with revitalized purpose and ambition. Suddenly, with one swift move, the demons regarded their victory as a nearer possibility than they had dared to before.

"Make no mistake! Our plan to corrupt and defile humanity will have many offensives, which I've dedicated Kumail's troops to contrive more and more of. You see, humans are much more complex than they seem and will grow too attached to their pitiful mortal lives. They will never commune with their God again, so the doubt regarding his very existence will be easy to sow. Moreover, we will make humans increasingly aware of their limited years and convince them that their self-satisfaction is the most important thing they should tend to. We will make him feel that the pursuit of pleasure is the ultimate achievement, and he must indulge his passions in whatever makes him feel good, regardless of the consequences. This will lead him to believe that money, fame, power, control, and leisure will fulfill his desires and make him happy."

After expounding these aspects of hell's retaliatory scheme, Satan's face betrayed signs of uncertainty. He seemed to be mulling over some unexpressed thought and then shook his head in a decisive movement before continuing.

"Well, we must not perceive this plan as foolproof, but we must strive to achieve it with our utmost capacity and strength. No doubt, the seed of disobedience has already been planted. Remember, however, that man can disregard our invitation to moral and spiritual disobedience and cling to God. If he stays close to his maker and follows his leadership, he will recognize our deception and reject our invitations to commit more sin. But if you fail once or twice, you must keep trying until you derail his spiritual position and godly intent. At the same time, you will run into some spiritually well-grounded people who won't budge.

"Nevertheless, you will be able to influence more humans than you can imagine. And when you do, they will do my bidding and end up in hell with the rest of us. My fellow demons, fallen angels, the best of your kind! I assure you that if you take heed of my instructions and abide by them, our inevitable victory will be closer than you can imagine. I count on your unswerving obedience and steadfast resolution. You must not falter, no matter the nature of the obstructions that befall your path. I assure you that your invaluable favors for me will not go unrewarded. With your irreplaceable aid, it's only a matter of time before you see me, your one and only lord, seated on the most dignified and elevated throne in the universe!"

While proclaiming the last statement, Satan raised an undaunted fist into the air, implicitly inciting the herd of demons to follow suit. The swarm of fallen angels raised their arms in tandem, which evoked some sense of the glory of their heavenly days and almost resembled an oath of allegiance. They kept their hands raised, waiting for their lord's initiative in letting it drop. He did so after a long moment of admiring the magnificent sight before him, which momentarily drowned out their lackluster surroundings.

"With that, I give you all leave. Return to your stations and your assigned duties with diligence. There is not a moment to rest. We have a whole universe and its flawed order to overturn!"

With one last collective hail that concluded the assembly, the swarm of demons began to disperse through the same paths they had arrived through, which led to the various cities of hell. Meanwhile, the demon chiefs, namely Akar, Damyan, Andras, and Kumail, stayed behind and surrounded their King to offer their congratulations and devise their next action plan.

Chapter 9

The Growth of Humans and Corruption

When Adam and Eve were expelled from Eden, they found their world significantly altered and reduced to barren land filled with dull, prickly plants and thistles compared to Eden's fragrant and colorful gardens, which were no less than paradise on earth. Though eating the forbidden fruit from the Tree of Knowledge elevated their awareness about the world and themselves, it also snatched their childlike curiosity and wonder and made them much more conscious of their mortality. Their initial feeling of shame was shrouded by God's benevolent act of making garments out of skin to cover themselves with. But the seed of disobedience that Satan sowed bore more poisonous fruits in the form of regret, humiliation, and enslavement to their carnal desires. God knew that sin deprived the humans of the state of innocence with which he wanted them to know the world, and he did not wish for Eden to be stained further by the depraved and sinful acts that he knew their generations would commit. As punishment, he made Eve's role of child-bearing much more agonizing than was initially intended, and the ground beneath their feet was cursed so that it no longer produced the endless variety of fruit that had satiated their palettes and nourished their bodies in Eden. Instead, Eve had to labor and toil away to reap herbs from the ground to sustain themselves.

I, Sabrael, curse Satan ten times over for this rift he engendered between God and his cherished creation, and if it were left in my power to intervene before Eve bit into the fruit, I would have surely done so. I'm sure God's providence still persevered in letting the events unfold this way. Though the humans were yet immature, their free will had to be tested at some point or another, for the Almighty knew that his nemesis would seek revenge at some point. Since Lucifer had been banished from heaven's premises and hell did not contain anything of significance through which Satan could hurt God, the earthly realm became the only playground in which he could enact his diabolical schemes.

Surely, Satan is also cunning and efficient, despite his earlier oversight in attempting to defeat heaven through direct battle. This time, by leading the humans astray and sullying their purity, he targeted the only chink in God's armor, which was dependent on the decision-making prowess of the humans who were made in his image. All of God's children, from the Cherubims to the angels and even the beasts of the field, watched with helpless consternation how much God's pride and gaiety were wounded by Adam and Eve's misconduct. In fact, the most disheartening tragedy of humankind has been its inability, since the golden days of Eden, to realize how Satan continues to sever the precious bond that existed between God and humanity in its inception by consistently enticing them to defy God's commandments in favor of momentary and selfish pleasures, which are but a mere glimpse of the eternal blessings they could attain by practicing temperance and subservience instead.

While Adam and Eve grew accustomed to their new lives, there was a sexual tension between them, along with the urge to reproduce and ensure the continuation of their bloodline. After being separated from God's enlightened presence, they spent more time together and developed a closer bond. They familiarized themselves with the functioning of their bodies and the pleasures of interacting with one another, and before long, Eve gave birth to their first son, Cain. The two humans were enamored by the process of childbirth and their ability to create new life with each other, which echoed both of their images. After some time, Eve gave birth to another son named Abel, and the two children provided each other invaluable companionship while growing up with each other.

Cain learned the practice of cultivation from his father, and following in his footsteps, he grew up to be a tiller of the ground, producing new types of fruit and herbs from the ground. On the other hand, Abel pursued a different way of life. Since a young age, he displayed a peculiar familiarity with God's animals and grew up to be a keeper of sheep, breeding and rearing them for meat, as well as their soft woolen skin that made for warm and comfortable garments. Though a significant amount of time passed by peacefully, there came a point when Cain and Abel grew envious of the time Adam and Eve spent with their creator. They were heavily disheartened upon hearing about the grave sin that their parents had committed, which had incurred the curse of the earth on all their generations to come. In order to make up for the disobedience and in hopes of reuniting with their maker, the two brothers sought to please their Lord.

One day, what transpired was that Cain brought an offering to the Lord in the form of fruit that he had harvested from the ground. Abel, the younger brother, also followed in the elder's footsteps and brought the firstborn of his flock of sheep, specifically the choicest and fattiest parts of the animal, as his offering. The Lord God conveyed to the brothers through a messenger that he respected Abel's offering and the intentional thought put into it, whereas he had the opposite reaction to Cain's offering and did not respect the indifference with which Cain simply offered plain fruits without taking the time out to select the finest ones from the bunch. Cain did not receive this reaction well, and his blood boiled at the thought of Abel's offering being accepted, even though it achieved the purpose the brothers set out to do: to please their Lord. Moreover, Cain had taken the initiative, from which Abel got to reap the rewards. From then on, Cain carried a dejected countenance and low spirits wherever he went.

The all-knowing and merciful did not fail to notice this shift in Cain's demeanor and wanted to nip the poison in the bud before it had the chance to grow and influence Cain's actions. What the humans did not know was that Satan's shadow still loomed over them, looking for the opportune moment to inspire hatred and contempt. Much to Akar's satisfaction, the tempter and his demon chief observed this situation unfolding from a distance, waiting for the perfect moment to strike. Cain's lapse in judgment was merely a human error, by which he did not realize that God deserved special treatment as compared to a gift that he might've offered to another human being, and this scenario could've served as a valuable lesson for the elder brother. Satan's malicious eye, on the other hand, saw the opportunity to exacerbate Cain's feelings and engender another sin through it.

The Lord God asked Cain, "Why are you angry, and why has your countenance fallen?"

He clarified that he had nothing against Cain in particular and would surely accept his offerings if he learned to do good. On the other hand, he warned Cain that if he did not do well, which was sure to inspire difficult emotions as part of the human makeup, then Cain would be susceptible to committing sin like his parents did.

"You must remember," the Lord God continued, "that the force of sin desires to be embodied by you, and when it opens its fangs, you should rule over it."

Paying heed to God's advice, Cain went over to his brother, Abel, in an attempt to dissolve animosity by conversing with him. They met in an empty field, which quickly turned into a stage for humanity's second test. Unbeknownst to man, Satan and Akar also descended to the field and incited intense jealousy and disdain in Cain's heart. The conversation took a dreadful turn when Abel expressed his intention to give more offerings to their Lord, and behind the surface of their outward behavior, Akar convinced Cain that the only way he could secure God's approval was by getting rid of the competition that threatened to outdo him once more. He persuaded Cain to believe that his offering of fruit would always remain inferior to the flesh that Abel was able to furnish. Of course, Cain could not see the fiendish presence influencing him, and their whispers manifested in his being as strong urges that he struggled to contain. Thereby, Cain let his emotions get the better of him, and he resolved to physically hurt his brother. In their time growing up on earth, the two brothers had observed scuffles between other beasts of the field, and various accidents and illnesses had revealed to them the capacity of living beings to experience pain and suffering. Cain grabbed a jagged rock from the field and hurled it toward his brother, making him lose his balance and fall. Then, as if Abel were a sworn enemy, Cain got on top of him and smashed his head in with a bigger piece of rock. He kept striking Abel's limp body despite the splatters of blood and crushing of bones, and he did not stop until he had practically dug Abel into the ground. While watching the first humans being created, I did not dare imagine that they'd be capable of such brutal and violent acts, which made me wonder whether God had made a mistake by creating them in the first place.

When he returned to his senses, Cain could not dare look at the state in which he had left his brother. He got back on his feet and walked the other way, having no idea of the demonic chuckles that reverberated through the air as Satan and Akar celebrated their second victory against God. The Lord God was utterly disappointed by this gruesome and barbaric act and momentarily descended to the earthly realm to speak to Cain.

He said to Cain, "Where is Abel, your brother?"

The guilt-ridden son found it easier to lie than to admit to the heinous act he had committed and responded, "I do not know. Am I my brother's keeper?"

The Lord God was infuriated more so upon receiving a dishonest response from the wrongdoer and wanted to ensure that this sin was punished so as to discourage future generations from killing, especially of their own blood.

"What have you done?" he growled.

"The voice of your brother's blood cries out to me from the ground. Now, you will be cursed by the earth, which has opened its mouth to receive your brother's blood from your hand. From now on, when you till the ground, it will no longer yield its strength to you. Gone are the fruits that you cared not to offer the first or the best of as if your God had not generously bestowed them upon you. And now, you have spilled the sacred blood of one who was dear to us. A fugitive and a vagabond, you shall be on the earth."

Cain could not bear the weight of this punishment, as it rendered his motivation for killing his brother utterly void. Instead of being favored, God rejected him, and he would no longer get a chance to offer anything to please him. He told God that his punishment was greater than he could bear and admitted to his mistake. By being driven out of the face of the ground, he realized that he was losing the audience of God's only perceptible face as well, in the form of his creations. He accepted his fate as a fugitive and vagrant on earth and feared that anyone who came in his way might kill him the way he had killed Abel. When God heard Cain's trepidation, he ordained that whoever dared to kill Cain, vengeance would be taken on that person sevenfold. In order to ensure that no one mistook Cain for someone else, God put a mark on Cain that would declare the fratricide he had committed and remind its beholder of the punishment promised for anyone who dared to kill him.

Hence, Satan succeeded in sowing the seed of violence that would sprout and burgeon into more instances of fighting, bloodshed, and barbarity among the future generations that would descend from the corrupted blood of Cain. Ashamed of the disapproval he had incurred, Cain went far from the place where he had murdered his brother and dwelt instead in the land of Nod, toward the east of Eden.

Cain's evildoing drove the lush gardens even further away from humanity's reach. God's justification for expelling Adam and Eve from Eden was amplified tenfold. From there on, Cain split up from his parents, who were like the root of humanity. In the land of Nod, he managed to start a new life. He took a wife and got to know her intimately like Adam knew Eve. Slowly and gradually, the humans began to proliferate and occupy the vast expanse of the earth, as God had intended.

Cain's wife conceived a son named Enoch, after which Cain built a city that he named after his son. The bloodline carried on through a succession of sons, namely, Irad, who was conceived by Enoch, then Mehujael, then Methushael, and then Lamech. Lamech took two wives who were named Adah and Zillah, and they produced sons who redeemed the bloodline to some degree, though their father also killed two men for wounding or hurting him. Adah's son was named Jabal, who was the father of nomads who dwelt in tents and raised livestock, and Zillah bore Tubal-Cain, who became the instructor of every craftsman in bronze and iron.

Meanwhile, after the loss of their second son, Adam and Eve conceived another child, and soon Eve bore another son named Seth. Seth's bloodline carried on much like Cain's, and his son was named Enosh, who then begot Cainan, who gave birth to Mahalalel, and then came Jared, then Enoch, who was the only one that walked with God and lived for a much lesser number of years, for then God took him. He had a boy named Methuselah, who, in turn, bore one named Lamech. Though both Cain and Seth also gave birth to several other sons, daughters, and grandchildren, these were the prominent sons in the two-family branches, with Seth's eventually leading to Noah.

As the human population on earth increased, so did their propensity to commit vile and shameful acts, which disappointed God enough for him to start questioning the very existence of creatures with free will and volition. Satan and his companions continued to pull the strings of human desire and temptation in more imaginative ways, though the Lord God must have considered all possibilities. At some points, they seemed to control the humans almost as if they were puppets. Only a few of them lived out their lives as God had wanted them to. The sons of God saw the daughters of men and found them beautiful, so they took the ones they desired as their wives. The world's population at the time also comprised giants, specifically when the sons of God conceived children with the daughters of men, and their sons made for mighty men like none other have appeared since. Still, there came a day when God saw clearly the baseness of human existence.

He said, "My spirit shall not strive with man forever, for he is indeed flesh; yet his days shall be one hundred and twenty years."

With time, he saw that the wickedness of man on earth was great, and the fire of his wrath was aggravated by their godlessness and denial of truth despite the endless signs that God had bestowed on them and made plain. God's eternal power, divine nature, and perfection were clearly visible in all of creation, so the people had no excuse. Even if they knew God, they neither glorified him nor expressed gratitude, and Satan's misdirection darkened their hearts till they were rendered fools. They replaced their immortal God with images that were made to look like humans, birds, animals, and reptiles. Instead of the creator, they began to worship the created, and in turn, God gave them over to sexual impurity and shameful lusts, upon which they acted readily. The two genders abandoned their natural sexual relations, and women laid with women, and men laid with men. The human race became filled with every kind of evil, greed, and depravity, which extended into acts such as murder, deceit, gossip, slandering, disobedience, infidelity, and a pitiful deficit of venerable qualities such as love, mercy, and trust. Even those who knew God and were well aware that such acts were deserving of death continued to act against their own wisdom, nudged deeper into the darkness by Satan's machinations, and encouraged others to do the same.

It wasn't long before God saw that the intent of human thoughts and actions was consistently evil, and there seemed to be no attempt on their part for repentance or redemption. Our Lord God was terribly aggrieved and became sorry that he had made man on earth. Satan's implicit war was successful in pushing God to a point from which there was no turning back.

He announced, "I will destroy man whom I have created from the face of the earth, both man and beast, creeping things and birds of the air, for I am sorry that I had made them."

Upon hearing this judgment, Satan was overly pleased with himself, for he had successfully replaced God's endless love for his creation with regret and retribution. Thus far, from the first sin committed by Adam and Eve to Abel's murder at the hands of

Cain, everything was going according to plan.

Chapter 10

Flooding the Earth to Fix a Problem

Generation after generation, Satan and his army of demon chiefs succeeded in corrupting t h e genealogy of Adam. God hoped, with each successive descendant, that humankind's free will might prevail against the dark forces tempting it toward sin, but he was only disappointed each time. It was as if the first disobedience committed by Adam and Eve had induced a new kind of desire that was only satiated by evil acts motivated by greed, lust, and violence. This moral corruptness afflicted both Cain and Seth's bloodline, with Enoch being the only grandchild, five generations down Seth's lineage, who had the honor of walking with God. Enoch pleased God with his unwavering faith and dedication to the right path, and for that virtue, God took him away from the earth so that he would not see death.

After Enoch, the earth did not witness another righteous person like him until his great-grandson, Noah. When Noah was born, his father, Lamech, said, "This one will comfort us concerning our work and the toil of our hands because of the ground which the Lord has cursed." In Noah's first five hundred years, he bore three sons named Shem, Ham, and Japheth. Moreover, Noah was a just man, the most perfect in his generation, so he also had the privilege of walking and communing with his creator. Still, these individuals' piety was insufficient to alter God's outlook on the rest of humankind, which was falling further into the abyss of wrongdoing. When he looked upon the earth, he saw that indeed it was corrupt, for all flesh had corrupted its way on earth. When God resolved to destroy humankind, Noah was the only person whom he considered worthy enough to save and use as a vantage point whence the human race could undertake a new beginning.

Indeed, Noah was taken aback by his good fortune when God announced the drastic measures by which he would remedy the problem while letting Noah live on. In God's eyes, Noah was the only man who was able to insulate himself from the widespread depravity and retain his spiritual purity.

God said to Noah, "The end of all flesh has come before Me, for the earth is filled with violence through them; and behold, I will destroy them with the earth."

Noah was prepared to have his bloodline erased and understood God's concern regarding the rampant perverseness that had befouled man's purpose on earth. Instead, God revealed his intention to save Noah's bloodline and assigned him a mission as part of his grand design.

He provided Noah with precise and detailed instructions, "Make yourself an ark of gopherwood; make rooms in the ark, and cover it inside and outside with pitch. And this is how you shall make it: The length of the ark shall be three hundred cubits, its width fifty cubits, and its height thirty cubits. You shall make a window for the ark, and you shall finish it with a cubit from above and set the door of the ark on its side. You shall make it with the lower, second, and third decks. And behold, I myself am bringing floodwaters on the earth, to destroy from under heaven all flesh in which is the breath of life; everything that is on the earth shall die."

Initially, Noah was horrified by God's plan to destroy all of humanity and could not comprehend the reason for building such an ark as God was asking him to, but then God clarified, "But I will establish My covenant with you; and you shall go into the ark—you, your sons, your wife, and your sons' wives with you. And of every living thing of all flesh, you shall bring two of every sort into the ark to keep them alive with you; they shall be male and female. Of the birds after their kind, animals after their kind, and every creeping thing of the earth after its kind, two of every kind will come to you to keep them alive. And you shall take for yourself all food that is eaten, and you shall gather it to yourself; it shall be food for you and them."

Of course, Noah's insurmountable faith and trust in God immediately accepted this mission, and he condemned the world and the stain of human life on it before proceeding to fulfill God's wishes exactly as they had been conveyed.

Satan's soldiers tried their best to get Noah to question God's providence, to make him perceive God's plan as cruel and unforgiving, but Noah was unmoved and displayed steadfast obedience. He heeded the warning of things not yet seen, and he moved with godly fear to prepare an ark for saving his family along with pairs of every bird, animal, and creeping thing on earth. In doing so, Noah became a subject of mockery and ridicule for the godless community that surrounded him.

The rest of Noah's days after that point were spent in anticipation of the great flood that God had promised. He enlisted the help of his family to build the massive ark, which took more than five decades to build from scratch, even though they labored from morning to night, day after day. At the same time, Noah tried time and time again to warn the people around him of God's displeasure and the impending doom that would befall them, but they continued along the path of sin that Satan and his demons had laid out for them.

This period was wrought with vile and sinful actions. His neighbors fought with one another over trivial matters such as one's land yielding more crops than the other's or a dispute between their children during play. Owing to Akar and Kumail's ploys, petty quarrels wouldn't take long to escalate into long-drawn family feuds whereby countless lives would be lost. Once, when one of Noah's elder relatives, Jecamiah, passed away, Akar grasped the opportunity to inspire greed in the deceased man's three sons, who each wanted to inherit the wealth of land that had kept their family affluent over centuries. Meanwhile, Kumail undertook a scheme to weaken the brothers' sense of sympathy and fraternal care for one another and swayed them toward savage, murderous solutions. Motivated by their hankering avarice, the brothers conspired and plotted against each other until tensions reached a boiling point, and they were forced to take up arms.

It was as if the earth was replaying Cain and Abel's tragedy, for the brothers did not stop and question their urges until the youngest ended up murdering the other two. He forced his brothers' families to relinquish control of whatever land they still had and drove them out of their homes with no regard for how they would survive without shelter or food for themselves. Noah was utterly dejected after numerous vain attempts to get the brothers to act with empathy and consideration. When the youngest brother triumphed over the others, many community members congratulated him for his victory. Still, Noah was the only one who went to him and reprimanded the unnecessary violence. Noah told him that God would curse both his bloodline and the land he had usurped and that his spoils owing to fratricide would not last long, but the young boy overlooked this warning and proceeded with his brutal plans to seize his brothers' shares of inheritance.

During the years in which Noah built the ark, he also continued to teach God's commandments to the people in his community. Despite trusting that God would deliver his promised punishment on humanity, he wanted to do everything in his power to avert the catastrophe if possible. Noah was of the opinion that if humanity fixed its ways, it might be able to achieve salvation by invoking God's mercy. Still, Satan and his demon chiefs were adamant in bringing about humanity's downfall. They encouraged Noah's community members to mock him and his family publicly, along with those who had agreed to help Noah build the ark for satisfactory compensation even though they didn't believe in his God or the prophecy that had called on him to build such an ark in the first place. Owing to this public disdain, some of the workers who had taken on the job of assisting Noah deserted him a few years before the ark was about to be completed. His family and a few trusted companions continued to toil away at the gopherwood structure to see it to its conclusion.

Akar sparked a fire of contempt in the hearts of Noah's onlookers. With each passing year, the public derision and taunting against him intensified until the larger part of the community regarded Noah as a senile old man who had lost his bearings. They sneered at him for putting his family through undue hardship in order to construct a large ship on dry land, which seemed to have no purpose. At some point, the people in Noah's hometown were so infuriated by his supposed obedience to God that they threatened to kill him and his family if he did not put a halt to his project and destroy the ridiculous ark that he was building. Of course, God was always there to protect him and his family, and any time someone came close to harming them, he intervened and averted the danger. Despite the strong opposition from all directions, Noah's family stuck by his side, becoming prime examples of God's expectation of unquestioning faith, and indeed, they were rewarded for it.

Finally, the day arrived when Noah had completed the ark, and his team of workers watched in awe as he hammered the final nail into the window of the ark, just as God had designed it. The Lord God was certainly pleased upon seeing Noah's efforts reach fruition despite years of criticism and discouragement in various forms. The construction of the ark was a test in itself, and God determined that Noah was worth saving and would make for the best progenitor of humankind from thereon. He was six hundred years old at the time.

The Lord God instructed Noah further, "Come into the ark, you and all your household, because I have seen that you are righteous before Me in this generation. You shall take with you seven each of every clean animal, a male, and his female; two each of animals that are unclean, a male and his female; and seven each of birds of the air, male and female, to keep the species alive on the face of all the earth. For after seven more days, I will cause it to rain on the earth forty days and forty nights, and I will destroy from the face of the earth all living things that I have made."

When Noah heard of the impending doom of forty days of endless rain, he grew concerned for the earth's inhabitants, animals, and humans, including those who made him endure terrible hardships. The Lord God had anticipated this softness of heart from Noah, who was too pure to wish for misfortune upon any living organism. Therefore, Noah was given limited time to gather specific numbers and pairs of each animal, as God had ordained. After seven days, Noah, his wife, and their three sons, Shem, Ham, and Japheth, and the three wives of his sons, entered the ark along with every beast, cattle, bird, and creeping thing of every sort. Following God's orders, they each went into the ark with Noah, two by two, male and female of all flesh. Noah also ensured he kept enough food for his family and all the creatures that were supposed to accompany him. Once all the intended passengers of the ark were safely boarded, the Lord God shut the door of the ark himself, knowing well that when Noah saw the suffering and destruction of humanity during the flood, his pure heart would not be able to stop empathizing with them and trying to save them by letting them into the ark.

As God had promised, on the seventh day, all the fountains of the great deep were broken up, and the windows of heaven were opened so that it rained relentlessly on earth for the next forty days and nights. The resulting deluge was so fiercely destructive that I wondered whether God planned to destroy the earth itself. The flood swelled till its tides reached the highest mountains of earth, but the ark was constructed with God's blessings, so the water carried it safely on its surface. Within a few days, all of earth was covered by water, which prevailed fifteen cubits upward. The rain brought so much water that it covered the earth for a hundred and fifty days, and the resulting flood killed all flesh that moved on the earth, including man, birds, cattle, beasts, and creeping things that crept the earth. Only Noah and those who were on the ark with him remained alive.

Once the flood had surely killed every living being on earth, the fountains of the deep and the windows of heaven were shut, and the rain from heaven was subdued. The Lord God caused strong winds to blow over the earth, owing to which the flood water gradually subsided. Around the seventh month mark, the ark rested around the peaks of the mountains of Ararat. The water took so much time to drain and evaporate that it wasn't until the tenth month that the peaks of the mountains became visible. Only then, when the first glimpses of land were seen, did Noah open the window of the ark that he had made and send out a raven to fly to and fro above the water. He also sent out a dove as a test to see how much water had receded from the face of the earth. The dove found no place to perch or rest, so it returned to Noah in the ark, which informed him that the earth was still submerged. When the dove returned, Noah put his hand out for her to sit on and drew her into the ark. He waited another seven days and then sent out the dove again. This time, the dove returned with a freshly plucked olive leaf, and Noah knew that the water from the flood was finally beginning to recede. He waited another seven days to be sure, then sent the dove out again. This time, the dove did not return, which was sufficient to confirm that there was enough dry land and a place to rest on the earth.

In the sixth hundred and first year, on the first day of the first month, Noah opened the covering of the ark to reveal a clear and sunny sky. He looked around and was pleased to find the surface of the earth mostly dry, and by the end of the second month of the year, the land on earth was entirely dry. Indeed, our Lord God is the most merciful, and the elements of the earth behave exactly as he ordains them to.

When the Lord God deemed the time to be right, he said to Noah, "Go out of the ark, you and your wife, and your sons and your sons' wives with you. Bring out with you every living thing of all flesh that is with you: birds and cattle and every creeping thing that creeps on the earth, so that they may abound on the earth, be fruitful and multiply on the earth."

Indeed, this rebirth of life on earth from the womb of the ark was an echo of the genesis of humanity through Adam and Eve, whom God had also intended to be fruitful and multiply on the earth, except their sin had unsettled the perfect harmony of God's creation. This time, the progenitor had already witnessed the human propensity for good and evil and had firsthand experienced the punishment for disobedience as well as the rewards of submitting to God's will. Indeed, Noah and his family were the only humans whom God considered worthy of life, and the mercy of our Lord made it so that they survived the cataclysm of the great flood, the force of which destroyed all other life on earth. When Noah stepped out of the ark, he breathed the fresh air of a new world purified of all the burgeoning evil that Satan and his fiendish demons had propagated across the earth.

Since the root of sin was planted in Eden, this was God's first attempt to rescue humanity from the vicious reins of Satan's ongoing war. Even though the flood was a drastic measure taken by God to rid the world of sin, Satan knew that the seed of wrongdoing that he had firmly planted in Adam and Eve wasn't going to be easily uprooted. For him, the destruction of the world's population was only a minor setback, and there being fewer people allowed his team of demons to focus their malevolent energies on a select few, just like they had done in the case of Cain and Abel.

Satan knew that it was only a matter of time before the shoot of sin broke out of its husk and sprouted up through the fresh soil of the earth, and he was willing to play this game for as long as time went on.

Chapter 11

Starting Over with One Family

When Noah and his family stepped out of the ark along with the pairs of birds, cattle, and creeping things that had accompanied them, they were each filled with renewed awe and reverence for their Lord.

The seemingly limitless expanse of the world unfolded before their eyes, and no matter how far into the distance they looked, there were no signs of conscious life or movement in whichever direction. The earth was covered by a blanket of lush green vegetation that had not only withstood the great flood by the mercy of God but gleamed brighter owing to the nourishing minerals that the inundation had dispersed across the land. Meadows and plains without trees or shrubbery had been wiped clean, but fresh new blades of grass were already breaking through the soil, which filled the goats and cattle with relief and exhilaration. Their hooves were glad to touch the earth's textures after months, leading them to the nearest pasture for fresh nutrition. Having remained confined in the ark for months, the fowl of the air dove out into the air and fluttered their wings a few times before they rediscovered the rhythm of flight. Once they were comfortably buoyant, they rose up to the clouds and stretched their wings out under the gleaming sun, their feathers preened and radiant, rejoicing in the pleasures of unbounded flight.

Noah and his family were grateful beyond measure. They were astounded by the ark's ability to save them from the calamitous flood, and their hearts beat in their chests with reaffirmed faith and in constant praise of their Lord. He wanted to express his gratitude in a tangible manner, so the first task Noah undertook was to build an altar in God's name where he and his family would worship their God every day. Over the next few months, our Lord God watched the repopulation of earth originating from his chosen humans and animals, hoping that they would learn from their mistakes this time. Noah also waited for the right time to make use of the altar to express his thankfulness to God for saving his life along with his kin. One day, unknowingly following in the footsteps of Abel, he collected the flesh of all the clean animals and birds available to him and burned it on the altar as an offering to the most benevolent. The Lord smelled a soothing aroma, with which he was incredibly pleased, as it reminded him of the wonder and innocence of earthly life as he had created it, removed from the wavering free will of man. Still, he was satisfied with the lot he had saved, and their thankfulness reaffirmed his plan to give humanity a fresh start. He said to his children in heaven, "I will never again curse the ground for man's sake, although the imagination of man's heart is evil from his youth; nor will I again destroy every living thing as I have done."

On that day, God promised that as long as earth remained, it would carry on with its seasons and cycles of seedtime and harvest, cold and heat, winter and summer, and the diurnal pendulum of day and night. Whether humans would continue to inhabit the earth or not was to be seen, but the rest of earthly life did not deserve to be destroyed or punished for the sins of humankind. He still hoped that the hearts of men would be purified by the swift deliverance of retribution in the form of the flood, and he wanted the chosen best to restart life with unrestrained access to the well of God's love and kindness.

In response to Noah's offering, God blessed him and his sons and then repeated the same instructions as he had given to Adam and Eve. He told them to be fruitful and multiply till they had filled the earth with more of their kind. In addition, he told them that because of the deeds of their ancestors, every beast of the earth, bird of the air, fish of the sea, and the rest of conscious life would live in fear and dread of humans.

"They are given into your hand," he said to Noah. "Every moving thing that lives shall be food for you.

I have given you all things, even the green herbs."

Indeed, it is the unmatched benevolence of our Lord that the humans' dominion over everything on earth was retained. If he wanted, he could've reduced man's stature and made it even with the rest of earthly life or even shifted the world's hierarchy so that humans were subordinated to the beasts of the earth. Somewhere in his heart, humans still remained his favorite creation despite their fallibility and inclination for evil. He knew that the human will was being tampered with by his nemesis, Satan, who was hell-bent on alienating God from all of his creation. At the same time, he expected humans to practice steadfast resolve, obedience, and strength of will for their own good more than his. Though Satan was pleased by God's decision to destroy most of his creation, there was a providence in the act that could not be grasped except by unquestioning faith. God works in mysterious ways, but so does Satan, who was already devising his next plan of action to lead Noah's family astray as they prepared to start life anew.

Although God permitted Noah to use the creatures inhabiting earth as he pleased, he did set some restrictions. Man was told never to consume the flesh of animals with its life, which was their blood. God promised that he would demand a reckoning from the hands of every beast and man, and each of their deeds would be accounted for. In order to discourage violence, which had haunted Adam's bloodline like a plague, God announced that whoever spilled man's blood would put his own life at stake, for he had made man in the pure image of God, and the spilling of his blood was an attack on God's image.

"And as for you," he said to Noah and his sons, "be fruitful and multiply; and bring forth abundantly in the earth and multiply in it."

As much as Noah wanted to follow this divine instruction, he felt apprehensive about humanity's future, for he feared that they would fall into the same depravity that had brought the curse of the flood upon the entire earth. Little did Noah know that human degeneracy could far surpass the extent he had beheld, which I've had the misfortune of recording until now. Thankfully, much to Noah's surprise and mine, God resumed his instruction and set limitations for himself as well.

"And as for me," he continued, "Behold, I establish my covenant with you and with your descendants after you, and with every living creature that is with you: the birds, the cattle, and every beast of the earth with you, of all that go out of the ark. Thus, I establish my covenant with you: Never again shall all flesh be cut off by the waters of the flood; never again shall there be a flood to destroy the earth."

God sanctified his promise by generating one of the most beautiful images that humankind has ever seen. He unleashed the hidden miracles in the light of the sun and set a rainbow in the cloud as a sign of his covenant with man. He ordained it so that anytime he brought rainclouds over the earth, a vibrant rainbow would shine as a blessing and reminder of the covenant so that God would prevent the water from the clouds from turning into a flood that might destroy all flesh. After Eden, this was one of the only things that made earth feel like heaven, and since that day, I have always revered the sight whenever it has emerged. God promised Noah that this covenant would last till the end of time.

Upon hearing these words and observing the fantastic rainbow emerging from the clouds, the burdens on Noah's heart were lifted, and he allowed himself to feel more hopeful regarding the fate of his bloodline. Noah and his family set out into the open arms of the world. The small group of eight, including Noah and his wife, their sons Ham, Shem, and Japheth, and each of their wives, started off from the east to find a perfect place to settle down. Satan, who was observing this exchange with Akar from the furthest edges of earth's horizon, spat in contempt upon hearing the pact before hastening back to his headquarters in Hell to devise ways of tarnishing the covenant. He had wished to keep humanity entrapped in a cycle of sin and vengeance, but God managed to avert the possibility by promising that he would not upend life on earth until he had demanded reckoning from the hands of every beast and man in the last of their days.

Although Satan knew that God would uphold his end of the contract, he began planning ways to make man forget about this unprecedented deliverance from punishment.

Chapter 12

The Curse of Canaan

In response to God's new covenant, Satan called an urgent meeting of his demon chieftains. Damyan, Andras, Kuraim, Akar, and Azrail stood before their master, seated comfortably on his throne, to receive instructions pertaining to their next action plan. They knew that God had destroyed most of humanity in the flood, as most of their souls were punished by being sent to hell. They also knew that God had spared Noah and his family, so the chieftains came prepared with their own suggestions and ideas for how best to deceive and manipulate Noah's family to make them defy their covenant with God.

Satan began, "Welcome, my loyal soldiers. Much has transpired in the earthly realm since we last spoke. Before we delve into our master plan, what has become of the souls of the people who died in the flood?"

Damyan, who had been assigned the responsibility of handling souls arriving in hell, stepped forward to answer, "My Lord, the flood has been an absolute blessing for hell's chambers! The swarm of souls that arrived at our gates during the flood was no less than a deluge itself. My guards frothed at the mouth upon the sight of so many helpless souls to play with. As per your instructions, my soldiers at the gates greeted the newcomers in the most gruesome and tormenting ways. They took on fiendish forms that roared and hissed at the frightened souls as they passed through the gates. We also marked their passage on both sides by a blazing fire, and I stationed troops to fan the flames in the souls' direction to make hell feel hotter to them than it already is."

Satan's countenance revealed signs of deep satisfaction when he heard the agony of God's favorite creation. In response, Damyan became much more animated and invigorated as he recounted the torturous welcome that he arranged for the human souls, "Ah! You would have been pleased to see the horror on their faces as they regretted the actions on earth that had brought this fate upon them. They walked in shame with their heads downcast as we cursed at them and told them how they were the worst of all creation, that they made a grave mistake by defying God's commandments, and how they would suffer till the end of time with no semblance of respite. We bound their limbs in chains that they could barely lift, and we struck them with lashes when they took too long in between steps. They are now confined in their respective cells, and since their arrival, hell has resounded with a soothing symphony of cries, imploration, and self-loathing."

Satan smiled and nodded his head. "Ay! It brings me great happiness to see God's creation undergo such anguish.

You have done well, Damyan. Keep experimenting with your methods of torture till you've tested the limits of the human soul. Indeed, we will make them despise their very existence till they curse God for creating them and giving them free will."

Damyan took proud steps backward to join his co- conspirators. Azrail patted him on the back. Satan continued, "As for the developments on earth, the flood has finally come to an end, and our playground is open for business again. God has announced a new useless covenant with Noah, which he hopes will keep his dismal creation on track. I believe you all know what we're supposed to do."

He regarded his chieftains with a critical eye and waited for them to respond, wanting to make sure that they were thinking along the same lines as him.

"Of course," Damyan responded, "we should aim to get Noah to defy the covenant with God. Indeed, God has promised that he will never destroy humanity in the same way again, but we can make him regret that promise. If only we can get Noah to do something terrible…"

Satan's mouth stretched into a subtle smirk as he noticed the growing suspense among his chieftains, who now anxiously waited for him to respond to Damyan's suggestion. I couldn't help but notice all the subtle ways in which Satan maintained a sense of power and superiority over his companions. From his choice of words to the lengthy silences, every syllable and intonation was meticulously thought out.

"Indeed, you have spoken well, my esteemed warrior!" Satan validated Damyan's contribution, "We will get humanity to defy their covenant with God and make him wish that he could destroy them again. But Noah will only be the seed. If everything proceeds according to my design, entire generations descending from Noah will compel God's wrath and punishment."

Upon hearing Satan's remarks, Akar stepped forward and asked, "My king! I wholly support your plan to turn this into a long-drawn battle. We are likely to inflict much more damage that way instead of rushing humanity into corruption. For now, the earth is inhabited by a select few, and even if we manage to lead them astray, God may correct the issue by means other than destruction. But, as you have contrived, if we wait for the human population to grow and then contaminate them in larger numbers, the matter will quickly go out of God's hands. My lord, if there is one thing I am unsure about, it is with regard to Noah's role in your scheme. He has been pious enough to be chosen as the leader of humankind's second generation. How do you plan on sowing the seed of dissent through him?"

Satan closed his eyes and nodded for a few seconds, contemplating each and every point that Akar had raised. He was pleased to have his plan approved and stood up from his throne to address Akar's query.

"Noah has a new passion," Satan told his chiefs. "He has been working as a farmer and is trying to grow a vineyard. My plan is to get him drunk beyond his senses and do something wrong. From his drunken stupor, I will expose his nakedness to his children and magnify his shame, causing him to curse his grandchild— Canaan. This is how it's going to happen: a day after the wine-testing ceremony, Noah will be alone that afternoon. I will muse with him, recalling the time of the flood: his bravery, the people who died, God's love, the health and welfare of his family, and how fortunate he is to be alive.

"I will let him relax in the moment, convincing him that he deserves to have another drink, and another, and another. Time will pass as he consumes the wine, obliviously disconnecting from reality. At some time, he will undress himself, pretending to be getting ready for bed but unaware that he is naked. Then, I will engender some reason for his son, Ham, to visit his tent and become witness to his nudity. Indeed, this will be an awkward encounter for both father and son, and Noah, in his drunken stupor, will make a lasting decision that will afflict all the generations that hail from Ham's bloodline. I will make Noah resent Ham and curse his entire lineage. Ham's son, Canaan, who has only recently been born, shall be the root through which this curse will unfold.

"With this curse, we will augment Canaan's fame and fortune on the earth as well as his calamity. Through events manipulated by us, we will help the Canaanites become a technologically and scientifically advanced nation compared to their neighbors. We shall make them fall in love with arts, music, architecture, and ceramics, and we will make them rich in ivory, gold, and alabaster. In this way, we will make them fall in love with their material, worldly life to the point that they will forget about God, his covenants, and the many sins that they have been discouraged from committing. We will make them successful and raise their stature higher than the rest so that they feel invincible and no longer remember God's favor upon them through Noah.

"Additionally, we will have them become immoral, antitheocratic, and hostile to God and his people. In fact, the Canaanites will become the most depraved culture, attempting to impede God's plan in the world for humanity."

Damyan stomped on the ground and dug the talons in his feet into the ground as a show of power and resilience. Visualizing the sort of reality that Satan described, his mouth began to froth, and the marred surface of his skin started to steam.

Andras, who had specifically been assigned to pressure people into committing sins and undesirable acts of corruption, stepped forward with his question, "My lord! Did we not get Adam's descendants to behave in exceedingly immoral and corrupt ways as well? What will be different this time? Would our lord elaborate on what is meant by immoral and depraved?"

"Ay! The sort of acts that Adam's descendants committed were only the beginning. We all have witnessed the human propensity for evil. There are many unexplored ways through which they may harm themselves, their families, and the world in general.

"For one, we will encourage their hostility toward parents, much of which will be rooted in low self-esteem, emotional imbalance, and anger. These humans are fragile— not having a proper view of self can lead them to develop unrealistic expectations in interpersonal relationships and other aspects of life. People can become less resilient if there is a lack of a proper sense of self, leading to confusion and further resentment in parent-child relationships. Adults who grow up with these lacks and deep-seated flaws often undergo failed relationships, fear of taking healthy risks for development and growth, and poor engagement with their own children.

"Moreover, we shall employ whatever means are necessary to push them away from God. They will soon be relying solely on idol worship to seek answers to their problems. God hates idol worship. He gets jealous when people turn their backs on him and worship images made of stone, gold, and other substances. I must admit, it is abominable. Man making God with his own hands depicts his ignorance of the spirit world and how far he has fallen from grace. These images can't see, they can't hear, they have no life, and they provide no help. Those who worship them are just as dead as the images themselves but don't know it. Yet, idol worshipers can become obsessed with the image, so much so that some will sacrifice their children to the idols for spiritual favors that will never materialize. God will indeed be alarmed by such loss of precious, innocent life."

Andras stepped forward and added, "Ay, my lord! I am beginning to grasp what you mean by corrupting man and leading him to his own demise. We will lead them so far away from God's covenant that they stop turning to him even in times of need. We will distract them with other names, concepts, and systems, and we will make use of the sciences to invalidate all the signs that reaffirm God's covenant, such as the rainbow. We will get man to believe that it is simply a natural phenomenon with no significance. Ah, yes! I have another idea if my lord should entertain it."

Andras paused for a brief moment to ascertain whether Satan

appreciated this contribution or if he wanted everyone to shut up and listen. Upon receiving an affirming nod, he continued, "We shall lead them into the occult, ignoring God and seeking guidance through mediums such as astrology, witchcraft, and seances, which may appear as harmless hobbies but unknowingly dabbling in our world. What they don't know is the attempt to speak with the dead is opening the door for evil spirits, one that may encourage demonic possession and, ultimately, self-destruction. This will present us with so many more opportunities to interfere in the world. Ah! Once we manage to invade their foundational beliefs and ideologies, their actions will quickly follow suit!"

"Yes! Yes!" Satan responded as his body sprang into motion. He started to walk around the chieftains, who were lined up next to one another. They followed his movements, and he looked each of them in the eye to note their reactions, for he knew that the next few points he was going to raise should make his followers' blood rush with excitement.

He continued, "Above all, we will compel the Canaanites into gross sexual immorality, including some of the most unnatural, breath-taking behaviors. They will have sex with their father, mother, mother-in-law, neighbors' wives and husbands, sisters, and children. Among other things, these practices will promote pedophilia, and if all goes well, the problem shall spread more quickly in the world than wildfire. In time, most cultures will pass laws against these taboo conducts primarily because they lead to an increased risk of genetic disorders in children during their parents' pregnancy. Even so, we will encourage the behavior as though the idea came from heaven itself.

"We shall make them practice homosexuality, which is an abomination to God, our adversary who holds firm that the conduct deserves death. Yet, we will persuade the Canaanites to participate in the exercise, making them feel God created them that way and, therefore, feel helpless when faced with the temptation. The way to advance the idea is to make them feel that resisting their sexual urges, wherever it may lead, is to deny their very freedom and happiness, which God himself has ordained since the beginning of time. If an individual chooses to lay with the same sex, let it be; the very essence of the act will rile our enemy. Nonetheless, within that unrestrained freedom is the most debased of human behavior, one plagued with our influence and wrapped with guilt, shame, and embarrassment, saying nothing of the potential health problems and the depravity of human dignity. Make them believe that unrestrained sex is the road to freedom and happiness. As long as the act is consented to, there should be no law denying the person this intimate pleasure.

"Lastly, as impossible as it sounds," Satan paused as his companions puckered their ears in anticipation of a challenge. "We will make them have sex with animals, which is another ritual that our maker despises and calls for death as a punishment. Here, we are driving man to insanity. The thought of it is enough to elicit reactions ranging from discomfort and disgust to moral outrage and ethical condemnation. Yet, we will press the issue until some people accept and practice it. And they will. Who knows what happens in the dark, secret world of human sexual confines, except our maker, who sees all? And as taboo as it may be for some, others will gladly take the chance to relieve the unrestrained sexual compulsion with an animal when the opportunity arises."

Satan made sure that by the time he was done with his speech, he was situated directly in front of his throne, which served as an encouraging reminder of the power that lay behind these schemes. His companions knew better than ever that even though Satan had failed in defeating God in direct battle, he had been relatively successful in making God's creation an implicit part of his war. Slowly and surely, humankind was turning into the proxy through which God and Satan conducted their offenses against one another.

***

A few years after the flood, Noah became a farmer to sustain the family through their semi-nomadic life. At some point, he planted a vineyard. The latter decision was inspired by Satan's suggestions, who, unbeknownst to Noah, carried on whispering twisted ideas in his mind to lead him away from the covenant he had made with God. Noah's conscience was yet troubled by the destruction of everyone he knew on earth, and he began drinking wine to drown out his sorrows. Once, as Satan had planned, Ham found Noah naked in his tent while he was drunk and got extremely embarrassed by witnessing his father in such a vulnerable state. When he told his brothers, Shem and Japheth, they responsibly carried a garment to his tent and covered him with their faces turned away so that they would not witness his nudity. When Noah heard about the behavior of his sons while he was still in a drunken stupor, he cursed the descendants of Ham, which at that time comprised a son named Canaan, while he prayed for blessings for Shem and Japheth. He wished that Canaan would become a servant to his brethren. After the flood, Noah lived for another three hundred and fifty years as a drunkard before he died.

In the meantime, many sons were born to the three brothers, which swiftly expanded Noah's bloodline, and the human population on earth started to grow. They continued their journey from the east until they came across a large empty plain in the land of Shinar and decided to settle down there. Here, Satan found an opening to make another move and strike back. Even though God had told the family that humanity would never again be destroyed by water, the ancestor to whom they owed their lives was gone and no longer able to remind his children and grandchildren about the covenant promised by God. Satan's demon chieftains got to work and started to instill deceptive thoughts in the minds of Noah's descendants. Kumail instructed his troops to remind the humans time and time again of God's harsh punishment of their ancestors and began to convince them that such destruction was unnecessarily ruthless on God's part and undeserved by humanity. In the minds of Noah's children, Kumail's stratagems made God seem like an angry and emotional being who might lose his temper at any small mistake that they might commit.

Despite countless periods of rain and the sign of God's covenant with man shining in all its colors and glory, Satan's forces managed to convince humankind that the complete and utter destruction of everything was not only possible but likely to occur. Thereby, they managed to implant a deep mistrust of God's word in the residents of Shinar, which made them perceive the covenant as a disposable agreement, the validity of which seemed to depend on God's mood. Akar's soldiers convinced the sons of Ham, Shem, and Japheth that instead of trusting God to stick true to his word, they should establish the flatlands they had discovered in Shinar as their permanent residence and make arrangements for their own protection from an event as destructive as the flood.

Thus, after pondering those thoughts enough, the family devised a plan to cater to their fears. At that time, all the inhabitants of earth shared one language and were able to understand each other completely. They said to one another, "Come, let us make bricks and bake them thoroughly. Come, let us build ourselves a city and a tower whose top is in the heavens. Let us make a name for ourselves, lest we be scattered abroad over the face of the whole Earth."

The Lord God had specifically instructed Noah and his sons to bring forth abundantly in the earth and multiply in it, expecting them to spread out as their populations increased, so he was surprised to hear their intention to concentrate and settle in one area. Still, he exercised patience and let Man proceed with his idea before gauging whether he needed to intervene. Of course, he did not appreciate man's mistrust in his word and their feeble attempt to protect themselves from a potential punishment from God. It was truly a mockery on man's part to think that anything he could construct would suffice as a form of defense against God's insurmountable power. Inevitably, they gathered materials for construction from earth's abundant resources, all of which were created by God himself. Indeed, he could destroy it all in one swift move if he so willed.

The humans used brick for stone and asphalt for mortar, and bands of men worked together to construct a tower that would reach the heavens. When the construction of it was finished, Satan and his companions contemplated it with pride. As far as their machinations were concerned, they had succeeded; Satan understood that the entire endeavor was an unnecessary safety net against something that God had sworn would not happen. The tower that man built became a tall and overreaching proclamation of their mistrust of God. When the tower was completed, the Lord God descended upon earth to take a look at what the sons of man had built. As expected, he did not like the idea of all of humanity being concentrated in one tiny part of the extensive earth. He feared that such a disposition would lead man along the same path that corrupted Noah's generation, inviting chastisement onto them. Indeed, through my observations of human life and Satan's forces at work over several millennia, I have concluded that Satan finds it easier to corrupt populations that are concentrated in one settlement. On the other hand, establishing distance between human societies prevents the spread of vices and allows different societies to keep each other in check. He witnessed how the human minds in a collective were already starting to go astray and succumb to their pride and oversight.

The Lord God said, "Indeed, the people are one, and they all have one language, and this is what they begin to do; now nothing that they propose to do will be withheld from them. Come, let us go down, and there confuse their language, that they may not understand one another's speech."

So, the Lord God took the humans from the land of Shinar and scattered them abroad across the face of the whole earth. Therefore, they stopped building the city, which would have surely brought about their demise. In light of these events, the tower has since come to be known as Babel, for that was the site where our God confused the language of earth's residents and dispersed them until they were out of reach of one another. The sons of Ham, Shem, and Japheth started settling in distant nations in their own lands with their own languages, according to their families, which led to their own separate bloodlines. Each of these nations then went on to establish their own governments, policies of law and order, and traditions.

Satan's companions celebrated on the sidelines and struggled to contain their excitement for returning to Hell and reporting their advances to their master. Indeed, the prudence of our Lord succeeded in averting a situation that could've easily turned into a great catastrophe, but at the same time, there was a strength to humanity's oneness, which was lost upon their being scattered across the earth. In staying near each other, they could've held each other accountable, but not for long. Based on the directions God had given man to propagate on the earth, even if God hadn't intervened, there would've come a time when Shinar would've become overly populated, and man would've had to venture outward, away from the first semblances of civilization. On the other hand, God's nemesis loved the idea of division and confusion. The chaos of different strands of humanity being separated from each other made it easier for him to stir up envy, greed, and jealousy among the groups. Additionally, their differing languages made it more difficult for humans to understand one another. Of course, Satan had enough legions of demons that could scour the earth in a heartbeat and implement his malicious schemes.

While it is possible that Satan wanted God to do exactly what he did, to create divisions between men by which their differences would only grow, God is still the all- knowing and most powerful, and his foresight cannot be questioned. It is also highly possible that humanity's being in one place could've made for easier targets for Satan, and then he might've managed to corrupt all of them instead of a select few. How things might've proceeded is mere speculation, and what's more certain, as demonstrated by humanity's progress over time to the present day, is that God's intervention did not prevent but delayed what was inevitable.

It wasn't long before men hailing from the disparate nations began to attack each other for wealth, power, and control, wreaking havoc upon the earth.

Chapter 13

A Promise for Life

"My loyal confidants! Much of what I discussed with you centuries ago about the Canaanites has come to pass," Satan boasted at the start of his next meeting with his demon chieftains. "They are mired in wretchedness and human filth, so much so that their stench has reached heaven, exciting our adversary to a state of disgust. Indeed, the Canaanites are intelligent, prosperous, and wealthy people. Still, God is not impressed in the least by their success and sophisticated culture. Instead, he is nauseated by their extreme corruption and immorality, and he is most likely planning to end their civilization as a result of their sin. Like Sodom and Gomorrah, which were part of the Canaanites and have been destroyed, the rest of civilization has become decadent and ripe for destruction."

"Ay!" Kumail raised a fist in celebration as he spoke, "Weakening their conscience was so much easier after the advent of science. They care way more about their worldly lives than their return to God. Indeed, it serves our plans well that the human population has propagated tenfold after Noah's family. Now, we have many more targets and angles from which to attack."

"Yes, it was a great decision to wait, my lord. We have inflicted so much more damage that way," Akar added to inflate his master's pride.

Satan had a smug, self-content look on his face, for it was his idea to wait for Noah's bloodline to multiply before corrupting their way of life. It allowed the problem to snowball out of hand quicker than it otherwise would have.

"It's a good thing you mentioned Noah's descendants, Kumail. We must keep track of all our targets as well as their propensity for evil, especially now that they have been dispersed away from Babel. Here's how the lineage has progressed thus far: Ham's bloodline was carried forth by his sons Cush, Mizraim, Put, and Canaan. Though Cush gave birth to many sons, one of the notable names was Nimrod, who came to be known as a mighty one on earth. Even our nemesis recognized him as a mighty hunter, and so Nimrod gave birth to his own kingdom. The foundations of his kingdom were laid in the land of Shinar itself, specifically in the areas known as Babel, Erech, Accad, and Calneh, but after some time, Nimrod migrated his kingdom to Assyria, where he built new cities that were named Nineveh, Rehoboth Ir, Calah, and Resen.

"From the son Canaan, whom I accurately predicted as the next source of our victory, came the Canaanites, which contain various family branches such as the Jebusites, Amorites, Girgashites, Hivites, Arkites, Sinites, and so on. The Canaanites increased in population so rapidly that I had to disperse their families further, and they settled in lands all the way from Sidon to Gaza in the direction of Gerar and in the direction of Sodom and Gomorrah, as far as Lasha. Still, I am proud to state that all has proceeded according to plan; we made Ham see the nakedness of his father, and in response, Noah cursed Canaan's bloodline to be servants to the descendants of Shem and Japheth. Since then, the Canaanites have time and time again committed scrumptious acts of sin."

"Moreover, we corrupted Ham's descendants so much that the part of the lineage known as the Philistines, hailing from Mizraim, has become uncouth and savage barbarians. Another instrumental branch of the lineage has been Sodom and Gomorrah, whom

Akar's forces were able to tempt into one of the vilest acts of disobedience. Instead of the natural order of life ordained by God, in which men mate with women and produce children in their collective image, men began to engage in sexual relations with men, and they lost interest in their women. Their homosexual conduct spread like a plague until our attacks managed to convert the whole nation to homosexuality. We normalized this sinful manner of sexual engagement enough that, as the population grew, each new male was afflicted by the same twisted desire and was unable to resist the lusts of the flesh, however deranged and unnatural they happened to be in the eyes of God. I amplified their depravity to such an extent that they began to violate other people's sexual consent, and during the time of Lot, they wanted to impose themselves on the two angels who visited Lot. As a result, I am pleased to inform you that God has wiped the entire group off the face of the earth."

Upon hearing the last piece of information, the demon chieftains erupted in celebration. They saw the development as a crack in God's covenant, in which he had promised never to destroy humanity again.

"Ay! It seems like we're close to pushing God to destroy humanity all over again!" Damyan added arrogantly.

"Indeed, we will soon make God wish he had destroyed all of them," Satan continued. "Had they all remained in Babel, we might just have managed to afflict the entire population with the plague of depravity. Anyway, the children born to Japheth, who was the elder son, were named Gomer, Magog, Madai, Javan, Tubal, Meshech, and Tiras. From these, Gomer had more sons named Ashkenaz, Riphath, and Togarmah, whereas Javan also begot sons named Elishah, Tarshish, Kittim, and Dodanim. It was from these descendants of Noah that the coastland peoples, who became known as Gentiles, were separated into their own lands according to their languages, families, and nations. While I've kept a close eye on Ham and Japheth's descendants, I'm afraid I've ignored the third son. Akar, what became of his bloodline?"

Akar stepped forward to give his report. "Of course, my lord. Children were also born to Shem, the third brother, named Elam, Asshur, Arphaxad, Lud, and Aram. After moving out of Shinar, the sons of Shem chose the area starting from Mesha toward Sephar, the mountain of the east, as their dwelling place. The sons of Shem were also divided into separate families according to their languages, lands, and nations.

"As the human population has ballooned, we have increased our presence and interference in their settlements. In fact, we have achieved so many instances of demonic deception and manipulation that it would take ages to recount all of them. Out of the three bloodlines, the weak descendants of Japheth and Ham, in particular, gave in to our temptations on numerous occasions, incurring God's displeasure. The Gentiles have nauseated God with their tendency to disregard him. They've become slanderers, gossipers, arrogant boasters, deceitful God-haters, and murderers, all of which surfaced as a result of our deception. Their lifestyle has demonstrated that it is much easier for humans to succumb to the lusts of the flesh, what pleases their eyes, and the pride of life than to adhere to what has been ordained holy and morally sound."

Akar's tone took on a somber disposition as he continued, "My lord, we haven't succeeded with all of Noah's descendants, though. Of the three sons of Noah, Shem's descendants have ended up being as God-fearing and pious as our rival had hoped for Noah's descendants to be. They practice patience, successfully resist the temptations we bring on, and keep away from sin most of the time. What shall we do?"

Satan closed his eyes in contemplation for a brief moment, then responded, "Do not worry. Though they may be better than the descendants of Ham and Japheth, they are not spiritually perfect. As ordained by our adversary, no flesh will be justified before him despite working by the law, for the law also brings knowledge of sin, which humans find too difficult to resist. Keep an eye on Shem's descendants. I have good reason to believe that his bloodline will lead us to our next point of interest, Abram. The time is nigh for us to inflict another blow to God's pitiful attempts at saving humanity."

***

While all these events were developing, God was watching, listening, and planning. He was highly dissatisfied with the unfolding events: the effects of sin and the continued depravity of nations giving in to fleshly whims and demonic influences with no thought of consequence. Though the all-knowing was prepared for all the directions in which humans could possibly progress, I wondered if his disappointment and mercy were starting to reach a limit. When it came to the question of dealing with humanity's downfall, God wasn't left with many options. Once, he had already destroyed most of humanity, hoping to grant it a fresh start through Noah's family. Unfortunately, sin and demonic infiltration had once again contaminated humankind to the point of disgust despite being separated into numerous nations. Since God had promised that never again would such a flood destroy life on earth, he contemplated an alternate course of action to resolve the problem. He contacted Abram with a plan.

He said to Abram, "Get out of your country, from your family, and from your father's house to a land that I will show you. I will make you a great nation; I will bless you and make your name great; and you shall be a blessing. I will bless those who bless you, and I will curse him who curses you, and in you, all the families of the earth shall be blessed."

So, Abram departed as the Lord had instructed him to, and Lot went with him. Abram was merely seventy-five years old when he departed from Haran. This promise was another attempt to solve the problem of sin on earth. God had already tried the approach of destroying every corrupted being on earth and restarting the human race through one pious bloodline—that of Noah's—but that approach had failed to stand the test of time. Instead, our Lord God now wanted to use Abram as a means of salvation against sin by giving him all the necessary resources to mediate God's blessings for the rest of the earth. Through Abram, all the families and nations on earth would be blessed.

God's instructions to Abram were determined to bear fruit in multiple parts. Firstly, Abram had been promised land, for which he was told to leave his ancestral home. This land would come to be named Canaan. Once Abram reached the land that was destined for him and his family, the Lord promised he would give that land to Abram's descendants.

Thus far, Abram's wife Sarai had been unable to conceive children, so there were no descendants in question. But the Lord also promised that he would turn Abram's bloodline into a great nation, which meant that Abram was meant to have offspring at some point in the future. This was God's way of ensuring that Abram's bloodline was elevated to a stature higher than any other nation on earth. He promised Abram that his name would be revered and remembered throughout the land. Indeed, Abram is now regarded as the father of all nations. Lastly, God's promise decreed that Abram would be the head of one great family, through which all the families on earth would be blessed. Indeed, Abram's bloodline was blessed with multiple prophets and messengers who brought forth God's commandments and instructions for the rest of humankind.

Meanwhile, Satan started to devise his counterattack against God's elaborate plan. The Devil could not stomach humanity acquiring salvation by any means. He wanted to thwart this plan from its very inception and briefed his companions regarding the steps they would take to give free rein to sin, which would, in turn, ravage human dignity and prevent humankind's spiritual reunification.

Although it would take a long time—in fact, centuries—to materialize completely, Abram was duly rewarded for trusting God's promise and resisting the distractions that Satan contrived to meddle with God's plan. Indeed, the Lord God blesses those who prove themselves worthy by obeying his commandments and seeking his favor.

Chapter 14

Sabotaging the Promise

A fter all, how many generations will he attempt to save?" voiced Akar, carefully observing his king's movements.

"We will defile each and every one of them. I spit on this great nation that he has promised Abram," snarled Satan, seated comfortably on his throne atop the wall with his eyes closed.

In the vast expanse of hell behind them, the landscape overflowed with vigorous activity. Over time, Hell's cities had evolved into self-sustaining pieces of land, in stark contrast to the barren and desolate terrain that Satan and his companions had landed in after the fall. Each city had developed its own systems, routines, and training regimes, depending on the demon chieftains who had organized them. Elaborate structures had been constructed surrounding the cells in each city, containing torture chambers for new souls, training arenas for demons, and even offices, where the demons maintained records of all human souls and devised new strategies of manipulation to present to their king. There was a regular exchange of tactics, information, and other resources between them. Each day, the localities generated a list of their observations and achievements pertaining to the earthly realm to be reported to Satan by the leaders of the separate factions.

"I am astounded by our adversary's resilience," Akar attempted to reassure Satan.

"Has he not learned, from the fate of Abram's ancestors, that humankind is doomed to failure?"

Satan smirked and opened his eyes. He was pleased to be greeted by the stage of hell's operations in full bloom.

"Sounds like we need to drive the point home again and again," replied Satan, followed by a hearty, menacing laughter between the two.

Akar was still persistent in his attempts to gain his master's favor. Although he had more or less become the King's de facto right-hand man, he wished and hoped for an official promotion that would place him above the other demon chieftains in the hierarchy.

"Do you wish for me to send forces to obstruct Abram from reaching his destination? Or better yet, should we lead them astray?"

Satan stood up from his throne, poised and self- assured, as if he had some infallible plan up his sleeve.

"Nay," he answered without bothering to look at Akar even once.

"This attempt by our adversary could turn out to be a vital turning point in man's relationship with God. I know he will be following their movements closely. The unfolding of this so-called promise has to be sabotaged with utmost precision and delicacy. Reassign your forces elsewhere. It's time for me to go myself."

***

When Abram reached the land of Canaan, he saw the land that God Almighty had promised to be the dwelling place of his descendants.

The Lord's benevolence moved Abram, so one of the first things he did on the land was to build an altar in his Lord's name. Then Abram moved to the mountain east of Bethel and pitched his tent there between Bethel and Ai. There, too, he built an altar to the Lord. He continued to journey toward the South to demarcate the land of his descendants and gain a better sense of what God had left in store for him. Although the land did not seem nearly as lush or abundant as Haran, which Abram, his family, and Lot alongside him had left behind, Abram reminded himself of God's reassurances and started life anew.

Not long after that, the land where they had settled was infected by a severe, life-threatening famine. Abram and his family struggled to find enough sustenance to get through their days. They traversed countless miles each day in hopes of acquiring at least a few morsels of food. Some days, they would return with a few figs, dates, or cherries that they would distribute evenly among themselves, even if that meant getting by on mere crumbs. On other days, they would return empty-handed. Satan enjoyed watching God's creation suffer, and he was quick to realize that the trying times inspired difficult feelings in the hearts of men that he could capitalize on.

"You fool!" Satan whispered in Abram's thoughts one night when his resolve was rendered meek by hunger.

"You left your good home, trusted in a God you haven't seen, and came out here to die in this famine. God promised to make you a great nation, and here you are, barely managing to survive. You need to abandon this land and this mission, move to Egypt, and save yourself and your family from death."

Satan's words managed to sow a seed of doubt in Abram's heart. Indeed, he had placed blind faith in God's commandments and risked the lives of his people in hopes that the migration would raise their stature and improve their quality of life. As far as he could tell, only the opposite effect had taken place, which made it near impossible not to consider Satan's suggestion. He spent some days fearfully mulling over the idea. One night, when the family became extremely irritated by hunger and were unable to find any food whatsoever and the relentless desert chill with its wailing winds pierced their skin and made them shiver, Abram cursed the land for being so unforgiving and made an impulsive decision.

The next morning, he announced to his people that they would migrate to Egypt because the famine threatened their existence. They wrapped up their tents, gathered their belongings, and mustered the last ounces of energy in their bodies to undergo the arduous journey. While they were on their way to Egypt, they came across a variety of small fruit- bearing trees and shrubs, which filled their stomachs with nourishment and their hearts with hope. While watching Abram's decision unfold, Satan found another opportunity for intervention.

"Just so you know," he interjected in Abram's thoughts, though Abram had no idea that the very source of evil in the universe was directing him like a puppet.

"Egyptians love beautiful women like Sarai. So, when you arrive, you must lie and say Sarai is your sister. That way, they will not kill you and possess her."

The thought entered Abram's mind like a plague and festered into a fear that compelled him to share his apprehension with his wife.

When the group was close to entering Egypt, he said to Sarai, "Indeed, I know that you are a woman of beautiful countenance. Therefore, it will happen when the Egyptians see you that they will say, 'This is his wife'; and they will kill me, but they will let you live. Please say you are my sister, that it may be well with me for your sake, and that I may live because of you."

So it was when Abram came to Egypt that the Egyptians saw the woman and found her extremely beautiful. When the princes of Pharaoh saw her, they commended her to Pharaoh, and the woman was taken to Pharaoh's house. She claimed to be Abram's sister, and the Pharaoh treated Abram well for her sake. He had sheep, oxen, male donkeys, male and female servants, female donkeys, and camels, of which he gave some share to Abram to feed his followers and tend to their needs.

When God considered the meeting between the Egyptians and Abram's people, he saw that Abram had deviated from the plan that the divine promise was contingent on. God knew that this was the work of his nemesis and was greatly dissatisfied that Abram's will had not only succumbed to Satan's bluffs and abandoned the covenant between them but also been dishonest with the people who welcomed them with open arms based on unmerited and irrational fears. The all-knowing God perceived this development as an injurious deviation from the plan he had devised for humankind's salvation and decided to intervene.

He plagued Pharoah and his house with a fatal infestation because of Sarai. One day, the Pharaoh called Abram and reprimanded him for the ghastly betrayal.

"What is this you have done to me?" he roared. "Why did you not tell me that she was your wife? Why did you say, 'She is my sister'? I might have taken her as my wife. Now, therefore, here is your wife. Take her and go your way!"

The Pharaoh commanded his men to drive Abram and his people out of their land. He told them to ensure that Abram took his wife along with him, as well as his belongings. In this way, God rescued both Abram and his mission from a grave disaster. In fact, both Abram and Pharoah had much to lose if God did not intervene. Satan was excitedly anticipating the fruits of his contrivance before God averted the dreadful scenario at the very last minute.

When Abram was driven out of Egypt, he had no choice but to return to Canaan, the place that God had intended as his dwelling place for generations to come. By the time Abram arrived in Canaan, the famine was over, and the land was covered in fresh green vegetation that heralded a time period of nourishment and prosperity. I knew that the initial famine was only God's way of testing Abram's faith to see how much he could rely on him, but Abram's decisions only proved that he was exceedingly prone to be led astray. Abram pitched his tent in Bethel, reestablished communion with God, and began the process of settling down. Of course, Satan was disappointed by this turn of events, especially after he had managed to push Abram to the edge of a precipice. When he returned to hell, he reported God's intervention as a minor setback in his plan, reassuring his companions that the opportunity to strike again would soon arise. He rested for a few days before returning to the earthly realm and waiting for the opportune moment.

Owing to the renewed abundance of land, Abram became wealthy. He acquired all that he could ask for, including livestock, gold, servants, and herdsmen—all signs of God's promise to turn Abram's bloodline into a great nation. The only fundamental lack was that of a bloodline itself. Abram had no heir, and the issue became more troubling with each passing year as Sarai grew older and became more and more likely to lose her ability to conceive. When the couple was unable to conceive for ten years after the promise, the dilemma started to invade their daily reality.

Satan, who continued to monitor Abram's life and progress, noted the growing despair and hopelessness in the couple's hearts and decided to take advantage of the situation. One day, when Sarai pondered the family's dilemma in the solitude of her tent, Satan attempted to rile her up against God.

"God hasn't been entirely honest with you," he said to her in a pitying way, as if she had been subjected to an act of divine deception.

"He forgot to mention that you are beyond the child- bearing age, which keeps you waiting and longing for something that will never happen. But you can fix the problem. If you really want a child, you can use your maidservant for that. Give Hagar to your husband. Then, if she conceives and bears a child, you can claim the child as your own."

Sarai was taken aback by the advent of such thoughts in her mind.

"I can't do such a thing," she said out loud, as if she had a listening audience in the tent. "Besides, my husband would never agree to it."

"You don't know that," replied Satan. "Ask him and see what he says."

So, after giving the matter more thought, Sarai approached Abram and broached the subject.

"See now, the Lord has restrained me from bearing children. Please, go to my maid; perhaps I shall obtain children from her."

Abram heeded the voice of Sarai, not knowing that it was actually the voice of Satan. His own misery because of the lack of a descendant clouded his judgment in gauging how such an act would likely displease God. Then Sarai, Abram's wife, took Hagar, her maid, the Egyptian, and gave her to her husband, Abram, to be his wife. As Sarai had suggested, Abram married Hagar, and she conceived his first child. When Hagar saw that she had conceived, she began to despise her mistress, Sarai.

In response, Sarai regretted the plan she had made with Abram to acquire an heir and how it caused a rift between them—now, the woman who was starting to despise her was also the mother of Abram's child. She realized that she had been misguided into permitting such an interlude between her husband and maidservant. She voiced her concerns to Abram, who saw that Hagar's negative feelings toward Sarai were not the result they had hoped to achieve.

He said to his wife, Sarai, "Indeed, your maid is in your hands. Deal with her as you please."

Upon receiving this reassurance from Abram and realizing that he had developed no preference for Hagar or a desire to defend her, Sarai considered it best to get rid of Hagar before her loathing for Sarai spilled over onto other members of their family. Sarai started to be extremely harsh in her interactions with Hagar, to the point that Hagar was left with no option but to flee from Sarai's presence.

One day, an angel of our Lord found Hagar by a spring of water in the wilderness on the way to Shur. He inquired where she had come from and where she was headed, upon which Hagar revealed her intentions of escaping Sarai's unfair treatment, even though she had only acted according to Sarai's wishes. God recognized Hagar's predicament, sympathized with her, and conveyed a set of instructions to her through his angel.

The angel said to Hagar, "Return to your mistress and submit yourself under her hand. We will multiply your descendants exceedingly, so much so that you will not be able to count them. Behold, you are with a child, and you shall bear a son. You shall call his name Ishmael because the Lord has heard of your affliction. He shall be a wild man; his hand shall be against every man, and every man's hand against him. And he shall dwell in the presence of all his brethren."

Hagar was relieved to hear this news and decided to trust the blessings that God had in store for her. She returned to the land of Bethel, where Abram had pitched his settlement, and she submitted to her mistress, Sarai. Hagar shed her hostility toward Sarai for wanting to take her son and offered to behave however she wanted. Indeed, it was better for Hagar and her unborn child to be nursed in Abram's settlement than in the land to which she had planned to flee. The rest of her time until childbirth passed much more amicably, and there finally came a day when she gave birth to Abram's heir, whom she named Ishmael according to God's wishes.

At eighty-six-year-old, Abram was still vibrantly healthy and strong when Hagar gave birth to Ishmael, whereas Sarai, who was younger by a decade, was roughly seventy-six years old. Still, Abram and Sarai placed their faith in God and waited patiently to be rewarded for heeding God's wishes. In one exchange with God after a violent rebellion in the Valley of Siddim, when Abram was ninety- nine years old, he expressed his perturbation regarding his lack of a declared heir, upon which God established an everlasting covenant with him. God asked for every male child in Abram's descendants to be circumcised, along with those servants who might have been bought from foreigners. At the same time, God informed Abram that his name would be Abraham from then on and assured him once again that he would be the father of many nations. God also changed Sarai's name and told Abraham that he should call her Sarah from that point on. He told Abraham that Sarah would be the mother of nations, and many kings would descend from their bloodline.

When Abraham heard God repeating his promise of a child after more than a decade of patience on his part, he fell on his face and laughed.

"Shall a child be born to a man who is a hundred years old? And Sarah, who is ninety years old, will bear a child?"

God assured Abraham that that was indeed what he had planned and that when Sarah gave birth to Abraham's son, he should name him Isaac. He assured Abraham that his son would be born around the same time period as the succeeding year. God promised that he would make Ishmael fruitful as well and multiply him exceedingly through his bloodline, but at the same time, his covenant would be with Abraham and Sarah's son, Isaac. As much as Abraham and Sarah found it difficult to trust this promise, I knew that he would surely deliver it as long as Abraham paid heed to the divine instruction.

Abraham adhered to God's commandments and had every male in his family, along with Ishmael, circumcised in the flesh of their foreskin. Indeed, the next year, Sarah gave birth to a son named Isaac, by the mercy of our Lord and his ordinance. God's promise was finally fulfilled, despite Satan's numerous attempts to derail his providence by getting Abraham and Sarah to act against his wishes. Still, it cannot be said that Satan failed in his objectives.

Indeed, Satan was successful in deceiving Sarah, much like he had deceived Eve and caused the first rift in man's communion with God. The birth of Isaac was a miracle that demonstrated the unrivaled power of God, by which he can make happen whatever he pleases, no matter how difficult it may seem. Through Isaac, God also bestowed countless blessings on Abraham and Sarah and finally initiated the prophecy of turning Abraham's descendants into a great nation. Still, Satan was at least partly successful when he influenced Sarah into making Abraham conceive a child with her maidservant, Hagar.

Given that Ishmael was not part of God's initial plan, his birth was no small feat for Satan, who would find some way or another to amplify the problem and use it to his advantage. Ishmael, being the firstborn child, made him the rightful heir to Abraham's legacy, but God made it known that he intended Isaac to be Abraham's rightful successor. As God's promise moved forward, it engendered a lifelong rivalry between Ishmael and Isaac, who waged war against each other based on their separate claims over the Promised Land.

This land would eventually come to be known as Israel, and owing to Satan's successful ploy, the conflict between the two bloodlines would plague the land until the end of time.

Chapter 15

Four Hundred Years of Servitude

Long before the birth of Isaac or Ishmael, and before Abram and Sarai's names were changed, God had caused a deep sleep to fall upon Abram and told him, "Know certainly that your descendants will be strangers in a land that is not theirs and will serve them, and they will afflict them four hundred years. And also the nation whom they serve I will judge; afterward, they shall come out with great possessions. Now, as for you, you shall go to your fathers in peace; you shall be buried at a good old age. But in the fourth generation, your descendants shall return here, for the iniquity of the Amorites is not yet complete."

On the same day, God had also told Abram, "To your descendants, I have given this land, from the river of Egypt to the great river, the river Euphrates—the Kenites, the Kenizzites, the Kadmonites, the Hittites, the Perizzites, the Rephaim, the Amorites, the Canaanites, the Girgashites, and the Jebusites."

This land would come to be known as the Promised Land, which, as God had ordained, would become a source of great conflict between the nations of Isaac and Ishmael. After Abraham and Sarah were miraculously blessed with a son, Sarah lived until the age of one hundred and twenty- seven. When she died, Abraham mourned and wept for her and then purchased property in Machpelah to bury Sarah out of his sight. He himself lived on until the age of one hundred and seventy-five, after which he was buried in the same tomb as his wife, Sarah. By then, Ishmael was well-established with a family of his own, and Isaac was well in his prime. Though Abraham was no longer there to witness it, God's covenants with him were yet to unfold.

When he was forty years old, Isaac married a woman named Rebekah. For the first few years of their marriage, Rebekah remained barren, which became a source of great distress for the couple. Isaac pleaded with the Lord for his wife, and since God had promised to turn Isaac's descendants into a great nation (and indeed, he is the best keeper of promises), he granted Isaac's plea, and his wife conceived. Then, it came to pass that her children struggled within her womb. She wondered if something was wrong with her, so she inquired from the Lord.

The Lord said to her, "Two nations are in your womb. Two people shall be separated from your body. One people shall be stronger than the other, and the older shall serve the younger."

After Rebekah's gestation period was over, she gave birth to twins, as the Lord God had foretold. The older brother was named Esau, and the younger one was named Jacob. The two boys engaged in many squabbles and conflicts throughout their childhood, eventually growing apart into two independent nations. Esau eventually came to be known as Edom, whereas Jacob was eventually named Israel, whereby he became the progenitor of the people that God had promised to turn into a great nation. Indeed, as God had predicted, the Edomites inevitably became Israel's enemy.

Unfortunately, Israel's own family was not devoid of enmity. His sons became jealous of one of their brothers named Joseph, and owing to Satan's corrupting influence, they devised a plan to get rid of their brother so that they may be favored in the eyes of their father. The brothers sold Joseph into slavery, and he was taken to Egypt, where he ended up working as a steward to one of

Pharaoh's officials, Potiphar. Now, Satan knew that Joseph was destined to play a significant role in saving Israel, and in order to derail Joseph's purpose, he made one of Potiphar's wives become infatuated with Joseph. She tried to seduce him, but Joseph was careful not to overstep any boundaries as he knew that in Pharoah's court, he was at the mercy of his superiors. Despite the clarity of Joseph's intentions, Potiphar's wife leveled false accusations of indecency against him, and he was imprisoned. After some time, through members of Pharaoh's court who were imprisoned with Joseph for various reasons, it came to be known that Joseph possessed the gift of interpreting dreams accurately.

It then came to pass that God showed Pharaoh strange and repetitive dreams that he struggled to understand. When he shared the perturbation with his companions, they told him about Joseph, so Pharaoh summoned Joseph from prison and told him to interpret the dream. Joseph informed Pharaoh that the dream foretold seven years of plenty in the land of Egypt, which would be followed by seven years of terrible famine, thereby allowing Pharaoh to make the necessary preparations to sustain his kingdom through that time. Pharaoh was so satisfied with Joseph that he made him second-in-command. He gave his signet to Joseph, clothed him in fine garments and jewelry, and gave him a wife. He then assigned Joseph the task of going about Egypt's lands to gather food and save Egyptians during the incoming crisis. In the meantime, Jacob continued to long for his son, trying to accept with a heavy heart that Joseph might be dead and he might never see his son again.

When the territory of Egypt was struck by famine, the surrounding area of Canaan, where Jacob's family resided, was also affected. Jacob asked his sons to go to Egypt and try to find food there. When they reached Egypt, they were informed by well-meaning people that the governor managed the main store of food, and unknowingly, they found themselves in dialogue with their brother, Joseph. Joseph recognized them but kept his identity secret for some time. He tested his brothers first, and once he was sure that he could trust them, he called on them to bring their father and the rest of the family to Egypt. Even Pharaoh was pleased to hear that Joseph's brothers had arrived from Canaan. Jacob could not believe his ears when the brothers told him that Joseph was still alive, but God reassured him that he should not fear going to Egypt. By that point, Jacob's household had grown to nearly seventy people. They placed their fate in God's hands, took all their possessions, livestock, and descendants, and made their way to Egypt.

Owing to this sequence of events, the people of Israel ended up living in Egypt for the next four hundred years. In the meantime, God permitted Edomites and other Canaanites to remain in the Promised Land, and their population grew into various factions. They defied God's commandments and spread mischief on the land for four centuries, and God patiently tolerated their misconduct. Longsuffering and gracious as he is, he would have allowed the people to relocate if they had repented of their sins. However, falling victim to continued demonic temptations, their iniquity grew worse with time, reaching a point of deserving condemnation and punishment. With the help of Israel, God decided to utterly destroy and wipe the Canaanites from the earth.

When the Israelites made their way to the Promised Land, they were led by one of God's most precious servants, Moses. Much like Jacob and Joseph, Satan knew that Moses was a significant figure in God's long-term plan for humanity, so he set about making treacherous plans to interfere with Moses' mission on earth.

***

"Did I not make it clear that I do not want to see my adversary fulfill his covenant with Israel?" Satan roared from his throne atop the wall, which made the flames in the surrounding torches crackle and flare.

The demon chieftains stood in a line with their heads bowed in shame. They regarded one another from the corner of their eyes, silently nudging the others to speak up. Behind them, the streets of hell's cities resounded with haunting screams of tortured souls trapped in their cells. The sky above them alternated between hues of grey and violent red.

"My lord!" Damyan mustered the courage to respond. "They have not yet left Egypt. We managed to keep them in Egypt for four whole centuries, and rest assured, we have defiled the Promised Land beyond reparation. It was all going according to plan, but the birth of this Moses has rekindled Israel's hopes to return to their ancestors' land. We almost managed to kill him as a child. You would not believe it; he was rescued by the Pharaoh's own daughter!"

Upon hearing Moses' name, Satan turned to his side and spat on the ground. "May the Pharaoh's daughter be cursed! I thought he was supposed to aid our objectives."

Akar, scared that his silence might be perceived as incompetency, spoke up, "My lord! If everything goes according to plan, the Pharaoh will indeed help us. Moses' survival can work in our favor if we make his people lose faith in him. Besides, we have made Egypt's society wholly dependent on the people of Israel. The natives keep their hands clean, resting in opulent rooms and cushioned seats, while the people of Israel toil away to sustain Egypt. They pay a heavy price for being granted refuge, and the Pharaoh would not let them go easily."

"Ay, do not by any means let Israel leave Egypt," Satan

commanded. "Should this Moses fellow make his way to Canaan, he will surely purify the land and dismantle the centuries of work that your forces have accomplished."

Kumail stepped forward in an attempt to placate his master. "Your majesty! Should you approve of it, I shall make the Israelites fearful of ever leaving the familiar grounds of Egypt. Just as we did with Noah's descendants, we shall make the Israelites lose faith in God's covenant, and they shall consider their life in Egypt to be the best circumstances they could live in, despite all their hardships."

"That will do well," Satan said while nodding his head in contemplation. "As for the mission of marring Moses' name in the lands of Egypt, Akar, what's the update on the special team I asked you to put together?"

Akar stepped forward with determination. "Yes, my lord. I have picked out the best and most conniving of my soldiers for this task of utmost importance. I present to you all Protos and Dagon, who have thus far displayed an unmatched and manic enthusiasm for leading humans astray."

"Here they come," Akar added as he turned to face hell and pointed toward the horizon.

The chieftains turned their heads and perceived two figures in flight soaring high above the unforgiving landscape. They flapped their wings vigorously as they flew in various mesmerizing patterns on their trajectory toward Satan's throne room. At times, they came so close to one another that it looked like they would collide, but then one of them would flip upside down and circle around the other, or fold his wings and descend several cubits, or they both would conduct some stunt that made their flight seem more like a harmonious dance than a monotonous flapping of wings.

"Don't mind them," Akar expressed with a smirk. "They love to show off."

As they approached, they disappeared behind the wall briefly before they emerged above the edge with one final flap and landed in the clearing near Satan and his chieftains. Protos landed first, followed by Dagon barely a few milliseconds later. As Protos heaved and caught his breath, his proud smile overflowed with thick, mucky slime. Dagon, on the other hand, bared his sharp canines venomously, making his bloodthirsty intentions clear. They then turned their attention to the assembly.

"Master," Dagon spoke up in his raspy voice as the two bowed their wings. "We are at your service."

Satan smiled.

***

By the time Moses was declared the Prince of Egypt, he was well aware of his ancestry, leading all the way back to Jacob. Trusting that his being revered by the Pharaoh's family must be God's providence in some mysterious way, he continued pretending to be Pharaoh's son. One day, he took off on a casual walk from the King's court to visit his relatives.

When he went out to his relatives' neighborhood, he was shocked to see the state of his people. He saw that an Egyptian was beating up a Hebrew, who happened to be one of his brethren. Unbeknownst to him, he was being trailed by the venomous shadows, Dagon and Protos.

"This is it…" Dagon whispered to his co-conspirator. "This is the chance we've been waiting for! Do something, Protos!"

Protos specialized in pressuring people and causing them to sin, motivating them through extreme emotions such as anger, hate, compulsiveness, and fear. He whispered to Moses, "Don't just stand there and watch your brethren being violated! Bring an end to this brutality. Kill the Egyptian and hide the body. Given your stature, no one would dare suspect you."

Witnessing the suffering of his relative made Moses' blood boil. Having grown up in Pharaoh's court, Moses was not perfect by any means. He was born in sin and shaped in iniquity like every other human on earth, and his only chance of salvation would require some form of miracle from God. The slightest suggestion from Protos was enough to make Moses consider the idea of violence as a viable solution to the injustice unfolding before his eyes. He looked both ways to ensure that no one else was looking and, without once considering the ramifications, picked up a heavy rock to smash the Egyptian's head in with a decisive blow. He confirmed that the Egyptian had stopped breathing and then buried him in the sand with the help of his Hebrew relative. Though Moses had not realized the gravity of his actions yet, Protos and Dagon celebrated on the sidelines, elated by their success in getting one of God's most precious humans to commit first-degree murder. Though Moses was satisfied by the result of his intervention, he hoped that no one had witnessed him in the act of hitting the Egyptian.

The following day, Moses went out again during the daytime and was surprised to find that two Hebrew men were fighting each other. He asked the onlookers to figure out what had happened, then said to the one who had wronged the other, "Why are you striking your companion?"

Moses was surprised that the men did not immediately stop fighting, even though he was perceived in Egypt as the Pharaoh's grandson. Instead, they looked at Moses with disdain.

Then, the one who was in the wrong spoke up, "Who made you a prince and a judge over us? Do you intend to kill me as you killed the Egyptian?"

Moses was shocked by the man's statement. His breathing became rapid, and beads of sweat appeared on his brows fear. His spoke up, "Surely this thing is known!"

Soon after that incident, as Moses expected, Pharaoh heard of Moses' crimes. Overcome by anger and disappointment, he blamed his daughter, who had found Moses in the river, for bringing filth into his court. Wishing to rid his court of any aspect that might bring his authority into question, he immediately ordered Moses to be killed. When Moses received this news, he hastily made preparations and fled the city with his trusted companions' help. He made his way alone to the land of Midian and sat down by a well. Though God disapproved of Moses' actions and weakness of will, he still planned on using Moses to lead his people from Egypt to the promised land.

The merciful Lord granted refuge to Moses at the house of the priest of Midian. The priest, Jethro, was so impressed by Moses' selflessness that he even gave him his daughter, who blessed Moses with a son named Gershom. One day, when Moses was tending the flock of his father-in- law, God spoke to him from the burning bush near Mount Horeb and instructed him to implore the elders of Israel to follow him to the Promised Land.

God said to Moses, "Say to the Israelites, 'The Lord, the God of your fathers—the God of Abraham, the God of Isaac, and the God of Jacob—has sent me to you. Tell them that God appeared before you and told you that he intended to fulfill his promise of rescuing the Israelites from their misery in Egypt and giving them the land of the Canaanites, Hittites, Amorites, Perizzites, Hivites, and Jebusites—a land flowing with milk and honey."

He also added, "Say to Pharaoh, 'This is what the Lord says:

Israel is my firstborn son, and I told you: let my son go, so he may worship me. But you refused to let him go, so I will kill your firstborn son.'"

God expected that Pharaoh would not let go of Israel so easily, as the Israelite workers had practically become the backbone of Egypt's economy. He asked Moses to take the elders along with him and request the Pharaoh to let them go on a three-day journey in the wilderness so that they could offer sacrifices to their God. In order to help Moses' case, God blessed him with the ability to perform wonders and miracles that he may demonstrate in Pharaoh's court to convince him that God had indeed spoken to Moses. On his way to Egypt, God made Moses meet with his brother, Aaron the Levite, who accompanied him to speak to Pharaoh.

Here, the all-knowing God devised a larger plan to make the people of Egypt suffer. Indeed, he had told Abraham that he would punish the nation that held his people captive and brutalized them. Moses and Aaron went to Pharaoh and did as their God had asked them to. At the same time, God hardened Pharaoh's heart to delay the departure of the Israelites from Egypt. Pharaoh did not even bother listening to Moses and Aaron's arguments, nor did he wait to witness the miracles that they had been instructed to perform. Instead, he gave orders to slave owners and overseers in Egypt to treat the Israelites even more harshly. Pharaoh believed that the Israelites were becoming lazy, which was why they had such absurd ideas as taking a three- day vacation to offer sacrifices to their Lord. He thought that keeping them burdened by work would prevent them from taking Moses and Aaron seriously. Their work was doubled, and their resources were reduced, making it nearly impossible for the Israelites to fulfill the work expected of them.

The demons working alongside Protos and Dagon took note of this event and immediately saw the opportunity to engender a rift between the Israelites and the people who were supposed to lead them. Prink, Tygress, and Protos stirred the emotions of the Israelites and pushed them to confront Moses. They said in unison to each member, "See what this Moses and the mentioning of his God is doing to your people? You are now getting whipped, and your workload has doubled since he arrived. Don't listen to him."

The people of Israel were angered. This was the opposite of what Moses had promised, so they went up to Moses and Aaron and expressed their grievances, "May the Lord look on you and judge you! You have made us abhorrent in the sight of Pharaoh and in the sight of his servants to put a sword in their hand to kill us."

Satan's forces succeeded in making the Israelites believe that Moses was the root of their troubles, not Pharaoh. They lost sight of how they were already oppressed under the rulers of Egypt and how Moses intended to free them and lead them to the better life promised to them. This reaction was in line with Satan's strategy: to make the people of Israel blame Moses and God for everything that went wrong during this development. Little did Satan know this was only the beginning.

In the following months, our Lord God made Moses and Aaron plead to the Pharaoh numerous times, and each time he refused to let the Israelites go, our Lord sent a plague on the people of Egypt. First, their water was turned into blood, then there was a plague of frogs, then lice, followed by flies. Then the Lord sent a plague of livestock disease, in which all the animals that belonged to Israelites were spared. The sixth plague was that of boils that afflicted all the people of Egypt, but the Pharaoh remained stubborn. Then, the Lord sent destructive hail upon Egypt, which made the Pharaoh lose his resolve, and he permitted Moses and Aaron to leave the city. The hail was stopped as soon as they left, but then Pharaoh returned to his sinful and oppressive ways. Then there was a plague of locusts, then darkness that lasted for three whole days except for the dwellings of the children of Israel. By that point, the signs of our all-powerful God were abundant and undeniable, so Pharaoh began to fear for his Kingdom and finally told Moses and Aaron to take their people and leave Egypt. As the Israelites prepared to leave Egypt, the Lord God fulfilled his covenant with Abraham by inflicting one last plague on Egypt. The night before Moses and Aaron left, the Lord brought death upon every firstborn in Egypt, which included the Pharaoh's own son. After this point, Pharaoh had no option but to let the people of Israel go. Though his heart was still hardened, it became clearer to him that his defiance was inviting curse after curse upon the land and people of Egypt.

The day finally came when Moses and Aaron led the people of Israel out of Egypt toward the Promised Land. The sacrifices made by the people of Israel came to be known as the Passover, and the Exodus was underway.

***

"My lord…" Akar spoke up, breaking the heavy silence.

The demon chieftains stood in front of their king in a line. Satan regarded their faces critically, trying to decipher why they looked so grim and downcast. He was seated comfortably on his throne with his wings retracted and two worker demons standing on his sides, gently waving large fans to direct air at Satan.

"Ay! My companions!" Satan greeted them enthusiastically. "What news have you brought me today? Have Protos and Dagon succeeded? Have the Israelites been trapped in Egypt till the end of time? Come on! Don't stand there like dumb boles. Speak up!"

"My lord," Akar continued, albeit clenching his fists to keep himself from shaking. "Protos and Dagon did succeed in marring Moses' name, but only in Egypt. We got Moses to commit murder, which tarnished his respectability. And then, in response to Moses' request to leave Egypt, the Pharaoh doubled the workload of Israelites, making them despise Moses."

Satan was confused by the doleful countenances. "Well, that's great news! Why do you all look so miserable? Doesn't that mean the Israelites will stay in Egypt? Surely, that gives us more time to defile the Canaanites, yes?"

"I wish I could affirm that, my lord," Akar replied. "I'm afraid the Israelites are on their way to the Promised Land as we speak…"

Satan's eyes became bloodshot. He slammed his hands on his throne's armrest and stood up aggressively. He pursed his lips in disgust, and suddenly, his glorious white wings popped out of his back, towering above all who were present in the throne room.

"And how have you failed so horribly? Would you care to explain?"

"My lord…" Damyan mustered the courage to respond on Akar's behalf. "It was for the same reason that we lost the battle in heaven. Our adversary intervened on Moses' behalf despite Moses demonstrating committing one of the worst sins. He granted numerous miracles to Moses and his brother, Aaron, each of which we got the Pharaoh to disbelieve. But then he sent down plague after plague after plague. Ten whole plagues he sent, weakening our hold on Pharaoh until he gave in and allowed Moses to take the Israelites and leave Egypt."

Satan hissed and looked up at the sky with explosive wrath. He raised his fists up to the sky and let out a loud, shrieking roar as his demon chieftains stood by and watched fearfully.

When he looked down, he spoke in a stern voice through teeth clenched in repugnance.

"Well, then, why are you standing here and wasting my time? Go stop them!"

Chapter 16

A Mass Departure

Compelled by the havoc wreaked upon Egypt by the plagues sent down by our Lord, Pharaoh summoned Moses and Aaron and said to them, "Rise, go out from among my people, both you and the children of Israel. And go, serve the Lord as you have said. Also, take your flocks and your herds, as you have said, and be gone, and bless me also."

At the same time, the Lord God instituted the Passover as his final judgment over Egypt before fulfilling the promise that he had made to Abraham. The Israelites were instructed to take a lamb for each household. All the lambs were supposed to be males and must not be more than a year old. The month of April was declared as the first month of the year for the Israelites, and they were instructed to kill their lambs on the fourteenth night. The Israelites were asked to take some of the blood and place it outside their homes, to eat the rest of the animal at night, and to burn whatever was left of it by morning.

The Lord said, "For I will pass through the land of Egypt on that night and will strike all the firstborn in the land of Egypt, both man and beast; and against all the gods of Egypt I will execute judgment: I am the Lord. Now, the blood shall be a sign for you on the houses where you are. And when I see the blood, I will pass over you, and the plague shall not be on you to destroy you when I strike the land of Egypt."

That day was marked as a memorial for the Israelites, and they were told to keep those days as a feast by an everlasting ordinance throughout their generations. For seven days, the Israelites were instructed to eat only unleavened bread and anyone who ate yeast in the seven days after the fourteenth was to be cut off from the congregation of Israel.

Moses and Aaron conveyed these instructions to the people of Israel.

"And it shall be," said Moses to the elders of Israel after summoning them, "when your children say to you, 'What do you mean by this service?' that you shall say, 'it is the Passover sacrifice of the Lord, who passed over the houses of the children of Israel in Egypt when He struck the Egyptians and delivered our households.'"

So, the people of Israel, who were readier than ever to leave Egypt, bowed their heads and worshipped. Then, they went away and did as the Lord had commanded Moses and Aaron. At night, the Lord struck all the firstborns of Egypt, including the firstborns of livestock, and there was a great cry in Egypt. The entire nation wailed in unison, for there was not one house where there was not at least one dead. By God, I, Sabrael, had never heard such a piercing cry emanating from the human realm, and never have I heard such a thing since then. Only the Israelites who had followed the Passover rites were spared. The Egyptians began to fear the Lord's punishment and urged the people of Israel to leave the land in haste.

Moses and Aaron had also instructed the children of Israel to ask the Egyptians for articles of silver, gold, and clothing. By inflicting the plagues upon Egypt, the Lord gave the Israelites favor in the sight of Egyptians, so they granted the children of Israel what they requested. Thus, the children of Israel plundered the Egyptians, and they were finally prepared to journey out of

Egypt.

Besides women and children, nearly six hundred thousand people traveled on foot from Rameses to Succoth. A mixed multitude of flocks, birds, and livestock went with them, too, and though Pharaoh did not realize it then, some Egyptians also left with them — those who had grown to like the people of God and wanted to be with them. For four hundred and thirty years, the people of Israel lived in Egypt and suffered at the hands of their masters. At last, they were freed from the oppression of the Egyptians by being expelled from the country by the same people who relied on them for labor.

The Israelites initially regarded the Exodus as an unnecessary risk that threatened the life, they had gotten used to despite all its miseries. They were highly cautious before placing their trust in Moses, and though their emancipation reassured them that this leap of faith reaped rewards, they still proceeded with caution. Satan, on the other hand, was prepared to do whatever it took to prevent God's covenant with Abraham from being fulfilled. A holy nation set aside to worship God would be a huge blow to his war against heaven, and he did not want Moses' followers to perceive his God as someone who fulfilled his promises or was looking after them. He implored his demons to do everything in their power to lead the Israelites astray.

The estimated distance from Egypt to the land of Canaan through Philistia was not long and could have been covered by the Israelites in two months, but God did not lead them through the land of the Philistines. A large group of instigating demons, among them Dagon, Ragno, Bush, and others, had ignited a deadly war in the land by inciting the leaders of the opposing factions. So, God avoided Satan's trap by leading the Israelites through the wilderness around the Red Sea. The children of Israel went out of the land of Egypt in orderly ranks, and Moses carried the bones of Joseph along with him, for he had asked to be buried in the land of his ancestors.

After a long, arduous journey, the Israelites arrived at the Red Sea shores and were asked to camp there. Throughout the journey, Satan's forces trailed the Israelites and stirred poisonous emotions in their hearts, such as fear, regret, and displeasure. They criticized Moses and complained to him every step of the way for putting them through such an unnecessarily demanding journey. They could not understand the providence of the Lord in sending them through the way of the wilderness and craved instead the familiar lands of Egypt. In fact, God also directed them through a longer path to purify their hearts before they arrived in the Promised Land.

During their four centuries in Egypt, many Israelites succumbed to worshipping Egyptian gods and fell into unhealthy eating habits. This was why the Passover feast was instituted with stringent rules concerning their meals. In the same way, the long journey presented an opportunity for both cultural and spiritual renewal. Unfortunately, the Israelites lost their patience, and their accusations drove Moses to the point of madness and forced God to reconsider his promise to Abraham.

One particular event during this journey directly opposed the Israelites to Moses. Shortly after Pharaoh allowed the Israelites to leave Egypt, Akar's soldiers surrounded him in an attempt to make him regret his decision to let Israel go. Prink, Tygress, and Protos hovered above him and filled his heart with fear and bewilderment, convincing him that letting his slaves go would be his worst mistake. They showed him gruesome images of his people turning against him and seeking to sever his head.

After carefully choosing the words by consulting his companions, Protos whispered in Pharoah's ear, "You fool! Why have you let them go after they mired your lands in devastating plagues and took your firstborn sons? How easily you have submitted to the will of your own slaves! And now, their freedom comes at the cost of your economy. Have you not heard that the dull-witted Moses has led his people away from the obvious path of the Philistines, and they camp now next to the Red Sea, closed in by the wilderness, where they would make for defenseless targets for your offense? Do not tarry! Now is the time for you to crush them, once and for all!"

At the same time, the demons turned the hearts of Pharoah's people against the Israelites, and they were quick to forget the consequences of their non-compliance with God's chosen ones. They asked their king, "Why have we done this, that we have let Israel go from serving us?"

Thus, I watched with perturbation as Pharaoh's heart was hardened, and he changed his mind and decided to pursue the Israelites instead. He chose six hundred of the best chariots of his kingdom and went out of Egypt with his people to chase the children of Israel. Their horses and chariots were much faster than the Israelites traveling on foot, and it wasn't long before they reached dangerously close to their target.

Meanwhile, another group of demons surrounded Israel; among them were Protos, Dagon, Tygress, Bush, and Ragno to instigate fear in the hearts of the people. "Did we not warn you that this Moses would lead you to your death?" they said. "Here, in this wilderness, you are going to perish. With the Red Sea ahead and Pharaoh's army behind you, there is no way for you to escape. Die, oh Israel, Die!"

Then the children of Israel lifted their eyes, and behold, the Egyptians marched after them. So they were very afraid, and the children of Israel cried out to the Lord. Then they said to Moses,

"Because there were no graves in Egypt, have you taken us away to die in the wilderness? Why have you so dealt with us, to bring us up out of Egypt? Is this not the word that we told you in Egypt, saying, 'Let us alone that we may serve the Egyptians'? For it would have been better for us to serve the Egyptians than that we should die in the wilderness."

Moses had not expected Pharaoh to change his mind, but he had faith in God's providence and told his people to exercise patience. "The Lord will fight for you," he told them, reassuring them that not only would the salvation of the Lord prevail, but they would also never see the Egyptians again. Then, the events that unfolded reminded everyone, including myself, of the insurmountable power of our Lord by which all those who obey him are protected and rewarded.

The Lord instructed Moses to lift his rod, stretch out his hand over the Red Sea, and divide it. He instructed the Israelites to proceed through the dry land that would emerge, where Moses would split the sea. In the meantime, an angel of God stood behind the Israelites, dousing them in divine light, while a pillar of cloud came between the Israelites and the Egyptians so that Pharaoh's army was left shrouded in darkness.

So, Moses did as God instructed, and the entire Red Sea was divided into two. The children of Israel, mesmerized by the miracle, went into the midst of the sea through the dry land. God hardened the hearts of the Egyptians, and when they realized their enemy was on the brink of escape, they followed after the Israelites with all their horses and chariots. While the Egyptians were midway through the sea, God made their chariot wheels disappear, significantly hindering their movements. Then he asked Moses to stretch his hand out over the Red Sea again so that the waters rejoin and drown the Egyptians.

The Israelites watched as the sea returned to its full depth, and all the Egyptians, including the horses and chariots, were destroyed. The people of Israel saw the great work that the Lord did to save them, and having witnessed the decisive punishment inflicted on Pharaoh's forces, they began to fear their Lord and believe his servant, Moses. They celebrated their salvation from Pharaoh and sang beautiful hymns depicting God's might and benevolence in times of great need.

***

"He did what?" Satan roared when his demon chieftains visited the throne room to update him about the latest developments.

"Yes, my lord, we could hardly believe our eyes," Akar explained with his head lowered. "We had set up two traps for them that they were bound to run into. Had they taken the way of the Philistines, the Philistines would have perceived them as disobedient slaves deserting their masters. They would have either returned them to Egypt or simply killed them. And if they were to take the way of the wilderness, which they did, they were surrounded by nature's obstructions and would've easily been destroyed by Pharaoh's army."

"But they were not?" Satan asked while pacing back and forth in front of his throne.

"No, my lord," answered Akar. "As we said, Moses raised his hand toward the sea and, in a godlike gesture, split the water into two. His people traversed the dry seabed, leaving it behind. So we compelled Pharaoh to follow them. As soon as the Israelites reached the other end of the sea, Moses raised his hand again, and the waters came together, crashing into one body again. All of Pharaoh's forces were killed on the spot."

Satan grimaced. He progressively lost faith in his forces' abilities.

The rest of the demon chieftains stood with their arms crossed, prepared to receive their master's displeasure. Satan stopped pacing and stood with his legs wide apart, facing his best soldiers.

"So, you mean to tell me that God's promise to Abraham is well on its way to being fulfilled? That there was but one task I asked you all to undertake, and you have exceptionally failed?"

"My lord..." Akar began and fumbled. "I understand this is a great inconvenience to our plans. I assure you, we had the Israelites within our reach before our adversary intervened. He has consistently thwarted our plans. He must know by now that the strings of humanity's will are firmly tied to our hands."

An awkward silence ensued as Satan contemplated the next course of action. The demon chieftains stole sidelong glances at one another and hoped to present some idea to make the defeat look like a step forward in the larger plan. Finally, Andras stepped forward and directed the conversation away from regret and criticism.

"My lord, what are we to do next? Moses and his people are on their way to the Promised Land."

Satan raised his bloodshot eyes, clenching his fists to contain his anger. He huffed through his nose, pursed his lips, and said, "We will have to take drastic measures to prevent Abraham's nation from succeeding. I will devise our next few steps. In the meantime, make the promise seem as empty as you possibly can."

"Yes, my lord. We will do so right away," Akar responded before marching off and rushing down the stairway on the wall.

***

Merely three days after they departed from Egypt and were saved from the forces of Pharaoh, the Israelites started complaining

167

to Moses again. Protos and Tygress charted their route to the Promised Land, removing all nourishment and provisions they would have encountered in their path. The Israelites traveled for three days through the wilderness and did not find enough water to satiate all of them. The children cried of thirst, and the women lost their will to proceed further.

They stumbled upon some water in an area called Marah but discovered that the water was bitter and not drinkable.

"What shall we drink?" they asked Moses accusatorily, blaming him for the hardships resulting from his encouragement to leave Egypt.

Moses cried out to the Lord in his helplessness, and the merciful Lord showed him a special tree. Moses cast the tree into the waters of Marah, which made the water sweet and refreshing. Indeed, the Lord's blessings on Moses and his people were beyond measure despite their lack of gratitude. The Lord God also reassured them that if they paid attention to his commandments and kept his statutes, he would protect them from the sort of diseases that he brought on the Egyptians.

The Israelites rested for some time before carrying on with their journey. They eventually came to Elim, where there were twelve wells of water and seventy palm trees, which was enough supply of food and hydration for the Israelites to live comfortably for a few days. They decided to camp at Elim and rest some more to recover their energy.

For most people traveling with Moses, Egypt was the only reality they had witnessed. They had grown accustomed to idol worship, and when they found themselves relieved of immediate responsibilities, they considered the difficulties they had encountered on their way and feared that their gods were displeased with their betrayal of Egypt.

During those days, God summoned Moses to the top of Mount Sinai for a meeting, where he received two tablets of stone with the Ten Commandments and was told to construct a tabernacle for worship and offerings during their journey. Moses was gone for forty whole days, during which a group of demons comprising Pratt, Deanglo, and Tempo took the opportunity to incur God's disapproval again. These demons also belonged to Akar's regiment and were well- versed in the art of tempting humanity toward sin. They convinced the Israelites that Moses would not be able to protect them and made them turn to their old, primitive ways.

"Moses is dead," the demons whispered into the hearts of Israel's tribe leaders. "No one goes away for forty days without bread and water and survives. Take matters into your own hands. Go to Aaron and have him build you a golden calf that will lead you the rest of the way."

They listened to the demonic prompt and readily believed the suggestion, for Moses was indeed delayed. They approached Aaron and said to him, "Come, make us gods that shall go before us; for as for this Moses, the man who brought us up out of the land of Egypt, we do not know what has become of him."

Had Aaron not been influenced by the demons, he might have reassured his people that Moses was alive and would return soon. Alas, he was also manipulated by Akar's soldiers and took his people's fear as a realistic possibility. He knew not how else to console them, so he said to his people, "Break off the golden earrings which are in the ears of your wives, your sons, and your daughters, and bring them to me."

So, all the people broke off the golden earrings in their ears, bringing them to Aaron. He received the gold from their hand, fashioned it with an engraving tool, and made a molded calf.

When the Israelites saw the molded calf, they were reminded of the spiritual practices they had been indoctrinated with. The tribe leaders congregated and said to their people, "This is your god, O Israel, that brought you out of the land of Egypt!"

When Aaron heard their proclamation, he built an altar before it. Then Aaron announced that they would arrange a feast in the name of their lord the following day. They rose early the next day, made offerings to their god, and sat down to eat and drink of the feast. While they were busy with these rituals, Moses descended from the mountain.

Both Moses and our God were astonished when they saw how quickly the people of Israel turned away from their God and forgot the miracle and benevolence which had saved them from the ruthless Egyptian forces. Moses was so enraged that he broke the two stone tablets he had received atop the mountain. He marched into the feast area, took the molded calf the Israelites had made, and burnt it in fire. He then ground the calf into powder, scattered it on the water, and made the Israelites drink from it. While they obeyed, albeit confused, Moses asked Aaron, "What did these people do to you that you have brought so great a sin upon them?"

Aaron did not have a response to give. Moses, who was still infuriated, was willing to take any steps necessary to eradicate the problem of sin from Israel. In a fit of rage, he ordered all those who were involved in reigniting idol worship in Israel to be killed. What unfolded before my eyes that day was no less than carnage: three thousand people were slaughtered with no chance to repent. As God became more aware of Israel's tendency to sin, he realized that harsher measures would be needed to keep them on the right path.

Moses announced that the people of Israel had rested for enough days, and it was time for them to continue their journey to the

Promised Land. During the rest of the journey, God fed Israel with Manna from heaven. It was like white coriander seed, and it tasted like wafers made with honey, but eating the same thing day after day, the people eventually became weary of the food and wanted more.

The demon forces took note of this rising feeling in Israel and promptly took action to exacerbate it.

Chapter 17

The Devine Struggle with Israel

W ell..." Pratt began, floating high above the mass of Moses' followers along with the demons Deanglo and Tempo.

From their vantage point, the earth looked a lot different than it did during the time of Adam and Eve. Vast terrains filled with mountains, deserts, foliage, and water bodies of varying sizes stretched out before them. Every few kilometers, the land was marked by civilizations that numbered hundreds of thousands with their unique methods and systems of agriculture, government, community, and warfare. Two giant civilizations, namely Egypt and Canaan, encapsulated their target subjects: the Israelites. They had hoped that Moses' absence would allow them to corrupt his followers irreparably, least expecting that their adversary would outright execute the corrupted individuals to save the nation.

"Well?" Deanglo roared in response. "Is that what you will say when our master asks why we failed?"

"Can't blame us! Who knew our adversary would kill off three thousand of his favorite creations?"

"Do you not remember the flood?" Deanglo asked in a mocking way.

"As if one could forget!" Pratt scowled. "But don't you see that any time we get close to triumph, our adversary steps in unannounced to redeem them all over again? Besides, it's a good thing we don't have to answer to him directly."

While the other two carried on with their banter, Tempo had his malicious gaze fixed on the children of Israel, looking for any possible avenues to inspire dissent. He took note of their growing dissatisfaction with the daily monotonous diet. Every time they'd see the Manna falling from heaven, scores of them would look up with disappointment, as if God had missed another chance to excite and satiate their appetites. He overheard some of them having thoughts along the lines of, "Is this all Moses' God can send? If he is all-powerful as he likes to claim, why not send us more delicious food?"

Tempo nudged his companions to pay attention. "You fools!" he called out to them. "All is not yet lost. So what if our target has crossed the Red Sea? And so

what if our adversary has killed all those we compelled to return to the ways of the slave masters? Surely, he would not kill the entire nation that he has vowed to save, and they have not yet reached the Promised Land! Look at how their ingratitude makes them forget God even though he sent them food from the sky! While you were so busy recounting your failures, I devised our next attack plan. Though their discontentment with their diet through this journey may seem miniscule, it is a disease that can plague the entire nation! I see no way that Moses could handle it."

"Indeed, Moses and Aaron can do no better than sweet Manna falling from heaven. Do you think our adversary might kill the whole nation?"

"Well…that would mean breaking his covenant with Abraham," answered Deanglo. "Let's find out!"

Just as the children of Israel sat down to consume their nightly meal before sleep, the demons approached the group and said to the tribe leaders, "Remember your diet in Egypt: the cucumbers, the melons, the leeks, the onions, and the garlic? Don't you miss that? Now, all you have is this dried-up, tasteless Manna before your eyes! Isn't it time for a change?"

Then, almost in unison, the people started crying and wailing about their plight in a wilderness that may lead to their eventual death. A mixed multitude approached Moses to voice their complaints.

"Who will give us meat to eat? We remember the fish that we ate freely in Egypt, the cucumbers, the melons, the leeks, the onions, and the garlic, but now our whole being is dried up. There is nothing at all except this manna before our eyes! Why did we ever come out of Egypt? Give us meat that we may eat."

Hearing about the issue, Moses became exasperated with his people and considered whether the burden of leading Israel was too heavy for him to bear. Out of sheer helplessness, he asked God to kill him to relieve him of the responsibility. God acknowledged Moses' plight, and that day, He asked Moses to gather seventy men from the elders of Israel so that they may share Moses' burdens. He also promised that the children of Israel would be provided meat for consumption—quails—albeit more out of disdain than as a reward.

The Lord said to Moses, "Say to your people that I shall give you meat. You shall eat, not one day, nor two days, nor five days, nor ten, nor twenty, but for a whole month, until it comes out of your nostrils and becomes loathsome to you, because you have despised the Lord who is among you, and wept before him, saying, 'Why did we ever come out of Egypt?'"

Initially, Moses had no idea how this would be possible, as the

Israelites numbered a staggering six hundred thousand, and it would require a lot of animals to feed meat to all of them. Then it came to pass that a wind went out from the Lord, bringing so many quail from the sea that they spread out for the length of a day's journey on both sides of the camp. The children of Israel toiled for two whole days and a night to gather the quails, after which they spread them out for everyone to eat. As they started to consume the meat, while it was still between their teeth and barely chewed, the wrath of the Lord was aroused against the people, and he struck them with a great plague.

Shortly after this experience, Aaron and Mariam started questioning Moses' leadership because he married an Ethiopian woman. Influenced by the treacherous demons and their ever-present shadow on Israel, they said, "Has the Lord indeed spoken only through Moses? Has he not spoken through us also?"

God realized that this question could lead to internal conflict in Israel, which would lead to the nation's inevitable collapse. He immediately called Moses, Aaron, and Mariam to the tabernacle of meeting and came down to them in a pillar of cloud to explain how the system of messengers was supposed to work. He informed them that when it comes to prophets, God makes his message known to them through dreams and visions and explained that his servant Moses, on the other hand, was an exception to the rule, for he spoke with Moses face to face. He told them that that should have been enough for them to trust in the leadership of Moses and be scared of defying or speaking against him.

Angered by Aaron and Mariam's actions, God turned Mariam into a leper as he departed. Aaron and Moses were horrified, and they both begged God to forgive their sins and prayed to him to heal Mariam. God responded to Moses directly, expressing that he considered it necessary for Mariam to be punished for some time. He told Moses to shut her out of the camp for seven days, after which she could be received. The people of Israel halted their journey till Mariam returned, and surely, the incident warned them not to criticize Moses or attempt to disobey him. When Mariam was brought in again, the people of Israel moved from Hazeroth and camped in the wilderness of Paran.

Several instances of demonic interference marked the rest of the group's journey to Israel. At one point, Akar's soldiers convinced Korah, Dathan, and Abiram to assemble two hundred and fifty tribal leaders of Israel to question Moses and Aaron's leadership once again.

They said, "You take too much upon yourselves, for all the congregation is holy, every one of them, and the Lord is among them. Why, then, do you exalt yourselves above the assembly of the Lord?"

Moses was disappointed by the question and tried to reason with them at first. He asked them whether they did not see the countless favors their Lord had bestowed on them, but in their response, they complained that they felt cursed more than blessed.

They said, "Is it a small thing that you have brought us up out of a land flowing with milk and honey to kill us in the wilderness, that you should keep acting like a prince over us? Moreover, you have not brought us into a land flowing with milk and honey nor given us an inheritance of fields and vineyards. Will you put out the eyes of these men? "

Moses knew that God was losing his patience with the people of Israel, who found one reason after the other to complain about their status, unwilling to wait for the blessings of the Promised Land. Moses instructed Korah's company to bring censers the next day so as to make offerings to their Lord at the Tabernacle of the meeting. As they approached the Tabernacle, they were intercepted by Korah, who gathered the entire congregation of two hundred and fifty against Moses and Aaron. Upon witnessing this open challenge, God became angry and reacted with deadly force.

He said to Moses, "Separate yourself from among this congregation, that I may consume them in a moment."

When Moses pleaded with his Lord to have mercy and refrain from punishing the whole congregation for the sins of a few, God told him to instruct everyone to step away from Korah, Dathan, and Abiram. That day, the ground opened and swallowed alive all of those two hundred and fifty people. In response, the people of Israel complained to Moses and Aaron and blamed them for killing the "people of the Lord." God's wrath unfurled further, and he sent a plague on the children of Israel that consumed another fourteen thousand and seven hundred. From what I gathered, it seemed like God no longer wanted to leave any room for delay or failure. Any and all evil influences were swiftly dealt with and removed from the path to the Promised Land.

Throughout the rest of their journey, countless demonic interferences threatened the fulfillment of God's covenant with Abraham. God was so disappointed by Israel's consistent straying from the right path that he delayed their travel to the new land by purposely allowing the unbelieving generation who left Egypt to die in the wilderness. Joshua and Caleb were the only survivors who crossed the Red Sea into the Promised Land. Those born on the journey were led to the new land under the leadership of Joshua.

Even so, the disobedience, rebellion, murmuring, and complaining against God and the leadership never stopped, leading God to conclude that humankind would never change. The very nation he cultivated from the ground up became a thorn in his flesh, and he called them a still- necked people.

After arriving at the Promised Land, the people of Israel did not behave as God had instructed them to. Although they successfully drove out all the inhabitants of the land from before them with God's help, they didn't destroy all their figured stones, their molten images, and all their high places. They took possession of the land but kept some of the Canaanites' properties.

God had obligated them to take those steps because he did not want Israel to be corrupted by the sinful ways of the Canaanites, whose demonic influences had misled through the entire duration that Israel resided in Egypt.

God said to Israel, "You shall not follow the customs of the nation, which I will drive out before you, for they did all these things, and therefore I have abhorred them."

It wasn't long before Israel itself became an abhorrent nation to God, and he decided to deal with the problem in a decisive manner.

Even in the days of Moses, he gave a fair warning, "Say to the children of Israel, 'I could come up into your midst in one moment and consume you. Now, therefore, take off your ornaments, that I may know what to do to you.'"

So, the children of Israel mourned God's reaction and stripped themselves of their ornaments by Mount Horeb. The Lord God clarified to the children of Israel that he had not given them the Promised Land because of their righteousness, for they had only repeatedly disappointed him. He had only driven Canaanites out of their land and protected Israel thus far because of his promise to Israel's ancestors, namely Abraham, Isaac, and Jacob.

"Remember!" the Lord said, "Do not forget how you provoked the Lord your God to wrath in the wilderness. From the day that you departed from the land of Egypt until you came to this place, you have been rebellious against the Lord."

Owing to their sins and demonic influence, God eventually ended up splitting the nation of Israel into two kingdoms: Israel and Judah. This split inevitably led to more hostilities and conflict, pitting families against their relatives. It wasn't before a great dispute arose in Israel with regard to the succession of kings. Rehoboam, Solomon's son, was the rightful heir to the throne and reigned after Solomon's death. On the other hand, Jeroboam was a servant who rebelled against Solomon. Both of them laid claim to the kingdom, causing an irreconcilable rift among the tribes of Israel. Ten tribes of Israel swore their oath to Jeroboam as their king, whereas the tribes of Judah, Benjamin, and the Levites remained with Rehoboam. The northern ten tribes who took Jeroboam as their king kept the name of Israel.

The once unified tribes of Jacob were now two nations—two houses, or two brothers if you will—that had become enemies. The prophets wept over Israel's fate—they were a people of God, after all, but their pride and hunger for power had led them to their own demise.

Satan and his warriors had successfully turned ancient Israel into a mockery before God on their journey to the Promised Land. At every opportunity, demons exploited the people's weaknesses, reminding God again and again that the poisoning of the seed of humanity in the Garden of Eden was no small thing and had made the 'human will' susceptible to demonic manipulation till the end of time. Humanity was so far gone that it would probably require another miracle to pull them out of depravity and waywardness.

***

"Finally! Some good news!" Satan exclaimed while celebrating in his throne room with his chieftains.

Worker demons stood on the sidelines, fanning the leaders to relieve them of the unrelenting heat. Behind them, the landscape danced through evaporating vapors, revealing structures and establishments that rose up higher than the holding cells for human souls. Worker demons could be seen dragging carts filled with weapons and marked stone slabs containing records of earthly life from one city to another.

As the human soul population swelled into incalculable numbers, it significantly increased the amount of labor expected of hell's demons regardless of the regiments. Even within the regiments, troops were delegated to specialized units that were responsible for monitoring and meddling with separate nations on earth. Hell had successfully been transformed into a full-fledged, sophisticated base of operations.

"Ay, my lord," Akar cheered, "I promised you our success was inevitable. Though our adversary had to intervene numerous times just to lug the children of Israel to the damned Promised Land, he cannot claim that he has fulfilled his covenant with Abraham. Back in Canaan, they may be, but by no means are they a great nation!"

Celebratory chants and applause resounded from Satan's throne room, echoing through the harsh terrain. Demons in various parts of hell looked toward the throne room, starting to anticipate good tidings.

Damyan stepped forward. "My lord! I'm also pleased to inform you that human souls have been arriving in our realm at a faster rate than ever. Whenever it pleases your temper, I suggest you walk through your kingdom. No corner of hell remains untouched by the cries of pitiful souls tortured beyond their capacity at our behest. I assure you, it is the most soothing harmony I have ever heard!"

"I am pleased, Damyan," Satan lauded his formidable soldier. "Indeed, each time I hear a distant cry, especially the ones emitted by newly arriving souls, it fills my very being with vigor. Their cries are proof of our triumph!"

Upon seeing their master in a cheerful mood, the demon chieftains felt lighter than they had in a long time and sighed in relief. Their fear of Satan's admonishment was, at least momentarily, alleviated. After they had recounted their favorite exploits and exchanged more compliments to boost each other's egos, Akar redirected the conversation to business.

"My lord, what shall be our next course of action?"

Satan's laughter slowly faded in contemplation, settling on a subtle and contented smile. After a few seconds, he responded, "We will have to wait for our adversary to make the next move. I speculate he will try to save his creation once again through some new covenant or medium of intervention. In the meantime, I believe our brave soldiers deserve a day off. Tell them they may spend tomorrow purging or resting however they prefer. As much as earth is our battlefield, we must not forget to have fun. We shall return to work the day after."

Chapter 18
A Unique Approach to an Old Problem

The next few generations of the tribes of Judah and Israel disappointed God in the same way as the Israelites who left Egypt with Moses. Satan's forces had successfully corrupted the nation into a warped sense of pride and distorted thinking. They became a group plagued with corrupt priests and wicked practices, and a false sense of security mingled in their privileged relationship with God. I watched in dismay as our benevolent Lord sent prophets and messengers one after the other, but to no avail. The people of Israel seemed adamant about defying God's commandments and inevitably leading the nation to its own demise. No matter how many among them were punished for their sins or forgiven instead, every approach taken by God failed in the face of Satan's machinations.

After Solomon, several kings and messengers attempted to turn the people back to the one true God. Some of the notable ones were named Azariah, Elijah, Isaiah, Jeremiah, Ezekiel, Zechariah, and Mordecai. When Prophet Malachi came to try and save Israel, he delved deep into their lifestyle and discovered that they were mired in hypocrisy, infidelity, mixed marriages, divorce, false worship, and arrogance, much of which emerged from the Canaanites' way of life.

Malachi began to fear that the people of Israel were beyond the possibility of acquiring redemption. Satan had indeed laid strong foundations for leading the nation astray. They became so sinful that God's word had no effect on their behavior, and he, too, quietly withdrew himself for a breath of fresh air. He sent them one last message through Malachi, informing them of the reasons why they had lost God's favor.

He told them that he loved those before them who followed his commandments, such as Jacob, whereas he hated the likes of Esau, who laid waste to his blessings. He blamed the priests for offering defiled food at his altar and condemned them for sacrificing the blind, lame, and sick animals instead of the healthy males from their flocks, as he had asked. He warned them that he would no longer accept their offerings.

As for the corrupt priests, God rebuked their descendants and cursed them along with their blessings, for they were supposed to be the messengers of God's words but had instead caused many to stumble from the law and corrupted God's covenants. He made them base and contemptible before all the people. He blamed Judah for having profaned the institution of marriage by marrying the daughter of a foreign god. He condemned all those who dealt with their wives treacherously and reminded them how much he hated divorce or blemishes on the sanctified bond between a man and a woman.

Still, he reaffirmed that his covenant with Levi would continue, for the Levites were truthful and just and walked with God in peace and equity while turning many away from iniquity. For that, God said, they deserved the life and peace promised to them in the covenant.

He said to them, "Behold, I send my messenger, and he will prepare the way before me. And the Lord you seek will suddenly come to his temple. Even the Messenger of the covenant, in whom you delight. Behold, he is coming!"

He also told them that he would send Elijah, the prophet, before the coming of the great and dreadful day of the Lord. Elijah would remedy the corruption on the land lest God should strike the earth with a curse. The Sun of Righteousness, he promised, would arise on the day when God would burn up all the wicked and those who fear his name would trample over them.

Even then, the ungrateful children of Israel felt that it would be too much for them to wait for the messenger's arrival and began to speak harshly against God, claiming that it was useless to serve him. There was no profit for keeping his ordinance. Still, God ordered that a book of remembrance be written for those who feared his name and meditated on his name. He reassured me that there would come a day when those people would be like his jewels, and he would spare them from punishment.

At this point, I wondered whether God's patience was reaching a limit. He had already tried to save them more times than anyone had expected. From the flood around Noah's time to Israel's deliverance from their slave masters in Egypt, Abraham's descendants were indebted to God in more ways than they cared to remember. If he wanted, he could've abandoned the nation and humanity as a whole forever.

Doing so would automatically mean eternal condemnation for every person who walked upon the earth. The only reason he held back was because of his eternal covenant with Abraham and his undying love for his creation, no matter how flawed it turned out to be. Owing to the pious ancestors who preceded the children of Israel, God held his wrath back, took time to think, and decided to wait for the right time to reconnect with humanity.

Nearly four centuries passed during which God withheld intervention. During those years, all the angelic beings in heaven slowly became increasingly concerned, for the fate of humanity seemed to be on a downward trajectory. Then, one day, God called the leaders of his regiments to the Hall of Gems near his throne for a decisive meeting. He intended to discuss his strategy and next action plan with those well-versed in Satan's methods.

I can hardly express the hope and optimism that witnessing this congregation filled me with. I couldn't deny that after all these years of watching the progress and demise of humanity, I had grown to care about them and wanted what was in their best interest. Still, I had unfaltering faith in God's providence, for, despite the corruptible free will of human beings, the all-knowing must have foreseen all possibilities and made adequate preparations to deal with them. Michael, Gabriel, Raphael, Uriel, and a few others attended this meeting.

As I watched the discussion unfold, I noticed from the corner of my eye a creeping shadow approaching the gates of heaven. I identified the shadow as Satan, who seemed but a pitiful visage of his past glory. The unrelenting heat of hell seemed to have taken its toll on his body, which once stood as a dazzling emblem of God's majestic powers of creation.

Though Satan was banned from entering heaven ever again, I could tell that even from that distance, he could hear everything that was being said in the meeting. God himself seemed more than aware of his presence; he seemed to have almost expected it. I could tell because as soon as Satan arrived and stationed himself at an ideal vantage point, God began to speak about his plans in even more detail, allowing his adversary to hear all the privileged information.

"I will send a new prophet," he explained to his angels, "who will be known as John the Baptist. He will be the harbinger of our plan. Shortly thereafter, the world will experience the unique birth of a child called Immanuel, meaning 'God with us.' He will eventually come to be known as Jesus, and he will save humanity from the pit of hell. Jesus will serve as the vessel through which I will inhabit earth and help humanity directly."

Once again, God was proactively contriving a way to save his beloved creation — man. I think it was a surprise to all of us that he was willing to use himself as the instrument this time. If all went according to plan, he would become flesh, allow himself to be manipulated by man, die on a cross, rise from the grave on the third day, and return to heaven. Through this process, he would rescue humanity from the clutches of Satan.

"The audacity!" I heard Satan roaring under his breath. "Even after all this, he is still trying to make a comeback? Once again, he will attempt to rescue this pitiful bunch called humanity. What a waste of time!"

Vanishing in a flash, Satan made his way back to hell, raging uncontrollably. So much so that no sooner had he reached than his companions started trying to console him.

***

"I can't believe he is planning to go down himself!" Satan hissed.

Akar stepped forward in an attempt to calm him down. "My lord! Our adversary may take all sorts of steps to save his dismal creation from failure. We must not lose our resolve. Let's consider what new opportunities this scenario presents us with."

"Ay! I agree," Damyan chimed in, "I say this gives us the chance to make him look weak and powerless. Imagine if this Jesus, which you say will be God's own embodiment, fails in his mission? Would that not convey to the rest of heaven, plain and clear, that their so-called leader has lost touch with his abilities?

Besides, he has been failing over and over again, and each time, he manages to blame the humans for being disobedient. This time, when they fail despite his direct aid, our victory will be all the more consequential."

While the demons were lost in reveries of vanquishing their foe once and for all, Satan seemed to be more grounded in his expectations. He knew that God's presence in the flesh would be a force to be reckoned with. He could overturn humanity's fate in a single blow if he wanted. The only silver lining to this plan was that while God was constrained in human flesh, his clairvoyant and manifesting powers would be limited, giving Satan's forces a chance to carry out elaborate offensives that might derail humanity for the rest of time to come. Still, Satan felt like it was too risky an affair that he would be better off avoiding altogether.

"Nay! You think we can tempt our adversary the same way as we have with the rest of our targets?" Satan snarled. "I'm sure he's better than his creation at distinguishing his thoughts from those that we feed. We have witnessed the miraculous powers his chosen ones have displayed, managing to derail our plots on numerous occasions. Indeed, the people of Israel would never have left Egypt if not for the merciless plagues that he sent down upon the entire population. He would not relinquish those powers while residing in our playground."

His companions took a step back and looked at one another in perturbation. Satan was seething with anger, seeming almost on the verge of exploding. They knew not how to placate him.

"My lord!" Kumail attempted to make him feel more in control. "What do you suggest we should do? We cannot sit back and accept defeat so easily. We have to fight back some way or the other!"

"Ay! You have spoken well, Kumail. Soldiers like you keep

their leaders focused on the way forward, no matter how many obstructions lay in their path. I just know this Jesus is going to be a problem, and I have to nip that problem from the very bud!"

While Kumail noticed the underlying envy in his companions' eyes, he was quick to respond to their more immediate reaction, which was to nudge him to carry on as his approach seemed to finally be working. Satan was no longer bellowing mindlessly at the advent of unprecedented maneuvers. Instead, they had managed to redirect his focus to the steps that they could take to resolve the issue.

"My lord," Akar saw the opportunity to contribute, "You might be pleased to know that we maintain a stronghold in the area where he is supposed to be born. Herod, the king of Bethlehem, is but one of our many puppets in the region. I'm sure we can use his influence to nip the problem in the bud."

Satan turned around to look at Akar, albeit lost in contemplation at the same time. It seemed as though the whole scenario played out behind his eyes in that split second, with all its possible variations and unforeseen complications. I was sure that, by this point, Satan must have started to anticipate interventions from his adversary. As time went on, the strategizing on both sides became more and more elaborate.

"That's a great idea, Akar. As things stand, our adversary is probably unaware that we are privy to his plans thanks to my spying faculties. Start making Herod seem like he is on our adversary's side. We must ensure that this Jesus is born in Herod's domain so that we may make Herod seek the child with feigned intentions of protecting and worshipping him. Once Herod has the child in his possession, we may allow Herod to show his true colors by killing him!"

As Satan continued to describe each progressive step of his plan, his fists tightened, his wings stretched out wider and wider, and his eyes took on a deep red hue that made even his companions grow wary. Satan, much like his adversary, was losing his patience as well. As far as he was concerned, humanity had already lived on way longer than it deserved.

"Our adversary won't see it coming, but I'll kill this child before he sees daylight!" Satan growled.

Chapter 19

The Lamb of God

Just as God had ordained, Jesus was born in the same bloodline as Abraham and David, coming soon after the Prophet, John the Baptist, who was a harbinger of the coming Messiah. Not only was John's coming foretold by Isaiah, but John, in turn, prophesized Jesus' coming. He preached God's final judgment and baptized repentant followers in preparation for it.

He told the people of Israel, "One mightier than I is coming after me. I have baptized you with water; he will baptize you with fire and the Holy Spirit."

Indeed, by the miracles of our God, John's mother, Elizabeth, had a relative named Mary, who was betrothed to one named Joseph. By God's will, the Virgin Mary conceived a child before Joseph, and she consummated their marriage. Joseph was cautioned by the people surrounding him and was thinking about putting Mary away secretly.

At that point, an angel of the Lord appeared to Joseph and informed him of the nature of Mary's pregnancy. The angel told Joseph not to be afraid to take Mary as his wife and that the child she conceived was from the Holy Spirit. The angel also conveyed that he should name the child Jesus, as he was the same child that Isaiah had spoken of, saying, "Behold, the virgin shall be with child, and bear a son whom they shall call Immanuel, meaning 'God with us.'"

Therefore, Joseph mustered courage and heeded the word of God, taking Mary as his wife. He did not know her till she brought forth the child of the Holy Spirit, whom he was supposed to name Jesus. Satan's strategy was to ensure Jesus' upbringing in a region that was well under the control of his demons. He got the Roman Emperor, Caesar Augustus, to decree that all the world should be registered. The first census took place when Quirinius was governing Syria. Joseph, who belonged to the lineage of David, went up from Galilee into the city of David in Judea, called Bethlehem, where he got himself registered along with his wife, Mary.

Indeed, as Satan had planned, Mary's pregnancy was concluded in those days, and Jesus was born in Bethlehem of Judea in the days of Herod the King, whom Satan's forces had secured under their reins. When Jesus was born, three wise kings from the East visited Jerusalem bearing gifts and asked for the child that had been born as king of the Jews. They claimed that they had seen his star in the East and had come to worship him. When Herod the King heard of this, he was troubled by the threat it posed to his rule. Demons quickly took the opportunity to exacerbate this situation.

"This child is going to be your demise," whispered Protos and Dagon into Herod's ear. "They call him 'King of the Jews,' meaning he is going to take your throne and rule over the nation forever. You must do something about this problem immediately. You must find a way to kill him while he is an infant."

The demonic prompting compelled Herod into a defensive position. "No one is going to take my throne while I'm alive! Not even the so-called 'King of the Jews.' How can someone even dare to imagine subordinating me while I still live and breathe? Such offense must not go unchecked. I will show them what it means to be king!"

Satan's forces instructed Herod to refrain from taking immediate action and feign cooperation with the visitors so as to find the child. Herod asked the visitors to look for the child and inform him of its whereabouts so that he could also worship the child.

God noted Satan's attempt to hinder his plans and swiftly took action to avert the danger. After they departed from Herod's court, the three kings, who would eventually come to be known as the Magi, beheld the same star that had informed them of Jesus' birth. This time, the star went and stood right above where the child was. They struggled to contain their jubilation and headed over to the destination to which the star pointed them.

When they reached the house and saw the child with his mother, Mary, they fell to their knees and worshipped him before presenting gifts of gold, frankincense, and myrrh. Though their exhilaration upon sighting Jesus was pure and innocent, I feared that they would unknowingly become an instrument for Herod's evil intentions, in turn fulfilling Satan's diabolical schemes.

Indeed, the providence of our Lord triumphed before Satan's plans could materialize. He foresaw Satan's plans and sent a divine warning to the Magi through a dream, instructing them not to return to Herod. They abided with the Lord's wishes and departed for their own country through another route. God knew that Herod would continue to seek the child, so he sent a similar warning to his father, Joseph. An angel of the Lord appeared in his dream and said, "Arise, take the young Child and his mother, flee to Egypt, and stay there until I bring you word, for Herod will seek the young child to destroy him."

Joseph sprang to action and took his wife along with the child to Egypt, intending to stay there until Herod's death. Herod was enraged when he realized that he had been deceived by the wise men. Fearing that the child might survive because of being unidentified, Herod ordered the death of all the male children in Bethlehem who were younger than two years old. On that day, the area of Ramah resounded with haunting cries of mothers grieving after the heartless slaughter of their newborn sons. Little did Herod know Jesus and his family were already way out of his reach.

Herod was unable to find the child till the last of his days, and after his death, the same angel of the Lord appeared to Joseph in a dream and said to him, "Arise, take the young child and his mother and take them to the land of Israel, for those who sought your child's life are now dead."

While on the way to Israel, God warned him once again concerning the ruler of Judea at the time, upon which Joseph turned aside into the region of Galilee. Instead of Judea, Joseph and his family ended up dwelling in a city called Nazareth. In those days, John the Baptist preached in the wilderness of Judea, where all of Jerusalem and Judea went to him to be baptized in the Jordan River. Much to John's surprise, Jesus of Nazareth also came to be baptized by him.

John immediately tried to discourage him. "I need to be baptized by you, and you are coming to me?"

Jesus, guided by the wisdom of our all-knowing God, responded, "Permit it to be so now, for thus it is fitting for us to fulfill all righteousness."

Then, John agreed to baptize the promised Messiah and baptized him in the Jordan River, just like the repenting children of Israel. When Jesus came up from the water, he saw the spirit of God descending to the earth and alighting upon him. Indeed, our Lord was pleased with him.

Satan, who had been watching these developments with a

contemptuous eye, planned another attempt to stifle Jesus' mission on earth. He no longer trusted his demons to handle this time-sensitive objective of utmost importance. When Jesus was returning from the Jordan River, Satan approached him directly. As Jesus traversed through the wilderness, he was tempted by Satan for forty whole days, testing his patience, resolve, and obedience to God. Jesus fasted consistently for those forty days and nights, after which he was hungry, so Satan said to him, "If you are the son of God, command this stone to become bread."

Of course, God's son and servant knew better than to trust the tempter, so he responded, "It is written that man shall not live by bread alone but by every word of God."

Almost instantly, Satan realized that there was no point in convincing him to renounce his fasting ritual. He also noted Jesus's great faith in the written word and realized that incorporating it in his next attempt would help his objective. So he led Jesus high above the city of Jerusalem, placed him on the pinnacle of the temple, and said, "If you are the son of God, throw yourself down from here, for it is written, 'He shall give his angels charge over you, to keep you,' and, 'In their hands, they shall bear you up, lest you dash your foot against a stone.'"

Though Jesus instinctively knew that God would protect him, even through angelic beings, if necessary, he considered the matter briefly before realizing that doing so would inevitably test God, which would be unnecessary. Because of his faith in his father, he needed no physical demonstration to affirm his resolve. He refused the tempter's invitation by saying, "It has also been said, 'You shall not tempt the Lord your God.'"

Starting to lose patience, Satan took the Son of God up on a high mountain and showed him all the kingdoms of the world in a single moment. Satan offered to give all the kingdoms and their authority to Jesus if he agreed to worship him, and though the temptation of that much power was strong, Jesus remained steadfast in his resolve. He refused the offer and admonished Satan for attempting to lead him astray from God's purpose.

He replied, "Get behind me, Satan! It is written that I shall worship only God. And it is him that I serve."

I was filled with delight upon witnessing Satan's disappointment at this response. After a long time, God's plan of reviving Israel seemed to unfold as intended, without unnecessary meddling or interference. This sequence of events was a testament to God's omnipotence and insurmountable power. When Satan realized that this approach would not bear any fruit, he returned to hell and delivered a frenzied rant about Jesus' loyalty and devotion.

***

"Have I lost my charm? Does the world no longer care for my influence?" Satan let out a screeching cry out of helplessness before continuing, "Tell me! Have I lost touch with the abilities that brought us thus far? Why won't the son of God give ear to my temptations?"

Never before had his power been challenged so overtly by beings he perceived as less than him. The demon chieftains gathered around their leader in the throne room, the torch fires burning bright, almost as if reinvigorated by Satan's explosive fury. Akar, Damyan, Kuraim, and others glanced at one another in dismay, evidently at a loss for how to placate the king of hell.

Damyan, the loyal soldier, rested a hand on his master's shoulder, taking a moment to indulge his wonder at the glorious wings of one of God's most beautiful creations. After encouragement from his companions, while Satan's eyes were downcast, he spoke eagerly, "My lord! Never again should you doubt your capabilities.

Look at the critical point to which we have driven our adversary's project, so much so that he himself had to descend to the realm to try and save it. We have successfully intercepted most of his covenants with humanity.

"So what if we were unable to prevent Jesus' advent or to kill him? Remember that it is only so because Jesus is no ordinary human; it is our adversary himself in the flesh. This very act proves that his so-called favorite creation has fallen short of his hopes and expectations. Why else would the king of the universe take such a lowly form as the humans? It is no less than a loud and clear proclamation that though God's love for his creation may have no bounds, they do not, in turn, love him nearly as much. I regard that state of affairs as nothing but your victory."

"Ay, master!" Akar interjected, "Damyan has a good point there. We will surely find a way to hinder this futile mission. Even if Jesus manages to fulfill his purpose somehow, look at what it entails! Imagine the extent of depravity we can make humans descend to once they know that God has promised to save them from the pit of hell! I'm sure we can get our adversary to regret all the favors he has bestowed on them."

After a long time, Satan finally looked up, pleased to find his companions by his side. He could perceive hell's landscape stretching far and wide through the spaces between them, a testament to his kingdom's progress since their fall from heaven. An orchestra of eerie cries emanated from every nook and corner, overshadowed now and then by the deafening screeches originating from the bottomless pit. One by one, he looked at each one of his chieftains' faces, and I wondered if I saw some semblance of gratitude in his eyes.

He responded, "My treasured companions! Let it be known when we will surely sit on the highermost throne above the heavens that the king of the universe was aided by the strongest and most trustworthy soldiers. Indeed, life on earth owes most of its pleasures to our machinations, unknowingly facilitating our war against heaven, the mirage they will long for when they atone for their sins at our home. We must use them as tools to impede Jesus' mission. I believe this is our adversary's last attempt to circumvent humanity's imminent downfall. If we manage to succeed now, he will have no defenses left to save his pitiful handiwork."

Indeed, God's son was not as easy to sway as those who preceded him, but the humans remained as susceptible as ever. Still, Satan asked his chieftains to instruct their demon soldiers to maintain vigilance on Jesus around the clock and to inform him of opportunities that might allow them to thwart God's mission.

He paused for a moment before squinting his eyes into purpose and closing his fists. "Let us not stop till we have brought our adversary to his knees!"

***

In the meantime, Jesus continued to preach the ways of his God to his followers. He demonstrated several miracles that proved his favor with God. He healed the sick, the blind, those who suffered from leprosy, and those who were demon-possessed. He also displayed extraordinary powers that defied laws of physics, such as walking on water, feeding five thousand people with merely five loaves of bread, and even raising the dead back to life for them to speak to their loved ones. Jesus also appointed twelve disciples to disperse across the land, spread his message, and carry out similar feats, such as healing the sick and casting out unclean spirits that afflicted innocent people.

When Jesus came to the region of Caesarea Philippi, he asked his disciples what people identified him as. Some said John the

Baptist, some said Elijah or Jeremiah, while some named other prophets of our Lord.

Jesus then asked his disciples what they identified him as, to which Simon Peter answered, "You are the Christ, the Son of the living God."

While he was pleased to hear this answer, Jesus knew he was soon headed to his own demise. Not long after, he began to tell his disciples that he would have to head to Jerusalem and suffer many things at the hands of the priests, elders, and scribes. He informed them that he would inevitably be killed and then be raised back to life on the third day. Peter was greatly displeased at the son of God expecting to be treated in such a way. When he got the chance, he took Jesus aside and rebuked him, "Far be it from you, lord. This shall not happen to you!"

Jesus's response to this admonishment surprised Peter. Indeed, the Son of God had clarity of vision enough to see that those words were not spoken by his trusted companion, Peter, except under the influence of God's adversary, Satan.

Even though Peter's attempt was to express concern and compassion for his lord, Jesus saw how it posed a risk of influencing the course of God's mission. He had already accepted his fate of being mistreated and killed as a necessary step for fulfilling his mission on earth, and what he needed instead from his companions was reassurance and encouragement for adhering to God's wishes.

Jesus turned and said to Peter, "Get behind me, Satan! You are an offense to me, for you are not mindful of the things of God, but the things of men."

Indeed, Peter had not even considered that his words might have been motivated by demonic manipulation. Jesus could see through Satan's tactical maneuvers even when they manifested through his most trusted companions, even if the companions themselves failed to notice it.

Peter realized that even his innermost thoughts and feelings that felt autonomous were susceptible to demonic influence, and it took a wise and critical eye to differentiate between human will and Satan's machinations. The son of God possessed enough wisdom to rebuke the progenitor of evil instead of blaming his companion, who was under the influence of external forces.

Moving forward, Satan resorted to another strategy to intercept God's divine ordinance. Since Jesus was destined to die at a specific moment, Satan figured that killing him before the predetermined time would likely impede God's plan to save humanity from sin. When Jesus returned from the Jordan River after being baptized by John, he resided in his home city, Nazareth. On Sabbath day, he went into the synagogue and stood up to read the word of God. He was handed the book of the prophet Isaiah, and he read from it.

Jesus recited the divine word, "The spirit of the Lord is upon me because he has anointed me to preach the gospel to the poor. He has sent me to heal the brokenhearted, to proclaim liberty to the captives, and recovery of sight to the blind, to set at liberty those who are oppressed, and to proclaim the acceptable year of the Lord."

When he gave the book to an attendant and returned to his seat, all the heads present in the congregation turned and fixed their gaze on him. He added, "Today, this Scripture is fulfilled in your hearing."

The multitude experienced a variety of feelings in response to his proclamation. Their interest grew stronger, and they marveled at his words, albeit with disbelief. Surrounding demons suddenly found an avenue to topple Jesus at that moment by discrediting or killing him. Igniting disapproval, hate, and disbelief in the congregation's heart, they whispered to the crowd, "Is this not Joseph's son, Jesus, who grew up in the neighborhood with your children? What nonsense is he talking about?"

Sensing their disapproval, Jesus replied, "Assuredly, I say to you, no prophet is accepted in his own country…, meaning whatever I do or say to you will have no effect because you've made up your mind to reject me."

When all those in the synagogue heard these things, they were filled with wrath, and they rose up and thrust him out of the city. They led him to the brow of the hill on which their city was built so that they might throw him down over the cliff. Having near Godly powers, Jesus was able to pass through them and avoid the tragedy. Then, without delay, he made his way to other cities where he would gain more respect. Again, being God, Jesus was able to anticipate demons' attacks and flee from them.

Having failed in this instance to pose a realistic threat to Christ's life and, being afraid of upsetting their master in hell, the demons soon found another occasion to stir people up against him. The Jews had grown up believing that "God is one" and that no one else on earth, not even his prophets and messengers, had the right to claim that exalted stature. When Jesus appeared on earth in the same shape and form as everyone else, yet claiming to be God, some of the staunch Jews were enraged.

Akar's soldiers sought to capitalize on their hostile emotions and approached them to whisper in their minds, "Look, this man is violating the very sacred thing you've believed to be true since birth. He makes himself God, which is blasphemous. He is likely possessed by a demon and is insane. Why do you listen to him? Stone him to death! Before he has the chance to garner support."

One day, during the Feast of Dedication in Jerusalem, Jesus walked into Solomon's porch for a break from the chilling winter. Then the Jews found him and said, "How long do you keep us in doubt? If you are the Christ, tell us plainly."

Jesus answered them, "I told you, and you do not believe. The work that I do in my father's name bears witness to me. But you do not believe because you are not of my sheep, as I said to you. My sheep hear my voice, and I know them, and they follow me. I give them eternal life, and they shall never perish. Neither shall anyone snatch them out of my hand. My Father, who has given them to me, is greater than all, and no one is able to snatch them out of my Father's hand. My father and I are one."

Then, the Jews took up stones again to stone him. Jesus answered them, "Many good works I have shown you from my Father. For which of those works do you stone me?"

The Jews responded with condemnation, "For a good work we do not stone you, but for blasphemy, and because you, being a Man, make yourself God."

Once again, Jesus managed to escape before the situation got out of hand. The Jews were baffled by his ability to slip away unharmed despite their strength of arms and greatness in number. They sought to seize him again but were unable to get hold of him to carry out their violent plans.

***

The demon chieftains trailed Satan as he took a stroll through the city of hell dedicated to murderous souls.

Wretched faces peered through the rusting bars of the holding cells. Some of the cells had lifeless arms hanging out as if some savior might come and rescue them from their misery. Their wide, unblinking eyes spoke of the unbearable pain and anguish they had endured during their time in hell. From other cells, meek voices could be heard of repenting souls begging God for mercy and forgiveness.

Though the king of hell usually derived pleasure at the sight of God's favorite creation in such a mournful state, during this particular walk, he was visibly preoccupied with the limits of his own ability, as well as repeated demon failures in preventing Jesus from fulfilling his mission. The time was nigh for Jesus to be killed, paving the way for all humans to gain God's forgiveness for sin through repentance.

"So you're telling me…" Satan grunted, "That we were unable to get even a single Jew to throw a stone at him?"

Before responding, Akar glanced at Damyan and Kuraim, who were walking alongside him, almost as if to ensure that he had their support in case Satan misconstrued his answer.

"My lord," he mustered the courage to respond, "The Jews were more than prepared to do so. He seems to possess powers unlike any other human we've dealt with before. Any time we're close to vanquishing him, he slips away unnoticed. We're not sure of how to contain him in a place whence he can't escape, except for approaching him directly rather than employing humans to do our dirty work."

"Dammit! I should have gotten him in Judea. It comes as no surprise that our adversary has granted him special protection. I know he's God's son, but he is also human, and I can't believe it's proving to be so difficult to kill this character," Satan roared. "I don't see why the spirit that inhabits it should make any difference. Surely, the human form must make our adversary weaker in some way. If he performs miracles, portray them as unlawful magic. If he preaches any lessons, expose their contradictions with the

Jewish Scripture. This is an unprecedented opportunity to make God himself seem like a flawed being!"

Azrail chimed in to relieve the pressure off Akar's soldiers, "Indeed, my lord. We even tried approaching him through demonic possession, but our soldier, Malphas, was dispossessed of the host body before he saw it coming. What if we send all the forces of hell to possess the humans surrounding Jesus?"

"Nay! That would be an announcement of an all-out war on earth, but that will come much later. Besides, I don't suppose our regiments are ready for another battle. We have witnessed the hard way what happens when our adversary interferes. He is like an obsessive father, unable to leave his offspring to sort their differences between themselves."

Seeing no way out, Satan shrieked out loud, piercing hell's air with such intensity that cells in every corner of every city were rattled as their inhabitants feared that some divine punishment was upon them. Though Andras and Kuraim flinched ever so slightly, their nerves were calmed by other chieftains' robust and anchoring presence. Only the bravest of them all, Damyan, bared his fangs at the mention of war. The grief of his companions lost in the heavenly battle still manifested on his countenance every now and then, and he had been waiting for an opportunity to avenge their deaths.

Damyan joined in the conversation. "My lord! If this Jesus is really God's embodiment in human form, and he has to die, I say we somehow bring him to hell. You would salivate at the elaborate welcome ceremony I would arrange for him."

Satan sneered at the suggestion, though he dismissed it quickly. "Damyan, if that were possible, I would not waste a single moment before delivering our adversary to hell. I would have you make a special cell right next to his throne in the highest firmament. Alas, for now, our battleground is the earthly realm."

***

While Satan and his chieftains convened in hell to decide their next plan of action, God's angels guided Jesus away from strongholds of demonic influence so as to protect his mission from unforeseen interferences. During his escape, Jesus ran into people who were possessed by demons and had to come to their rescue. There, he demonstrated his authority over the evil spirits through exorcism, showing the world his power over demons and hell.

First, he traveled by boat to the other side of the sea, to the country of Gadarenes. When he stepped on shore, he immediately perceived a man with an unclean spirit exiting the nearby tombs. No one had been able to bind this man, not even with chains. Each time people had attempted to, the man had used brute demonic force to break those chains and shackles into pieces.

When he saw Jesus from afar, he ran and worshiped him. And he cried out with a loud voice and said, "What have I to do with you, Jesus, Son of the Most High God? I implore you by God that you do not torment me."

In response, Jesus said to him, "Come out of the man, unclean spirit!" Then he asked him, "What is your name?"

The man answered, "My name is Legion, for we are many."

Jesus realized that hell's attempts to hinder his mission were intensifying. The legion continued to beg Jesus earnestly not to send them out of the country. Jesus perceived that the imploration originated from the demons more so than the man. The demons begged him to send them instead to the swine so that they may enter them, and Jesus readily permitted them.

Nearly two thousand unclean spirits departed from the man's

body and bolted straight toward the herd of swine feeding near the mountains. As soon as they possessed the swine, the herd ran violently down the steep mountainside and drowned in the sea next to it. When the city's people saw the man of the tombs sitting clothed and in his right mind, they grew apprehensive. They feared something was wrong with the man and pleaded with him to leave the country.

Jesus then made his way to Capernaum, a city of Galilee, to teach the people about the Sabbaths. The people were almost unanimously wonderstruck by Christ's teachings and the authority in his voice. In the synagogue, there was one man who had the spirit of an unclean demon. He cried out with a loud voice, saying, "Let us alone! What have we to do with you, Jesus of Nazareth? Did you come to destroy us? I know who you are—the holy one of God!"

Jesus immediately rebuked him, saying, "Be quiet, and come out of him!" And when the demon had thrown him in their midst, the demon came out of him and did not hurt him. Then, the people of Capernaum were all amazed and spoke among themselves, saying, "What a word this is! He commands the unclean spirits with authority and power, and they come out." And the report about him went out into every place in the surrounding region.

With that exorcism, the demonic forces were momentarily vanquished and no longer possessed any power to interfere with Jesus' mission. Fortunately, from there on, God's plan for Jesus' sacrifice unfolded as intended. The time for the feast of the unleavened bread drew nearer as the Jews prepared for the Passover in celebration of Moses' exodus from Egypt to the promised land.

Jesus asked his disciples to prepare for the Passover as well. Jesus was aware that his death was near, and he also predicted that his trusted companion, Peter, would deny him thrice instead of trying to save him. Peter was baffled by such a suggestion being made by the son of God, for such a betrayal would be akin to betraying God himself. Yet, as much as Peter was loyal to Jesus, the prediction was based on the human instinct to survive, especially in the face of death.

Indeed, the Jewish religious leaders and teachers of the law took note of this man named Jesus, who claimed to be the king of Jews. They planned to arrest and kill him and corroborated with one of Jesus' disciples, Judas, whom they found ready to betray the son of God. After arresting Jesus, they held him near a courtyard where Peter was also taken. While the religious leaders looked for concrete offenses to accuse Jesus, his companion Peter was asked by one of the servant-leaders about Jesus, in response to which Peter also fulfilled the prophecy of denying the son of God. In the meantime, the religious leaders tore Jesus' clothes and attempted to rile him, but he placed his faith in God's providence and said nothing.

Finally, they settled on the offense of Jesus calling himself God and handed him over to one named Pilate, who then prepared Jesus to be nailed on the cross. The people then took Jesus to a place called Golgotha, where he was nailed to the cross and then left to die. Despite Satan's efforts to defeat Christ and render God's plan null and void, the mission was accomplished. The death of Christ was a clear sign of God's victory. Heaven had successfully triumphed over the grip of Satan and hell, paving the road to humanity's salvation.

The death of Christ symbolically paid the ransom for sin, allowing humanity to continue its fellowship with God through repentance, averting their eternal condemnation after death.

***

The demon chieftains congregated in Satan's throne room atop the wall in hell to celebrate Christ's death. Even though Jesus' departure from earth transpired at its preordained time, his removal from the earthly realm was a relief for Satan's forces, whose plans and strategies had run into repeated obstructions owing to Jesus' exceptional wisdom and prudence.

Even before his life was sacrificed to redeem humanity's sins, he had delivered manifold from strife, debilitating illnesses, demonic manipulation, and possession. After his death, Satan and his forces rejoiced at regaining their influence over humanity's actions, albeit the consequences of sin had been greatly diminished as a result of Christ's death on the cross.

Damyan, Kuraim, Andras, Azrail, and Akar laughed in unison with their master as the demon workers in hell's cities, who could hear the malicious laughter several cubits away, discussed the possible reasons behind the joyful atmosphere. Given the rumors of victory on earth, they began anticipating good tidings from their immediate superiors.

"Ay!" Satan remarked, "It pleases me to see that even the son of God was not immune to abuse and ridicule at the hands of God's creation. The cross was truly a cherry on top. This is a job well done, my loyal soldiers!"

Over time, the demon chieftains had adopted a ritual of recounting their favorite moments from their exploits about humanity.

Akar stepped forward with his hand raised in triumph. "My lord! Every moment after the son of God was handed over to Pilate was a sight to witness. Deanglo and Tempo had lots of fun ridiculing God in human form. Oh, how the Jewish soldiers twisted a crown of thorns for his head and dressed him in a purple robe! He looked more like a buffoon than the supposed 'king of the Jews.' It's a pity that the world will remember him as the one who was hanged on the cross."

"Indeed! You have spoken well, Akar," Satan expressed his approval. "Let the world remember what becomes of God's most loyal servants. No doubt, the son of God would have expected a more respectful farewell after all his efforts and sacrifices for humanity's sake. Had he joined our forces instead, we would have shown him what being a king truly means!"

Andres stepped forward and chipped in, "My lord! Your leadership has helped us expose all the flaws and weaknesses of God's favorite creation. So much the son of God did to save others but could not save himself! Indeed, it's a pity he became more of a sacrificial lamb than a king. My lord, what do you make of the forgiveness of humanity's sins through his demise? Should we be worried?"

Satan nodded his head in approval before responding, "You have raised an important concern, Andras. But worry not! Our objective was never to fill hell's holding cells with more human souls, as much as the sight does please my eye. Our adversary might have made a terrible mistake by forgiving humanity's sins in advance. Now that the son of God has borne the brunt of the punishment, which was a strong deterrent, we will make the people who succeed him even more sinful in their ways. Their forgiveness is still contingent on maintaining unwavering faith in the Son of God and unrestrained repentance. Since humans still possess the freedom to accept or reject God, so as far as our mission is concerned, nothing has changed.

"Nay! We will drown them in so many distractions that they will forget the word 'faith' altogether. We will continue to tempt humans with the unbounded pleasures of lust, avarice, and power. Let's see how much sin our adversary is willing to overlook, especially when most of them refuse to invoke his name. I speculate there is a limit, and we may just push him to the point of wanting to abandon or destroy his treasured subjects all over again! Either way, we shall make humanity get in the way of its own salvation. The war is not yet over, and I can already foresee the scales tipping in our favor."

Damyan flapped his wings to draw everyone's attention. Raising his fists to the sky, he chanted, "Hail! The king of the hidden kingdom! Hail, the most exalted of them all!"

Chapter 20
Agitating the Family

Several centuries after the resurrection and ascension of Christ, Christianity had become a well-established religion around the globe. It spread across nations and continents, mountains and valleys, villages and metropolises, yet human souls continued pouring into the abyss as before as if Christ's sacrifice had been futile.

The immediate torture upon arrival would jolt the newcomers into a strange reality, making them realize that death is by no means the end of their existence. Those before them appeared hopeless in cells of bondage, resigned to a condition far worse than they could have imagined, yet having to endure the pain and suffering infinitely. They were murderers, deceivers, prideful, unrepentant souls—though not any worse than the others who arrived there—and each group was isolated by the nature of sin that caused their hellish transgression. There, they relived their worst moments over and over again, gnashing their teeth as they writhed in unbearable agony.

From the deep recesses of hell, demons started to assemble for their first demonic council in the great arena. There, they would called to order by their king—Satan. For what seemed to span six days in the human realm, the conference was a welcome break for the regiments of demons that had scoured the earth tirelessly. Their wicked duties were temporarily placed on hold as sin itself continued to ravage humanity without their immediate intervention.

In the open arena—a space larger than any earthly kingdom—legions of demons awaited, crowded around the center stage where their king would soon appear. Their chatter rumbled like a plague of locusts, a low yet incessant drone that bounced off the craggy, disintegrating walls of hell. The sheer volume of their buzzing was enough to drown the anguished wails of tormented human souls echoing from the cells, but still, the screeching cries from the Bottomless Pit broke through the din intermittently.

For the lesser demons, this was a rare opportunity to lay eyes on their king—a being whom they had not seen for centuries. Only the chief demons, those appointed as Satan's most trusted, had the honor of direct audience with him. The chieftains stood at the forefront of the simmering mass, adorned in grotesque emblems of prestige—tattoos that marked their centuries of vile accomplishments and metal jewelry studded with vibrant gems they had collected during their time on earth. Proud and dignified, their darkened eyes glowed faintly as they gazed toward the empty stage where Satan's throne awaited.

The arena was too vast for me to even dare to count the legions that filled it. Demons of all shapes, sizes, and forms stretched from one horizon to the next. Pratt, Tygress, Prink, and Protos stood among them, eager for their king's approval, though deep down, they knew he rarely singled out anyone. In the sea of grotesque creatures, they were nothing more than specks, unworthy of even a glance from their ruler.

Still, the hope lingered.

The demons rejoiced. For them, humanity's agony was the sweetest victory of all. Suddenly, the murmur of conversation began to die down. A collective shift rippled through the crowd as the throne at the center of the stage started to glow with an unnatural, malevolent light.

When Satan arrived, no one seemed to know where he had emerged from—not even me. The king of hell strode confidently across the raised platform with strands of his jet- black hair waving subtlely under the weight of his pristine crown, bedecked with some of the most valuable gems his demons had found on earth.

A wave of gasps passed through the sea of demons before rows upon rows started to chant his praise. When he reached the center of the stage and turned to face the crowd, his weathered, olive skin glowed bright despite bearing the hellish realm's relentless heat for centuries.

Given the occasion, he had gone the extra mile to wear an extravagant battle attire—a fine choice, in my opinion, considering how much it amplified both his authority and beauty. He was delighted to see hell's meeting arena filled with the legions of his fallen brothers, all gathered to witness their master's proclamation. The air was heavy with tension, anticipation, and oppressive heat. His blueish-grey eyes gleamed at the sight of hell's numbers, and with a slight smirk, he began.

"My loyal subjects, my companions in battle, my faithful legion," Satan's voice boomed, commanding the attention of all present and casting an eerie hush over the crowd. His tone carried the weight of eons of war, suffering, and rebellion. "Welcome to a time of unprecedented victory and celebration!"

The crowd erupted into cheers, the force of their approval making the very ground beneath them shake. Demons of every rank, shape, and form bellowed their allegiance. Their faces were twisted with malice and delight, and their eyes burned with a newfound fervor upon sighting their exalted leader.

Satan allowed the noise to continue for a moment, his eyes scanning the sea of demons before him. He fed off their energy, devotion, and hunger for the destruction of everything that their former home, heaven, once stood for.

"Much has happened," he continued, his voice lowering into a darker, more sinister tone, "since we were cast out of heaven and made to reign here in this dismal realm. But through your loyal service and tireless effort, we have achieved what once seemed impossible."

He paused, savoring the moment. The demons leaned forward, impatient for his next words.

"We forced God—our eternal adversary, the very one who once cast us down—to do the unthinkable. He died to save the very creatures he had so much faith in, and we successfully corrupted. Through my carefully planned whispers, through sin introduced in Eden, I brought his perfect creation to its knees."

A new wave of laughter and cheering rolled through the crowd, louder this time, as the legions reveled in the humiliation of their shared enemy. Satan's smile grew wider, radiating the same irresistible charm that had swayed generations upon generations against their God's wishes.

"And yet," he continued, lifting his hand to silence them, "our triumph goes beyond that singular event. Yes, he sacrificed himself, but even in that, he underestimated us. He underestimated me. For in all his wisdom, his foresight, and his power, he never truly understood the nature of humankind as I did."

Satan's voice dripped with disdain as he spoke of humanity. His contempt for God's creation was palpable, and the demons drank his words like a sweet poison.

"The first time I laid eyes on man, immediately after his creation, I saw the truth—something God failed to see in all his self-righteousness. Man is selfish. He is a creature driven by desire, hunger for more, and the insatiable urge to possess what he does not have. I saw this, and I knew it would be the key to their downfall."

Satan's words were met with approving nods and murmurs from his audience. Some demons hissed and clapped their clawed hands in satisfaction, recalling their roles in the great deception of humankind.

"It began in Eden," Satan said, his tone turning conspiratorial as though sharing a secret only he and his most trusted followers knew. "The woman, Eve—so eager, so curious. It was almost too easy to bend her will, to twist her thoughts, to plant that seed of doubt in her mind. With just a single whisper, she was mine. And then, through her, the man fell as well. Their disobedience opened the floodgates of sin."

A collective sigh of satisfaction rippled through the arena as demons reminisced about the early victories of their war against humanity.

"But what came next," Satan's voice dropped even lower, filled with both satisfaction and mockery, "was far more satisfying. Their fall was only the beginning. With sin came curiosity, and with curiosity came discontent, rebellion, and ambition. They sought pleasures beyond what God allowed them, and in doing so, they tore at the very fabric of the world he had designed for them."

He raised his hand to the sky as though grasping at the remnants of humanity's goodwill, now crumbling under his influence.

"Our greatest tool has always been man's selfishness. His greed.

His constant yearning for more. He cannot help himself. Even when faced with the consequences of his actions, he continues down the same destructive path, time and time again."

Satan began pacing again, his wings enlarging behind him as a demonstration of his inflating pride upon recalling his victories. His eyes gleamed with malevolence as he prepared to share the greatest victory of all.

"And nowhere," he said, voice rising, "is this more evident than in the destruction of the human family."

At the mention of the family, silence fell over the gathered demons. They knew where this was heading. The dissolution of the family was among their most prized achievements, a slow but devastating blow to the very foundation of human society.

Satan paused, letting the weight of his words settle in before continuing.

"Our adversary, in his infinite arrogance, believed that the family would be the unshakable core of human civilization. A man, a woman, and their children. It was a perfect plan in his mind—a reflection of his love for humankind and his desire to nurture and guide them."

The demons hissed and growled at the mention of God's supposed 'love,' their loathing for him evident.

"But," Satan sneered, "He failed to consider the one thing that would unravel it all: man's free will."

At this, the crowd let out a guttural cheer. I had to agree — free will had been their greatest ally in the war against God.

"The first time I saw man," Satan continued, his voice a low, malevolent growl, "I knew that his free will would be his undoing. He is a selfish, gullible creature. He will always choose what benefits him, even if it means betraying his own kind. It was with this understanding that I laid my trap. The moment Eve disobeyed, the sanctity of the family was doomed."

The demons clapped and cheered, relishing the destruction of something so precious to their enemy.

"And so," Satan said, spreading his arms wide, "we have invested much in the family, not to preserve it, but to destroy it. We have warped the idea of marriage, turning what was meant to be a sacred, lifelong union into something fragile, something easily broken by greed, lust, and selfishness. Infidelity runs rampant, trust erodes, and divorce—once unthinkable—has become common. And through this, the children suffer, becoming ripe for our influence. Marriage was meant to be a reflection of God's character and his affinity for his creation, but instead, it has become one of the primary sources of their troubles."

The demons cackled with delight, their voices rising in a cacophony of dark joy. They had witnessed the truth of Satan's words firsthand, working tirelessly to break apart families, to sow discord and pain.

Satan grinned, his voice dripping with satisfaction. "Today, the so-called family unit is nothing more than a dysfunctional assemblage. There is no moral or ethical

center. No foundation. It is a mockery of what it once was. And it is all thanks to us. Though he tried to save them time and time again, through the choicest of humans, such as Noah, Abraham, Isaac, and Jacob, we have successfully managed to lead all those attempts to failure. Though our adversary intended the family unit to be a channel through which newborn children would receive his so-called love for the first time, we have successfully turned it into a playground of the worst human atrocities. Though Cain was the first person to murder his own family member, he was certainly not the last."

The crowd erupted in applause once more, the demons exulting in their shared victory, their confidence swelling with each word from their master.

Satan's eyes burned with triumph as he raised his hand again, signaling for silence. The demons obeyed instantly.

"And this," he said, his voice a low, sinister rumble, "is only the beginning."

The silence that followed Satan's proclamation was teeming with suspense. His declaration of victory over the human family had sent a wave of euphoria through the demonic assembly, but now they leaned forward, eager for the next revelation. They knew that when their master said something was "only the beginning," greater and darker schemes were yet to be revealed.

Satan paced deliberately, the clinking of his feet on the stone floor echoing through the vast landscape. His wings flexed slightly, casting long, sinister shadows against the flickering flames. His smile broadened as he reveled in the attention of his audience.

"Our triumph," he said slowly, savoring each word, "is not confined to the destruction of the family alone. No— our influence has spread like cancer through every aspect of human life. What once stood as the pillars of their society— trust, unity, faith—are now crumbling under the influence of our work. You, demons, have been in every domicile in the world of man, listening and looking for opportunities to take advantage of vulnerable situations in the family. Often, you arouse conflict out of nothing when one doesn't exist, pushing the family into a morally distorted bunch of self- centered individuals. Throughout the ages, your approach has been deceptively simple: Through various modes of communication such as their relatives, friends, colleagues, and your own impressions, you push the idea of self- awareness, personal freedom, empowerment, independence, economic freedom, control, etc., all concentrated around personal ambition, which they feel the need to fulfill under any circumstances.

"Through your relentless pursuit of human ruination, you discovered various ways to amplify greed in human lives, mainly using fear as a base. Fear of not having enough, hoarding what is needed, losing what they have, and living without recognition are keeping humankind buzzing around like bees. The search for more money, material possessions, fame, power, control, and happiness is endless. The perpetual cycle keeps them anxious, stressed, and exhausted, not even realizing that most of these are transitory objects thrown in their path as distractions to keep them away from the truth."

He paused again, his menacing eyes sweeping the crowd. "Look around you," he continued, his voice growing darker, more insidious. "What do you see in the world above?"

The demons looked around with curious eyes to see if anyone had the courage to respond to their master. Though the question was rather open-ended, it remained to be seen if Satan was expecting to hear something specific. One of the worker demons from the front rows raised his charred and dusty hand, catching Satan's astute gaze.

"Yes, my formidable solder! What do you see?" the god of his age asked again.

A collective sigh emanated from the crowd at the phenomenon of one of the lower-stature demons being addressed directly by their king. Most of them had never imagined even being able to lay eyes on him, let alone speak to him face-to-face.

"My lord! The god of this age! King of the hidden kingdom!" the demon responded, taking some time to praise the king before trying to choose his words wisely. "In front of my eyes…I see the most beautiful creature in the entire universe. As for the world above…I see pitiful creatures living for nothing but themselves. I see that they do not obey their master…and they hurt each other just to possess more things which will outlast them."

Satan closed his eyes while listening to the answer, letting the contentment on his lips express his approval of the demon's words.

"Indeed! You have observed and spoken well, my soldier. Selfishness, greed, and lust—these are now the driving forces of humankind. Every decision they make is rooted in their desire for more. They only crave wealth, power, fame, and comfort—things that will rot away in the end. Their appetites are endless, and it is their weakness. We have fed their desires, stoked the fires of their ambition, and watched as they destroy themselves in pursuit of fleeting pleasure. To make it even worse, they compare what they have with their neighbors, attempting to outperform those around them to feel valued and accepted, even when doing so creates economic hardship."

Numerous demons approached the worker demon who had dared to speak and patted his back to commend his effort. A shuffling restlessness passed through the crowd as more and more demons wished to speak with their king and awaited their turn.

Satan continued, "Tantalizing humans in ceaseless pursuits of self-gratification is not only positively exalting for us but further damning for the family. Moreover, since most of their possessions cost money, they habitually purchase them with credit, building debt in the process that eventually causes family conflict that ends in tragedy. As the pressure builds in the home, spouses cultivate relationships in the workplace that often lead to infidelity, complicating matters even more and leading to family dysfunction and breakups. All that leads to familial chaos, and our adversary is often blamed for either causing the problem or refusing to answer prayers to help fix the mess.

"Most often, family dissolution goes beyond the home, which further contributes to our purpose. Those impacted by divorce because of economic hardship, infidelity, or other self-inflection initially triggered by greed or fear must reach out to others for help—relatives, friends, and the community. The spilling of the problem destabilizes everyone involved—spouses, children, and society.

"While society gradually decays over time with dysfunctional families, more immediately, spouses suffer from loneliness, regret, and distrust, making them even more vulnerable targets for bad decisions induced by demonic temptations. Struggling to regain control over their fragmented lives, parents lose control over their children, who now see them as greedy, self-destructive, and weak. Lacking good role models for improvement, the children begin to make decisions about their lives, leaving them wide open for demonic intervention.

"In those moments, and for as long as it takes, you, demons, push the children to self-destruction, reminding them daily of their predicament: Neglected by unloving, selfish parents and abandoned for life. The gentle prodding leads them to seek love, affection, comfort, and guidance wherever they can find it, even from misguided, ill-minded influencers. There, they are led astray: stealing, vandalizing, drinking, illegal drug use, crime, and sometimes murder. Those who get isolated and sidetracked fall into one of our permanent traps—demonic possession.

"They become hosts for indwelling demons who possess their

bodies and lead them to self-destruction and threats to others. Humans mistake that stage for insanity and place these individuals in mental institutions for the rest of their miserable lives. The demons stay in them until the humans die and end up here with us, which is why some of us are not here today."

Satan's eyes gleamed, the malice behind them barely contained. He continued, "As tragic as this scenario is for humans, the cycle repeats despite their efforts to prevent it. Lacking good role models, children who grow up unprotected, unloved, and resentful repeat the pattern in their own families. This further breaks down the moral fabric of society, leading to more distrust, vandalism, crime, and other related problems. While all this is taking place, we, instigators behind all this chaos, remain hidden from sight while God gets blamed for everything that's wrong in the world."

There was a murmur of agreement from the crowd, growing louder with each passing moment. Demons from every rank, from minor tempters to high-ranking generals of hell's legions, took pride in their part in this deception.

"Under our inescapable influence, the humans betray one another for material gain. They lie, they steal, they cheat—all in the name of personal satisfaction. They have turned their backs on their God, convinced that they can live without him, except when they need a subject to blame for their maladies. They have embraced the lie we gave them from the beginning: that they are gods unto themselves, masters of their own fate."

"But," Satan said, his voice rising above the din, "our greatest victory lies not just in the corruption of the individual or the family unit but in the destruction of the very things that could have saved them."

He paused, his grin widening. "Take, for instance, the notion of truth."

The arena grew still as the word lingered in the air. Another worker demon standing in the middle of the crowd raised his hand, inducing a nod from the king of hell, granting him permission to speak.

"My lord! Our savior!" the worker demon spoke in a shrill, guttural voice bursting with enthusiasm. "We have filled their world with so many truths, they find it difficult to tell which is the real one!"

"You are absolutely on point. Truth…" Satan repeated, his tone mocking. "Once upon a time, it held power. It was a force that could shape nations, unite people, and turn the tide in favor of righteousness. But today... today, truth has become a matter of opinion, a commodity to be bought and sold to the highest bidder."

A low hiss of approval rippled through the gathered demons. The demon who had spoken beamed with pride, having had a direct dialogue with one of God's best creations.

"They no longer seek the truth," Satan continued. "No. Now, they create their own versions of it, twisting it to fit their desires. What was once considered sacred and unchangeable has been reduced to mere perception. With every falsehood they believe, they stray further from their God and closer to us."

Satan's voice dropped to a near whisper, but it carried with an eerie resonance. "They no longer believe in anything but themselves."

At this, the masses erupted in applause once again. Satan allowed it to continue this time, relishing the sound of their approval. The thrill of their shared success washed over him like a refreshing wave, filling him with dark satisfaction. He had worked for millennia to bring humanity to this point—where the concept of absolute truth had been completely dismantled.

Finally, with a slow, deliberate gesture, he raised his hands to quiet them once more.

"And yet," Satan said, his voice dripping with smug satisfaction, "even this is not enough, though we have corrupted their desires, destroyed their families, and stripped away their belief in truth. We have far surpassed what our adversary considered us capable of."

At this, the demons erupted into a frenzy of malevolent excitement, howling with glee at the mention of all they had achieved. Satan's eyes burned with triumph as he let them revel in the moment. The demons cheered, some even stomping their feet in wild applause.

Satan's voice dropped to a near growl, his tone triumphant. "Through deception, through temptation, through pride, we have already turned their hearts away from their God and made them focus on themselves. We have to infiltrate every level of their institutions and continue to plant doubts, feed their egos, and stoke their desires."

The demons roared with approval, their collective pride swelling at the realization of how far they had come in their quest to dismantle what was once considered unbreakable.

Satan basked in the glow of their adoration, his dark heart swelling with pride. This was his moment—his ultimate victory over the enemy that had exiled him from heaven. The destruction of humankind's institutions, the corruption of their hearts, and the dismantling of the very foundations upon which they stood—all of it was his doing, and now, he stood before his legions as their triumphant leader.

But, as always, Satan had more to say.

Satan let the chorus of demonic cheers echo throughout the vast arena for a while longer, basking in the sheer malignance of it. The throngs of demons were enraptured, enthralled by their leader's words and the unending list of their collective accomplishments. But Satan, ever the master manipulator, had only scratched the surface of his grand address. He raised his hands once more, calling for silence, and the din subsided to a low murmur of expectation.

"You've done well, my loyal subjects," Satan said, his voice smoother and more seductive, as though he were uttering a lullaby rather than a battle cry. "But as we know, victory comes not from resting on one's laurels. Our work is never truly done, and there are always new heights of corruption to scale, new depths to plunge in our relentless pursuit of humanity's destruction."

He paced once again, his wings swishing behind him. His mind raced through the countless layers of human existence they had invaded and poisoned, from the family to their nations and the very soul of humanity itself.

"There is one other matter," Satan said, his voice dropping to a conspiratorial whisper, causing his audience to lean forward, hanging on his every word. "A matter that runs deeper than institutions, beyond families, beyond nations. I speak, of course, of the human soul."

The very mention of it sent a ripple of excitement through the demons, but this time, the reaction was hushed, more sinister, as though they sensed the gravity of what was about to be said.

"The soul," Satan continued, "is the core of humanity. It is the one thing that links them, albeit tenuously, to our enemy. It is where they draw their strength, their hope, their desire to seek something beyond the material world."

Satan paused for dramatic effect, watching as his words sank into the expectant ears of his assembly.

"For centuries, we have waged war on the human soul," he said, his voice growing darker. "We have polluted it with greed, lust, pride, and fear. And yet... there remains within each man and woman a flicker, a spark of something... beyond our reach. Faith."

He spat the word as though it were venom on his tongue.

"Faith," he repeated, his tone dripping with disdain. "That wishy-washy belief that there is something greater, something transcendent, something worth fighting for. It is faith that has kept humanity tethered to our enemy, even in their darkest hours. It is faith that drives them to seek redemption, to return to him, even after they've fallen into the traps we've set.

"But fear not," Satan said, his tone shifting, a sly grin spreading across his face. "For we have devised ways to extinguish even that. We have exploited their doubts, their uncertainties, their fears. We have introduced endless distractions so that their focus is not on the divine but on the mundane, the trivial, the fleeting pleasures of this world."

He held out his hands as though presenting an invisible prize. "Look at them now. Faith, for most, has become a relic of the past, something quaint, a crutch for the weak. They no longer seek truth in faith; they seek comfort in possessions, in status, in fleeting experiences. They have replaced faith in the divine with faith in themselves, in their technology, in their science, in their ability to control the world around them."

The crowd rumbled with appreciation. They had seen the fruits of this labor, watching with glee as humanity became increasingly secular, increasingly detached from any notion of a higher power.

"But," Satan continued, his voice growing more intense, "our greatest weapon against faith has been fear itself. Fear of the unknown. Fear of death. Fear of suffering. We have fanned the flames of these fears in their hearts, so much so that they will do anything—anything—to avoid them."

He laughed, a low, sinister sound. "Look at how they scramble in the face of sickness, in the face of economic uncertainty, in the face of war and disaster. Their fear drives them to madness, and in that madness, they turn away from faith and grasp at whatever straw we dangle before them."

The demons roared in approval, their dark hearts swelling with pride at the thought of all the souls lost to despair and fear.

"But there is more," Satan said, his eyes glowing with malevolent fire. "We have not just driven them to fear; we have taught them to worship it."

The demons quieted, intrigued by this bold statement.

"Yes," Satan said, his grin widening. "Fear has become their new god. They build their lives around it, make decisions based on it, and allow it to dictate their every move. They fear for their health, their safety, and their financial security. They fear the judgment of others, failure, and the unknown. And in doing so, they have built altars to their fears, sacrificing their faith, joy, and hope upon them."

He paused, letting the gravity of his words sink in. "And we, my friends, have made this possible. We have fed their fears, cultivated them, and nurtured them until they became all-consuming. And now, humanity is trapped in a prison of their own making, unable to see beyond the bars of their own terror."

The demons erupted into applause once more, their shrieks of approval echoing off the walls.

"But we are not done," Satan said, raising his hand for silence once more. "No, our work is far from complete. While we have driven humanity into the depths of despair, there are still those who cling to hope and hold onto faith, however fragile it may be."

He sneered, his eyes narrowing. "But that hope is nothing more than a dying ember, and it is our task to snuff it out completely."

The demons leaned forward, eager to hear the next phase of Satan's grand plan.

"Our next objective," Satan continued, his voice taking on a chilling finality, "is to ensure that humanity's faith, or at least whatever remains of it, is utterly destroyed. We will continue to exploit their fears, but we will also attack their very ability to believe."

He paused, his red eyes gleaming with malice.

"We will sow seeds of doubt in their minds, make them question everything they once held dear. We will twist their understanding of good and evil until they can no longer discern the difference. We will bombard them with conflicting messages, false prophets, and empty promises until they are so confused and disillusioned that they turn away from faith altogether."The demons were almost trembling with excitement, their anticipation rising with every word.

"And when that day comes," Satan said, his voice rising to a crescendo, "when humanity no longer believes in anything but their own desires, when they are so consumed by their own selfishness, their own fears, their own doubts— we will have won."

The crowd erupted into wild applause, their cheers and hisses filling the air like a symphony of evil.

Satan stood before them, basking in the glory of his vision. The demons were on their feet now, cheering their master's name, their eyes gleaming with anticipation for the ruin they would soon unleash.

"And on that day," Satan said, his voice now a whisper that carried through the deafening roar, "we will celebrate, for we will have achieved what we set out to do from the beginning. We will have taken humanity, God's beloved creation, and turned them into creatures of darkness."

The demons cheered louder, the very walls of hell's cities trembling with their elation.

Satan's smile grew wider in satisfaction.

"This," he said, raising his arms triumphantly, "is the beginning of the end for humanity. And when they fall and are lost forever, it will be because we made it so."

The demons erupted in a frenzy of celebration, their victory over humanity now within reach. Satan turned from the crowd, his wings unfurling in a display of power and dominance as he strode back to his throne room atop the wall.

Hell was filled with the sound of demons cheering, celebrating their successes, reveling in the destruction they had wrought upon the world.

Satan sat upon his throne, his face etched with gloating triumph as he looked over the frenzied crowd. His plan was working. Hell's mission was thriving, and the downfall of humanity was inevitable.

With a final glance at his loyal followers, Satan leaned back in contentment, absorbing the sounds of celebration reverberating through the sweltering air.

Chapter 21

Attacking from the Top

The aftermath of Satan's first address left the legions of demons in a state of exhilaration. After he departed into temporary seclusion, the masses dispersed into smaller quarters, eager to revel in their collective victories. Even in the bowels of hell, the atmosphere was electric—charged with the excitement of conquest, the intoxication of pride, and the deep satisfaction of having twisted humanity into their image.

The quarters they gathered in were cavernous, jagged halls of stone illuminated by the fiery firmament that served as their realm's canopy. Demons of every rank, size, and shape, each uniquely scarred from centuries of war and corruption, filled the spaces with their raucous chatter. Their voices, though capable of speaking every human and angelic language with terrifying fluency, defaulted to their favorite dialect—gestures combined with harsh, guttural tongue sounds and clicks—one that communicated not just words but intent and emotion with terrifying precision.

Clusters of demons gathered in small groups, gesticulating wildly as they shared stories of their most recent conquests on earth. They boasted of souls they had claimed, families they had torn apart, and societies they had thrown into chaos. Satan's speech had validated their exploits tenfold, revealing to them the pleasures of boasting about their achievements. Before that address, though they were individually aware of their own actions on earth, they had little exposure to the maneuvers of countless other demon regiments that were also employed in corrupting the earthly realm.

Their voices blended into a cacophony that echoed through the halls, punctuated by bursts of dark laughter and the occasional flash of infernal light as one demon or another demonstrated some newly perfected skill in manipulation or torment.

As incorporeal beings who operated above the laws of the natural world, the demons did not need food, drink, or sleep to fuel their endeavors; they found sustenance in their own malevolence. Their revelry took on the form of acrobatic displays, their grotesque forms twisting and spinning through the air with unnatural agility. Some demons, eager to impress their comrades, performed elaborate stunts, launching themselves from the walls of the cavern, their wings unfurling at the last second in displays of skill. Others conjured up nightmarish illusions, images of human suffering, or distorted visions of paradise that drew gasps of approval and applause from the crowd.

In one corner, a group of demons debated which human nation they had most successfully corrupted, their words laced with arrogance. "The West," growled Alastor, a demon with eyes like burning coals. "They think themselves so free, but we've twisted that freedom into bondage. Look at their so-called democracies, collapsing under the weight of their greed."

Moloch, another demon with spiked, leathery wings and a reputation for propagating child sacrifice and pagan rituals, scoffed. "You speak of the West, but look to the East. Totalitarian rule, mass suffering—we've turned entire populations into slaves. There, our control is absolute."

The discussions, though competitive, shared one common thread—pride. Each demon relished in the havoc they had wrought, and as the night in human terms stretched on, their zeal only grew. They waited with eager anticipation for the next session, where they would once again lay eyes on their king. The time between his appearances was long, but it only served to stoke their devotion and inflate their sense of accomplishment.

As what seemed like a full night and day passed in the human realm, the great arena began to fill once more. Demons returned from their various quarters, assembling in the colossal space before Satan's throne, which stood in the center, ominous and dark. The anticipation in the air was palpable—an oppressive force that seemed to press down on the gathering crowd.

The moment of Satan's return drew near, and with it, a surge of energy rippled through the assembly. The closer they were to their master, the more invigorated they became. The thrill of victory mingled with the deep need to be recognized by him, to be validated in their purpose. Many of them—those of lower ranks—would never be called by name, but even the briefest glance in their direction would be enough to fuel their arrogance for centuries.

Then, at last, it happened. A familiar, bone-chilling silence fell over the crowd, extinguishing the low murmurs of conversation. The air itself seemed to crackle with the weight of his presence. The shadows around the throne deepened, growing darker and denser. Satan had returned.

The darkness that swirled around the throne was thick and suffocating, seeming to devour the very light from the torch fires of hell. As Satan's presence imposed itself on the atmosphere, every demon in the vast arena instinctively bowed their heads, lowering their eyes to the scorching ground. The reverence they showed was not born of love but of awe—an awe that came from knowing they stood in the presence of their master, the one who had defied heaven itself.

Satan emerged from the shadows slowly, his form materializing as if pulled from the abyss. His tall frame towered over the assembly, his wings casting long, jagged shadows that rippled across the floor like creeping tendrils of darkness. His skin, pale and smooth as alabaster, contrasted sharply with the blackness that surrounded him, and his eyes—icy blue, cold and calculating—scanned the crowd with a gaze that could freeze the soul. His jet-black hair fell in perfect waves down his shoulders, framing a face that, even in its darkness, retained a beauty so terrifying it could only have been crafted by divine hands.

The silence was deafening, broken only by the faint sound of distant wails from the damned souls who writhed in torment in the deeper recesses of hell. But here, in this moment, the focus was singular. All eyes were on Satan.

The demons, trembling with anticipation, began to stir. First, the lowest of the ranks, the foot soldiers and tempters raised their heads, their eyes wide with adoration and fear. Then, slowly, the higher-ranking demons followed, their movements synchronized as if directed by some unseen force. The air filled with a low rumble of excitement, the tension mounting as the legions prepared to welcome their king.

Then, as though a dam had burst, the crowd erupted into frenzied adulation. Demons leaped into the air, their grotesque wings unfurling as they performed acrobatic stunts in tribute. Some spiraled high above the throne, flipping and twisting, while others contorted their bodies in unnatural ways, showcasing their dexterity and skill. The more powerful among them conjured fire and shadow, hurling them into the sky in an infernal display of loyalty. Torch flames danced across the arena, and the heat in the air intensified, turning the space into a cauldron of raw energy.

Satan stood motionless, watching his followers with a cold, detached satisfaction. He allowed them their moment of celebration, knowing that their need for recognition, their desperation for his approval, would only fuel their desire to serve him more fervently.

After several minutes of wild displays, the demon chiefs, clad in their intricate emblems of authority, stepped forward. They moved with a practiced grace, their tattoos glowing faintly in the dim light as they raised their hands to quiet the crowd. The roar of the assembly gradually subsided, and the demons settled into an eerie silence, their eyes now fixed on the throne.

Satan did not speak immediately. Instead, he let the silence linger, building the anticipation to its peak. When he finally opened his mouth, his voice was a low, resonant rumble that seemed to echo from the very depths of the abyss.

"My loyal subjects and battle companions," he began, his words slow and deliberate, "it seems that the previous report on the family has served you well. You are joyful, and that brings me gladness."

The demons responded with murmurs of agreement, their faces alight with pride. For a moment, Satan let his gaze sweep across them, his eyes lingering on the chiefs who stood at the front, their chests puffed out with self- importance.

"In our last meeting," Satan continued, his voice rising slightly, "I spoke of the chaos within the human home—chaos you have all worked tirelessly to bring about. The destruction of the family, once a cornerstone of human civilization, now stands as a testament to your dedication, your cunning, and your relentless pursuit of our cause."

A ripple of applause broke out, but it was subdued, for the demons knew there was more to come. They waited, their anticipation growing with each passing second.

Satan's lips curled into a smirk as he saw their eagerness. "Today," he said, his voice taking on a more sinister tone, "I will bring you more information— information that will expand your victory beyond the home, beyond the family. As you know, the world of humankind is made up of many facets, all intertwined to form a cohesive system. The family, while important, is only one part of that system."

The crowd shifted, eager to hear what new victory lay on the horizon.

"The next critical segment of human civilization," Satan continued, "is their government."

The mention of government sent a wave of excitement through the demons. Many of them had spent centuries working within the labyrinthine structures of human governments, sowing corruption, greed, and division. They had long known the power that came from controlling those who made the laws and who wielded authority over entire nations. But they also sensed that their king was about to reveal something new—something that would take their efforts to an even greater level.

Satan raised a hand, signaling for calm, though his followers were already hanging on his every word.

"Human government," he said, "is where laws are enacted, enforced, and adjudicated. They think of themselves as Gods, making commandments for the rest of humanity to follow. It is the pillar upon which the rest of human society is built. The men and women in the highest positions of power control everything— families, businesses, churches, schools. And it is through them that we have the greatest opportunity to extend our influence."

He paused, allowing the gravity of his words to sink in. Then, with a predatory gleam in his eyes, he added, "But before we discuss how we have infiltrated and corrupted human government, we must first understand our adversary's intent for it."

A murmur of discontent passed through the crowd at the mention of God, but Satan raised his hand to quiet them once more.

"Human government," Satan said, his voice dripping with disdain, "was divinely decreed. It was meant to replicate the established authority we once knew in heaven. In his infinite arrogance, our adversary set it up to reflect his so-called perfect order. There, in the heavens, he remains the only absolute authority—something I fought against, something I despised, and something I will one day challenge again."

The demons growled in approval, their hatred for the rigid hierarchy of heaven simmering beneath the surface.

"But," Satan continued, his tone shifting, "I have to admit, even I saw the logic in his organizational structure. And so, I implemented a similar system here in our kingdom. As you can see, it has served us well."

He gestured to the demon chiefs, who stood at attention, their glowing tattoos a mark of their rank and authority. They nodded in agreement, their eyes gleaming with pride.

"Our adversary," Satan went on, "helped humanity structure their government in much the same way. They have their kings and queens, presidents and legislators, civil servants, judges, law enforcement officers, all working together to maintain order, to promote what they call the common good."

Satan's voice was thick with sarcasm as he spoke the words. The demons hissed and snickered, knowing full well how they had twisted that very structure to serve their own ends.

"The first responsibility of human government," Satan said, "is to promote what is good and healthy for society. Something I like to refer to as the 'right agenda.' It comprises laws that promote morality, spirituality, and human dignity—these are what our adversary intended. But…"

Satan's eyes darkened, and his voice took on a more menacing tone. "We have changed all of that."

The arena buzzed with dark excitement as Satan's words hung in the air, casting a shadow over the assembled legions. The demons, fully engaged now, leaned in closer, eager to hear the next phase of their master's speech. The flickering fires of hell illuminated their grotesque features, casting eerie reflections of their eager faces across the cavern walls.

Satan, watching them with cold satisfaction, continued. "Human government was originally designed to promote morality, righteousness, and what our adversary calls 'the greater good.' These governments were meant to protect the weak, ensure justice, and provide freedom for all. Our adversary intended laws to guide men toward what he believes is spiritual health and ethical behavior."

The crowd hissed in mockery at the very idea. Several demons sneered openly, knowing well how far they had perverted such noble aspirations.

"The second duty of government," Satan said, his tone darkening, "is to restrain and punish lawbreakers. Those who violate these laws—laws intended to reflect the will of the heavens—are swiftly judged and brought to justice. On the other hand, those who uphold government laws are considered law-abiding residents and are treated kindly, respectfully, and safely. But we, my loyal subjects, saw the flaw in this system. We knew that human nature—riddled with greed, ambition, and pride—would never allow for perfect governance."

Satan paused, his eyes gleaming as the murmurs of agreement rose once more.

"Seeing it from our adversary's point of view, no matter who humans are, where they come from, how much wealth they possess, or how much status they have, if they break the law and are found guilty, they must be punished. The opposite is also true. No matter who humans are, what they look like, where they come from, how much wealth they possess, or how much status they have, if they obey the rules and do what is good, the government should protect them with ample freedom and opportunity for growth and success.

"Now, imagine a world where these principles— morality, righteousness, justice—actually worked," he said, his voice dripping with disdain. "Imagine a world full of humans, promoting love, harmony, and peace. That world would exalt our adversary and undermine everything we stand for!"

A collective growl of disgust rippled through the arena as the very thought of such a world filled the demons with revulsion.

"That," Satan continued, "was the world our adversary envisioned. But we... we had other plans."

A murmur of excitement passed through the crowd as Satan's words took on a more sinister edge.

"Just as we have ruined the family unit," he said, "we have infiltrated human government. We have corrupted it, twisted it, and used it to serve our purpose."

He paused for a moment, watching the demons as they absorbed the full impact of his declaration. Their excitement was palpable, but Satan could see they were hungry for more—more details, more victories.

"Through careful manipulation," Satan explained, his voice silky smooth, "we have turned the very concept of government against humanity. Our left agenda, as I call it, has taken root in governments across the world. Where once leaders promoted morality and freedom, they now promote pride—self-indulgence, arrogance, narcissism, selfishness."

The demons nodded in agreement, some even chuckling to themselves at the thought of how easy it had been to twist human leaders toward these vices.

"Instead of humility," Satan continued, "we have instilled in them a sense of superiority. Instead of selflessness, we have encouraged self-serving ambition. The very leaders who were once meant to protect their people now look only to their own power, desires, and greed. And the people suffer under their rule.

"Today, I'm pleased to inform you that we have succeeded in a big way, partly because of your assistance and the contributions of human government. Using human greed mixed with power-hungry politicians and other influencers who desperately feel the need to control others, we have deceptively confused the public into believing that what is moral, decent, and righteous is ultimately bad for humanity."

Satan's words hit with force, drawing approving howls from his audience. The atmosphere was charged with the thrill of victory, and yet Satan knew his followers craved more examples of their conquest.

A demon named Orobas, tall and gangly with long, sinewy arms, raised a clawed hand and spoke with an unsettling hiss. "Master, could you share an example of one such leader? Perhaps one who fell particularly well to our designs?"

The demons around him nodded vigorously, curious to hear a more detailed recounting of their victories. Satan, always pleased to indulge their thirst for recognition, inclined his head slightly in acknowledgment.

"Ah, a fine question," Satan said, his voice laced with a dark humor. "There are so many to choose from. But one of the more notable examples... is none other than Judas Iscariot."

At the mention of the name, a ripple of recognition swept through the crowd, followed by a collective gasp of excitement. Judas's betrayal of Christ was one of the most infamous moments in human history, and the demons were eager to hear how their master had played a role in it.

Satan allowed himself a small, satisfied smile. "Judas, of course, was not a political leader, but he was an influencer—a man with the power to shape history. You see, I worked on him for a duration of three years in human time, slowly isolating him, planting the seeds of doubt and hatred in his mind."

The demons were silent now, hanging on every word.

"None of his companions suspected a thing," Satan continued, his voice taking on a conspiratorial tone. "On the outside, everything appeared normal. Judas was just another follower of the Nazarene. But within him, the fires of betrayal were burning, and I fanned those flames until the moment was ripe."

The demons hissed with delight, and Satan's eyes gleamed as he spoke the words that sealed Judas' fate.

"Then, on that fateful night, I entered Judas. I took control of his mind, his body, and led him directly into the arms of the priests, where he betrayed Christ for a handful of silver."

Satan's voice grew darker, his smile more wicked. "And thus, with one act of treachery, I set into motion a series of events that changed the course of history. Judas fell, as did many others. Even today, countless leaders— politicians, kings, tyrants—fall into the same trap."

The crowd erupted into applause, their admiration for Satan's cunning on full display. The atmosphere was electric with celebration as the demons reveled in their collective victory.

Satan raised his hand once more, signaling for calm.

When the arena was quiet again, he continued.

"But Judas was just one. There are many more. Politicians who have risen to power only to bring misery and death to their people. One such leader, known to you all, is Adolf Hitler."

At the mention of the name, the arena shuddered with excitement. Hitler's legacy of destruction was infamous, and many demons had played a part in his rise to power. Satan's eyes darkened as he recounted the story.

"Hitler, a man driven by hatred, greed, and an obsession with racial purity, was one of our most prized creations. We fed his rage, twisted his ambitions, and watched as he led millions to their deaths. Under his rule, the world was engulfed in war, and the Holocaust became one of our greatest triumphs. When he thought he was purifying the earth of bad human blood, he was forging his own fate into hell, where he now resides and is being controlled by you. Even more serious is what our adversary has in store for him when he leaves this place. Some humans say Adolf Hitler was crazy—a madman, they called him. This is because they couldn't see the evil spirits that possessed his being, intensifying his rage and driving him to madness. "

The crowd erupted again, demons leaping into the air with glee at the mention of such widespread devastation. Their laughter and applause filled the chamber, echoing off the stone walls like a symphony of despair.

Satan let them revel for a moment before continuing. "And it wasn't just Hitler. There was also Joseph Stalin, another notable soul who is also here with us, locked in his cell, regretting the day he was born. He was a political leader of the Soviet Union whose decision led to the killing of millions of people.

"In his quest to industrialize the Soviet Union, he implemented a series of Five-Year Plans that were aimed at rapid growth. The plans were successful in turning the Soviet Union into a major industrial power but at a great cost to human lives. His greed opened the door for demon possession, pushing him to the brink of insanity. Power was everything to him, so we gave him as much as he could handle and some more. His policies led to widespread famine, essentially controlling the food supply by feeding the urban population and military while deliberately starving others. Many of us had the pleasure of watching all of this unfold.

"About twenty million people perished through genocide, most of whom were Russians. Anyone or everyone who opposed his rule was senselessly murdered. Today, he is wailing in his cell, desperately wanting to change the past and finding it impossible to do so."

Rows of demons cheered in unison upon hearing the conclusion of Stalin's life. Indeed, it seemed like demonic manipulation and human corruption had spread to the furthest corners of earth— essentially, wherever human life had spread and settled.

Satan continued, "There was also Mao Zedong, who came to

power during a time that seemed to favor tyrants and genocidal maniacs in leadership positions. Like Stalin, he seemed to prefer killing his own people. He got busy as soon as he came to power and killed four to six million people within the first four years of his rule.

"His policies, like the Great Leap Forward and the Cultural Revolution, caused the deaths of around forty-nine million people. Overall, he contributed to the deaths of about seventy-eight million people, surpassing both Hitler and Stalin. He, too, is one of our occupants, grouped with the same deceived, genocidal leaders in human times.

"By his own admission, he thought death would have ended everything but was shocked by the afterlife. Somehow, still very much conscious and riddled with endless pain and suffering, he regrets his decisions but finds it impossible to undo them. Like the others, his memories haunt him day and night, and they will continue to torment him forever. There are countless others like them—each one a puppet in our hands, driven by their own greed and ambition. Each one was responsible for the deaths of millions. And now, where are they? Here. Locked in our cells, writhing in endless torment.

"I could tell you about more greedy politicians who have sold their souls for power and brought misery and death to millions of people as a result, but I believe you get the picture. In almost all these cases, we had something to do with it. We look for these twisted, troubled, weak, and desperate humans who feel that they need to take control of their lives, often by taking revenge on others, and we fuel their desire, giving them what they want while gradually pushing them into the abyss. Often, their actions include bringing pain, suffering, and death upon people while they themselves slowly make their way to hell where they belong. This is one way we use humans to destroy other humans while remaining invisible. When this happens, they end up right here in the end. The humans might think that the worst ones are behind them, but of course, there are more to come."

The demons cheered wildly, their voices rising in a chaotic crescendo. Satan's smile widened as he surveyed the crowd. The energy of their excitement was palpable, and he knew that their work on earth would only intensify after this.

"And so," Satan concluded, his voice booming over the roar of the crowd, "we will continue to use human government to achieve our ends. We will corrupt their leaders, twist their laws, and destroy their societies from within. For every soul that enters our domain, we grow stronger, and the world above grows weaker. Looking at the millions and millions of human souls who now occupy our cells, I'll say you ought to pat yourself on the back for your achievements. This is a direct result of your unflinching loyalty to me, your comrades, and our mission."

The demons roared in approval, their eyes gleaming with dark anticipation. Satan stood tall before them, his wings unfurling in a display of power as he surveyed the legions below him.

"Through human suffering, dead or alive, we demonstrate to man and our adversary that we are determined to fight back and win. Even as I speak, human souls are pouring into our kingdom. This means those who end up here most likely never took the time to pray, go to church, or worship God, things you prevented them from doing while they were alive. Worse, many of them didn't even believe God existed, denying his presence and sovereign rule in the universe, which I plan to possess during our second battle. Fortunately for us, these souls will never reach heaven... not ever.

"Mind you, some of the strategies we've used in the past to manipulate humans are no longer effective. Although we can always depend on their greed and fear for success, humans have become smarter over the years. We, too, have adjusted our tactics to outsmart them.

"Today, we're on the prowl, searching for all types of government employees—kings, presidents, legislators, judges, lawyers, curriculum developers, and so on—to give them a chance to do our bidding. As always, we look for the greedy, desperate ones and push them in front of the line, quietly proposing and directing them toward deals that will bring them power, fame, money, and recognition. As always, the arrangement must include the propagation of our left agenda, which includes the destruction of morality, religious freedom, family values, law and order, and hatred for God, among other things. How is that for cleverness?"

After the dramatic and rhetorical question, Satan swept his eyes across the mass of demons gathered in the meeting arena. A wave of contentment washed over him upon witnessing the approving nods, chants, and other gestures from the fallen angels who had followed him blindly since his war with heaven.

As the crowd settled into anticipation, Satan resumed his speech. "For example, by deceptively manipulating some politicians, judges, and government employees who then influence those below them, we have banned the so-called 'Holy Bible' in some countries and incarcerated, tortured, and killed Christians, thereby curtailing the spread of our adversary's way of life for the masses. We have even managed to prohibit open worship in some countries, except in secluded areas, to prevent the proliferation of Christianity and thus reduce the threat to the government.

"As if that wasn't enough, we also got the governments of some countries to ban prayer in public schools because it infringes on the rights of other people. At the same time, we've cultivated demonically possessed individuals to create havoc in the institution with guns, knives, and other objects, killing people and disrupting the status quo. And while the public feels empathy for the deranged perpetrators, thinking they have been abused and misled as children, they can't see the evil spirits that are hidden inside them."

A round of hysterical laughter emanated from the crowd upon hearing about the human perception of the problems in their realm. The invisibility of hell's spirits allowed them to do their dirty work in the shadows, while the humans would usually end up regarding themselves or God as the root of discord. Once the racket died down, Satan took a moment to collect his thoughts and then continued.

"Of course, we cannot deny that human societies are complex, with layers upon layers of norms, institutions, and factions, which compel us to fight our war on several fronts. Of all their strata, children have always proved to be the most vulnerable and impressionable, so we have allocated considerable resources to corrupt their educational institutes. In some countries, we have developed school curriculums focusing on sexual adaptation, indoctrinating children and minors to reconsider their gender as designed by God. From a young age, they become homosexuals, bi-sexual, lesbians, and transgenders, all of which are devious sexual conduct to nauseate God and propagate our left agenda.

"Furthermore, we have destabilized families and society with unlimited alternative lifestyles. With the help of deluded members of government, we enable and promote the practice of same-sex marriages, proposed sexual orientation, gender confusion, reproductive rights, and a myriad of other duped concepts that go against the normal design that our nemesis has proposed. And while they relish in their debauchery, they remain blind about the physical and spiritual dangers ahead that occur after death.

"In fact, we have achieved feats that I had feared we might not be able to. In the name of individual freedom and choice, we've enabled the killing of children in some countries through abortion. Though the very act is murder, they assuage their guilt by calling the unborn a fetus, attempting to disregard the crime, which cannot be undone. However, neither their conscience nor our nemesis will overlook the offense, regardless of what they do or say. Negating the reality that human life begins at conception, they violate the sanctity of life by denying the unborn to live based on personal choice and inconvenience."

When the mass of demons heard their unending list of victories in the earthly realm, waves of mirth passed through them. Most of them had not yet realized how deeply they had struck human society, influencing their very laws and statutes to enable grave sins that their nemesis would never forgive.

"I know I mentioned that the humans have also grown smarter and found ways to identify our whispers and resist our temptations," Satan said, his voice now a low whisper that still somehow carried through the arena. "But you should have gathered by now that our multifaceted attack cannot be countered in its entirety. No matter their growing ability to resist our attacks. You must remember that, in the larger picture, we are undeniably winning!

"Never will humans understand that they are not wrestling against flesh and blood but against principalities, against powers, against the rulers of the darkness of this age, and against spiritual hosts of wickedness in the heavenly places. The truth is, most of them don't even believe we exist. To them, Satan, the Devil, and demons are all figments of the imagination—made-up cliches to create fear or entertainment, which works to our advantage.

"As you can see, the infiltration of human governments around the world has done us good in many ways since it was first established.

Through key government employees, we have corrupted the system, engendered distrust of government in the minds of the public, deluded the truth, propagated unnatural conduct that disgusts our archenemy, fragmentized human civilization into small, self-centered groups, killed countless innocent people, displaced humanity around the world, and established massive fear, unease, and distrust in the world.

"Today, humans don't trust each other unless they know the person well, and everyone feels uneasy about their life without understanding why. I'm proud to say that we are the ones in control of the world, not humans. And if they don't believe it, they can simply watch the carnage around them for proof. Of course, much of the work is due to your hard work and persistence, and I congratulate you once more for a job well done! In the next event, I will share more good news with you."

The arena erupted once more into chaotic applause as Satan turned and vanished into the shadows, his departure as swift and silent as his arrival. The demons, left to their own devices, began their celebration anew.

As Satan vanished from the platform, slipping back into the swirling shadows, the atmosphere in the arena shifted from one of reverent silence to outright celebration. The demons, still buzzing with the intoxicating thrill of their victories, broke into a frenzied display of wild applause, dark laughter, and hellish exuberance.

It was as though the very air itself had caught fire with the energy of their gloating, pride, and lust for more destruction. They were eager to continue their work of corruption and chaos in the human realm.

Chapter 22

Wealth for Power and Control

By the end of the second conference, hell was alive with an energy unlike anything it had seen for centuries.

After Satan's departure from the arena, the lower-ranking demons, eager to impress and prove their worth, launched themselves into the air with a ferocity that bordered on madness. They flipped, spun, and contorted their bodies into grotesque shapes, showcasing their physical prowess with reckless abandon. Others conjured up visions of devastation—cities on fire, families torn apart, leaders brought to their knees in agony—only to be met with approving cheers from their comrades.

In one corner of the arena, a group of demons gathered around a figure who had conjured a massive illusion of a battlefield where humans clashed and died in droves, their blood staining the earth. The demon manipulating the vision smirked as he added flashes of fire and brimstone to the scene, sending the onlookers into fits of applause.

"See how they tear each other apart!" one demon shrieked, his forked tongue flicking out in excitement. "All it took was a whisper here, a seed of doubt there. Now look at them—slaughtering one another over nothing!"

His companions nodded eagerly, their faces twisted into malicious grins.

Some of the more seasoned demons gathered in clusters in other parts of the arena. Their conversations focused on the tactical implications of Satan's speech. While the younger demons reveled in their immediate triumphs, the older ones knew that their king's words signaled a shift in strategy—a deepening of their involvement in human government, which required finesse, patience, and relentless manipulation.

One such group, led by a demon with the appearance of a withered serpent, huddled close, their voices low but filled with intensity. "The corruption of government has always been one of our most effective tools," the serpent- like demon hissed. "But now, we must take it further. We must focus on infiltrating every aspect of their laws, twisting them until what is evil is declared good, and what is righteous is cast aside."

A smaller demon with wings that flickered like dying embers raised a hand. "But haven't we already achieved that? In so many places, laws have been enacted that glorify greed, promote selfishness, and punish morality. What more can we do?"

The serpent demon fixed him with a cold, calculating stare. "What more can we do? Everything. We must ensure that the people no longer trust their leaders. We must drive a wedge between them—leaders against the public, the public against the laws. Make them feel betrayed. Make them feel that the only way to gain freedom is through rebellion, through chaos. Once that seed is planted, we simply stand back and watch them tear their own governments to pieces."

The embers in the smaller demon's wings flared brighter, and he nodded eagerly. "Yes... yes, that makes sense. Divide and conquer from within."

Nearby, another demon chimed in. "Our king mentioned the 'left agenda.' We have to push it even harder. Pride, greed, and indulgence—they are already ingrained, but we need to ensure these leaders embrace these vices fully. Once they do, they will sell out their own people without hesitation."

The group cackled at the thought, imagining the devastation they could wreak upon the fragile human governments, already teetering on the brink of collapse.

All around the arena, similar conversations unfolded. Demons were discussing their next moves, eagerly planning how they would corrupt more leaders, infiltrate more institutions, and bring about greater suffering on earth. The energy was feverish, fueled by their unholy drive to see the world above them crumble into darkness.

Suddenly, Damyan's massive, dragon-like figure stepped forward, his presence commanding immediate attention. His enormous wings stretched wide as he addressed the gathering. "You have heard our king's words. His plan is clear. Human government is our next great battleground. It is where we shall plant our strongest agents, twist every law, decision, and action to suit our purpose."

The crowd of demons roared in agreement, their voices filling the cavernous space with a cacophony of devotion.

"But," the chief continued, his voice booming over the din, "you must be subtle. Governments crumble not through overt chaos but through quiet, insidious corruption. You must whisper in the ears of those in power. You must guide them slowly and carefully down the path to destruction. And when they fall, when their laws no longer protect but persecute, then we shall celebrate."

His words sent a shiver of excitement through the crowd. The demons could already envision the destruction they would cause. They could see the leaders they would turn into puppets, the laws they would warp, and the people they would push toward rebellion and despair.

The chief spread his arms wide, his wings casting long, menacing shadows across the arena. "Go now! Get everyone to prepare for tomorrow's session. If you pay heed to his words and efficiently implement the strategies he outlines, it won't be long before you stand next to our king and are rewarded with the knowledge that you were the instruments of humanity's downfall!"

The demons erupted into hilarity once more, their voices rising in a triumphant roar. As the chief stepped back, the arena descended into a whirl of activity. Groups of demons dispersed, heading toward the lower chambers in hell's cities to plot, plan, and prepare for their next moves on earth.

The air was thick with the promise of destruction, and as the last of the demons departed the arena, a lingering echo of their triumph remained, bouncing off the stone walls like the reverberation of a dark, unholy hymn.

***

The following day, the demons of hell carried themselves with renewed purpose, their infernal zeal inflamed by the good news that had poured forth from their king's throne. The knowledge of humanity's continued descent into depravity, fueled by sin and greed, swelled their egos, making them feel as if the torches of hell burned just a little brighter in celebration of their work.

In the shadowy recesses of the cavernous quarters where the demons retreated after each session, the atmosphere was nothing short of chaotic jubilation. Some demons, whose grotesque forms seemed to writhe and shift like living shadows, took to refreshing their ghastly tattoos, which resembled splattered paint on canvas. These tattoos weren't just markings—they were the visual representation of their victories. Dark, distorted human faces, each twisted in agony, were etched into the flesh of their demonic hosts, their mouths open in silent screams as they reflected the pain and suffering that these demons had inflicted on the world above. For some, the tattoos seemed to bleed, the designs dripping at the edges as if they were alive, oozing malevolent energy.

Others reshaped their entire physical forms, their bodies morphing and contorting to better embody their mood. The wildest of them all leaped through the air, performing acrobatic feats that defied natural laws. They spun and twisted through the suffocating darkness of the cavern, their laughter reverberating off the jagged walls as they created illusions of massive cities burning, of gold pouring from broken vaults, of men and women fighting each other for scraps of wealth. Their displays were met with thunderous applause from their comrades, their eyes glowing with the dark light of triumph.

The atmosphere around them was constantly charged with tension, anticipation, and glee. They fed off each other's excitement, their twisted forms growing more vibrant with every boast, every laugh, and every dark thought. The mood was intoxicating, an endless celebration of their success and the continued unraveling of humanity.

As before, their revelry did not stop until the anticipation of their king's return consumed them. Word spread quickly through the twisted corridors of hell that Satan would soon reemerge to deliver yet another address, another update on their progress against the world of men.

On the day of the third session, the demons began to assemble in the great arena once more, their grotesque wings and monstrous forms jostling for front-row positions. There was a palpable sense of expectation hanging in the air, a shared belief that whatever came next would be even greater than what had already been revealed. The low hum of their excited chatter echoed through the arena like the distant buzz of insects, growing louder with every passing moment as they waited for their master's return.

Then, without warning, the familiar cold hush fell over the gathering, signaling the imminent arrival of their king. It was as though hell itself held its breath. The demons fell silent, their monstrous forms rigid with attention, their glowing eyes turned toward the throne. In the oppressive darkness, the flames of the torches cast long, distorted shadows across the jagged stone walls.

Suddenly, from the depths of the swirling darkness, Satan emerged.

The effect was immediate and electrifying. The moment his towering, infernal figure became visible, a wave of energy swept through the arena. Demons erupted into a frenzy of praise, their voices rising in a deafening clamor that echoed off the stone walls, echoing through every crevice of the underworld. Their cries of adoration rang out like the roar of a thousand storms, shaking the very ground beneath their feet.

The scene was pure chaos—demons leaping into the air, wings spread wide in grotesque displays of loyalty, while others performed flips and spirals high above the crowd. It was a spectacle of unrestrained adulation. Demons of every rank, from the lowest tempters to the highest chiefs, threw themselves into displays of loyalty and devotion, eager to earn even a passing glance from their king. Some demons slithered along the ground, their serpentine forms writhing in outlandish patterns as they whispered chants of praise.

Others conjured visions of despair, showcasing the suffering of human souls in hell, each one a testament to their success.

For several long minutes, the arena was filled with noise, movement, and the pulsating energy of the gathered legions. Yet, despite the wildness of the display, there was an underlying order to it all—an unspoken understanding that they were performing for one purpose alone: to please their king.

Eventually, the demon chiefs stepped forward, their forms larger and more imposing than the rest. Clad in their prestigious emblems of authority—tattoos and brands that shimmered with a dark glow—they raised their clawed hands to signal the crowd to simmer down. Slowly, reluctantly, the noise began to subside. The demons, their eyes still fixed on Satan, quieted themselves, though the air was still thick with the lingering remnants of their excitement.

Satan stood before them, towering and motionless, his eyes glowing like embers as he surveyed the crowd. His gaze was cold, probing, as though he were silently assessing each of his subjects, ensuring that no one was absent, that every eye was on him. The tension in the arena mounted as the demons waited for him to speak.

In the stillness that followed, a group of lesser demons whispered among themselves, their voices low and filled with anticipation.

"Do you think he's pleased with us?" one asked, his forked tongue flicking nervously.

"Of course he is," another hissed. "Look at him—he hasn't left us in the dark for long. If he wasn't pleased, we wouldn't be celebrating like this. He feeds on our success, just as we feed on his power."

A third demon, his eyes wide with admiration, nodded in agreement. "He's watching us. He sees everything. You can feel it, can't you? The way he looks through you. It's as if he knows every thought, every action. There's no hiding from him."

The demons fell silent as Satan's gaze swept over their section of the arena, his eyes lingering for a moment before moving on. Finally, after what felt like an eternity of suspense, Satan spoke.

His voice, deep and resonant, echoed through the vast arena like the rumbling of an approaching storm. "It is good," he began slowly, "to see you bubbling with contentment. It looks like you are happy, and believe me, you deserve to be." His words were laced with a dark satisfaction, the kind that spread through the crowd like fire, igniting their spirits.

The demons, though silent, visibly swelled with pride. Their monstrous forms seemed to shimmer with the energy of their victories. Every one of them, from the smallest imp to the most fearsome chief, waited eagerly for the words of their king to pour over them like molten lava— burning yet nourishing their dark desires.

"You have worked hard," Satan continued, his tone both patronizing and menacing. "And I am ecstatic about your progress. In fact, this celebration is a time to feast on your success."

A ripple of approving murmurs ran through the assembled crowd, demons exchanging glances of shared triumph. Some stood straighter, their wings flexing in anticipation, while others glanced at their newly altered tattoos, their faces twisted in malicious glee at the images of human suffering they bore.

"But," Satan's voice grew darker, "let me make one thing clear: there are better days ahead. Because of human greed, we have endless possibilities to degrade them into self-destructive mortals, turning every man, woman, and child into God-defying, egotistical beings. They zealously push our left agenda as their own and, at the same time, curse the very God who gave them life."

The demons erupted in delighted snarls and cheers, the sound like the howling of a thousand tortured souls. The air crackled with their excitement as they imagined the endless torment they had inflicted upon humanity and the thought of more to come.

Satan allowed their outbursts for a few moments before continuing, his voice cutting through the noise like a blade. "The amusing part of all this," he said, his lips curling into a sinister smile, "is that humans never know how much we influence their decisions. They believe they act of their own free will, that their desires are born from within."

Several demons cackled their laughter, producing a sickening, grating sound.

Satan's gaze swept the crowd, his eyes glowing with a malevolent fire. "We speak to their souls—whispering to their deepest desires, their fears, their ambitions. And what do we use to sway them? Their own arrogance. Their need for power, recognition, and independence. These, my subjects, are our greatest tools. The smarter they become, the more self-reliant they feel. And the more we feed their egos, the closer they come to destruction."

The demons nodded eagerly, the truth of Satan's words resonating deeply with their experiences. They had seen it firsthand—how a subtle whisper in a human's mind could lead them down a path of ruin, how their pride could blind them to the very chains they were wrapping around themselves.

"Indeed," Satan said, his voice rising with grim intensity, "you and I have caused unspeakable damage in the world of man. Every war, every act of violence, every instance of bloodshed and suffering—it all traces back to us. We have perpetrated it all. And the humans, in their blindness, continue to believe that they are in control."

A murmur of approval rippled through the crowd. The demons basked in the glow of their achievements, their twisted faces reflecting the joy they found in humanity's suffering.

Satan's expression grew colder, more calculating. "In the name of self-preservation, personal freedom, and individual choice, we have driven nations to defy the very God who could save them from this place." He paused, allowing his words to sink in. "But today, I will tell you about another critical way we have gained control over them. Something that will swell your pride and strengthen your resolve as we continue to retaliate against the one who banished us."

The crowd leaned in, eager to hear the next phase of their king's grand design.

Satan's eyes gleamed with dark delight as he continued. "Let me begin by saying this: nothing in the world of man gets his blood boiling hotter than the sight and sound of money."

The word echoed ominously through the chamber, and the demons stirred. They knew well the power that money held over humanity. It was a force that could drive men to betray their morals and commit unspeakable acts— all for the promise of wealth and power.

Satan grinned, a terrifying display of cold superiority. "Money, for humans, is like a sixth sense—it enhances the other five, giving them the means to indulge their desires. And those who have it usually want more. It is the ultimate tool for control, influence, and power."

He paused, letting the weight of his words settle over the crowd before he added, "By itself, money is neither good nor bad. It is simply a tool. In the hands of those with pure motives, it can do good—heal the sick, feed the hungry, and yes, even spread the gospel of salvation."

The demons hissed at the mention of salvation, their faces contorting with hatred at the very idea.

"But in the hands of our followers," Satan continued, his voice growing darker, "money becomes a weapon of destruction. A tool for manipulation, greed, and power. And this, my subjects, is where we thrive."

He began pacing slowly across the platform, his presence looming over the crowd like a shadow. "Everything begins with the economy," he said, his tone instructive, as if he were speaking to students eager to learn. "The economy is the arena where all humans—rich, poor, and middle class—bring their resources into one system for trade. And this, my loyal subjects, is our next playground."

A wave of agreement passed through the crowd, demons nodding in understanding.

"We look for the humans with the greatest ambition," Satan explained, his voice smooth as silk. "Those who are hungry for more—more money, more power, more control. Once we find them, we place persuasive demons around them, anticipating their needs, proposing solutions, and pushing them ahead of the line. And then, we dangle the carrot before them—the promise of wealth, the allure of success."

Several demons laughed, imagining how they had successfully led countless humans into the traps of greed and ambition.

"Once hooked," Satan said, his voice laced with satisfaction, "their greed takes over. And we, with our whispers, stoke the fire.

We tempt them with glimpses of the power they could have, the freedom, the control. And they will do anything—lie, steal, cheat, kill—just to get more. The more they get, the more we tighten our grip."

He stopped pacing and turned his gaze once again on the crowd. "And that is only one of the instruments through which we control them. With money."

Satan's words flowed through the arena like venom, each one sinking deep into the eager minds of the demons who hung on his every syllable. The idea of controlling humanity through something as simple as money had become a cornerstone of their tactics, and hearing it spoken by their king filled them with renewed purpose.

Satan continued, his voice growing more intense as he spoke. "Our adversary himself acknowledged the power of money in his Scriptures. He warned humanity of the dangers inherent in the love of wealth, yet they are too blind to heed his warnings."

His voice dropped into a mocking tone as he quoted, "For the love of money is a root of all kinds of evil… for which some have strayed from the faith in their greediness and pierced themselves through with many sorrows."

A low rumble of approving laughter rolled through the crowd. The demons understood the power of money better than anyone. They had seen firsthand how it could drive a man to ruin and how the desire for wealth could overshadow morality, family, and faith. They had whispered into the ears of rulers and beggars alike, and each time, the outcome was the same—destruction.

Satan allowed the laughter to die down before continuing, his voice now a smooth, chilling tone. "For most humans, that passage is nothing more than a cliché, something they quote without understanding its gravity. But we know better. We know how easily their greed can be exploited. We know that with the right push, even the most righteous will sell their souls for the promise of wealth."

The demons nodded in agreement, their eyes gleaming with malice as they recalled their successes. They had taken ordinary men and women—people with dreams, families, and ambitions—and twisted them into monsters, all for the sake of money.

"There are many wealthy humans in the world," Satan said, his voice taking on a darker edge. "Some have earned their wealth honestly, through hard work and perseverance. But many more have made deals with us— deals that cannot be undone."

He paused, letting his words hang ominously in the air. The demons were silent now, their anticipation building.

"When a human crosses that line, when they choose wealth over righteousness, they are ours. They step into a world where morality no longer matters, where their conscience is nothing more than an obstacle to be overcome. And once they are in our grasp, they are lost. They will do anything—anything—to keep their wealth, to increase it, even if it means destroying everyone around them."

The demons shifted, their twisted faces alight with dark glee. They had seen the truth of this in countless human souls, each one corrupted and consumed by greed. They had watched as families were torn apart, businesses crumbled, and nations fell, all in the pursuit of wealth.

Satan's expression grew colder, more calculated. "These humans are driven by an insatiable hunger. They crave the luxury and freedom that money brings. But they fail to realize that every step they take toward wealth brings them closer to us—closer to their eternal torment."

A demon with elongated limbs and a twisted grin leaned toward his companion, whispering with satisfaction. "It's true. I've seen it myself. The richer they get, the more paranoid they become. They're always afraid of losing it all."

His companion, a creature with wings that flickered like dying embers, nodded in agreement. "Yes, and that fear makes them easy to manipulate. We plant the seed of doubt in their minds, and they begin to trust no one. Not their family, not their friends—no one but the money they cling to."

The murmurs of agreement spread throughout the arena as the demons recognized the brilliance of their strategy. Fear, greed, and the insatiable desire for wealth had turned humans into their own worst enemies. And the more they struggled, the deeper they fell into the abyss.

Satan's voice cut through the murmurs, drawing the crowd's attention back to him. "Indeed, these humans have chosen their path. They have forsaken their souls for the temporary pleasures of wealth. And when their time comes, when death claims them, they will join us here, just as all the others have."

The mention of the damned souls in hell sent a shiver of excitement through the crowd. They knew the fate of those who had sold their souls for money—those whose lives had been spent in pursuit of wealth at the expense of everything else.

Satan's eyes gleamed as he spoke of the condition of these souls. "The ones who have made their deals with us, the ones who sacrificed everything for wealth, they now writhe in agony, tormented by the memories of their greed. Their pain and suffering reverberate through this kingdom, their wails a constant reminder of their foolishness."

A low growl of satisfaction rippled through the demons at the mention of the tormented souls, whose anguish filled the caverns of hell with a never-ending symphony. The images of these souls, once powerful and wealthy on earth, now reduced to eternal suffering, only served to strengthen the demons' resolve.

"Today," Satan explained, "most of the world's wealth is controlled by a small group of humans—many of whom have made their deals with us. On their journey to success, they stepped on, lied to, and abused other humans; they broke laws and disregarded authorities, destroyed properties and blatantly stole from others, conducted illegal activities, and shed innocent human blood. Humans who do these things have little sympathy for their victims. This is because their conscience is seared by demonic influence, resulting in a void of spiritual consciousness whereby they feel no remorse about their actions. They remain steadfast on their path to success while destroying other people's lives to get where they want to be.

"These are the ones who control the stock markets, the banks, and the corporations. They hold the power, and with that power, they spread our influence."

The demons listened intently, fully aware of the magnitude of their achievements. They had spent centuries weaving their influence into the fabric of human society, and now, their reach extended into every corner of the economy.

"But it doesn't end with wealth alone," Satan said, his voice growing more intense. "These humans use their money to manipulate governments, to control entire nations. They corrupt politicians, fund wars, and create policies that keep the rich richer and the poor in chains. And while they build their empires, they leave devastation in their wake."

A demon near the front raised a clawed hand, its voice hissing through sharp fangs. "Master, what about those who resist? The ones who don't succumb to greed?"

Satan's expression hardened as his eyes narrowed toward the demon who had put forth the question. "A good question indeed. I ask you to consider: has the resistance of others in the past managed to thwart any of our plans? There will always be some who resist. But even they can be broken. We plant seeds of doubt, fear, and disillusionment. We isolate them and make them feel powerless. And for those who truly resist, we use the greed of others to crush them." He replied.

The demon nodded, satisfied with the answer, while the others grinned wickedly at the thought of destroying even the most resilient of humans.

Satan stepped forward, his wings unfurling slightly as he addressed his followers. "This, my subjects, is how we control the world of man. Through wealth, we twist their ambitions, drive their greed, and ensure their destruction. We have corrupted the very foundation of their society, and they are too blind to see it."

He paused, letting his words sink in before delivering the final blow. "And when they fall, when their wealth and power crumbles around them, they will find themselves here, in this kingdom, where they will suffer for eternity."

The demons burst into wild applause, their voices rising in a chaotic symphony of triumph. They had done it— they had successfully infiltrated the very heart of human society, turning wealth into a weapon of destruction.

Satan stood before them, his eyes gleaming with dark pride as he watched his legions celebrate their victories. His smile widened as he surveyed the crowd, knowing that the battle was far from over. The world of man was theirs for the taking, and with every passing day, more souls would fall into their grasp….

The cacophony of demonic celebration filled the arena, echoing off the jagged stone walls of hell. The demons were intoxicated with their own success, their egos swelling to match the infernal heat around them. Each of them reveled in the knowledge that they had contributed to the ruin of humanity, that their whispers of greed and power had pushed countless souls into the abyss.

Satan stood at the head of it all, his towering presence commanding attention, though he now appeared to be deep in thought. His eyes, those chilling blue orbs that could pierce the soul, scanned the crowd with a deliberate, calculated gaze. The noise of the celebration began to dwindle as though the very air around them knew to quiet itself in the presence of its master's contemplation.

The chiefs shared a knowing look. To please Satan was to live in the glow of his favor, but to disappoint him meant a fate worse than anything they could devise for the human souls they tormented. They had seen his wrath, his fury when expectations were not met. The heat of hell paled in comparison to the burning disappointment of their king. Moreover, he was their only hope, however faint, of returning to the glory of their former days.

As the demons around the chiefs continued their murmured discussions, Satan stepped forward again, his movements slow and deliberate. The atmosphere in the arena shifted once more, silence falling over the crowd like a thick blanket. Every demon turned his attention back to the throne, waiting for the next decree from their master.

Satan's voice, when it came, was quiet but forceful, each word dripping with dark power. "You have heard me speak of how we control the wealthy and manipulate their greed to further our cause. But let us not forget—this is only the beginning. Money alone does not destroy souls. What men do with it and how they wield it ultimately condemns them."

The demons shifted, eager to hear more.

"Our greatest success," Satan continued, his voice rising with malevolent energy, "comes not from merely enriching men but from driving them to use that wealth for our purposes. With money comes power. With power comes control. And it is through control that we truly own them."

The demons nodded, understanding now that wealth was not the final goal—it was the means to an end. Control was the true prize, the way to bend humanity to their will. They had seen it in the highest offices of the human world, where leaders, businessmen, and influencers used their wealth to shape policies, manipulate governments, and spread chaos.

Satan's lips curled into a thin, sinister smile as he began to pace the platform, his wings casting long shadows across the ground. "Humans," he spat the word with contempt, "are obsessed with control. They believe that with enough money, they can bend the world to their will. They think themselves untouchable, above the laws that govern the weak. And we, my loyal subjects, have encouraged this delusion."

He paused, looking out over the sea of demonic faces, each one contorted in twisted admiration. "We have created a world where the rich feed on the poor, where the powerful crush the powerless, and where the very systems designed to protect humanity serve only to enslave them. We have also created a system by which most opulent human families have held onto their wealth. Although most of the older ones have passed on and are now residing here, in this kingdom, their blood money stays within the family, filtering down through descendants who are also determined to preserve it at all costs. Many of these families now control the stock market, own some of the largest corporations in the world, and run banks, mortgage companies, and lending institutions. In other words, because of their massive wealth, they, along with corrupt government officials, control the bulk of the economy, which works in our favor."

Balam, a demon near the center of the crowd, raised his voice, emboldened by the dark energy that flowed from Satan's speech. "Master, how do we ensure that this control remains in our hands? How do we prevent them from seeing through the illusion?"

Satan turned toward the demon, his gaze locking onto the creature like a predator. "The key," he said, his voice dangerously calm, "is in making them believe that they are in control. We give them the illusion of choice. We present them with options that all lead to the same outcome—ours."

The crowd erupted into dark laughter, their amusement at the simplicity of human manipulation filling the arena with a chilling sound.

Satan's eyes gleamed with satisfaction as he continued. "When they believe they have power, when they believe they are the architects of their own success, they become blind to the chains that bind them. Their wealth gives them a sense of security, a false belief that they are in control of their own destiny. But we know better, don't we?"

The demons nodded eagerly, their faces alight with cruel understanding. They had seen how easy it was to manipulate humanity, how fragile the illusion of control truly was.

Satan's voice dropped to a low, menacing growl. "We feed their ambition, their desire for more, and we watch as they destroy themselves. These days, apart from wars, which are often perpetrated by human greed, not much blood is being shed for wealth. However, there are other punitive methods that demonically inspire wealthy humans to take advantage of others. Since money is the source of their power and status, they are afraid to lose it. So, they protect it by the most secure means available.

"Moreover, they use some of it to create more wealth by lending it to cash-poor, desperate humans for houses, automobiles, food, clothing, toys, etc., at confiscatory interest rates. Those who impulsively mismanage their funds often find themselves borrowing cash from them at subprime lending rates. Of course, all this borrowing subjugates borrowers to financial slavery while giving meaning to the phrase: "…the rich get richer." Making matters worse, humans who build a habit of borrowing money rely on the rich for cash, further perpetuating their dependency on a system that's designed to keep them poor.

"Just as before, the rich show little empathy for delinquent borrowers. A rating system that monitors everyone penalizes those who struggle to meet their financial obligations. In some cases, their assets are repossessed, and others are pushed into bankruptcy. And while the rich get richer, borrowers struggle to pay their bills and become economically paralyzed. Meanwhile, the rich climb higher and higher, believing they are untouchable, only to find that the ladder they've been climbing leads straight to the depths of hell."

The crowd roared in approval, the demons throwing their heads back in raucous laughter. They reveled in the idea of watching humanity's most powerful figures fall from their self-constructed thrones, their wealth and influence crumbling into nothing.

Satan let the applause die down before delivering his final blow. "What you, demons, should know is that blood money eventually serves our purpose. The thinking of those who control it often aligns with our left agenda and promotes our purpose. Remember, these humans are selected for financial dominance primarily because of their tendency to lean in our favor. Therefore, a large part of their wealth is devoted to programs that are against godliness and family values. They channel millions of dollars to elect corrupt politicians, promote abortion rights, endorse devious sexual conduct, support alternate family lifestyles, destroy religious freedom, and push other programs that undermine morality. This is where we are today, and your labor in influencing the rich has contributed to the continued decay of human society.

"The humans who align themselves with us, who sacrifice their souls for wealth and power, they are fools.

Broadly, they disregard their creator, negate the existence of their souls, and cause pain and misery to others for the sake of money. But their very conduct is wrapped in deception. They believe that they are supporting 'change' for the good of society, and if there is a chance they have done something wrong, their money will buy them forgiveness. They believe that once death comes, they will escape their mortal existence and find peace. But as you all know…" He paused, letting the weight of his words sink in. "… they are mistaken."

The demons howled with glee, the sound reverberating through the arena like a symphony of madness. They could feel the truth of Satan's words deep in their bones, the certainty that those who had fallen into their trap would suffer for eternity.

Satan's smile widened, a grotesque display of triumph. "All the humans we've worked with through the ages are here, in this kingdom. They endure pain and anguish beyond imagining, tormented by their past decisions. And it is their suffering, my subjects, that is your victory."

The demons erupted into wild cheers, their voices rising in a chaotic cacophony of triumph and celebration. Their success was undeniable, and the eternal torment of human souls was proof of their power and influence.

Satan stood tall, spreading his wings out wide as he surveyed the arena filled with the legions of demons who had followed him in his rebellion against the heavens. His heart swelled with pride at their loyalty, their devotion to the cause. They had achieved so much, and yet, there was still more to come.

"As we continue," Satan said, his voice booming over the cheers, "remember that this is only the beginning. The world above is still ripe for corruption, still vulnerable to our influence. Through wealth, power, and control, we will continue to twist humanity to our will."

The demons cheered louder, their anticipation for future victories fueling their celebration.

"And when the time comes," Satan continued, his eyes gleaming with dark promise, "we will surely bring the world of man to its knees."

With that final declaration, the demons erupted into frenzied applause, their twisted forms writhing in celebration of their king's words. They knew that under Satan's rule, there would be no end to the suffering they could inflict on humanity, no limit to the souls they could claim. As the celebration peaked, Satan turned and disappeared into the shadows again, leaving his legions to bask in the glow of their success.

No sooner than he had departed, the air in the arena buzzed with the promise of more destruction, chaos, and souls to claim in the name of their dark king.

Chapter 23

In Pursuit of Pleasure

The firestorm of Satan's war against heaven never dimmed. The infernal torches danced and flickered along the jagged edges of the cavernous kingdom. Given the scorching heat spread throughout hell's landscape, the torches' warmth was barely felt by its inhabitants, but their light cast a constant, haunting glow over their surroundings. It had been three days since the grand conference began, and by now, the demonic legions were more than drunk on their victories—they were utterly intoxicated by their king's words.

In the moments after Satan's departure at the end of the third day, the legions of hell had dispersed into their usual groups, forming pockets of chaos and celebration. Every corner of the damned realm echoed with their howls of triumph, their boastful laughter, and the clatter of grotesque limbs as they danced in cruel delight. It was a time of reflection—each demon recalling his own malicious victories over humankind, trading stories as if they were treasured jewels.

"Do you remember the plague I stirred up in the village of Karthon?" snarled one demon named Dantalion, his massive wings adding a sense of terror to his form. "The humans wept for days, crying out to their so-called God, but I made sure none of their prayers were heard."

A smaller demon named Eligos, his body adorned with pulsating tattoos of screaming faces, hissed in response. "That's nothing compared to the families I tore apart. I whispered lies into the ears of the father until he struck his wife in anger. She fled with the children, and their home crumbled into ruin."

Nearby, a twisted creature named Gamigin, with wings like tattered leather, boasted, "I lured the young to drink and take their own lives. Their anguish was exquisite, their souls ripe for the taking."

The demons relished in these memories, basking in their shared accomplishments, yet even amidst the frenzy, there were murmurings of those who faced obstacles— humans who resisted, those who prayed, and the righteous warriors who had delayed their plans.

"I nearly had him," growled Camio, a demon with cracked, hardened skin that looked almost like scales, "but then one of those blasted angels intervened, his sword drawn, his presence blinding. I had to flee before I could finish my work."

The others nodded, some muttering in agreement. They had all encountered resistance at some point—holy interferences that delayed their conquests. But tonight, none of that mattered. Tonight, they celebrated their dominance, their king's approval, and the insidious ways in which they had twisted the hearts of humans.

On the following day of the conference, the air was heavy with anticipation. Word had spread that their king was to return soon, and with that news, the atmosphere in hell shifted once again. Palpable excitement surged throughout the realm. Whispers echoed in the darkness—speculations about what Satan's mood might be like this time or what new revelations he would share.

"He's been different these last few days," murmured Dantalion, his eyes gleaming with dark curiosity. "Have you seen how he watches us? His gaze feels… colder."

Camio, whose claws scraped the ground as he slithered across the molten stones, nodded. "Perhaps he expects more. Perhaps we haven't done enough."

"But haven't we been triumphant?" Gamigin interjected, his voice low and uncertain. "We have brought ruin to humanity. We have turned their hearts to greed, lust, and power. What more could he want?"

"He always wants more," came the reply from Akar, his form larger and more terrifying than the others. His voice was a deep rumble that made the ground tremble slightly beneath them. "We are his instruments of destruction, and until the world is fully in our grasp, he will never be satisfied."

The other demons fell silent at the chief's words. They knew them to be true. Their work was far from over, and their king's ambition knew no bounds.

Then, as if summoned by their very thoughts, the air around them thickened with a familiar, ominous presence.

Distant torch light shimmered on the jagged rocks more fiercely, and the shadows along the stone walls grew darker, sharper. It was the signal they had all been waiting for. Satan was returning.

As the king of hell stepped into view, his towering figure cloaked in darkness, a ripple of awe surged through the crowd. His appearance was as magnificent and terrifying as ever—his white skin gleaming against the backdrop of hell's darkness, his jet-black hair falling in smooth waves past his shoulders, and his cold, piercing eyes a shade of bluish-gray that seemed to see through everything.

The demons erupted in applause, their bodies writhing in ecstatic obedience and emitting deafening cheers. Some threw themselves to the ground in worship, while others twisted and contorted their forms in grotesque displays of reverence. From every corner of the arena, demons performed acrobatic stunts, leaping into the air and flipping their grotesque bodies as a tribute to their master's might.

For a long time, the arena was filled with nothing but the sounds of celebration—an overwhelming cacophony of shrieks, howls, and applause. The noise reverberated through the great hall, bouncing off the walls like the wails of the damned. The demons were on the verge of frenzy, their anticipation reaching fever pitch as they awaited their king's next decree.

Finally, the demon chiefs, adorned in their most fearsome attire, raised their arms to quiet the crowd. Slowly, reluctantly, the noise began to die down until the arena was filled with an eerie silence. All eyes turned toward the stage, where Satan stood with his wings partially unfurled, casting long, shadowy shapes across the meeting arena.

His eyes scanned the crowd with a quiet intensity, his expression unreadable. He allowed the silence to stretch as if measuring each demon's resolve and ensuring that every one of them understood the gravity of the moment.

Then, with a voice that dripped like molten lava, Satan spoke. "It is good to see you bubbling with contentment," he began, his tone cold yet laced with satisfaction. "It seems you are happy, and believe me, you deserve to be."

Satan's voice reverberated through the arena, commanding full, undivided attention. His gaze refused to leave the horde of demons before him. The demons shuddered with pride at his words, but they knew there was more to come.

"You have worked hard," he continued, his words slow and deliberate. "And I am ecstatic about your progress. Indeed, this celebration is a feast on your success. But understand—this is just the beginning. Better days lie ahead."

A murmur of excitement rippled through the crowd, a mixture of hisses, snarls, and whispers as the demons processed his words. Their king, in his cold magnificence, promised more victories. Their appetite for destruction grew with every syllable.

"Today, we shall talk about a unique term in human language," Satan went on, "which they use to justify their indulgence in pleasure, no matter how grotesque. They call it hedonism—a philosophy that elevates pleasure as the highest good. It is a seductive idea that suggests individuals have the right to pursue enjoyment at any cost. Pain and suffering are to be avoided, while pleasure is sought after like the nectar of life."

Satan's lips curled into a sneer. "Of course, they do not realize that this philosophy is one of our finest tools. Hedonism, in its true form, leads to chaos—immorality, selfishness, and the very destruction of the soul. It was first proposed by Aristippus of Cyrene, a man who, under our influence, pursued luxury until his death. A student of Socrates, yet one who strayed from the path of virtue."

A deep, guttural laugh emerged from the crowd. The demons delighted in the thought of yet another human philosopher manipulated by their hand.

"And where does Aristippus reside now?" Satan asked, even though the answer was self-explanatory. "Here, among us, writhing in pain and suffering! Yet, his philosophy lives on, having passed through generations and adapted by others. Humans are so easily deceived. They embrace the pursuit of pleasure without realizing it leads them into our hands."

Upon hearing this statement, a demon near the front, Ose, raised his head. His voice slithered through the sudden silence. "Master, what of the humans who seek pleasure through righteous means? Those who indulge in the simple joys given to them by their maker?"

Satan's eyes narrowed, his gaze piercing the demon who dared to speak. "Ah, yes," he drawled, his voice dripping with disdain. "The countless fools who believe they can find pleasure within the boundaries of morality. Indeed, their creator has given them many avenues for pleasure— wholesome ones, like the beauty of nature, the joy of family, or the satisfaction of hard work. But these pleasures are fleeting, and, most importantly, they grow boring."

The demons hissed in agreement. Boredom was a human weakness they had exploited for millennia.

"Humans are insatiable creatures," Satan continued, "always searching for the next thrill, the next pleasure to dull the emptiness inside. And it is there, in that desperation, that we thrive. They grow weary of the simple joys, and so we offer them something… darker."

The air grew thicker with anticipation as Satan's voice dropped to a whisper, barely audible yet charged with power. "We tempt them with pleasures they dare not speak of. We offer them indulgences that will consume their souls, and they accept it willingly. We have turned humankind into pleasure mongers, driven by the basest of desires."

A ripple of satisfaction surged through the crowd. The demons knew the truth of Satan's words well. They had been at the forefront of this effort, whispering temptations into the ears of humanity, guiding their hands toward sin. They had seen the effects—the gluttony, the drunkenness, and the indulgence in illicit pleasures. All of it was a testament to their success.

Satan continued, his tone now more reflective, as though savoring the scope of his work. "Through the ages, we have introduced humanity to the pleasures of excess— eating, drinking, gambling, and fornication. Each of these indulgences has become a prison for their souls, binding them to us. They no longer seek redemption; they seek more pleasure."

One of the winged demons near the center, Pruflas, raised his hand, cautiously addressing his king. "But, Master, what of those humans who recognize the dangers of such indulgence? Those who turn away from pleasure for the sake of righteousness?"

Satan's smile widened, and his voice oozed with malice. "Ah, yes, there are always a few. The ones who resist, pray to and worship the very God who seeks to save them from our clutches. They are the most stubborn, the most difficult. But even they cannot escape us forever."

The demon tilted his head, intrigued. "And how do we break them, Master?"

Satan's wings unfurled slightly, casting dark shadows over the rugged ground as he answered. "By making them believe their resistance is futile. We whisper doubts into their minds and fill their hearts with despair. We remind them of their weaknesses and failures. And when they fall... we are there to catch them, dragging them back into the pit of their desires."

The demons erupted into dark applause, their laughter echoing through the hall like a storm of madness. They understood now. Even the righteous could be broken. All it took was time, temptation, and eventual realization of their own twisted desires.

Satan raised a hand to silence the crowd, his expression now cold and focused. "But let us not forget the subtler pleasures that draw men to us—pleasures that, on the surface, seem harmless."

He paused, letting the silence stretch before continuing. "Publications, for instance. Books. Plays. In ancient times, they were a source of knowledge and entertainment. But we have turned them into something far more dangerous. Romance novels that fuel lust. Crime stories that glorify sin. Mysteries that tempt the mind into darkness. We have transformed literature into a playground of indulgence."

The demons nodded, their wicked faces gleaming in the dim light. They had witnessed the slow, insidious spread of their influence in every form of entertainment.

"And then," Satan said, his voice growing darker still, "there is the occult."

A collective hiss of excitement rose from the crowd. The occult had long been one of their most powerful tools, a direct link to the darkest corners of the human soul.

"Our adversary warned humanity of its dangers, but they never listen," Satan said, his voice tinged with mockery. "Sorcery, witchcraft, divination—these are the abominations that we have encouraged since the beginning. And how eagerly they fall into our trap."

Surgat, a gaunt figure with eyes like burning coals, leaned forward to speak up. "Master, what of the humans who claim to practice magic for good?"

Satan's laughter echoed through the hall, a sound so cold and malevolent that it chilled even the demons. "There is no such thing as 'good' magic. Those who dabble in the occult, no matter their intentions, are ours. They may cloak their practices in the guise of 'light,' but in the end, it is all darkness. And we welcome them with open arms."

The demons cackled in approval, their voices rising once more in celebration. They reveled in the thought of humans, oblivious to the dangers of their actions, unwittingly sealing their fate.

As Satan continued his monologue, the demons quieted once more and leaned in. His words were precise and deadly, like a blade cutting through the air. He relished the effect his speech had on his subjects, their glowing eyes fixed on him, their twisted forms overwhelmed by veneration.

"The occult," Satan repeated, his voice low but carrying immense power. "It has been one of our greatest successes. Remember how the people of Israel immersed themselves in the occult and later regretted their mistakes because of the physical, mental, and spiritual toll they endured? Humans, always seeking more knowledge and power, have wandered willingly into our trap. What began as a curiosity has become full-blown worship, though they deny it. They invoke the dead, seek answers from spirits, cast spells, and predict the future—foolish practices that bring them closer to us with each incantation."

The demons shifted excitedly. Some had directly influenced the rise of occult practices in various ancient civilizations—Ancient Egypt, Babylon, and even in the present day. They saw humans' desperation to control their fate, to know the unknown, as the perfect avenue for demonic influence.

"And yet," Satan continued, "there is an even deeper hunger within them, a hunger that has fueled their downfall from the beginning—sexual pleasure."

The mere mention of it caused a ripple of delight through the crowd. There was no greater tool, no more visceral way to enslave humanity than through their primal desires. Satan's smile turned sinister as he elaborated.

"Humans are fascinated with their bodies, with the bodies of others. Since the dawn of time, we have twisted their natural desires into something depraved. The original design was simple—sex to create life. But we corrupted that long ago. Now, sex is a means of control, a source of endless pleasure and, ultimately, destruction."

He let his words hang in the air momentarily, allowing the demons to bask in the shared memory of their corrupting influence over humanity's desires. The room was filled with wicked grins and whispers of approval.

Satan's eyes gleamed as he went on, "We encouraged the first humans to explore their bodies in ways they were never meant to. And it only grew from there. What was once sacred became common—images of sex displayed openly on pottery, tapestries, and paintings. By the time humans could write and draw, we had already poisoned their sense of modesty."

A demon with a menacing serpentine form hissed gleefully. "The first sculptures in Greece! Do you remember how they marveled at the human form? How they displayed their gods in all their nakedness? They called it art, but it was our influence all along."

Satan nodded, his smile spreading wider. "Exactly. From there, it was only a matter of time before we introduced pornography. It began as paintings and statues and eventually grew into books, films, and digital media. Today, humans have access to every kind of debauchery they could ever imagine, all at the tip of their fingers. It keeps them distracted, weakens their spirits, and distances them further from God."

The demons cackled in delight, their laughter sharp and grating.

They had wholly enjoyed witnessing the rise of pornography, and it had brought them more souls than they had ever hoped for.

"What humans don't realize," Satan continued, "is that their indulgence in sexual sin damages their spirit. Every time they watch or participate, they chip away at the essence of God in their souls. And when they believe no one sees their secret desires, we are there—always watching, whispering, and encouraging them to go further."

Valac, a demon with skin like a cracked stone, raised a clawed hand. "Master, what of the humans who repent? Those who turn away from such sins, seeking forgiveness?"

Satan's smile faltered for a brief moment, his eyes narrowing. "Yes, there are always a few who seek forgiveness, who crawl back to their God, begging for mercy. But," he paused, his voice dripping with vengeance, "we are patient. We wait for them to slip again, for their desires to creep back in. And they do. Oh, how they do!"

While recalling the perversity of human desires, Satan closed his eyes in satisfaction. The crowd murmured in agreement. It was a game of patience, and they had all learned that time was on their side.

"Even the most faithful," Satan mused, "are not immune to temptation. We are subtle and relentless, and eventually, even the strongest fall."

The demons hissed their approval. Most of them, who had struggled to achieve their goals with a few pious individuals, were relieved to find out that even the righteous could be led astray with enough persistence.

Satan's wings unfurled even more, casting a wider shadow over the arena. "Look at the world now," he commanded. "Pornography is not only accepted, it is celebrated. It is a billion-dollar industry that touches every home and device in its reach. Humans are so addicted to their pleasures that they cannot see how they enslave them. We are the puppet masters, and they dance for us, blind to the chains around their necks."

The demons howled in triumph, some pounding the ground in excitement. They lived for this—the slow, calculated destruction of humanity. Each indulgence, each sin, brought the humans closer to their grasp.

Satan raised a hand, and silence fell once more. "But sex is not the only pleasure we have twisted," he continued. "Think of the entertainment industry. Films, books, television shows—what once served as harmless distractions are now cesspools of sin. Humans fill their minds with violence, murder, and every kind of wickedness. And they enjoy it."

Dantalion stepped forward and spoke in a raspy voice. "Master, what of the children? Even they are exposed to such things."

Satan's smile grew darker, more sinister. "Ah, yes. The children. They are the easiest to corrupt, for they do not yet understand the world. We have filled their cartoons, games, and books with hidden messages—violence, rebellion, witchcraft. They see it as fun and entertainment, but it is so much more than they realize."

Gamigen flapped his wings like bat leather and croaked out, "Cruella de Vil! Stromboli! Scar!" He listed off some of the infamous characters from children's stories, their sinister deeds celebrated by young minds who couldn't yet comprehend the true nature of what they watched.

Satan chuckled darkly. "Yes, indeed. Villains who were inspired by some of the finest demons among us. Humans may think these stories are harmless, but we know better. The seeds of rebellion, greed, and hate are planted young. And once planted, they can't help but grow."

The demons erupted into laughter once more, delighting in the thought of corrupting the next generation so thoroughly. Each villainous character and every scene of violence was another step toward claiming their souls.

As Satan let the demonic outroar die down, the tension in the arena thickened, charged with the dark energy of his words. His voice took on a more triumphant tone, resonating with the sound of assured victory. The flickering torch flames along the rocky walls seemed to feed on his power, glowing brighter with each breath he took.

"But do not think," Satan said, his wings now fully extended, casting a vast shadow over the assembly, "that our efforts end with the children or the young. No, our influence touches every part of human society—every corner of their pleasure-seeking lives. Take music, for example."

At the mention of music, a hush fell over the crowd. "Music," Satan repeated, his voice smooth and dark.

"It is one of the most influential tools at our disposal.

Humans have always been drawn to rhythm, to sound, to song. It stirs their emotions, shapes their thoughts, and speaks to their very souls. Our adversary knows this as well. He uses music to inspire hope, love, worship, and devotion to himself. But we," he paused, his smile growing wider, "we have turned it into something else entirely."

He surveyed the crowd, his eyes gleaming as he spoke. "We have taken what was once pure and twisted it. Music that once lifted souls to the heavens now drags them into the depths of depravity. We fill their ears with songs of rebellion, hatred, lust, and greed. We make the most obscene, profane messages sound enticing. And the humans… they lap it up like the fools they are."

The demons hissed in delight, recalling the countless songs they had inspired—lyrics that glorified violence, drug use, and sexual immorality. They had woven their influence through every genre, from the slow-burning hatred of metal to the seductive rhythms of pop.

"And let us not forget," Satan continued, "those among humanity who have given themselves wholly to us through music. These so-called artists, obsessed with fame, fortune, and recognition, have made pacts with me, promising their allegiance in exchange for success. You see them on the grandest stages, adored by millions, spreading our messages to the masses with every word they sing."

Paimon, a demon with glowing red eyes, crawled forward, his voice dripping with excitement. "Master, what of the ones who openly praise you? The ones who speak your name in their music?"

Satan's grin grew more sinister. "Ah, yes. The bold ones. There are those who have no fear of admitting where their power comes from. They wear my symbols and openly speak my name in their songs, and the humans worship them for it. What they do not realize is that every time they sing my praises, they are dragging more souls into this place."

The demons roared with laughter, thrilled by the thought of humans unknowingly celebrating their own damnation. They had seen it time and again—musicians who courted darkness for fame and glory, their fans blindly following along, humming lyrics that led them further from salvation.

"But even beyond the explicit worship of darkness," Satan continued, "there are more subtle methods. Most of the music that fills the airwaves, the concerts, and the homes of humankind is designed to distract. To dull their senses. To keep them from hearing the voice of our enemy."

He paused, allowing his words to sink in. "Think of it. Humans spend hours, days, even years listening to songs that glorify nothing but themselves—songs of love lost and won, of shallow pleasure, of fleeting fame. And all the while, there remains an ever-widening rift between their minds and the things that truly matter. They do not pray. They do not reflect. They do not listen to the still, small voice that calls them to repentance. No, they are too busy singing."

A murmur of agreement spread through the crowd. The demons understood the power of distraction well. Music had become a constant presence in the lives of humans, a background noise that kept their thoughts unfocused and their spirits complacent.

"We have done well," Satan said, his voice growing softer, more reflective. "But our work is never done. There are still humans who resist, who see through the haze we have created. There are still those who cling to hope, turn to prayer, and fight against the pull of pleasure. These are the ones we must target. These are the ones who pose a threat to our kingdom."

Merihem, a demon with elongated limbs and a skeletal face, raised his hand. "But Master, how do we reach them? The ones who see through our deceptions?"

Satan's eyes flashed, his wings twitching slightly as he responded. "Ah, the righteous. They are indeed the hardest to corrupt, but not impossible. For these, we must be patient. We must wear them down over time, sowing seeds of doubt, fear, and frustration. When they face hardship, we are there, whispering that their

God has abandoned them. When they fall, we remind them of their failure, over and over, until they believe they are beyond redemption."

The demons nodded, understanding now. It was not brute force that would break the righteous, but subtlety— relentless whispers, quiet temptations, a slow erosion of faith.

"And remember," Satan said, his voice rising once more, "even the strongest can fall. Pride comes before the fall, and humans are nothing if not proud. They believe themselves invincible, untouchable, and it is in that moment that we strike!"

The crowd buzzed with excitement. They had seen it happen countless times—men and women who thought they were beyond temptation, only to be brought low by a single moment of weakness.

Satan's eyes shone with dark satisfaction. "Let them think they are safe. Let them believe they are righteous. And when they stumble, we will be there to catch them— dragging them down, as we always have."

The demons erupted into applause once more, their laughter echoing through the cavernous hall like the sound of breaking bones. Their king had spoken, and they were ready to continue their work and spread their influence further until they had stained every thread of the fabric of human society and no soul was left untouched by their presence.

Satan raised his hand, and the noise ceased instantly. His eyes scanned the crowd, his expression cold and calculating. "But there is more," he said, his voice soft but commanding. "Much more."

The demons waited, their anticipation palpable. They knew their king was not finished. There was always more work to be done, always new ways to corrupt and destroy.

Satan's gaze darkened, his voice dropping to a near- whisper as he continued. "Let us speak now of sports."

Satan paused, letting the tension build before continuing. His voice dropped to a low, ominous tone as he said, "Humans consider sports to be harmless entertainment. They call it recreation, a way to pass time, bond, build camaraderie, or stay healthy. But we know the truth. Sports, too, have become one of the most effective avenues through which we spread our influence."

A ripple of curiosity stirred among the demons. The idea of sports being a tool of damnation amused and intrigued them. Satan allowed their murmurs to fade before he elaborated, "Let me explain. It begins innocently enough—a game played in the fields that looks like a competition of strength and skill. But what humans fail to understand is that we have corrupted even this, turning a simple pastime into an all-consuming obsession. And in that obsession, they find only distraction, competition, and greed."

He paced slowly across the platform, his celestial wings rustling behind him. "Think of the money," he said, his voice sharp and cutting. "Sports, once a simple contest, now command billions of dollars. Humans will pay unimaginable sums just to watch others play, to sit in grand arenas and shout their devotion to athletes who have become nothing short of gods in their eyes."

The demons hissed in approval. They knew how deeply ingrained the obsession with sports had become in human society. They had seen the rise of stadiums, the fervor of fans, and the lengths people would go to idolize their favorite athletes.

Satan raised his hand as if holding the very concept of sports in his grip. "And in their devotion to these athletes, they forget everything else. Families are torn apart as fathers abandon their children to watch the next game. People neglect their work, responsibilities, and well-being, all for the sake of watching a contest unfold. They pour their money into it, their time, their very souls."

A demon near the front slithered forward, his voice a harsh whisper. "Master, what of the athletes themselves? Do they know they have become idols?"

Satan smirked. "Some do, but most are too blinded by their own fame and fortune to see it. They revel in the adoration, basking in the glory that should belong to their creator. And we are right there, feeding their egos, making sure they believe they are untouchable. They rise higher and higher, thinking they are gods among men—until they fall when they are least expecting it."

The crowd erupted into delighted laughter, the demons relishing the thought of humans idolizing other humans, only to see them fall from grace. It was a game they had played for centuries, watching the mighty fall and bringing them to their knees.

"And what happens," Satan continued, "when these idols fail? When they lose a game? When their performance falters? The humans who worship them are crushed. Their entire sense of identity, their happiness, and their very lives are tied to the success of these athletes. And when that success fades, they are left empty, hollow, ripe for our influence."

He let the words sink in, allowing the demons to imagine the devastation of a human soul left adrift after the failure of an idol. They knew it well—it was in these moments of weakness, of disillusionment, that they moved in, sowing seeds of despair, anger, and bitterness.

"But there is more," Satan said, his voice growing darker. "We have woven gambling into sports, turning what was once a mere game into a high-stakes gamble. Humans bet their money, their livelihoods, and sometimes even their lives on the outcome of a contest. And when they lose—as they so often do—they spiral into deeper desperation, driven to ruin by their own greed."

A winged demon raised his hand. "Master, what of the fans? Those who live for their teams, who wear their colors like a second skin?"

Satan's smile widened, showing the full predatory gleam of his teeth. "The fans! They are perhaps the most deceived of all. They wear the symbols of their teams with pride, shouting their loyalty as if it were a matter of life and death. They cheer, they fight, they riot—all for the sake of a game. It becomes their religion, their identity. And in doing so, they forget the very God who created them."

He paused, letting the total weight of his words hang in the air. "They spend more time worshiping their teams than they do worshiping their creator. Their stadiums are their churches, their athletes are their idols, and their games are their sacraments. They do not see the blasphemy in it because we have blinded them to the truth."

The demons hissed in excitement, thrilled by the idea of humans unknowingly turning sports into their religion. They had long known the power of distraction, the way humans could be led away from the truth by something as simple as a game.

"And then there is the violence," Satan continued, his tone growing darker still. "The fights that break out among fans, the hatred that festers between rival teams, the blood that is spilled over something as meaningless as a score. It is in these moments that we see the true power of our influence."

A demon in the back raised his voice, creating a rasping sound like metal on stone. "Master, what of those who resist? The ones who see through the deception, who refuse to idolize athletes or gamble on the outcome?"

Satan's eyes narrowed, his gaze cold and calculating. "There will always be some who resist. But they are few, and their numbers grow smaller with each passing generation. You must not let them discourage you from your mission. The power of sports, of distraction, is too great for most to ignore. They fall into the trap willingly, believing it to be harmless fun."

The demon seemed to hesitate for a moment, then asked, "And what of those who seek redemption after they have fallen into the trap?"

Satan's smile returned, more vicious than ever. "Redemption? It is a fleeting thing. Humans may seek it, but they are weak. Once they have tasted the pleasures we offer, they will always crave more. They may turn away for a time, but we are patient. We wait. And when they stumble and fall, we are there to catch them—dragging them back into the depths."

The crowd erupted into a frenzy of approval, their excitement palpable. They knew the truth of Satan's words—humans, once corrupted, rarely found their way back to the light. And those who did often fell again, their weakness exploited by the very desires they could not control.

Satan raised his hand once more, silencing the crowd. His voice dropped to a near whisper, though every word carried through loud and clear. "We have corrupted their pleasures, their pastimes, their very souls. And we will continue to do so. Humanity is weak, driven by desire, and it is through that desire that we control them."

He paused, his gaze sweeping over the legions of demons before him. "You have done well. Your efforts have not gone unnoticed. But there is still much work to be done. The world of man is vast, and there are still souls to claim, pleasures to corrupt, and hearts to lead astray. Rest assured, we will let no corner of their lives remain untouched by our influence!"

The demons erupted in wild cheers, their voices rising in a chaotic symphony of triumph. They pounded the ground, their wings flapping in unison, their grotesque forms moving in frenzied celebration.

Satan watched them with cold satisfaction, his black wings unfurled, casting a shadow over the entire arena. His eyes gleamed with the promise of further destruction, of more souls to be claimed. He knew that this battle was far from over and that victory was already within his grasp.

As the demons celebrated, Satan stepped back from the edge of the platform, his wings folding behind him like the cloak of a king preparing to retire to his dark throne. The echoes of demonic applause reverberated through the underworld, a symphony of devilry that marked the end of yet another successful assembly.

As the fourth day of the conference came to an end, the demons dispersed into the endless caverns of hell, their laughter and promises of destruction echoing into eternity. They had least expected how much this conference would aid them in better understanding their objectives and the pitiful subjects of their machinations—humans.

After one last glimpse at the raging flood of his forces, Satan turned, the smirk never leaving his lips. With the weight of millennia upon his shoulders, he walked back into the shadows of his domain.

For now, his kingdom was secure.

Chapter 24

The Fate of the Church

The previous session had stirred the demons with unparalleled pride. Yet, even after Satan's departure, their conversations pulsed with more than simple gloating. The gathering was electric with discussions of their proudest deeds, each demon recounting acts of corruption, cruelty, and calamity in a bid to outshine one another. Some told of inflaming men's passions until they descended into ruinous hedonism; others shared tales of stealthily whispering resentment and disobedience into human ears until families and friendships lay broken in their wake.

Those of the higher ranks—chieftains who stood at the helm of entire legions—hovered above, watching over the throngs with expressions as gnarled and twisted as their scars. Each of them bore marks that distinguished their rank, not just in the form of crowns or jewels but also as deeply etched lines, jagged, brand-like tattoos, and piercings.

Across the darkness, demons jostled and preened, exchanging wicked laughs or sharpening claws on the jagged rocks underfoot, eager for the next audience with their master. Above, the atmosphere churned with swarms of demons testing their wings in acrobatic feats, dive-bombing through clouds of sulphuric smoke, the afterimage of their forms etched in fiery trails.

Somewhere in the shrouded vastness, atop the highest of crags, Satan waited, alone and contemplative. His eyes, cold as starlight, scanned the roiling legions below. He was unmoving, unblinking, but his presence was overpowering, a shadow cast over the masses gathered at the foot of the wall. As he surveyed his kingdom, a smile curled at the edges of his mouth, though it was less an expression of joy than of satisfaction—like a general who sees his army swelling with power and zeal.

The crowd grew silent as Satan descended from his high perch, the sheer power of his presence enough to silence the most restless of spirits. He moved forward with a slow, commanding gait, each step stirring a murmur of anticipation. His appearance remained as magnificent and terrible as ever: robes of midnight black rippling around him like a liquid shadow, eyes piercing blue-gray, luminous yet devoid of warmth. The ancient lines etched into his face spoke of a beauty that had hardened into something cruel and uncompromising.

As he ascended the platform from which he had delivered his previous speeches, his tall, imposing frame was visible– cloaked in shadow, eyes glinting with malice as he surveyed the mass of his followers. Silence fell as his gaze swept over them—a gaze that had, in ages past, cowed kings and tempted prophets. Without speaking, he held their attention, a sense of malevolent pride filling the room.

"My loyal followers," he began, his voice deep and resonant, echoing against the vast chasms of hell, "our previous discussions have proven fruitful. You have performed well in cultivating depravity, greed, and self- indulgence among men. Humanity has, indeed, become ensnared in the delights of their own desires, none the wiser to our influence."

A low, hissing applause spread through the crowd, demons' faces lit with triumphant grins, some nodding in silent acknowledgment, others simply grinning in dark satisfaction.

"But today," Satan continued, his voice darkening, "we turn our eyes upon a more sacred target. The so-called church. An institution designed to be a haven for those seeking light and salvation." His shrill laughter resonated with bitter irony. "And yet, even this haven has not escaped our touch."

"Be seated," he commanded, his voice carrying the weight of countless dark victories. "This topic has been my pleasure and your labor across the centuries. Since the days of the church's founding, it has been my ambition to distort and ravage this institution, to make it a stumbling block rather than a refuge for its believers."

A murmur spread through the crowd, and one demon, Xalvox, known for his stealth in manipulating church councils, dared to ask, "Master, was there a reason we allowed humans to establish the church? Why did we not prevent the ordeal altogether?"

With a thin, satisfied smile, Satan nodded. "Indeed, during its infancy, we did not intervene with all our power. Though we tried to prevent its birth altogether, our adversary's protection kept its foundations intact. In retrospect, the sequence of events has aided our mission much more than thwarting it. Back then, eradicating the concept would not have brought us measurable benefits. We needed the institution to embed itself in human society before using it as a tool for our machinations. Do you remember Peter? When he denied our enemy three times, it was one of our first victories—a symbol of human weakness, which I exploited to expose their lack of resolve. And Judas," he added with a sneer, "a disciple we won with mere coins. His betrayal set in motion a thousand-year strategy, one we would use time and time again to sow discord from within."

The demons erupted in cruel laughter, recalling how they had replicated such betrayals over the ages in innumerable ways, transforming loyal followers into betrayers. With the demons' laughter still echoing through the hall, Satan raised a hand for silence, his expression as chilling as the words he prepared to deliver.

"Ah, the early days," he mused, eyes glinting with aged malice. "In the first century, it was almost too easy. We set before the disciples the cruelty of Rome—a kingdom of idols and emperors who cared nothing for this 'new faith' springing up among the commoners. Many followers of Christ were crushed underfoot, either through torture or by planting doubt in their minds. We whispered to emperors and Roman officials, urging them to see these believers as threats. Before long, we had the Romans condemning them to lions and burning them as torches in the night."

The audience murmured in approval, relishing these memories. Then, a demon named Razial, infamous for his role in inciting rebellion and dissent, raised his voice. "But lord, wasn't there a time when the church gained power? When it seemed to sway even the Empire itself?"

Satan's expression darkened, yet a cunning gleam flickered in his eye. "Yes, Razial, and therein lay another opportunity. It was Emperor Constantine who proclaimed himself a 'Christian,' mingling church and state into a single force, an alliance we exploited masterfully. His so-called conversion flooded the church with the proud and the ambitious, those who sought influence over truth. Through this union, I twisted the church's message. I turned their gatherings into arenas for political power and rivalries. Soon, church councils became battles, doctrines were debated not for clarity but control, and the very words of Christ were twisted and disputed."

The demons cheered, impressed by their leader's past work as a tempter and instigator.

"But that was only the beginning," Satan continued, his tone chilling. "By influencing Constantine, we set the stage for centuries of corruption. Wealth began flowing into the church, drawing the greedy and hypocritical into its ranks. We turned bishops into politicians, priests into merchants, and the church became not a place of refuge but one of power and wealth—a far cry from its humble beginnings. And we have continued this corruption even to this day."

A dark smile played on his lips, and Satan extended his arms in a sweeping gesture, the hall falling to an eerie silence. The demons knew the power of what he described: a perversion so complete that even the faithful could scarcely recognize what their beliefs had once been.

At that moment, a demon named Malik, who had once sown division among early theologians, stepped forward. "My lord, I have witnessed firsthand and participated in the confusion we sowed among their doctrines. Have we managed to create enough divisions among them?"

Satan nodded approvingly. "Indeed, Malik, for it was in the doctrines that we planted the seeds of discord. Through arguments on the nature of Christ, the Trinity, and salvation, we birthed factions: Gnostics, Arians, and Donatists—all disagreeing, all claiming authority. We stirred every theological debate with whispers, with pride, with the desire for a personal legacy. By setting men against men in the name of truth, we fractured what was once whole."

He paused, his voice softening to a hint of satisfaction. "Today, we see the fruits of this labor—a church splintered into countless sects, each claiming to hold the only true understanding, yet all mired in bitterness and separation. My servants, you have sown seeds of discord so thoroughly that the church itself no longer knows unity."

The legions howled in approval, shaking their fists in triumph. They had long known the pleasure of dividing believers and watching as they tore each other apart in the name of doctrine.

As the fervor in the hall died down, Satan leaned forward, his gaze piercing as he recalled the centuries of manipulation. His voice resonated with dark satisfaction, each word a reminder of the web of deceit he had woven over the ages.

"Power," he intoned, letting the word linger in the air. "In their pursuit of it, the church bartered away its soul. It was no longer enough to be a place of worship; the church sought influence over kings, and in doing so, they allowed us to slip further into their very foundation."

One demon, an imposing figure named Zaphiron, stepped forward with a question. "Master, how did we manage to get kings and priests to conspire together? Would that not have stirred doubts within them?"

Satan's smile deepened. "Ah, Zaphiron, their doubts were easily silenced by ambition. For centuries, we fanned the flames of greed and dominance. By promising security and wealth to kings and power to church leaders, we formed alliances that obscured the faith they claimed to defend. One such instance was during the age of Charlemagne. By cloaking his conquests in the guise of spreading Christianity, we had a leader who would take up the sword in our adversary's name yet spill blood at our behest."

The demons burst into malicious laughter as they reveled in the irony. Satan let them savor the victory for a moment before continuing.

"And yet, the church wanted more. With the rise of the Papal States, bishops transformed into rulers. My servants, do you realize the victory in that alone?" He paused, his gaze scanning the assembly. "For centuries, popes who preached humility and poverty wore crowns encrusted with jewels, sat upon thrones of gold, and commanded armies to kill and conquer. Through them, we replaced humility with pride, charity with taxation, and piety with pomp. Their moral decay became so ingrained that even when reformers emerged, they faced bitter opposition from within."

The crowd's enthusiasm reached a fever pitch, and another demon, Tygress—a master of manipulation—raised his voice. "But my lord," he inquired with curiosity, "what of the reformers? If I remember correctly, did they not put up an obstruction in our plans?"

Satan's eyes narrowed, a flicker of cold rage beneath his pride. "The reformers, ah yes," he said, a tinge of disdain in his tone. "Some of them were troublesome, indeed. But we had our own strategies. When Martin Luther defied Rome, we twisted his movement until Protestant factions warred with each other, just as we did with the church councils. Where there was one Luther, we gave them a hundred doctrines, all at odds, all breeding discord. We turned reform into rivalry, and division multiplied. Soon enough, the Protestants fractured into sects, each claiming superiority, each as vulnerable to our influence as Rome had been."

The legions hissed in approval, the brilliance of the strategy resonating among them. They could see how each schism and division had contributed to the weakening of the church as a whole.

With a sweeping motion, Satan resumed, his voice gaining an

even darker intensity. "Through this disunity, my servants, we have turned faith into an instrument of control. The so-called Crusades… Ah, those glorious massacres! What began as a mission for the faithful became a blood- soaked conquest in our favor. I whispered into the ears of kings and popes alike, convincing them that God willed the deaths of innocents, that the gates of heaven would open to those who slaughtered without mercy."

At this, Razial, who had a penchant for fueling violent religious fervor, grinned widely. "And the Inquisitions, Master?"

Satan chuckled softly, his eyes gleaming with cruel delight. "Yes, the Inquisitions—a tool to make the church despised even among those who should have loved it. I turned its leaders against their own, accusing believers of heresy and igniting a fear so deep that they tortured their own kind. Men and women who had served the church were denounced and made into examples of terror. Suspicion, betrayal, and death—all sanctioned by their own leaders."

The demons erupted into cheers, for this memory was particularly sweet. Through Satan's plan, the church had descended into depths from which it could scarcely recover, alienating those it sought to reach.

"Look at what we achieved," Satan continued, raising his voice. "For all their talk of love and salvation, we exposed their capacity for cruelty. And even now, in this modern age, we continue to exploit those very same weaknesses. We've twisted the teachings of charity and humility into the pursuit of wealth, power, and status. We've transformed the very gospel they preach."

The demons clapped and howled in sinister joy, each one struck by the brilliance of their centuries-old conquest.

Satisfied with the fervor of his audience, Satan's voice deepened as he spoke of the modern era. His words were deliberate, laced with malice as he recounted the recent victories that had taken centuries to bring to fruition.

"And so," he began, casting a dark gaze over the crowd, "we come to the modern church. In this age, my servants, we have achieved something remarkable. We've crafted a church that is virtually unrecognizable from its original form. Today, it thrives on wealth, influence, and the allure of fame—tools it once claimed to renounce."

Satan's expression softened with satisfaction, a cruel smile curling on his lips. "We have convinced some to treat their roles as preachers not as a calling but as a career. The 'celebrity pastor'—a term unheard of in the early days—is a result of our ingenuity. Through fame and influence, we have enticed them to preach messages that draw masses but are void of conviction. Prosperity has become their gospel, and wealth their god."

He paused, savoring the effect of his words. The demons were hanging on each one, their anticipation building as they relished the impact of their master's achievements.

"Look at how they speak," Satan continued, his tone laced with mockery. "They have rebranded the gospel as self-help, prosperity, and endless positivity—words that appeal but demand nothing. Gone is the talk of sacrifice, of humility. They preach what they know the crowds long to hear, and they ignore the substance that would bring true conviction."

Another demon, called Terath—known for corrupting sermons into messages of wealth and worldly success—grinned and asked, "And how do the followers react to this, my lord?"

"Ah, Terath," Satan said, chuckling darkly, "they flock to it.

For years, we have fed them a diluted message. Now, they sit comfortably, believing that their lives will be blessed simply for showing up. They are no longer taught of the soul's eternal journey, of the sin that corrupts within. They believe their faith is about earthly gain and success, which aligns perfectly with our left agenda."

The demons howled with delight, their celebration echoing through the vast hall. Satan had expertly crafted a counterfeit faith, and they had watched it thrive.

Satan raised a hand, calling for silence as his voice grew more intense. "But our greatest achievement in recent times," he announced, "has been in exposing their hypocrisy. Do you remember the scandals, my servants? Those dark secrets we helped them conceal, only to reveal when they were at their highest?"

The crowd erupted in approving laughter, and a demon named Fornax, a salient member of the regiment that specialized in sexual scandals, spoke up with pride. "Indeed, my lord. We planted those seeds years ago, nurtured them in secret, then brought them to light at the perfect moment."

Satan nodded, pleased. "Yes, Fornax, and how well you and your group have done. We watched as leaders fell— men and women who spoke of holiness but could not control their desires. Through them, we showed the world the truth behind their facades. When their sins were revealed, they lost not only their influence but their followers' trust, casting the entire church into disrepute. People see them now not as holy, but as hypocrites, and turn away from their teachings."

He paused, a glimmer of pride in his eyes as he recounted one particularly infamous scandal from recent years. "Do you recall when we influenced a high-profile minister, known for his fiery preaching, to succumb to greed and debauchery? He had gathered thousands, his voice filling stadiums, but his fall was so public that his followers scattered. We turned his influence into a weapon against the very faith he once preached."

The crowd roared in approval, every demon savoring the victory. In their eyes, no tactic was as powerful as exposing the hypocrisy of a leader.

As the cheers subsided, Satan's expression shifted to one of deep satisfaction. He raised his hands to quiet the crowd, his voice dripping with pride as he resumed his address.

"Next, we come to one of the salient features of our offensive—fragmentation," he began, letting the word reverberate through the hall. "This is among our greatest victories in modern times. While once the church was unified, its followers stood as one, it is fractured beyond recognition today. My servants, the division we have sown has spread like wildfire, creating factions, each with their own interpretations and doctrines.

"We introduced doubts, small at first, into the minds of scholars and theologians. We urged them to question the Scriptures, to analyze and dissect each word, until they could no longer agree on its meaning. Doctrines were challenged, interpretations varied, and before long, we had birthed countless sects—all claiming to hold the truth."

The demons erupted in applause, the scale of their influence astounding even to them. Satan's strategy had been nothing short of brilliant.

"Consider the debates over salvation itself," Satan continued, his eyes gleaming with malicious delight. "Some proclaim that salvation comes by faith alone; others insist it requires works. Some cling to grace, while others preach judgment and fire. The result? They stand opposed, unable to reconcile their differences, each condemning the other."

The demons grinned, relishing the irony. What should have been a message of unity had become a weapon of division.

Satan's tone grew darker as he continued, his words laced with mockery. "We took even the most fundamental teachings and turned them into points of contention. Baptism, for instance. Should it be for infants or adults? Should it involve immersion or sprinkling? By turning these simple acts into controversies, we splintered congregations."

Another demon named Malchir—part of a specialized legion that was known for igniting theological disputes—laughed as he spoke up. "My lord, it took only a few subtle suggestions. One question here, one doubt there, and soon they were calling each other heretics."

"Yes, Malchir," Satan replied with a nod, his voice echoing with approval. "And that is the beauty of it. We let them do the work for us. They argue over interpretations, condemn each other over trivialities, and splinter into new factions. Today, they are divided into thousands of denominations, each believing they hold the sole truth, each unwilling to stand together."

The demons roared in approval, their malevolent laughter filling the hall. It was clear they took pride in the splintering chaos they had unleashed.

"But there is more," Satan added, his tone lowering conspiratorially. "We did not stop at theological doctrines.

We pushed them further into political, cultural, and racial divisions. We encouraged them to attach their faith to their ideologies, nationalities, and biases. And so, the church is split along political lines, each side claiming to follow the same God while despising the other."

The arena fell silent as the gravity of Satan's manipulation sank in before erupting into applause. The demons knew this fragmentation reached beyond the church walls, breeding distrust and enmity among families, communities, and entire nations.

As the applause died down, Satan's expression shifted to one of devious anticipation. "Now, my loyal companions," he began, his voice soft yet commanding, "let us turn our attention to our infiltration of the church through secular wisdom. For nothing has weakened their resolve like the slow creep of worldly philosophy.

"It was a matter of subtlety. The church once believed itself distinct from the world, its teachings firmly rooted in divine instruction. So we brought them wisdom that sounded godly but was rooted in human pride. We urged theologians to weave in philosophies of self and enlightenment. They accepted it eagerly, thinking they were elevating their understanding."

He paused, his eyes gleaming as he recounted the slow erosion of traditional teachings. "Consider the introduction of self-help philosophies, which placed human will above divine will. We told them, 'God wants you to be happy, to prosper, to fulfill your own potential.' Slowly, they turned away from sacrifice and obedience, focusing instead on self-empowerment. Today, many see God as a tool for personal gain, a deity who exists to fulfill their desires."

The crowd responded with murmurs of approval, understanding the brilliance of the strategy. Self-empowerment had replaced self-sacrifice, a subtle yet destructive shift.

"And what of sin?" Satan continued, his voice dripping with disdain. "We taught them to see sin not as an offense to God but as a psychological flaw, a misstep on the path to self-fulfillment. It is no longer something to be confessed and purged but a simple hurdle to overcome. In this way, we've diluted the very concept of repentance."

The assembly leaned in closer, captivated as Satan revealed the full extent of his influence. "And so, they brought the world into their sacred spaces," he continued. "Today, they blur the line between holy and profane. They bring secular ideas into the pulpit, mixing doctrines of faith with psychology, sociology, and self-care. They rely on human solutions instead of divine guidance, and in so doing, they lose their conviction.

"For example, they have brought concerts, theatrical productions, and celebrity worship into their places of gathering. They call it 'engagement,' but it is a mere distraction. They sit through sermons that entertain but fail to convict. They want their senses stimulated, not their souls stirred. In their pursuit of relevance, they have traded depth for spectacle, and their altars have become stages."

The crowd erupted into laughter, savoring the irony of churches seeking to please rather than to purify and the eloquence with which their leader described it.

Satan let the laughter settle before continuing, his gaze steely. "Today, they are less concerned with doctrine than with personal beliefs. Faith has become a matter of preference rather than principle. They speak of 'finding their truth,' as though the truth could be molded to their liking."

A demon named Lothar, who delighted in turning believers away from Scripture, grinned as he asked, "And what of the Scriptures, my lord? Have they not noticed the drift?"

Satan's eyes flashed with satisfaction. "Ah, Lothar, we have ensured that many no longer cling to the Scriptures as they once did. We introduced them to interpretations that align with their desires. They now pick and choose verses to suit their needs, discarding the parts that demand discipline and accountability. And in some cases, they question whether Scripture is even divinely inspired at all."

A ripple of dark delight passed through the crowd. Satan had managed to turn believers' own understanding against them, severing their connection to what they once held as holy and infallible.

"In this way," he continued, "we have made Scripture an accessory, more of a suggestion than a command. And so, they drift, tethered to nothing but their capricious whims."

The demons cheered, understanding that these subtle shifts had left the church vulnerable, weakened from within. What was once a fortress of faith had become a crumbling edifice, eroded by compromise and complacency.

Satan's gaze darkened, his expression twisted with satisfaction. "My servants," he began, "if there is one element that brings me profound delight, it is our influence on the church's concept of morality. Once, they stood steadfast on principles, viewing right and wrong as absolutes. Today, they accept a diluted, flexible code of ethics—one that allows them to shape their beliefs according to the world around them."

The crowd of demons responded with approving murmurs, pleased by the success of this manipulation. The power of moral decay had proven effective across all aspects of human society, but nowhere was its impact as gratifying as within the church itself.

"It began slowly, as all of our best works do," Satan continued, his voice reverberating with a quiet intensity. "First, we planted the idea of tolerance above all else. 'Love,' we whispered to them. 'Love and acceptance for all.' At first, this sounded noble, in keeping with their doctrines. And so they embraced it, believing that tolerance was synonymous with compassion.

"Once, they viewed love as a force that confronted wrongdoing and sought to lead others away from sin. But we taught them a softer, more passive love that tolerates everything and judges nothing. It was simple: we persuaded them that calling out sin was 'judgmental' and that correcting the wayward was 'intolerant.' And they accepted this without question."

The crowd murmured in admiration, appreciating the subtlety of Satan's strategy. Through tolerance, they had managed to paralyze the church's moral backbone, turning it into an institution that preached acceptance at the cost of integrity.

Satan continued, his tone darkening further. "In this age, they preach compassion so fervently that it has crossed into compromise. They no longer call sin by its name but label it as 'personal choice' or 'freedom of expression.' Behaviors once considered disgraceful are now applauded as individuality. And worst of all," he added, his eyes gleaming, "they avoid all talk of divine judgment, for it is 'too harsh' a message."

The demons responded with a thunderous cheer. They understood well the power of a church unwilling to speak of judgment; it allowed people to live as they pleased, free from fear of accountability.

"Look at how they now embrace the world's values as their own," Satan continued. "They have adopted ideologies of humanism, celebrating humanity's accomplishments rather than their God's. They praise self- fulfillment, champion self-expression, and glorify self- discovery—all ideals rooted in pride and selfish ambition. Under the guise of love, they elevate humanity rather than divinity."

The crowd burst into applause, for nothing delighted them more than seeing the church corrupted into a mirror of the secular world.

Satan let the applause die down before continuing, his tone quieter yet sharper. "And now, they find themselves in a place of moral relativism, where right and wrong are a matter of opinion. They have left behind absolute truths; instead, they preach that 'each must find their own path.' They have abandoned the notion of universal sin, saying, 'What is wrong for one may not be wrong for another.' It is their own gospel of relativity."

A demon named Icaroth, skilled in twisting perceptions, raised his hand, eyes gleaming. "Master, you speak of sin. Have they truly lost their conviction on this entirely?"

Satan's face darkened with delight. "Indeed, Icaroth. Today, they speak of sin only in terms that suit their preferences. They address societal issues, systemic problems, and matters of conscience, yet they ignore the sins of the soul—pride, lust, envy, and greed. They brush these aside, for they are too uncomfortable to acknowledge their innermost desires. And without these truths, they have lost the very core of their faith."

The crowd's laughter echoed in waves, reverberating through the dark hall. Demons like Icaroth and Lothar relished the irony of a church unwilling to address the very issues that it was built to overcome.

Satan leaned in closer, his voice a low, menacing whisper. "They avoid repentance altogether, treating sin as a psychological flaw rather than a spiritual blight. They ask for healing rather than forgiveness, for restoration rather than transformation. In this way, they seek to 'better themselves' rather than submit to a God they hardly remember."

As the ensuing wave of applause faded, Satan's expression grew grave, his tone weighted with pride. "But the crowning achievement, my faithful servants, has been their silence on eternity itself. They no longer speak of the afterlife; they no longer preach of heaven or hell. We have made them silent on what lies beyond, content to live only in the present.

"We have made them creatures of the here and now, deaf to eternity's call," he continued, gloating. "They concern themselves only with earthly matters, as if life here were all that existed. They preach prosperity, happiness, and fulfillment but never remind their followers of the soul's destination. We have turned their faith into a tool for temporary gain, void of any lasting consequence."

The crowd erupted in dark joy, the satisfaction of victory palpable as the hall filled with their glee. The demons knew that without the fear of eternal consequence, humanity would easily fall to their influence, slipping ever further from any hope of redemption.

As the celebration reached a fever pitch, Satan's gaze swept across his followers, his face a mask of cruel satisfaction. His clear, commanding voice cut through the noise.

"And thus, my servants, we have achieved a triumph unmatched. We have turned the church from a sanctuary of truth into a haven of complacency. We have dulled their conviction, softened their resolve, and stripped them of the very truths that once empowered them. And as long as they remain lost in this haze, they are ours."

The hall erupted in applause, a thunderous, triumphant sound that reverberated across the darkness. The demons celebrated with fervor, their master's words validating their efforts over the centuries. They had eroded the foundation of faith, transformed truth into ambiguity, and left humanity adrift without hope of salvation. And in that moment, hell rejoiced.

Satan stood motionless as the last echo of his words settled over the assembly, his gaze fixed on the legions gathered before him. A deep silence filled the hall, thick with the weight of his final message. The demons held their breath, their faces alight with triumph yet tense with anticipation. For each of them knew this was no ordinary moment—this was a victory centuries in the making.

Sensing their devotion, Satan raised his arms in a slow, measured gesture, his dark robes unfurling like the spread of ominous wings. With a glint in his eye, he surveyed them one last time, his lips curling into a sinister smile. His presence seemed to grow, shadow stretching from his form, casting a dim pall over the already dark hall. The very air seemed to bow under his power, swirling like an ethereal mist, moving in rhythm with the collective pulse of hell's denizens.

"My faithful ones," he said, his voice resonating with a profound authority that seeped into every corner of the hall, "today, we do not merely claim victory; we affirm our dominion. Let the collapse of their altars and our triumph stand as a testament to our indomitable will."

A hum of reverence rippled through the crowd, their eyes fixed upon him with unwavering devotion. Then, in a swift motion, Satan brought his hands down in a decisive sweep, and the air around him erupted in a low, rolling thunder. Dark flames sparked at his feet, crawling up his figure, flickering around him as if the shadows themselves were alive, bowing to his command.

The flames licked upward, engulfing him and casting a scarlet glow over the hall. With one final look, Satan's gaze met each of the demon chiefs, his eyes sharp and cold—a reminder of the authority he wielded and the expectations he had set. "Continue your work with zeal," he commanded, his voice carrying a final note of warning. "For there is no end to our purpose. We thrive in their confusion, and as long as they stray, they are ours."

And with that, the flames swelled in a fierce burst, obscuring him completely. When the blaze subsided, he was gone—vanished into the shadows, leaving behind an empty space where his presence had loomed only moments before.

The arena was silent for a breath, a stunned stillness, until a demon named Protos released a feral, guttural shout, igniting the throng like a spark. In an instant, the arena erupted into a cacophony of exultation.

Demons of every rank and shape surged forward, filling the space with wild howls and cheers. Some leaped into the air, wings unfurled, twisting and turning in frenzied acrobatics as they traced trails of dark smoke through the atmosphere. Others stomped and drummed the ground, creating a rhythm that echoed through the chamber like the thundering of a war drum. Claws clashed, talons scraped, and guttural roars mingled into a brutal symphony of triumph.

A massive demon named Talnok, adorned with chains and charred metal sigils, raised a disfigured chalice, roaring, "To the king who has led us! To the triumph of our eternal cause!" His voice boomed across the expansive grounds, sparking a fresh wave of cheers.

Demons in the crowd took up his chant, raising their fists and voices in unison. "To the king! To the cause!" they shouted, their voices blending into a singular, unstoppable roar that reverberated across the realm. The chants grew louder, blending with the distant, tormented wails of the human souls who lingered in endless suffering—sounds that now seemed to join the rhythm, a dark undercurrent of despair beneath the celebration.

Demons began sharing their proudest achievements with one another in small clusters around the hall, reminiscing over tales of countless human souls they had led astray—or rather, led to the haunting cells of hell. Tygress, a sleek, serpentine demon known for his mastery of subtle temptations, hissed in satisfaction, recounting his influence over a family it had torn apart with whispered lies and jealousy. A smaller demon named Drix, his form wreathed in flickering shadows, bragged of his work corrupting youth through media and music, watching them embrace sin as though it were a badge of honor.

The chiefs gathered in an elevated alcove, gazing over the chaos below. There was a collective nod among them, a recognition of their labor's results. Azazel, a powerful demon who had recently been promoted to chief, whispered to his neighbor, "Never have we seen such unity in their realm. It is no longer just a foothold; it's a kingdom of ruin." His words elicited dark laughter from his companions.

Meanwhile, Eshbel and Morbus instigated a ritualistic dance, their figures shifting and swirling, flames trailing in their wake. They moved with precision, their dark eyes gleaming, their voices chanting praises to Satan as the infernal melody rose to a fever pitch.

Above them, daggers of flame materialized in the air, twisting and interweaving as if in rhythm with the celebration. Dark clouds coalesced, filling the sky and casting jagged lightning down into the pits of the underworld, a terrifying spectacle that added to the fervor of the gathering.

As the celebration wore on, the demons grew bolder, each feeding off the collective energy in displays of dark prowess. Some sparred with each other in mock battles, their blows resounding like thunder as they clawed and fought in gleeful abandon. Others created scenes of agony and despair, flickering images of humanity's suffering that danced through the shadows as if projected upon invisible walls. The cries of souls caught in endless torment rose, a reminder of the fate that awaited those led astray.

At the far end of the hall, a group of lesser demons lit pyres of black flame, circling around it in a frenzied dance. Their forms twisted and contorted, casting elongated shadows that seemed to writhe and reach outward, embodying the essence of their depravity.

The sounds grew louder, filling every corner of the great hall with an intensity that could have shaken the very foundations of creation. The celebration reached a fevered pitch as they continued, their revelry blending with the moans of the condemned souls in the background—a dark harmony of suffering and celebration that pulsed through the air like a living, malevolent organism.

As the night stretched on, the chiefs gathered once more, their voices rising in a chant of allegiance to Satan. Talnok, lifting his defaced chalice again, called out to the assembly, "To the king who has granted us power, to the one who reigns over this dark realm—our loyalty is eternal!"

The crowd joined in, shouting as one: "Our loyalty is eternal!"

At that moment, their chant became a living oath, a binding pledge that resonated through every corner of hell. And as their voices echoed, the demons knew that their mission and purpose would continue, unyielding and undeterred. They had tasted victory and reveled in it, and their fervor had only grown stronger. For as long as humanity remained vulnerable and shadows lingered upon the earth, they would carry out their master's will.

And so, beneath the sulfurous skies of hell, they celebrated—a feverish, infernal throng of darkness bound to their cause.

315

Chapter 25

A World In Chaos

In the depths of hell, the reverberations of demonic celebration echoed through every crevice and chamber, a cacophony of triumphant howls and screeches that seemed to shake the very foundations of the infernal realm. The sound wasn't merely loud - it was alive, a living entity that crawled through the sulfurous air and burrowed into the obsidian walls. Each cry carried notes of such profound malice that they formed harmonies of horror, creating an orchestra of darkness that would have driven any mortal mad with terror.

I, Sabrael, watched as demons from every hierarchy reveled in their perceived victory. Unlike their previous gatherings, where strategic planning dominated their interactions, this celebration carried an almost desperate intensity. They knew this marked the end of their extraordinary assembly, and this knowledge lent a frenzied quality to their festivities.

Through the sulfurous haze, I observed as demons who had maintained rigid formations in earlier sessions now abandoned all pretense of order. The higher-order demons, usually stoic in their bearing, were seen trading war stories with lesser demons, their voices carrying notes of pride previously masked by formality. The Chieftains, who typically kept to themselves, now mingled freely with the rank and file of hell's army, their shared triumph temporarily erasing hierarchical boundaries. Never before had the residents of hell interacted so much with one another.

The term "Spirited Boldness for Success" rippled through the gathering like a battle cry, each demon savoring the words as if tasting sweet wine. The term was intended as their collective title for the time to come. This new mandate seemed to intoxicate them with fresh purpose, and I could see in their eyes the calculating gleam of creatures plotting ever more audacious assaults on humanity's moral foundations.

Just as the light fails to penetrate the deepest ocean trenches, so too did the darkness in hell's conference chamber seem to deepen with each passing moment. The demons' shifting forms created living shadows that danced across the obsidian walls, their movements reflecting the restless anticipation building among them. Some took to the air, their wings creating currents of hot, acrid wind that stirred the flames burning in the corners of the meeting arena that had served as the conference's venue.

Suddenly, without warning, the celebration froze. The very air seemed to congeal as a presence began to manifest at the head of the chamber. Though it seemed impossible, the darkness grew even more profound, coalescing into a form that commanded absolute attention. Satan, the Fallen Morning Star, materialized before his assembled forces, but not in the battle-ready aspect they had grown accustomed to during the conference.

This time, their king appeared in a form that harkened back to his days as heaven's most beautiful angel, though twisted by eons of darkness. His wings, spread wide in terrible majesty, shimmered with an anti-light that seemed to absorb the very essence of illumination. His face, still bearing traces of its original beauty, now held an expression of such triumphant malice that even his most hardened lieutenants felt themselves tremble.

The fallen angel's presence commanded a silence so absolute that even the torch flames seemed to quiet their crackling. His form towered above the assembly, a dark radiance emanating from him in waves that made the very air ripple. The glistening crown upon his head, fashioned from what appeared to be the only semblance of beauty in hell, caught and gripped the attention of myriads who had grown accustomed to the dark.

"My faithful legions," Satan's voice resonated with a terrible allure that reminded me of the music he once made in heaven, now corrupted into something that made reality itself shudder. "We stand at the precipice of our greatest triumph since the garden." His words carried both silk and steel, each syllable calculated to bind his followers closer to him.

As he spoke of the world's disarray, his form shifted subtly, becoming more corporeal, more terrifyingly present. "Observe," he commanded, raising a hand that seemed to pull shadows from the very air. In the darkness above, images began to form—cities in chaos, humans scurrying like ants in their daily struggles, faces contorted with stress and fear.

"Our influence," he continued, his voice swelling with pride, "has done more than merely tempt individuals. We have corrupted the very foundations of human society." The images above shifted, showing scenes of moral decay that made even some of the lesser demons flinch. "The race they run—for wealth, status, for mere survival—is a maze of our design, and they scurry through it like blind rats. Though their position might seem to improve every now and then, make no mistake—the human world is in disarray. Centuries of our influence upon humanity, weaving through the crevices of their intentions and morals, have left them ripe for our design. What was once a stable creation is now crumbling beneath the weight of our pressures, fragmenting before our very eyes!"

"Their supposed sanctuary," he sneered, "has become our

playground. Their shepherds chase golden fleeces while their flocks scatter. What was supposed to be a space that reminds them of God and keeps them on the right path has turned into a fertile breeding ground for sin and a scheme for their self-proclaimed leaders to accumulate power and wealth. The line between good and evil grows more blurry with each day, and instead of giving them a sense of belonging, the modern Church has only gone to create further divisions and disagreements among our adversary's followers."

When he spoke of the church's decay, his expression shifted into such malevolent satisfaction that it seemed to darken the chamber, while his words about human isolation drew murmurs of appreciation from the assembled demons. The legion responsible for tempting humans with pride, particularly, preened at the mention of their successful strategy of turning self-preservation into selfishness. Different demon factions responded with increasing enthusiasm as Satan elaborated on each point of societal breakdown that marked their victories against heaven.

Instead of the usual chaos of demonic celebration, they maintained a terrible discipline, and their joy was expressed through an almost military precision of movement and sound. The very air seemed to pulse with their collective pride and anticipation. Satan's form seemed to expand as he delved deeper into each triumph, his shadow stretching across the chamber like a living organism. The assembled demons leaned forward, their eyes gleaming with unholy light as their king dissected each victory with surgical precision.

"Let us savor the fruits of our labor," he purred, his voice carrying notes of both velvet and venom. "When we speak of good becoming evil, look how magnificently we've twisted their moral compass!" Above him, the shadowy images shifted to show scenes of modern human confusion.

"Those who stand for traditional values are branded as bigots," he continued, genuine amusement coloring his tone. "Those who speak of absolute truth are labeled as extremists. We've created a world where virtue is vice, where speaking truth is hatred, where protecting innocence is seen as oppression." The demons responsible for moral confusion rose up, their forms writhing with pleasure as Satan detailed how 'good' had been renamed 'evil' and vice versa.

Satan looked upon his audience, and his piercing gaze fell on a demon named Leraje, whose specialty lay in war and conflict. "Leraje, remind them," he said, voice dripping with sardonic delight, "how one man's 'right' has become another's offense. How a single word can now ignite outrage."

Leraje nodded, bowing low, his eyes sparkling with wicked triumph. "Our tactics have spread in whispers, my lord. Every thought, every gesture, every trivial action is scrutinized. They live in perpetual fear of offending each other, and so they tiptoe through life, their words carefully chosen yet sharp as blades."

"Exactly," Satan replied, his voice low and pleased. "Our handiwork has fashioned a world where freedom of speech is but an illusion. One opinion is another's prison; each belief a point of attack." He let a long silence draw over his words, savoring the sensation of his audience's awe. The demons nodded, intoxicated by the dark beauty of this reality they had created.

Satan's expression turned calculating as he continued. "Watch how beautifully they tear each other apart! One group's expression of freedom becomes another's oppression. Religious freedom clashes with social progress. Personal rights war with the collective good. And in their desperate attempt to balance these competing freedoms, they've lost all of them. Once, they looked to their neighbors with goodwill, revered their lawgivers, and believed in the nobility of their leaders. But we have stripped away this trust, tarnishing every institution."

The demons were responsible for discord and emanated waves of cold pleasure, as Satan described how they had taught humans to disregard their neighbors. They chittered with glee at the mention of fractured communities and broken trust, creating an unsettling resonance that made hell's walls vibrate. At this, a young demon named Volac raised his voice, eyes alight with fervor. "We see it in the children, my lord. Their homes are barren of love, the guidance of their parents cold and sparse, their innocence ground underfoot by neglect."

Satan's laughter echoed, a sound that sent shivers through even his most hardened lieutenants. "Yes, Volac. Children no longer revere their parents. Families are adrift, and every neglected child is a potential soldier for our cause. The children," he closed his eyes in satisfaction, "are our masterpieces of manipulation. Parents chase careers and material success, believing they're securing their children's futures while actually sacrificing their present.

"The young ones grow up in emotional deserts, raised by screens and strangers, their hearts hollow and hungry. We have successfully ensured there remains an unbridgeable gap between their generations so that even when the elders try to impart valuable wisdom to their younglings, the latter's stubbornness perceives it as an attempt to control them. They deprive themselves of the chance to witness a glimpse of God's love and spend the rest of their lives trying to fill the void we leave in their pitiful lives."

His voice took on a particularly triumphant tone as he continued. "Let their souls rot in neglect. Let them thirst for love that shall never come!"

The demons tasked with destroying family bonds swelled with

dark pride as their king praised their work in separating parents from children. They performed a sinister dance of celebration, their shadows weaving complex patterns of darkness. The assembly's reaction grew more intense as their king detailed each victory. Their uproar and synchronicity, however, were unlike any of their responses in the preceding days of the conference.

Satan allowed the group to relish their accomplishments before addressing the next aspect of human society they had managed to corrupt. "Of course, this aspect of our achievement cannot be concluded without allocating due credit to one of their qualities that's supposed to cultivate genuine connection but that we rendered utterly useless: trust. That supposed foundation of human society lies in absolute ruins," he declared. "Remember the days when humans trusted each other as neighbors, as allies? Those days are but a relic. We have fostered suspicion so keen that now every relationship, every partnership trembles on the verge of betrayal.

"Husbands and wives live in a state of suspicion; friendships wear thin from distrust, and even children look upon their parents with doubt. They trust neither their leaders nor their neighbors, neither their priests nor their protectors. Each institution we've corrupted, each authority figure we've compromised, has driven another nail into the coffin of human fellowship. Now, it takes only a rumor, a slight misunderstanding, to bring their households to ruin. They believe they are enlightened by their wariness, but their hearts grow weary with each passing day. "

The demons responsible for dismantling trust and sincerity swelled visibly at these words, their forms growing more substantial with pride. While they had spent centuries chipping away at the bonds between humans, turning every successive attempt into a hollow monument, they had little idea of how their efforts contributed to hell's larger mission against humans. Satan's elaborate speeches finally enlightened them about how crucial and indispensable their regiment had been for ensuring the smooth progress of the rest of their strategies.

Satan took a few steps to his side, lost in contemplation, before returning to the center of the stage. When he spoke again, his voice dropped to a seductive whisper that nonetheless carried to every corner of the chamber. "We've perfected the art of justified apathy," he said. "Humans now walk past suffering with perfectly reasonable excuses: It's not my problem. Someone else will help. I have my own troubles. What if it's dangerous to get involved?"

Finally, touching on the matter of censorship and political correctness, Satan's expression became one of pure malicious delight. "Our greatest weapon," he declared, "is their own language turned against them. We've created a linguistic maze where every word is a potential trap, where simple truths cannot be spoken for fear of offense, and genuine discourse dies under the weight of artificial politeness. Our handiwork has fashioned a world where freedom of speech is but an illusion. One opinion is another's prison; each belief is a point of attack.

"And to add salt to their injury, we have promoted a culture of 'politically correct' language, which only serves to censure, manipulate, and coerce people into compliance. Our left agenda has seeped so deep into their life philosophies and communities that they have forgotten the essence of being human. They find it easier to reject and outcast individuals who dare to stand against the tide of majority opinion instead of trying to find a middle ground. The culture makes everyone fear for their public image so much that they would rather abandon their loved ones than risk losing the acceptance of others."

In response to the praise, demons responsible for confusion and manipulation performed an intricate aerial display, their forms weaving complex patterns that seemed to mock the very concept of clear communication. The mass of demons assembled in the arena cheered them on as they waited patiently for their master's acknowledgment of their area of expertise.

Satan's form seemed to multiply as he spoke of their worldwide influence, his shadows stretching to every corner of the arena like a dark web. The assembled demons watched in rapt attention as their king's presence filled the space with an oppressive weight of evil purpose.

"Our forces," he declared, his voice resonating with dark pride, "operate with unprecedented efficiency." Above him, the shadowy images coalesced into a global map, points of darkness pulsing wherever demonic activity was strongest. "From the highest towers of power to the lowest streets of despair, our brave, diligent agents never rest."

The visualization shifted to show scenes of their handiwork: a businessman's face contorting with road rage, his demon passenger feeding his fury; a troubled youth entering a school with deadly intent, surrounded by whispering spirits of violence; a vandal desecrating a church while demons of sacrilege danced around him in gleeful circles.

"Our success lies in simultaneous assaults," Satan continued, his expression one of masterful strategy. "We don't merely attack the individual - we assault their sense of security, their relationships, their beliefs, their hope, all at once. As we pester humans from every angle, it's no wonder they can pinpoint any one problem. This is because they are dealing with several damming issues simultaneously. What's even more interesting is that they can't see us—the perpetrators. What they see instead is the compliant human agents, driven by demonic spirits, whom we use for the jobs." The images above showed humans overwhelmed by multiple crises, their faces reflecting the confusion of those who cannot identify the source of their torment.

The atmosphere grew even darker as Satan's voice took on a tone of terrible anticipation. "But all of this - the corruption, the chaos, the confusion - serves our ultimate purpose." His body seemed to grow larger still, ever more bewitching and terrifying at the same time, as the assembled demons trembled with a mixture of fear and excitement, their forms rippling like heat waves in the sulfurous air.

"When the time comes," he promised, his voice dropping to a monotonous rhythm that somehow carried more weight than his loudest proclamation, "we will have an army of humans so disillusioned, so angry, so separated from their creator, that they will gladly march against heaven itself! We will garner a human force, motivated by extreme hatred toward our adversary, for the final battle. At the right time, we will fight our adversary and regain our rightful place in heaven, and I will reign as the supreme being – your king forever!"

The chamber erupted in a sound that was part cheer, part war cry, and part primal scream. The final moments of Satan's address transformed into something unprecedented in the conference. His beauty, terrible and corrupt, seemed to reach back toward its original glory as he praised his forces. The assembled demons witnessed their king in a display of what almost appeared to be genuine affection - a sight so rare and unsettling that even I, Sabrael, felt a chill of dread.

"My faithful ones," he intoned, his voice carrying notes of pride that reminded me hauntingly of his days as heaven's most beloved angel. "You have exceeded every expectation. Your cunning, your persistence, your creativity in corruption—you have proven yourselves worthy of the kingdom we will inevitably seize!"

The response from the assembled demons was unlike anything seen in the previous sessions. Instead of their usual chaotic celebrations, they moved in perfect, terrible synchronization. Ranks upon ranks of demons rose into the air, their wings' movements creating ghastly motifs that made light of the celestial choreography of heaven. The air filled with a harmony of dark praise that twisted the very concept of music into something that would drive mortals mad.

As Satan's praise washed over them, the demons' reaction transcended their previous displays of loyalty. The air itself seemed to crystallize with the intensity of their devotion. Even the most hardened warriors among them, those who fearless led the group in the original rebellion, showed signs of being moved by their king's unprecedented display of approval.

The chamber transformed into a kaleidoscope of dark energies as demons of every rank expressed their gratitude in unique ways. Some of the demons, once beings of the purest light, emanated waves of anti-light that created a cloud of impossible darkness. Some others manifested their joy through displays of corrupted knowledge, creating illusions of twisted wisdom that floated through the chamber like toxic smoke.

Yet beneath the exultation, I sensed an undercurrent of something I hadn't expected to observe in hell - a kind of melancholy. The realization that their extraordinary gathering was ending sparked an almost human-like sentiment among the demons. Legions that had spent millennia working in isolation had finally experienced a taste of their former unity, albeit in its corrupted form, and the impending return to their solitary missions cast a shadow even darker than their natural gloom.

However, this touch of sadness served only to intensify their commitment to their cause. Satan's approval had awakened something dangerous in his forces - a renewed sense of purpose that called on them to outdo their usual malevolence. The lesser demons, usually focused only on their immediate tasks of temptation and corruption, now saw themselves as part of a grand design. The greater demons, typically absorbed in their complex strategies of global destruction, felt reinvigorated and grounded by the reminder of their ultimate, unified goal.

The chamber pulsed with their collective determination. Demons who had maintained unnecessary hostilities for millennia clasped hands in dark brotherhood. Territorial boundaries dissolved as they shared strategies and formed new alliances. The hierarchy of hell, usually rigid and unforgiving, became fluid in these final moments as they all united under their king's vision.

Satan observed this transformation with evident satisfaction, his beautiful-terrible face reflecting a triumph that went beyond mere victory over human institutions. He had achieved something perhaps even more valuable - the complete and voluntary submission of his forces, unified not by fear or compulsion but by shared purpose and ruthless malintent.

As the conference drew to its close, the demons began their departures in waves of choreographed darkness. Unlike their usually chaotic dispersal, they left in defined formations, each group acknowledging their king with displays of power that made the very foundations of hell tremble. The chieftains departed in bursts of anti-light, the higher-order in spirals of shadow, and the lower-order demons in echoes of celestial mockery.

The very arena, which had housed their unprecedented gathering, seemed to resist their departure. Yet their exit carried none of the chaos and disorder of their arrival days before. Instead, they moved with the terrible precision of an army almost prepared for battle.

As the last demons vanished into the infernal darkness, Satan's final words echoed through the chamber: "Go forth with spirited boldness. Our victory approaches!" Then he too departed, not in a flash of power as before, but fading gradually, leaving behind an impression of his presence that would linger on the arena's stage for eons to come.

I, Sabrael, remained briefly in the empty arena, witnessing the aftereffects of this momentous gathering. The air still crackled with residual energy, and the distant walls seemed to echo reverberations of their depraved celebrations. As I prepared to depart, I couldn't shake the feeling that I had witnessed something unprecedented in the history of creation - the moment when hell's forces found perfect unity in their corruption.

Though their conference had ended, I knew their terrible work was far from over. If anything, it was about to intensify beyond anything humanity had yet experienced. The demons had departed not with their usual mindless eagerness for destruction but with calculated strategies and renewed dedication to their king's grand design.

May heaven help the world that would face these energized forces of darkness, now more coordinated and determined than ever before!

Chapter 26

The Misguided Deceiver

Through the corridors of eternity, I have watched the tale of humanity unfold—an elaborate, ever- extending fabric with both light and darkness. The

naïve creatures have little idea of how close the hourglass is to running out, the sands of their time on earth collecting gently on the shores of the afterlife. Yet, these days, the darkness appears to have overtaken the canvas, blotting out the threads of divine intent with the smudges of demonic corruption.

From my vantage point, the state of humanity teeters on a precipice. The echoes of Eden's fall resound through the ages, amplifying with each successive generation. What began as an isolated act of rebellion has now morphed into a cacophony of sin, greed, and despair, conducted by the hands of hell's unyielding maestro.

I have seen men and women, children and elders alike, ensnared by the cunning traps of demons. No life is spared the trials of temptation, for Satan's reach knows no boundary. Even those who call themselves faithful, the so- called followers of Christ, are tested relentlessly, their strength winnowed by the tempest of spiritual warfare. Some stand firm, like trees rooted deep against the gale, but far too many are swept away, lured by promises of wealth, power, and fleeting pleasure.

Millions upon millions of souls have perished under my watch.

While some have ascended to the realm of eternal peace, where the love of the creator enfolds them like the warm embrace of dawn, most have fallen into the abyss. They wander the halls of torment, gnashing their teeth in regret and agony. These are the ones who faltered, led astray by their own desires and the whispers of demons. Hell swells with their cries—anguished wails that reverberate through the unforgiving, jagged expanses of this cursed dominion. The sweltering air carries more and more agony every day, each haunting scream a melody to demonic ears. These tormented souls beg for release, clawing at the suffocating walls of their cells, but their pleas fall into the void. Their fates are sealed, their sentences set in stone; they must repent for their deeds on earth, but it's too late.

Yet, despite all the torment, there is a faint glimmer of hope—the judgment seat of Christ. It looms as a specter on the horizon of all existence, the divine tribunal before which every soul must stand. Each will account for their faith, choices, and, most importantly, the things done in the body. For those who pass the test, the gates of eternal glory await. But for the multitude who fail, an even graver sentence lies beyond—a place much worse than hell.

As for hell itself, it is a theater of cruelty, a grand arena where demons indulge their evil and malevolence. They revel in the suffering of God's disobedient creatures, their glee amplified tenfold by every newly doomed soul that arrives at the gates of hell. Every tortured scream is no less than an anthem for the forces of darkness, their unholy pride swelling with each victory against heaven.

Meanwhile, the chieftains of hell report their endeavors to the throne of their master. The flood of damned souls and the ever-expanding grip of demonic influence on the living inflate Satan's pride. From his infernal seat, he surveys his kingdom with eyes gleaming like molten sapphires, confident in the strength of his dominion. Yet I wonder: Is this the full story? Can this deceiver, this vainglorious tyrant, truly believe he has the upper hand? For all his boasting and his vaunted power, might he himself be ensnared in a greater deception?

I have watched him brood for eons, his ambition burning like an unquenchable fire. He seeks to unravel the creator's design, to rewrite the cosmos in his image. But for all his machinations, there remains a question that gnaws at the edges of his empire.

***

The realm of hell brims with activity, though not the kind known to the living. Fires lick the jagged terrain, their light flickering against walls of blackened stone, casting long, distorted shadows of demons at work. The sulfur- choked air vibrates with the moans of the tormented, a never- ending chorus of agony that rises and falls like the tide.

From deep within the pits, souls claw at the rock, their fingers bleeding and raw. Their wails echo through the caverns, carrying notes of anguish, regret, and the faintest whispers of despair-laden prayers that go unanswered. Among them are murderers, thieves, betrayers, and the arrogant who proclaimed, "There is no God." Now, their defiance is silenced, replaced with endless suffering.

The demons feed on this torment. They prowl the shadows, their eyes gleaming like embers as they revel in the anguish of their captives. Some lash the souls with weapons formed of living fire, while others whisper into their ears, reminding them of every sin, every failure, and every missed chance for redemption. Each shriek and sob fuels their delight.

The chieftains of hell oversee this infernal theater, adorned in their grotesque regalia of rusting armor and flowing—albeit tattered—cloaks. They walk the fields of despair, their presence commanding both fear and reverence from lesser demons. Their voices boom as they shout orders, orchestrating an elaborate choreography of torment.

Amidst this chaos, Satan sat on his throne of obsidian, its jagged edges pulsing with a faint crimson glow. He was resplendent; his form a constant paradox of beauty and terror. His alabaster skin gleamed under the dim firelight, his jet-black hair cascading like liquid night over his shoulders. His piercing eyes, the color of storm-tossed seas, seemed to see all and miss nothing. On his head rested his crown, made of twisted metal, each point tipped with a flickering ember, a cruel parody of celestial majesty.

For a moment, he remained motionless, the only sound the crackling of flames and the distant cries of anguish. His lips curled into a faint smile as reports from his chieftains and higher-order demons filtered through the throne room.

"Another thousand souls have crossed the gates today, my lord," said Dagon, his hulking form wreathed in smoke. "Many of them from lands that once swore allegiance to the enemy. Their priests have fallen silent, their temples deserted. The seeds of corruption you commanded us to plant have borne fruit."

Tygress, slender and serpentine, slithered forward next. His voice was a silken hiss. "The leaders of men are ours to command. They bend to whispers, which they think are their own thoughts. Their greed has become a noose around the neck of nations, and their people stumble blindly into ruin."

Prink, small and hunched yet deadly in his cunning, added with a grin, "And the children, my lord, are ours. They are fed lies and call them truth, poisoned by entertainment that we control. They grow up severed from any knowledge of their creator."

Satan listened, nodding slowly. His smile widened, but his eyes remained cold and discerning. "Good," he says, his voice a rumble that shook every stone beneath them. "The creator's little experiment falters. Humanity crumbles under its own weight, driven by the lusts we have fanned into flame. They destroy themselves, and in doing so, they glorify us."

The chieftains bowed, their twisted faces alight with pride. Around them, worker demons murmured approval, their voices rising into a cacophony of exultation. But then Satan raised a hand, and silence enveloped the throne room. His gaze swept the room, and his voice, though unstrained, commanded absolute attention.

"They believe they are free," he said, leaning forward on his throne, "but freedom is a lie. It is the chains we have wrapped around them, chains they wear willingly. Their defiance of God is their true prison, and we hold the keys."

Satan remained on his throne, his form a blend of unearthly beauty and menace, illuminated by the fiery glow of hell's torches and replenished by the demons' chants of approval. The air was thick with the scent of sulfur and the muffled cries of tortured souls. His piercing eyes scanned the gathered group of demons, lingering momentarily on their eager faces, each twisted with malevolent desires and intentions.

"My loyal subjects," Satan began, his voice resonating through the cavernous chamber, a perfect blend of charm and dread. "You have carried out my commands with brilliance, sowing ruin where once stood hope and turning humanity's brightest lights into dim, flickering embers. I am wholly impressed by your work in this realm, organizing legions upon legions of forlorn angels into formidable, malleable soldiers—beastly forms that are more suited to our objectives than the flowery aesthetics of our adversary."

The chieftains responded with guttural cheers, their voices rumbling and echoing like a thunderstorm. Akar patted Damyan on the back in a gesture of commendation while others pounded the ground with their clawed feet, shaking the very foundation of the throne wall.

"Let us speak of our triumphs," Satan continued, his tone now sharp and commanding. "The so-called moral compass of humanity is in shambles. What was once held sacred is now profaned, and virtue has been reduced to mockery."

Satan's lips curled into a smile as he leaned forward, his voice soft but seething with malice. "Freedom," he said, "is their chains. They preach autonomy while bowing to desires we have instilled. They believe themselves unshackled as they drown in indulgence and selfishness. The so-called freedom of expression, choice, and love are but our tools to strip them of reason and bind them tighter to despair."

The group erupted in cheers again, the sound rippling like a wave of fire through the torturous air. Out in the distance, heads turned in hell's cities out of curiosity toward Satan's plan of action following the monumental six-day conference.

"Consider this," Satan went on, his tone becoming colder. "Their children, innocent in appearance, are molded by our hands. We have infiltrated their homes, their schools, their temples. Through subtle whispers and glaring lies, we have taught them to forsake their elders, defile their own bodies, and worship only themselves. And the parents—too busy or too blind to intervene—have delivered them to us willingly."

A collective laugh rumbled through the assembly before Andras spoke up. "Master, what of the few who resist? My regiment has successfully manipulated most of them, save for a select few who have managed to avert the better part of our attacks. Ah, the things

I would do to them if I could get my hands on them in our realm."

Satan's eyes narrowed, and the air grew colder despite the omnipresent heat of the flames. "Let them resist," he spat. "It is futile. Even their strongest are but flickers of light in a sea of darkness we control. We are patient and relentless, whereas their faith can falter; their hope can be corrupted. Every prayer unanswered, every tragedy they endure—we turn it against them. Even their victories are but delays to their defeat."

The demons roared their approval, their voices rising in a hymn of despair. Satan rose from his throne, his towering presence radiating dominance. The worker demons standing along the sidelines lowered their heads in veneration.

"Understand this," he said, his voice growing more fervent, "the creator may claim to hold the ultimate power, but we have what matters most—humanity's hearts and minds. We drive them with fear, greed, lust, and envy. We promise them everything, and they sacrifice eternity for fleeting pleasures. This world, their world, is ours."

He raised his hand, and the entire gathering fell silent once more. "But this is not the end," he declared. "We are far from finished. The final confrontation looms, and when the time comes, we shall take the battle to the heavens themselves. Nay, little does our adversary know of what we have in store for him."

A hush fell over the demons as they exchanged eager, conspiratorial glances.

Satan's voice dropped to a whisper, yet it carried across the vast terrain if amplified by the sweltering air. "Prepare yourselves. Let the victories of today embolden you for tomorrow. We are eternal. We are unyielding. And we shall surely rise to the highest throne."

The announcement of Satan's final decree sent a ripple through the assembly, like a spark igniting a forest of dry kindling. The demons erupted in unbridled jubilation, their roars and howls reverberating through hell's cities.

For a brief moment, hell seemed alive with an infectious energy that burned as hot as the unquenchable fires surrounding the throne. Satan stood motionless, a dark monolith of authority, his eyes scanning the terrain below with a cold, satisfied gleam.

Several chieftains stepped forward, their infernal decorations glowing faintly in the dim light. Damyan, with his towering figure, gleaming red eyes, and aura of dread, bowed his head low before speaking. "Majesty, your words fill us with purpose anew! We shall descend with renewed vigor upon the earth, leaving no soul untouched by despair and corruption."

Satan inclined his head slightly in acknowledgment of their loyalty and indispensable contributions. "Do not falter, for the work before you is vast. Let your ambitions burn as brightly as these flames, and let no human walk untouched by our shadow. From the infant's cradle to the elder's deathbed, let our influence seep into every facet of their fleeting existence."

The throne room grew quieter as the demons hung on his every word with dripping anticipation. Satan stepped forward, approaching near enough to be mingling in their ranks.

"In you, my bravest soldiers," he said, his voice ringing clear and terrible, "I see the embodiment of our defiance, the emblems of our resilience! You are the architects of chaos, the harbingers of despair. Together, we have turned a garden of promise into a wasteland of broken dreams!"

The demons roared again, their voices uniting in a chorus of unbounded pride. This time, Satan joined in as well.

"But this is not the end!" Satan continued, his voice rising above the din. "Even as we stand victorious today, the adversary prepares…"

At the mention of his adversary, Satan pointed toward the sky, almost as if he had the audience of the one he addressed. He continued, "We cannot deny that his followers, though diminished, persist. They whisper hope into the ears of humans, sowing seeds of resistance. But know this—hope is fragile, and we are the uncontested masters of its destruction. We will extinguish every flicker of faith until nothing but darkness remains!"

"Master, what of the prophecy?" Azrail stepped forward and asked, his voice carrying hints of concern or fear; I could not tell. "The one foretold by their Scriptures— their so-called second coming? More of them seem to be obsessed with it each passing century."

The throne room fell silent. All eyes turned to Satan, whose face remained impassive. All of the chieftains, without exception, had struggled to answer their regiments' questions regarding Christian movements on earth and their implications for hell's long-term vision. The flickering flames seemed to dim for a moment, casting darker shadows across Satan's sharp, beautiful features.

Satan's lips curled into a slow, sinister smile. "Prophecies are weapons of the weak," he declared. "They cling to them like drowning men to driftwood, hoping they will be saved. But they forget that even prophecies can be twisted. We will exploit their expectations, turn their faith into doubt, and their unity into division. By the time their so- called savior arrives, they will be too fractured to receive him."

Toward the end of the sentence, Satan's eyes wavered to the distance, almost as if lost in a reverie in which the events he mentioned played out. The corner of his mouth extended into a subtle smirk before he continued, his voice sharp and commanding.

"The war is far from over, but our momentum is unstoppable. The adversary grows weary of humanity's failures, and his forces are spread thin. Now is the time to press our advantage, to strike at the heart of creation and claim what is rightfully ours."

He turned, halting directly above his throne in preparation to seat himself again. In response to the growing anticipation among his chieftains, he spread his arms wide, the flames behind him roaring higher as if in response to his command. I despised him at that moment—his awareness of humanity's persistent downfall before all of our exalted God's attempts to guide them back to the right path. After all, what would it take for them to heed all the love and benevolence he constantly showers on them? But never mind the digression.

"Go forth, my loyal legions," he declared. "Bring the world to its knees. Let no corner of the earth remain untouched by our dominion. For we are the storm that no shelter can withstand, the shadow that no light can dispel!"

The demons erupted once more in chaotic celebration, their cries shaking the very core of hell. Their grotesque faces were lit with purpose as they vowed to redouble their efforts, swearing loyalty to their king until the end of time. But as the jubilation reached its peak, I wondered if the moving display was a prelude to ultimate victory or (hopefully) a prelude to a greater fall.

Satan lowered himself to his throne and reclined, his piercing gaze fixed on the fiery horizon of his dominion. A cold smile lingered on his lips as he muttered to himself, barely audible over the chatter of the departing chieftains. "The heavens may have their plans, but so do I."

And at that moment, in the aftermath of hell's conference with its air of celebration, a question hung heavy in the air—a question that even the chieftains dared not voice: was this truly the end of humanity's hope or was God's once-favorite playing the greatest deception trick of all time, and that, too, on himself?

About the Author

Tom Graneau, an ordained minister, certified financial educator, and family counselor explores the intersection of faith, finances, and family dynamics

for personal growth and spiritual vibrancy. His books entertain, educate, and inspire, offering practical insights into financial strategies, spiritual vision, and perception.

Whether you're seeking financial wisdom, spiritual guidance, or helpful life advice, Tom Graneau's work will be valuable for your journey toward personal success and spiritual fulfillment.

341